THE TALES OF ZREN JANIN

EXILE:
A NEW
BEGINNING

BOOK 4

M. L. DUNKER

Publishing Services provided by Paper Raven Books LLC
Printed in the United States of America
First Printing, 2022

Hardcover ISBN: 979-8-9850536-6-1
Paperback ISBN: 979-8-9850536-7-8

Dedication:
For anyone who has watched a dream die,
grieved the loss, and began to dream again.

"No one is a villain in their own story."
– George R.R. Martin

TABLE OF CONTENTS

CHAPTER 1

CHUL'S GIFT TO THE KEREK KING

Rani, the Viklander softfoot, came to us one morning. It was so early only Rygee was awake—in the bakery starting the ovens. Rani had slipped in the side door and stood on the green with his hands spread wide in the air as he hailed the house. Siba had poked her head out of the bedroom window trying to figure out who spoke Conrosan so horribly they had to shout it out before sunrise. But it was only Rygee, Siba, Rell, and I that were at Manumina that day, so she had dressed and gone down just as Rygee joined the softfoot outside. Siba then came to our house and asked Rell and me to dress and come to the village green.

I wiped the sleep from my eyes, finger combed my hair, and patted down the wrinkles in my shirt as Rell and I walked in to join them. I stopped short when I saw Rani, or actually what lay on the ground in front of him: the largest bow I had ever seen. Even larger than Rell's crossbow but built like Tiju Tia's short bow. It had tiny pulleys at the top and bottom, like Piffik had in the workshop to maneuver the largest pieces of furniture about his tables.

I looked at Rell. "Is this the new weapon?"

Rell shook her head. "This is only part of it. I think I know why Rani is here." She looked at the softfoot. "You have the rest of it?"

Rani gave her a sly smile. "Not here. I value my life too much. It is hiding in the hills east of here. There is a Vik patrol guarding it—but not too closely. Can you come now?"

Rell nodded and turned to me. "Do you want to see this? I cannot promise your safety, but I think you should know what is coming."

I looked to Rygee. He smiled at me.

"You should go along in case Rell and Rani need your fine Conrosan face to rescue them from a dance with Trouble." Rani inhaled sharply but said nothing to Rygee's words.

I saddled the horses while Rell went back for her crossbow and a pocketful of bolts. She said she would shoot the compound bow—that was what she called it—but she would need to sight in the targets on the crossbow she was most familiar with. Rani had smiled and noted Chul had told him to do whatever Rell said. Rani said he was not so casual with his life that he would disregard any wisdom from Chul Swyler, a man he considered the cleverest firemaster in Juisiti.

Rell came back wearing a Conrosan dress and her hair tied up in a braided crown, carrying her crossbow. No one said anything more, we just mounted and rode out with Rygee and Siba watching us. We rode horses in a different direction than the shepherd's cottage, but it was still east and almost to the Vikland border. Rani seemed comfortable and relaxed, although I noticed his eyes never stopped watching our surroundings.

He looked at me once and asked if I spoke Vik. Before I could answer, Rell replied that they should speak Wester—a language I did not know, she claimed—if he had secrets he did not want Manumina to hear. I carefully kept my face down and marveled how everyone at Manumina could tell a falsehood with such ease and speed. I wondered if I could ever have the same ability, or if I was doomed to tell the truth for the rest of my life.

They slipped into Wester, and I pretended I didn't understand. I wondered what was so important that Rani had wanted me out of the conversation. He talked of the news in Juisiti and in the Diplo. There were names of people I didn't know and places I had never been. Battles fought, prisoners taken, land exchanged. It sounded boring so I amused myself by making up a story about Zren Janin and his Sword of Courage.

I thought the Conrosan folk hero should meet one of the Viklander Monsters of the Mountains, but I wasn't sure how that would happen. Should the Monster fly to Conrosa? Or should

Zren Janin take a long journey to Vikland? It would be too far to walk, so how should he get there? Should he travel alone or with his Legion of Heroes? Sail on the seas or fly through the skies? Was there magic in flying? How would that work?

There were three Viklander soldiers on horseback waiting for us. As we rode up, I could see that two held a compound bow like the one Rani had. The other had a crossbow, and all of them carried a jeong bong in a long scabbard the length of their horses, and a tahn bong across their back. None of them smiled.

Rell and Rani spoke with them for a long time. I didn't recognize any of the Vik words, but there were no formal greetings, and I wondered if they were no longer done because of the war or because we were in Kerek.

Rell turned to me, glanced at Rani, and began in Keresh, "I apologize for our bad manners. None of these soldiers speak Conrosan, I am sorry. We will dismount and look closely at Chul's invention and then step back and fire at it with our crossbows first. There will be a loud sound and some dirt will be kicked up. We will step further back until we can no longer hit the targets and then switch to the compound bows. We are trying to determine how far away the bowmaster can be and still be successful. The greater the distance, the better the chance of surviving." She gave me a sad smile. "Do you understand, Zren? Vikland does not want to win the war at the cost of every bowmaster she has."

"What do you want me to do?" I asked uneasily.

"Bear witness. If none of us survives this experiment, take our bodies to Ishes," Rani said gruffly. "Do you have the stomach for such a task?"

I was so shocked at his words, I kneed my horse by mistake. It took all my attention to get Old Dris calmed down from the indignity. By that time, all the others had dismounted and had walked to a huge circle drawn in the sand. All of the cheatgrass and shrubs had been cleared and multi-colored clay pots were cradled—singly and in clumps—in shallow depressions. It was nearly as large as the Manumina green inside the stockade walls.

The soldiers were speaking in Vik again and I watched them. Rani carefully pointed out the differently colored pots, and the soldiers repeated his motions. I assumed he was telling them in what order he wanted them fired. Rell picked up some coarse dirt and let it drift through her fingers. She looked at the sun still in front of us and kicked at the dirt with her feet. None of them stepped within a chain's length of the circle's edge.

I wondered what the Empress considered an acceptable loss to change the ways of the known world. We all knew it had to change. People could not be treated badly, killed, or robbed because of the color of their skin or the land of their birth. There could not be ten ways to describe Kereki metal poisoning to justify taking something that did not belong to you.

All my life, before I met Ngahuru, I had been treated as 'less than.' When it happened, I had run away because I was too small to fight for myself. And now others had stepped up to fight for themselves and others like me. Viklanders, West Islanders, even the Wrens were fighting the only way they knew how to make a better future. And yet, it wasn't easy.

Piffik said the Kerekis were fighting for their homes and their families. They couldn't see the pain their way of thinking inflicted on others. War was not meant to be easy, he said, it was why Conrosans practiced non-violence.

Rell had disagreed, saying sometimes non-violence was only apathy and collusion. Sometimes defending the defenseless meant taking up arms. But usually those discussions lasted far beyond the coffee and fingersweets. Piffik would go home to his bed convinced he was right, and Rell would mutter that if the Empress hadn't worn a crown with teeth, we would still all be living in fear along the Northern Track.

Siba told me once the Viklander Empress measured the war in blood. But it seemed to me like this battle for justice had very dry ground to soak up so much, so easily, for so long.

I watched as the Viklanders nodded to each other and walked back to me.

"Zren, please take the horses and go back to nearly that outcropping." Rell pointed about two furloughs away. "I will shoot first. Then we will try the compound bows to test how far away we can hide. The horses may get spooked. Chul told Rani the noise may be loud, but none of us know what that means—how loud, how long. Keep the horses under control and do not approach us. We do not know if any of the pots will misfire late. Rani will keep count of the firings and will signal you when it is safe to come back to us. Do you understand?"

"Are you in danger?" I asked. "Do you have to do this?" I slid off my horse and grabbed the reins of the others to lead them.

"If it could end the war sooner? Yes, Zren, I have to do this."

The Viklanders watched me as I took their horses and led them away. When I turned and faced them again, tucked behind the small hillock Rell had pointed to, they had already blurred into indistinct shapes. I could pick out Rell because of her dress. They paced off southwest of me, and I wondered if that was to avoid the sun in their eyes. When they stopped, I guessed that Rell was standing nearly the distance of the length of the walls of Manumina.

I did not see the release, but there was a pop of sound and large amounts of dirt kicked up. Another soldier tried it with the crossbow. This time there was a pop, pop, pop, and a much bigger curtain of dirt jumped into the air. Then the other two soldiers tried the compound bows. Single pops. I wondered how many pots Rani and the soldiers had brought.

Rell and the others paced back even further. She exchanged her crossbow for one of the compound bows, and I could see her listening carefully as the soldier explained how it worked. Rani pointed at the one he wanted her to hit. She fired and the arrow went so far beyond the target that it exceeded the circle completely. Laughter drifted over to me. She paced back even further and tried again.

The blast nearly knocked me off my feet. One of the Viklander horses reared, and I fought to bring it down without frightening or injuring the others. Old Dris pulled back on the reins as far as she could, trying to get away. I struggled to keep them all under control. When I finally could look over to the circle, I was amazed to see a shallow crater where there had been nothing but sandy dirt and pulled cheatgrass.

I looked to the Viklanders. They were as still as an outcropping of rocks. Rell had the compound bow lowered, but no one was talking or looking at one another. They were all staring at the hole in the ground that hadn't existed a moment before.

The soldiers paced back even further. Only one of the soldiers hit the pots with a small pop, pop. The other two had arrows that fell harmlessly short. Rani pointed to another clump, backed up Rell one more time, and then pointed again. This time the other soldiers crouched down and wrapped their arms over their head before Rell fired.

I heard the muffled blast and saw the dirt rain down. Soon the dust drifted my way and coated my shirt. I wiped my face and looked at the damage. This blast had been far quieter than the other, but the hole in the ground was larger, much larger. The soldiers stood up and dusted themselves off and all five of them walked toward the circle. They talked for a little while. I watched them gesturing as Rani looked to be writing something in a small book. The soldiers walked around the holes and called out to Rani. No one crossed the lines of the scuffed up circle, but one of the soldiers made a wide path around and picked up all the arrows and quarrels that had missed their targets.

I waited patiently with the horses. Rell looked over and waved her fingers at me. Rani turned and gestured for me to join them. I pulled the horses along and as we got closer I could smell the chemicals in the air. The horses didn't like the smell either, and I gratefully handed them off to the other soldiers.

Rani spoke first, "Well, Zren, how many riatas do you think you could make of these without blowing yourself up?"

I stared at him, and the group burst out laughing.

"He is joking, Zren. He said it was Chul's first idea, but to have the power needed to destroy a bridge, it could not be the pots of chemicals that sailed through the air, but only the arrow that would fire them. Rani said Inezi, one of theirs at Fortika, has been testing the compound bows. She is able to hit her target from a very great distance."

I found my voice. "Nelo says she shoots at those who would harm her or force her to give up her secrets. I think she is not treated so well at Fortika."

Rani gave me a tight smile. "That one is not afraid to bury a man in the dirt. Unfortunately, Inezi has learned to measure her power with the death of others. Bima will need to handle her carefully after the war."

The others switched back to Vik, so I walked closer to the holes in front of me. I recognized the broken shards of the clay fired pots. The designs and colors looked a little different than what I remembered from Miya's thirteenth crossing of the Northern Track. I wondered how Chul knew to change the pottery and the shapes for these new chemicals. I wondered how he could dream these things into existence and know what would be needed. I wondered if he thought of Rell because she could see from such a great distance, and of Inezi because she could test his compound bow without consequences. I realized Chul used his memories and everything and everyone about him in his inventions. I wondered how the mind worked to make one person an inventor, another a bowmaster, and yet another a softfoot.

It was quiet. I turned and noticed everyone was silently watching me. I was going to ask if Rell was going to have to go back to Vikland. I thought I already knew the answer. I wondered if the Empress was ready to sacrifice a member of the Diplo who was so much more to me than just a bowmaster. I wondered how many times we all failed to see the entire person in front of us. I wondered if Rell would miss me as much as I would miss her.

Rell gave me a lopsided grin and turned to the others.

"We should go back. Rygee will have midday ready by the time we return. It is never a good idea to keep Zren from his table. His clever tongue will tell you a fairy tale while he sneaks the fingersweets out of your saddlebags."

Rani laughed but nodded easily to the others. We all mounted our horses. The three soldiers were traveling back to Ishes, but Rani told them he would go with us to Manumina and meet them later. Without another word to us, the three turned and headed north.

***

During midday, Rani asked Siba many questions about burn treatments, medicinals she would need, experience she had. He told us things could go wrong: a bowmaster unable to escape and forced to fire while still too close to the pots, or a friend of Vikland in a stable or a busy market square too careless about slipping one unseen into a supply wagon. If there were burns among Viklanders, or friends of Viklanders, he hastily added, he wanted to know if we could care for them until they were stable enough to travel to the Academy of Healing in Juisiti.

Siba leaned back in her chair and looked at Rani. Without a flicker of unease, she stated she had learned everything she knew about caring for burns from Rell Huena. That Rell had gotten up from her own sickbed to care for Chul and his burns from the Battle at the Bridge. That Rani could test this knowledge by speaking with the Viklander Ambassador of Kerek City, if she was still alive, because she had been the one who knew of Rell's talents as a healer and sent her on the Northern Track. Rell had cared for Chul from Kerek City to Manumina, taught Siba at Manumina, and cared for those who were burned out of barns, and woods, and battles from east of Balza to the border or wherever Padro Morto's wagon found them. Siba thought her own skills with cutting out arrows, binding broken bones, and curing infections were quite good, but if Rani expected to keep so many of his bowmasters alive, he should consider what healers remained at Manumina.

Rani smiled at her. It wasn't kind.

"We all play our parts in this war, Siba Namikk. I know your lies were meant as a kindness, but Rell Huena needs no defense but her own. She knows the stakes in this war. I do agree she serves a better purpose here, but that is based on my assessment and not your words of friendship. I am not going to take her with me. Not yet."

Rygee had stiffened as Rani had scolded Siba. I knew that look from before, when Rygee fought with a stubborn goat who would not mind us, or when one of the iron plows broke and he would have to spend the day teaching me how to fix it. I wondered if Rani could read Rygee as well as the rest of us.

Rani asked, "When will Piffik Qanaq return?"

"We have no idea. He comes and goes." Rygee dipped his head about the table. "These four are the ones most likely to be here at any given day. More than that depends on the war itself."

Rani tightened his jaw. I tried to figure out why Rani and Rygee didn't like each other—because that's what it seemed like. Was it because Rani was a softfoot and not a soldier? A Viklander, who started this war with Kerek? The reason Manumina was going to have to change again? Did Rani think Rygee was someone who would turn against Vikland whenever the purse was rich enough? A Farm Manager instead of fighting? A traitor to Kerek? Or was it only they were both stubborn men used to getting their way by their own work and strong wills?

Suddenly, Rani leaned back in his chair and smiled.

"I think it would be best if I left for Ishes now. I will spend the night there before I head back to my little bit of woods. I see your white-haired boy often. I was glad to hear he recovered from his encounter with the crimpers. I have also exchanged words with your boy at Evensong. He is more than clever and well-placed. We could never have done so well without his many talents. Your girl at Regno stands alone, yet she is also formidable for being so young. I enjoy talking with her in the woods on her walks in the mornings and at end of day when I am about, although I must always be careful not to receive a knife wound as a greeting. You have been helpful to Vikland, and we are grateful for your information and your children. We will protect them just as you protect us."

Everyone stood up from the table, and I was going to remind the others about the fingersweets after the meal, but instead Rell led Rani to the porch. We stood about awkwardly and then Rani gave a short formal bow to Rell.

"We will meet again. For now, thank you for safely showing me the power of Chul's new gift for the Kerek King. I am more than pleased to know the Empress will not sacrifice a bowmaster each time we need a bridge to crumble, a supply train to never arrive, or a patrol to disappear from the Kerek countryside."

He smiled at each of us in turn. "Zren Janin, your Wrens of Manumina have so many talents. If you should cross their paths, please remind them to handle the pots very carefully. I would hate to lose any of them now when they have so cleverly survived Kerek City."

The four of us were speechless that he would consider using the Wrens to set the pots instead of Viklander softfoots. No one said anything more as he untied his horse from the railing, mounted, and left.

I realized Rani had smiled nearly the entire time he was with us. But not once had I felt warmth, or friendliness, kindness, or joy. Instead, I was reminded of those grabs for power in the gambling halls of Kerek City all those years and years ago. I thought back to the story I had dreamed up earlier while we were on the way to fire the pots. I wondered if Zren Janin and his Sword of Courage had just met a Viklander Monster of the Mountains.

CHAPTER 2

GHOSTFIRE

Rygee brought in the farmhands. There were eight of them. All second or third sons on small holdings where work was in far more abundance than food and care. Rygee had come out with me the first day to explain how it would be done.

Rygee said Conrosans believed in hard work and fair dealings, and he was sure they would agree. He said he would watch the first day to see what each man's strength was, and if any wanted to carry a soldier's pike rather than a farmer's pitchfork, they only had to be one of the four worst hands at the end of the planting. He would let them sort it out. If they had any other problems, he said I would take care of it. He had placed his hand on my shoulder then and I wondered what was going through each of their minds as they took my measure. No one said anything aloud, and most of them dipped their head to me. Just like that, I was in charge.

Lou helped us the first few days because he said he wanted to pick out his own man who would help him with the goats and cheese. So, Lou and I and the farmhands spent our days tilling the soil, turning it over, getting it ready for planting. After the first day, Rygee didn't come out again, but he fed me pastries every morning while we talked over the work to be done. He listened as I talked of the men and their skills and their words, and he guided me on what to say and how to act to be respected as their leader.

The fields began to look like fields again. Straight furrows, mounded soil. Piffik, and Tiju Tia, and Oro went out for a few days. Piffik to deliver his commission and check on the settlement south of Huk; Tiju Tia and Oro to discuss with Josef, Nelo, and Arden the new plans for the Wrens to shrink their territory.

The farmhands barely gave the old Kereki woman and her rag and bone cart a second look. They were too busy planting to be distracted by the comings and goings of Manumina.

I finally relaxed, believing that we might be able to get the fields planted without mishap. Then Lou had taken one of the horses and his cheese cart and gone on the road early in the morning without telling anyone. That left us with only two horses and three iron plows for the eight farmhands and me to work the remaining fields.

When I told Rygee, he had lost his temper and started slamming bread dough on the table in the bakery. After a few moments, he stopped and said this wasn't going to fall on my shoulders. He was the farm manager, and he would come out to talk to the farmhands.

As he washed up to come out with me, he said some farmhands would need to wear the traces and be the horses. I was appalled. But when he repeated what needed to be done to the farmhands, two of them had merely shrugged; their holdings were so poor, it had been the same on their land. And that was that. Some of the farmhands and I wore the traces and pulled the plows forward through the soil while others pushed and guided from behind. All three plows had teams—one with horses, two with men—up and down the fields, furrowing straight rows.

After two days of this, I ached everywhere. I was exhausted but I couldn't rest. Siba had given me something for the pain in my shoulders, but it didn't help me sleep. I left my bed and sat by the open window in the cool breeze to see if I would feel better or at least become tired enough to sleep beyond the ache.

The moon was full and the moonglow so bright, the houses and fences outside the stockade threw shadows. The nights were still cool. It was the beginning of the Dry after all. I pushed my head out further letting the breeze wash my face.

I thought about Rani's visit earlier and wondered how much longer Rell would be able to stay with us. I thought of myself as brave only because I knew she would stand behind me. She could protect me from any harm that could happen. What would I be like if she went away? I wondered where the Wrens were. I wondered if Rani had asked any of them to hide the ghostfire.

Would they refuse? Would they be hurt? I thought about Solkka Ulani and Jenny in the hunt and hobble group west of Balza. If the news from Sary was to be believed, they were nearly in the thick of the battles. Would it make sense for them to remain there? Or would Ven Wila move them to another place where they could disrupt supply trains, communications, and patrols? How long could Ven Wila keep them alive?

I realized so many people I knew could be hiding in the dark: tired, hungry, and afraid. Yes, my shoulders ached. Yes, I hoped beyond hope someone would come home tomorrow bringing back horses to take our place in the traces. But once I fell asleep tonight, I would be able to sleep until morning without setting a watch, without wondering if I would wake and see morning.

It was still better than Lowertown.

***

Rani's test east of Manumina must have only been to convince him of the distance a bowmaster could hide and still be successful. It seemed like only a matter of days before news of the Viklanders' new weapon traveled back to Manumina. A weapon so dangerous, entire patrols and supply wagons could be destroyed without a shot fired in return.

Lou had come back from his cheese route with the rumors. He said the taverns were full of Kereki soldiers who told stories of crossing the Huk River with landscapes so empty they could see furloughs in the distance and know they were alone. Suddenly, they would hear a whoosh, or even nothing at all, and then with a roar the bridge would disintegrate under them. Some Kerekis said it was an ambush from the very air around them. Survivors told of magic that would allow one soldier to be protected by a stone fallen just so, or standing at the opposite end of the bridge, or the other end of the supply train, or a tree that took the blast and left a soldier deaf but alive.

Lou said the Patrons at their shops gossiped of a grain train making its way along the Northern Track with food from the port. Without warning, the road exploded when the wagon wheels drove by. Lou said he encountered Justices, hard-eyed and angry, riding out looking for answers and coming back with broken bodies.

Rell and Rygee and I knew differently. When we had fought at the Battle at the Bridge, Chul Swyler had mixed his pots of chemicals together, and then I had thrown them as riatas toward the archers. Chul had taken those memories of the children hiding under the bridge and built a new weapon. No longer was it necessary to mix the chemicals only moments before they exploded. Now, the pots could be carefully buried in roads and nestled under bridges. Pots could be slipped into supply wagons by friends of Vikland and explode decons later if the goods were carelessly unloaded or the wagon lurched through a deep puddle. Some pots needed heat to explode, others needed pressure—from a quarrel or an arrow, driven over, or stepped on, or to be knocked about in a wagon on a track infested with shallow holes. Encampments would burn from the outside in as pots were rolled or tossed into watchfires or tucked between sentry points. And yet, there would be no Viklander forces nearby to fight.

The farmhands would talk of it as they worked in the fields, as we broke for midday, and as they gathered at the end of day to be paid in coin by Rygee.

Rygee grimly noted the remaining work in the fields took longer as everyone worked to avoid soldiering.

"It doesn't have to be perfect, Zren, it just needs to be planted," he huffed as he inspected the day's work after the farmhands had left for the night.

He walked with me over to the pens where Lou's goats were resting near the loafing shed. There were two kids already born, but I told Rygee I hadn't helped with either. One of the farmhands had come early to help Lou. The boy hadn't said anything about it, just came early and didn't ask for more coin for the extra work.

"They're afraid, Zren. They are afraid the work will be done too soon and four of them will be released to the army. They are afraid of ghostfire, Viklanders, and dying. I know their fear, but

I can't do anything about it. The more work we have them do about Manumina, the more likely they will see something they shouldn't know about."

"Rell is dressing as a Conrosan wife now. She and Siba have been making dresses for her to wear."

"That only works from a distance, Zren. Rell and Siba both have a self-assurance about themselves that a Kereki housewife would never have learned. Hiding them in Conrosan dresses will only act as a maskovesto. No. It's good we will finish the planting soon. I don't know how we will find the four best."

Piffik came back from his route and asked to have me help in the woodshop. Ghostfire had increased his business so much he could barely keep up with the demand for coffins. But truthfully, we mainly lived on the coin from the Kereki army paychest that Rygee and Nelo had brought back from the trip to redeem Nelo from the crimpers. Rygee said there was a certain ironic satisfaction to paying for our food, farmhands, and medicinals with the coin from the very ones who made our lives so difficult. Piffik said nothing at all, but I noticed he no longer grimaced when he asked Rygee for coin for his travels to rescue the Viklander soldiers and softfoots.

Tiju Tia needed me back on the carts, she said. The crops were in; the plows were idle. She argued with Rygee that the farmhands knew how to weed a simple field, ensure the orchards were visited by the ground bees, and care for animals. Rygee had grumbled that she now expected him to take on managing them as well as everything else he did as Farm Manager. When Siba suggested he give up the baking—we could forego the coin he brought in by selling to Sary—he had given her a long look.

"How can I be the *titiro mai ke ahau* of all that Manumina does to help Vikland, if I do not appear in Sary lolling about, eating pastries with my customers, and gossiping with everyone and the Justice of all the news that happens up and down the Northern Track and the great houses of the north? It's not about the coin, Siba. Or the baking."

I had dropped my head at that. It seemed everyone was risking their lives except me. I felt as useless as Lou the cheesemaker. He lived outside the settlement on the east side of Manumina, walked to his springhouses and the earthern caves he had dug out of the ground, and spent his days there. Sometimes I saw him milking his goats, sometimes harnessing a horse and cart in the stable on the way to sell his cheeses all along the Huntsman's Trail and the Northern Track or pick up rennet from the butcher in Sary. He barely talked to the rest of us anymore. We were not so foolish to believe he no longer knew what was happening, there were too many Viklander horses coming and going for that, but he silently agreed to pretend to see nothing if we would let him live at Manumina and not turn him in as a deserter. It was an uneasy peace.

Siba had taken a deep breath and said perhaps we were all doing too much. We knew there were those who would die because we were not there, those who would suffer because we did not find them in time, but for the ones we did find, we could not give up hope for them. She said we needed mercy and grace for ourselves as much as we needed to share it with others.

She said she could learn to do the manabout chores with Rell when they did not have soldiers and softfoots in the infirmary. If my pretty Conrosan face had to sit on a cart, or do anything else needed of me, she said she could learn whatever needed to be done. She knew the stories of the Conrosan folk hero as well as anyone, she said. She was not going to stand in the way of Zren Janin and his Sword of Courage.

It was decided I would drive with Tiju Tia on the rag and bone wagon to Cloa.

***

We left the next morning after the farmhands arrived. Rygee and I explained to them that I would be taking my mother to Balza to visit her ailing sister, and he would be looking for a leader among them who was interested in setting the day's work for all of them. They all could try for the foreman position—it would come with more coin, of course—and the certainty that they would not be going to war. I watched them as they looked carefully at one another and then back at Rygee.

One of them asked, "There is still enough work here for all of us. None of us will be released to the army so soon after the planting, is that not true? Doesn't Manumina need us?"

Rygee gave a hard smile. "There is always enough work on a settlement this size. It is only, are you more afraid of work or of ghostfire? I am not going to pay men who talk."

He nodded to me, just as we had rehearsed earlier in the bakery. "It will be done just as you told me it should be done. We all know Manumina is a Conrosan settlement neutral in the war between Vikland and Kerek. We will not disappoint you while you are protecting your mother as she travels across Vikland. May all your family be well."

Traveling with Tiju Tia felt different this time. She was quiet and we were both watchful. I asked her if we would see Piffik anywhere along the way, and she said she didn't know. I asked if we needed to worry about ghostfire on the roads and bridges we would be traveling, and she replied she didn't think so, but she didn't know for sure.

I started to ask her if… And she burst out, "I don't know, Zren, I don't know! I don't know what that fool of a Kerek King is thinking to believe he can win this war. I don't know if he is shut up in his castle with only those who agree with him, and they lick their lips at the gold they are getting from Matasi. I don't know if they drink themselves to sleep every night so they do not hear the cries of the mothers mourning their dead sons, and wives and girlfriends grieving the loss of their loves. I don't know!"

I didn't say another word as we traveled on Piffik's half-tracks to Cloa.

If I could have said, I was not afraid, I would have finally learned to tell a falsehood.

CHAPTER 3

THINGS TIJU TIA DOES NOT KNOW

We reached Cloa long after dark. Tiju Tia had me check the stables to see if we could stable our horse, but Arden wasn't there and she didn't want to leave the cart untended where anyone could help themselves to whatever caught their fancy. She thought we should have Arden bring the horse over after we had end of day meal, and he could ensure that it would be taken care of with those he knew and trusted.

Linna answered the door to our knock. She looked surprised to see me.

"Zren?" She opened the door a little wider and we both slipped in.

It was our turn to be surprised. Callis was standing in the doorway to Arden's bedroom, and I could smell the stringent scent of medicinals.

"What happened?" Tiju Tia questioned sharply. She hurried across the room and Callis stepped aside.

Arden lay on his cot, his blanket only pulled up to his waist. His ribs were wrapped, his arms, neck, and face covered in bruises and shallow cuts. In contrast, his long brown hair was neatly brushed and spread out over his pillow. His eyes were closed and his shallow breathing was slow.

"Is he still with us?" Tiju Tia tore her eyes away and looked at Callis.

"I am. But the light hurts my eyes, and I prefer sleeping to feeling my bones complain. Callis, if you would be so kind to shut the door with all of you on the other side of it, I would be grateful." Arden spoke in a hoarse voice, but he didn't open his eyes.

I shot a glance at Tiju Tia—who pursed her lips tightly together—and then at Linna and Callis who tried to hide their smiles at Arden's boldness. Linna offered to make something to eat, and Callis pulled the door shut firmly behind us.

Over end of day meal, Linna told us what had happened.

"It was night and I had been sleeping. I woke when Mother made a sound and began scratching at the door. I thought at first, she needed to go out, and I wondered if it was truly that close to morning. Then I heard her whimpering and snuffling along the bottom of the door. She scratched more frantically. Suddenly, Mother stood up on her hind legs and put her front paws on the bar. She gave a breathy woof. I had never seen her do anything like that before. So, I hurried down the ladder in my nightgown. I threw on my cloak and pulled on my boots and grabbed a broom to defend myself. I unbarred the door and peeked around the corner."

Linna took a deep breath before continuing, "A man-sized lump of clothes lay on the wooden pallet Arden had built to keep us from tracking in mud. Mother pushed past me and sniffed at the cloak. She began licking, and I realized it was Arden. I looked out into the dark and saw nothing. No one. There were footprints leading to the pallet but none leading away. I put my hand on his neck. He was cold and clammy, but I could feel a pulse. He didn't respond when I whispered his name.

"I pulled him into the house and on to the rug. Mother sniffed him once more and then dashed out the open door and into the dark. I didn't call her or go after her, I only pushed the door so it looked closed and then unfastened his cloak. I noted his knives were still in their inside pockets so he had been caught unawares." Linna stopped for a moment.

"He never got a chance to defend himself," she whispered.

I looked down at my empty bowl and pretended I didn't see the tears in her eyes.

"I didn't dare light a lamp until Mother got back and I could bar the door properly, but there was a little dawn coming in the window, so I could see to remove his clothes before taking him to his bed. The damage was everywhere. Bruising along his arms, his ribs. He had bands of bruises around his upper arms and chafing about his wrists. He had been held or tied, I thought. His purse was gone and the pocket of food about his waist had been cut away. They had only left the strings dangling from the belt around his shirt."

Linna colored a little. "It is one thing to say you live with another as brother and sister. But it is another thing entirely to undress a man when he cannot say to do so. But I needed to know how much worse…" She huffed. "I pulled down his baggy trousers and he had papers wrapped and tied all about his legs. I unwound the Kereki ties wrapped about his calves and ankles. There were more papers. I eased off his boots and boot linings and there were small coin purses and a tiny map no bigger than my palm."

Callis gave me a stern look. "So, tell me, Zren Janin, who would hold a man and beat him senseless but not search him for coin or profit? This was not the work of bandits."

"Nor anyone from Kerek City." I felt an unease growing. "Perhaps it was crimpers who had been interrupted in stealing him away?" *It was Viklanders. Who else would defend themselves against another in the night but not rob the unconscious body? I* wondered if Callis and Linna knew it as well, and they were showing Tiju Tia the danger the Wrens were in.

"What does Arden say?" Tiju Tia asked.

Callis snorted. "He says Koanga made such clever pockets and knife sleeves and cloaks for us, it would be a shame to use them for such a short time hunting those who do not need to be hunted. That Linna and I are not Spice Islanders who believe that family is family and a harm against one is a harm against all. He says we are too wise to waste ourselves on his behalf. That we should focus on teaching him to make biscuits while he is resting and taking his ease."

Tiju Tia narrowed her eyes. "When did Mother return?"

Linna tipped her head and gave us a thoughtful look. "About a decon later. She was not alone. When the Wrens were at Manumina, Arden worked to familiarize her with all of us. But we knew she would have to recognize more than just the Wrens. Friends and allies too.

"Arden had explained to all of us how everything Mother did was based on scent. I understood we had to make strangers smell like people we knew. The chandler at Manumina had already left for Vikland, so I purchased some soap here in Cloa, and we have given slivers to all of the Wrens. We needed it to be uncommon so I bought every one of the most expensive bars in the store. The

Wrens are to rub it on their boots and hems of their clothes so that Mother can find them if they are ever missing. Arden had also given some to people he meets frequently; Mother would need to know them by smell.

"When Mother finally returned, I had already undressed Arden to his small clothes, and all of the papers were untied and laid out on the floor as they were on his body. The door slid open, and I jumped up to grab the broom to defend myself.

"It was Lomes the softfoot. I said they couldn't be here. That we were too close to the center of Cloa and someone would see them and know we were friends of Vikland. They said they were to meet Arden in the woods, and when he didn't arrive as planned, they had taken the soap from their pack and rubbed it on their Kereki boots and baggy trousers. Mother had found them hiding. Lomes thought the dog was indicating that Arden was nearby but didn't want to be seen, so the softfoot had followed Mother. 'The dog led me here.'"

Linna described how together the two of them lifted Arden from the floor and took him to his bed. She had heated water, and Lomes bathed him and checked for broken bones. It was daylight by the time they finished. The two decided that Linna would go to work as usual and tell the stablemaster Arden was too sick to come to work that day. Lomes would stay inside and care for Arden. If anyone came and knocked on the door, Lomes would hide in the loft. The dog would stand between the door and the ladder, and no one would be permitted to go up. Linna said Arden had trained Mother to guard her so.

Linna gave me a sharp smile. "Truly, Zren, I did not know if Mother would allow Lomes to go up the ladder. But after seeing Arden's body after his beating, I was disinclined to warn them. The softfoot could take their chances just as the Wrens do."

Linna and Lomes both knew it was Viklanders who had beaten him. I just nodded slowly. We all had grown up in Kerek City. Whether shopkeeper's daughter or street child, we knew the feeling of helplessness…and perhaps, rage against that helplessness.

"Do you still have the papers Arden was carrying?" Tiju Tia asked.

Linna shook her head. "Lomes read them while I was at the shop. The softfoot said the documents were those Arden had gathered and needed to get to the battlefields north of Balza. I said we had a healer at Huk who could mend Arden. That I would need help. I knew it would be many days before Padro Morto or you would come here.

"Lomes agreed to tell Callis, took the Manumina mare we had here at the stable, and left that evening for Huk. Callis was here the next morning before I left for my position."

At our surprised expressions, Callis interrupted, "The softfoot gave me enough coin to take a fast horse. Ross took the mare Lomes had been riding to the stable and exchanged it for a fresh one and brought me another. The softfoot regretted not being able to accompany me to Cloa, but needed to go on to the battlefields north of Balza. Arden's stolen papers were too important to wait. We saddled up and were both gone within the decon of their arrival."

Callis exchanged a look with Linna. It was unreadable to me, but Tiju Tia took note of it.

"What is happening now? What is the word in Cloa about Arden's absences?"

"I have heard the Patron on our doorstep as he walks Linna home to her cottage," Callis began. "He complains how Arden has failed yet again to walk his sister home. He laments that her brother has no sense of responsibility at all. He wonders why the stablemaster is such a fool to let his daughter walk out with such a one as that. What would become of her if her brother continued to be so careless of Kereki custom?" Callis had tried to use a voice like Josef would do, but she did not have his skill, and we did not laugh at her mimicry.

Callis added only that Arden would take a long time to mend, but he refused to travel to Manumina to do it. The idea of a male protector needed to be maintained even if he could do nothing but be present in the house and give commands to Mother to defend their home.

Linna began slowly, "You should know, Tiju Tia, Ross had been found by Viklander soldiers setting ghostfire pots along the half-track to a Kereki encampment. They did not believe him that he was a friend of Vikland, but they didn't want to hurt him in case he truly was. They took him with them so he couldn't warn others of what they had done."

"He has returned," Callis added. "He takes care of his rabbits." No one said anything more and the silence stretched uncomfortably.

What no one said, is that with Callis in Cloa trying to heal Arden, and Ross refusing to help at all, Huk was no longer a place of refuge in Tiju Tia's network. And that meant, Falan and Jenny and Josef were now isolated in the worst of the battlegrounds north and west of Balza. There was no way to get word to any of them of the danger they were in.

Tiju Tia said nothing for a very long time. "I see I have to make other plans, but at this moment, I do not know what they should be. I will go to the great houses—dressed as Will—and I will learn what is happening there. I will leave Zren here to be sent to Manumina if help or another healer is needed. When I come back this way, Callis, I think you should travel with me, and we will return you to Huk. I want to talk to Ross. I want to see for myself what is happening west of us. I want to know what is happening with the hunt and hobble groups and with Falan and Josef. I know they claim they have many friends of Vikland to keep them safe, but that also means there are many mouths whose words can condemn them to a traitor's death. Once I know where everyone stands, then I can move them to another location."

I noticed she didn't say a safer place. But then she asked me to unhitch the horses and take them to the stable. We would keep the cart outside the door and spend the night.

It felt strange the next morning to see Tiju Tia drive the cart away without me. We had reconfigured the little cart to be pulled by one so that I would have a horse if needed, although I still preferred a wagon seat to a saddle. Linna had me walk her to her shop. She introduced me as a cousin sent by her family to be her male protector since her brother needed to travel home.

The Patron looked me up and down and narrowed his eyes at me. "A cousin."

Of course, she had replied. Her mother's brother had sailed on the seas to the edge of the world and came back with a Conrosan bride and child. It was all quite romantic and if he liked she could tell him the very long story of how it all happened. But then the Justice came in to talk with his friend. Linna tipped her head at the door, and I quickly left.

Callis and Arden and Mother were all in his room when I let myself back in the house. I called out so they would not have Mother leap out with teeth bared. Instead, Callis opened the door and invited me in to sit with them. Arden pushed himself up to lean against the wall. His long brown hair was again neatly brushed, his face clean but still pocked with bruises. He smelled of the infirmary at Manumina, and I wondered what medicinals Callis used that smelled so similar.

They asked me for all the news at Manumina and what I heard about the war. I told them of the morning spent with Rani the softfoot and the soldiers and the different types of ghostfire. I repeated Rani's warning that if the Wrens handled the pots to be very, very careful. I asked Callis more about Ross and if the Wrens were in danger without his help.

"Ross hasn't gone out on Wren business for a long time, Zren. He takes care of his rabbits and that is all. I bet no one asked what he was doing on that road when he was found by the Viklanders. It could have been many things, but it wouldn't have been Wren business." She shook her head slowly.

"What will happen now to Huk? If you are here, and Ross will not open his door to anyone, what will Falan do so far away from anyone? Does Josef know? Does the hunt and hobble group with Jenny know?"

Callis looked sad. "No one has heard from Jenny for a very long time. We think they traveled somewhere else. But we must consider the entire group did not survive. There is no way to know for sure."

I sucked in a hard breath. I had met two of the soldiers in the hunt and hobble—Ven Willa and Solkka Ulani. I could not let myself think the worse. *They traveled someplace safer, I reassured myself. Much safer. They were all safe. They had to be safe.*

Callis interrupted my spiraling thoughts, "Josef is clever. If he does not see me in Huk, he may think I am at the settlement south of the Northern Track healing a soldier or a softfoot. He will not worry. And Falan cannot worry if she doesn't know. They have friends who help them, so they are not as alone as Tiju Tia thinks they are."

I looked at Arden. "Do the others know you are hurt? Tiju Tia said I was to learn your paths and if you visited some places often I should take your place until you can walk again and go yourself."

He gave me an appraising look, and then a sly smile. "Ah, Zren. I am as useless as Ross. It is Mother who knows where to travel and what to do. I accompany her to roast the birds and rabbits she catches for us to eat. I carry the documents and mapcases too heavy for her to take from place to place. Although neither she nor I speak enough Vik to keep us safe, sometimes I can warn the soldiers we are there to help before Mother frightens them into running away." He stiffly spread his arms to take in his bed. "You see what happens when she is not there."

"Viklanders did this?" I had known this when Linna had told the story, but I had not wanted it to be true. "I had hoped you and Viklanders were caught out on a night rescue."

Both Callis and Arden laughed at my words.

"Ah, Zren, I miss your words of comfort." He sobered. "It was a night rescue. But the soldiers did not believe me that I was there to help them. They were in too much of a hurry to do more than to take the pocket of food and coins I was carrying for them. They did not search me once they knew I was too injured to follow them or alert others they were near. They may make it back to a place of safety."

I didn't know what to say to that. I knew the Viklanders had to trust strangers—the friends of Vikland and the Wrens, but I never thought what would happen if the Viklanders didn't believe those who were sent to help them. How many Viklanders were lost because they trusted too easily—or were not helped because they didn't trust at all? It was the first time I realized Truth and Trust were weapons as deadly as a crossbow and Sailor's Curse.

"I think it would be best if you stayed with Linna and walked about Cloa with her so many people see you and know she is not alone. It will also help that so many will see others coming and going. I will not be in bed so much longer." Arden gave me an odd smile. "There are many who want to see me away from Cloa."

I tried to think what Arden was not telling me. I remembered how Nelo had told me that Arden was thick-skulled and had barely learned to read and write Keresh. Even Falan, who had mocked Linna for living with a dog in the house, claimed Mother was smarter than the entire Kereki army and definitely smarter than Arden. I didn't know if this was a great game the Wrens played among themselves to escape notice, or if there were some secrets that needed to be hidden. But I decided I could play along as well.

I asked if Linna came home for midday or if we should eat without her. I had noticed that no one seemed to be about the kitchen cooking, and I worried that they were not the cooks that Siba and Rygee were. Callis laughed and said she thought I was to be the cook for them all as she was busy with Arden and he was too unwell to leave his bed. I laughed back and pretended she had told a great joke. Thankfully, she soon made midday for the three of us.

The next days passed. Tiju Tia came and went—in her disguise as a Kereki boy named Will—taking Callis back to Huk. Arden still refused to go to Manumina for healing, but he was much nicer to Tiju Tia this time. He assured us he would be well enough to get up and travel the hidden trails of Kerek, most likely as soon as the weather turned miserable in the Wet.

I continued to walk Linna to and from her shop each day and made sure I greeted the Patron respectfully. I told stories in the evening: West Islands Constellation Tales, Conrosan tales of Zren Janin, and the Matasi parables that I could remember from Bima Ritwik. I even repeated the Kereki tales I knew and asked Linna and Arden if they had ever heard of any. They had and shared those they knew with me. I truly didn't like the Trickster.

Linna and Arden had both given me their blankets to make my bed on the floor in the front room. That's why I was the first one to hear the scritch scratch at the door one night long after we had gone to sleep. Mother awakened immediately after and bounded over me to put her face down by the crack at the bottom of the door. She gave a soft woof but made no anxious sounds. I thought it had to be someone she knew well, so I carefully unbarred the door.

I opened it to a stranger. A Matasi man as far as I could tell in the dark, but that was based more on how he was dressed and his short curly hair. He looked startled to see me and started backing away from the door apologizing. Then he saw Mother standing beside me and stopped. He stood there uncertainly, and I wondered what I should do or say.

"*Bonan matenon,*" I heard Arden say behind me.

The man visibly relaxed. "*Bonan matenon.*"

I turned and saw Arden fully dressed and leaning heavily on a thick staff like the ones we used at Manumina to sort out the goats. He nodded to me and then turned back to the Matasian and spoke quietly in Mata. The man bobbed his head and then came in. I closed the door behind him. I heard a "histt" and looked up to see Linna looking over the edge of the loft. She motioned me up the ladder. Unsure, I paused, and she waved at me again. At the top she moved aside so I could sit cross-legged on the floor beside her. She put her hands on both sides of my face and turned me to look at her.

Linna smiled broadly. "Ah, Zren, if you are here with me then you see nothing you should not see. If anyone asks you can tell the truth. You stayed at Linna's house. We all know Arden was badly injured in a fight. You never saw a stranger in the house because Mother would never allow anyone to enter who would harm Arden or me. We have all met Matasi missionaries and have heard their stories of the Lost God. You never saw Viklanders. You never saw anything at all. You know all this is true, Zren, do you not?"

I broke into a large grin as I realized what she had done for me. She knew how I struggled to make my tongue as clever as others. So, she made what I saw match what I would be forced to say to others. I shivered in the dark. She got up and brought the sheeting from her bed and wrapped it about both of us. Soon the voices below fell silent. I heard the door open and close. There was no sound from below, and the house felt empty.

The moonlight through the window was too dim to see much, but I felt Linna's sadness.

"You might as well go down and bar the door, Zren. Will you sleep lightly enough to hear him if they return? Arden will not say anything because voices might carry on the night air, but Mother will give a soft sound to let you know to unbar the door."

"Should he be out?"

"No, he shouldn't. But Mother responds best to him. If they need to find someone in a hurry, then Arden must go as well. At least he can ride in a wagon. Although the lurching about will do him no good. I do not care if you sleep up here or down below, but we might as well try to close our eyes, morning will come too soon."

I nodded and turned to go down the ladder.

"Zren?" Linna leaned forward and cupped my chin. She looked directly into my eyes. "Swear to me, Tiju Tia will never hear of this."

I was so surprised I rocked the ladder. She cupped my chin a little harder. "Swear it."

I nodded swiftly, and she let me go.

I barred the front door and then burrowed into my nest of blankets on the floor. But it felt like decons before my mind quieted enough for me to sleep.

Days passed. Once when Linna was working and I was alone, I looked at the battered books that rested on the small table in the front room. I had thought they might be the books Linna used to teach Arden to read Keresh. I wondered if she would have time to teach me.

I flipped open the books.

They were not written in Keresh.

I closed them softly and looked at the shut door to Arden's room. I wondered what was happening to the Wrens. When Nelo had first come back from the crimpers, he had said there were some things Tiju Tia did not know and some things she should not know. Or was there a reasonable explanation for all of this and I just didn't have enough of the pieces to puzzle it out?

***

Arden and Mother finally returned days later. Although he moved slowly, Arden no longer used his stick to get about and his bruises were mostly gone. He slept a long time, only waking to eat and for stories in the evening.

The next day, he unrolled maps on the table and asked me to join him. His maps were different than Piffik's, and I wondered where Arden had found them. He showed me where Josef's and Nelo's houses were, and where they had last heard of Jenny and the hunt and hobble group. He said the battle lines moved too quickly between Kereki and Viklander armies so he wasn't sure where it was safe to travel. He said it was why he did not risk sending me out to take his place. He said Mother did not know me well enough, and I would not understand her when she warned if they were going to meet Kereki soldiers or Viklander softfoots. He looked at my face as he said this to me, and I tried to decide if he was telling me the truth.

I asked if he could tell me about the Matasian who had come all those nights ago. Instead, he asked me when was the last time that Tiju Tia had come to Cloa and delivered anything: food, coin, or clothes for the Viklanders in hiding.

I realized she had not been back since she had taken Callis back to Huk. I asked how he and Linna got their needs met.

"We take care of our own. Now that I no longer work at the stables, I need to find another way to earn coin. Linna cannot…" He stopped. Then I heard it too—a soft rapping at the door.

Arden quickly rolled up the maps and whispered to me to take them up the ladder to Linna's loft…and hide.

I scrambled up the ladder one-handed as Arden noisily made his way to the door. He said something softly to Mother, and the dog rose stiff-legged and began a low rumbling that turned into a full growl as Arden unbarred the door. I peeked over the edge of the loft to see a small boy—about the age of eight or so—standing on the other side of the open door.

The boy looked at Mother and then back to Arden. "Will it bite me?"

Arden glanced at the dog and back at the boy. "I dunno, will you hurt me?"

The boy smiled weakly. "Josef sent me with a message. I live in Balza so you should know I am not afraid of very many things to travel so far by myself."

"Do I know someone named Josef?" Arden waited. He did not invite the boy inside.

"He said to tell you to kiss the stablemaster's daughter goodbye and clean the horse dung from your boots. You are going on a long journey. He will be coming the day after tomorrow with everything you need. He said to tell you I am Linna's new male protector to be in compliance with Kereki custom, and that according to a man called Zren Janin, I am to tell you I have more wits than a bowl of porridge."

Arden opened the door a little wider and invited the boy in. "That sounds like a Josef I may or may not know." He looked at the boy. "Do you have a traveling bag? Or a name?"

The boy smiled and darted back outside. I called to Arden and asked if I should remain hiding in the loft or come down. He said it still could be some trickery. The boy could be only checking to see if anyone was home and was even now bringing a dance with Trouble. I should remain in the loft and if the boy was bringing others, I should not climb down to help him, but jump out Linna's window. If I did not break both legs when I fell to the ground, I should hurry to the shop and take Linna to Manumina as fast as I could. She would tell Tiju Tia some things that needed to be done.

I waited nervously until the boy came back. He was alone and carried a small travel bag and a shiny West Islands metal flask. Arden asked him if he had been so foolish as to carry that flask so boldly on the Northern Track between Balza and Cloa.

The boy scoffed. "Of course not," he replied. No one took the Northern Track except soldiers, grain trains, and supply wagons.

Arden smiled.

The boy said he could be called, "Pike." He puffed out his chest a little and said he would be a fierce weapon between Linna and anyone who would harm her.

Arden's grin grew larger. "Josef told you to use a false name? Did he choose the name as well?"

The boy now called Pike nodded vigorously. "See? Now you know he is my friend, and he sent me to tell you to be ready to travel."

"Where I come from—in Kerek City—a pike is a fish as well as the name of a weapon. I don't doubt that Josef would call you his friend, but he would make someone laugh if he could, even if he was too many furloughs away to hear it." Arden looked up at me in the loft. "You can come down now, Zren. I no longer need you to protect me from our fierce stranger." He looked at Mother and put his hand flat and palm down. Just like that, Mother relaxed and moved back to her blanket in his room; her task as defender of the house done.

Arden asked questions of the boy the entire time he made the meal for the three of us. Pike was talkative about what he had seen and done on the way from Balza. He had stayed with friends in Huk, but did not say who they were, and refused to say anything of how he had met Josef, or how they came to be such good friends. He said his family was dead, but he had an aunt whom he guarded when she needed to go on her errands. When Arden said he seemed very young to take on such an important role as a Kereki male protector, Pike only responded that his aunt and uncle trusted him and therefore everyone else did too.

Arden put the soup pot right on the table and handed out bowls for us to serve ourselves. The boy asked for biscuits, but Arden replied he did not know how to make such things. He went back to the kitchen and brought out cold stonebread for us to eat with our soup.

Arden told Pike, Linna was a fine cook, and he should learn how if he ever had free time from all the chores she would have for him. The boy gave him a long look, but Arden never smiled or broke his somber face. I thought the boy looked dismayed at what he had gotten himself into.

That night after Pike had heard a handful of stories of Zren Janin and his Legion of Heroes, he had finally fallen asleep on Arden's bed. Linna, Arden, and I climbed the ladder to her loft to quietly discuss what should be done. It was clear Josef had not known of Arden's injuries or of my arrival, so that meant he had not been able to reconnect with Callis in Huk. He had not sounded like he was in danger and had not sent a warning that Falan and Jenny were dancing with Trouble.

Linna thought it was best to have me return to Manumina and let the others know Josef and Arden would be away for a while. I should also warn the others, with her unknown protector in the house, no one should expect to spend an unguarded night in Cloa. They talked back and forth whether I should wait for Josef's arrival. Linna was already worried the appearance of so many men coming and going would create gossip she didn't need.

They decided the story would be that Arden and I had both returned home for a while and Linna's family was so impressed with her Patron at the shop, they had only sent along Linna's youngest brother as a protector until either Arden or their cousin could return.

When I returned to Manumina, Arden said, I needed to make sure that someone, Padro Morto, Tiju Tia, or even Rygee or me, would come often enough that Linna would have a way to send a message for help if needed.

And that was the end of my life as Linna's cousin.

CHAPTER 4

ZREN JANIN AND HIS SWORD OF COURAGE

There were many advantages to traveling during the Dry. As my horse and I wandered along the half-track south of Cloa, I thought that the war should stop during the Wet. Everyone could stay home with a dry bed and eat good food with those we wanted to spend time with. Perhaps then, once the sun came out again, everyone would decide that it was so nice to be surrounded by those we loved, that the war could be over.

But how would there be a corridor of peace from Vikland to the sea? Would people change their mind on how others needed to be treated if they only spent time with those like them during the Wet? I managed to give myself a pain in the head just thinking about it.

After eating the midday Arden had packed for me, I started to look for a spot where I could find water for the horse and a shelter to close my eyes for just a moment. I thought I remembered a shallow ravine with a small stream through it a decon or less ahead of me. *That would be just the place.*

Somehow, I managed to get off the half-track I thought I was on, or perhaps I was on the wrong one altogether. I didn't find a ravine with water until almost dark and this one had a bramble fence about it that I hadn't remembered from before. My horse scented the water and eagerly picked her way down the steep side, and I barely waited for her to finish drinking before I filled my own waterskin.

I wondered if I should continue traveling and hope to find shelter closer to Manumina, or stay here where I could hide among the steep edges and finish my journey in the morning, or keep going after dark and use the stars to tell my way. I was hungry, but Arden hadn't given me much food, and I thought maybe I should save the little left for the next day. I wondered if I had wandered farther away from Manumina or if I was closer than I thought.

I heard horses. I looked around. The high sides of the ravine hid me if the travelers continued on, but if they were looking for a water source, there was only the one way in and I would be trapped.

The steps grew fainter and I thanked the Wester stars. I decided to travel on and see if I could find a barn or a deserted settlement closer to Manumina. I carefully led my horse out along the stream, and we headed up a gentle slope.

"I knew we only needed to be patient and you would save us the trouble of coming down after you."

I looked up to see three of them on horseback. The youngest one had a bow with an arrow nocked, but not pulled back. The talkative one had no weapons at all. I guessed her role was to be the *titiro mai ke ahau*. The one in the middle had his hands hidden in a cloak. I thought he might be the most dangerous one—with throwing knives, or perhaps a long dagger.

"You don't want me. I'm so poor I was going to go without my end of day meal. I'm sure you can find fatter purses on the Northern Track," I pleaded.

"You have a horse. You must have coin to feed that horse. Where are you from? Headed to market? Or away?"

"Neither. Just a manabout looking for work. My horse is as hungry as I am."

"Let's see about that." The man and woman dismounted; the youth pulled back the arrow. I got the message. I didn't move.

She patted me down and found my coin purse. Thankfully, I had left almost everything with Linna and Arden. Since I had planned to sleep rough along the half-track, I didn't think I would need it. It was only to make me feel that I was not destitute that I carried a single coin.

She scowled at me. "He's telling the truth."

"Perhaps." The man shrugged, and I was completely taken unaware when he slammed his fist into my stomach. I crumpled to the ground. The woman quickly grabbed my arms and yanked them apart. He patted me down, rougher than she did, and much more thoroughly. He found my Sailor's Curse and laughed.

"What's this? A little knife for a little boy? Is this all your mother allows you to play with?" He held the Sailor's Curse by the wooden knob between pinched fingertips and made a jab in the air. "Ooooh, look! Look how fierce I am! I can fight. Look, I can fight a moonbeam." He laughed at me. "You thought you could stand against a Viklander army with this little knife?" He spat at my feet and then took a closer look at my boots. "Those boots are worth taking." He looked at the one holding the bow and arrow. "They might fit you if you wish to have them." The woman pulled out a long dagger and held it to my neck as the youth put away his bow, dismounted, and sauntered up to me. Two hard tugs and I felt the breeze on my boot linings.

The youth considered. "Those linings are better than the ones I have on. I'll take those also." Soon my feet were bare.

"And the horse," the woman announced. "See? You are a man without gratitude. You claimed to be too poor to rob, and yet you have given us your horse, your boots, your little knife, and a single coin." She shook her head in mock despair. "The lessons we have to teach you." She pushed herself to her feet.

I could feel tears fighting to spill over. At least I was smaller than all of them, so I would be left my clothes. I cradled my injured stomach and rolled to my side as I heard them mount up and ride away.

Once it was quiet, I shakily stood up and tried to think what to do. I would dig myself a hole to hide in, I decided, and tear my shirt to wrap and protect my feet as I walked home in the morning. But first, I needed to be much further away from the water. I looked towards a little outcropping in the nearly featureless pasture and decided to tuck myself there for the night.

I had just reached the rock when I heard a distant shout and spun about. There were four soldiers on horses. I could see the setting sun glint off their weapons—pikes and long knives. They were fighting with the three who had robbed me. I wished I could see as far as Rell to know if the soldiers were those I could ask for help, or if I should hide. I decided if they would ride away, then I would go and rob the bodies of my belongings. I wanted my Sailor's Curse and my boots.

The soldiers won, I knew they would. They strung the extra horses and whooped and hollered as they headed to the ravine for water. Once their heads disappeared below the edge of dirt, I scurried over to the bodies on the ground, wincing as the coarse grass cut my tender feet. I searched for my Sailor's Curse first. Then I found the coin purses, they all had one plus mine, and my boot linings and boots. I was sitting on the ground tugging on my boot linings when I saw the soldiers galloping back to me. There was nowhere to run, so I sighed and waited for them as they rode closer and bunched in a circle about me. They were Kereki, regular army, not someone's home militia. My heart sank.

"Where did you come from?" one of them asked.

I pointed to the rock. "They had robbed me when I was at the ravine getting water for my horse. They left me barefoot and without food or coin. I thought to spend the night hiding and then walk to safety in the morning." I pointed to my boots. "I am only taking what is mine." I looked at the one holding the horses. "That's my horse—the old one. I would like it back, but only if it pleases you." I inwardly cringed at the wheedling tone in my voice.

The soldiers looked at each other and shrugged. The one holding the lines urged his horse forward and dropped the reins to my horse near my feet. I quickly tugged on my boots. I stood up with my hands wide to my side to show them I was unarmed.

"You shouldn't be traveling alone. There are bandits all along this trail. Why didn't you take the Northern Track?" The soldier sounded curious rather than accusatory.

"Because there are soldiers all along the Northern Track." I answered truthfully and then wished I could swallow my words.

They laughed. "True. Well, come travel with us. We are traveling from Pagta to guard grain fields and sheep from the Cold Mountains. No more eastern battlefields! Obviously, we were blessed by the Kerek King to receive such an assignment to Evensong. Perhaps our good luck will rub off on you. At least travel with us until the danger of bandits is past."

"It would be retracing my steps to go to the Northern Track." I hesitated.

He smiled easily at me. "Truly, you should not travel alone." The others nodded.

I wondered what they would think if I insisted on traveling by myself. Would they think I was working against them? Or would they just accept we were traveling in different directions? Would it be so bad for us to travel together? They had not harmed me so far and they certainly could have. Perhaps I could sleep tonight and let them set the watch. I sighed.

"Thank you. I accept the gift of your hospitality. I do not say this lightly. I already survived one encounter with bandits. I am not sure I would have survived another."

The dark-haired one laughed. "Well then. Let's find a place with food and beds!"

We had hardly traveled a decon when we reached a small settlement just south of the Northern Track. When I learned where we were, I realized I had been lost nearly the entire day. I had made barely any headway at all from Cloa to Manumina. I wondered if I could remember what half-track I had been on. I wanted to look it up on one of Piffik's maps to see if I could retrace my wanderings. Truly, it was a half-track I never wanted to see again.

The courtyard of the inn was small but clean. The stable boys reached eagerly for the reins as the soldiers dismounted. The dark-haired one pulled his purse and handed coins about. He told the boys tonight my horse was an army horse and to care for it as well as the others. I followed the others into the inn, and the barkeep called out greetings to the soldiers. There weren't many others inside, and we quickly had apple jack and cider. The barkeep himself came to our table. He looked me up and down, and I stiffened—waiting to hear abuse or to be refused food and shelter. Instead, he asked if I was a Conrosan from Manumina. He had his fine furniture made by a Conrosan thirty years ago when he was first starting his inn, and it was as strong and sturdy today as when it had been first delivered.

I weakly smiled and said I thought he might be thinking of Mr. Qanaq. The father of the one who ran the woodshop now, but I offered no more information than that.

"That's the name! I did not recollect it until you said it. Well, if you see the son, tell him his father's work has stood the test of men as rough as this bunch." He dropped a heavy hand on the soldier closest to him. They laughed.

The soldiers insisted on buying my meal, saying I had been the decoy to pull the bandits out of hiding so the soldiers would not get an arrow in their backs as they rode by. I offered to tell them a story in gratitude. I started with the one of Zren Janin and the Geese. I had told that story to Rell seasons ago. It still wasn't the right title for the story, but it was how I thought of it.

"In the days of long ago, the border between Conrosa and Fairyland was not so well guarded as it is today. Sprites and goblins, monsters without names, and mists without faces would dance in the land of the humans to cause trouble and strife.

In those times there was a hero born. No one in Conrosa knew his parents, his age, or his place of birth. He called himself Zren Janin."

As I told the story of Zren Janin meeting the townspeople who had handfuls of excuses of why the girl deserved the upset cart, the judgment of her circumstances, and the indifference of her neighbors, I wondered what it would take to heal Kerek after the war. What would it take for the countries to work together so that anyone could live with the ease of life I had experienced in Matasi, and the acceptance of others I had learned from the

Conrosans at Manumina, and the willingness to explore and travel Rell told me in her stories of growing up in Vikland? What would it take to provide the Wrens with a home of their own and an opportunity to practice Truth and Trust? I wondered if they would ever have a Manumina of their own.

"Once they were quite clear of the crowd of villagers, the girl said, "Thank you! I would have been happy just to have you walk back and find my crutch for me, but you did so much more! I can care for myself, but when I stumble, I need a little help from those around me."

Zren nodded in agreement. "I could have done only that. There are people in the world who are like geese. They squawk and honk but do nothing more than set up an alarm. There are neighbors who would pick up your cane and tip their cap as they handed it to you, leaving you to gather yourself and your cart and your pony and travel on your way. And there are friends, who help you gather yourself, ensure all is well, and then travel with you on your journey a little way or a lot."

He raised an eyebrow and mischievously smiled. "I didn't want to be one of the geese!" He stepped back from the cart as her pony started trotting down the road.

It took her a moment to rein in her little pony and turn back to look at the young man who helped her.

The road was empty except for her pony and cart.

She smiled to herself as she picked up the reins and continued on her way to her own hearth and home. She knew she had met Zren Janin, a changeling fae so in love with the humans, he stepped in to be their champion."

The others in the inn drummed their hands on the tabletops when I was finished and called for another.

The dark-haired soldier said, "Let the man eat!" and the barkeep brought me another bowl of stew.

Slowly, slowly, I relaxed. I told more stories—only Conrosan fairy tales, and drank nothing but water after the first cup of apple jack. When the night grew late, the soldiers said they would sleep in the common room and there was certainly enough room for me. The barkeep said they would not need to set a watch; no bandits ever struck the inn itself.

I curled myself into the corner and carefully hid my Sailor's Curse in my hand. I stayed awake long after I heard the soft snoring of the other soldiers. I wondered if this was what Nebs and Rygee had done every night along the Northern Track. How long had they wondered if each night would be their last? How long till morning? How long until they felt safe? And each day, they would wake up and see those they had thought were the enemies treat them with kindness.

I fell asleep sometime during the night. It was a wonder I didn't stab myself with my Sailor's Curse.

***

The next morning, as we saddled our horses and the dark-haired one spoke with the innkeeper, they waved away my coin and said the Kerek King was happy to pay my way.

I was grateful. I had stolen the bandits' purses along with my own, but truthfully they were all thin. I wasn't so innocent to believe I would have enough coin to pay my way for the next days if I continued to travel the Northern Track. We mounted our horses and rode east.

The soldiers told me of their travels about the countryside. They had foolishly thought the war would be exciting—although their fathers had warned them otherwise and their mothers had begged them to stay away from the fighting. They had been tired and hungry for much of it. When the orders came for them to go to the encampment south of Evensong, they had all praised their mothers' fervent prayers which must have made it so, for none of them had families so rich they could buy their way out of their conscriptions.

They talked about their favorite foods. Chaz, the dark-haired one, said his mother could make conchas so delicate he dreamed about them. I said I thought everyone dreamed about food. They laughed and agreed. Once they had joined the war, they had all dreamed about food, and soft beds, and even parents and siblings they had previously thought troublesome.

I asked about their families and when they asked about mine, I said I had been raised by a village. The one called Solenn made a joke about a dozen mothers with wooden spoons chasing after me when I stole fingersweets, and I laughed as hard as the rest of them.

They asked me what I had been doing wandering around in the dark when they found me. I said I was a manabout sent to see someone about buying another horse. They looked at the old horse I was riding and joked they hoped mine lived long enough to make my destination.

I listened as they told me more about themselves. Archie was saving his coin to marry when the war was over. Ria was a blacksmith. At midday, we stopped along the road at a simple cart with a fire and grilled meat. The Kerek King was happy to buy my meal again, the soldiers said. They were looking forward to more stories when we reached Sary for the night.

***

When we came over the small hill, I saw the bridge where we had been ambushed all those years ago. The Battle at the Bridge—that's how I still thought of it. I suddenly felt sweat everywhere on my body. Only once before had I been forced to cross that bridge, when the Tax Collectors had taken me away from Manumina, and I had been so sick with worry and sorry for myself I could not take it in. Now however, I was older, years older, but seeing the place where we had fought—and some of us had died—made me feel like a lost child.

I knew there were no children hiding underneath to stab us with their knives, no archers hiding in the shrubbery along the river to shoot us as we crossed. And yet...and yet...I couldn't make myself understand that I was safe.

Ria turned and looked at me. "Everything all right?"

I nodded and panted shallowly trying to get myself under control. He drew his brows together in a puzzled frown. "You don't look well."

I tried to shrug. "Perhaps I had some meat not cooked as well as yours."

He guffawed and turned to go down the hill.

I kneed my horse to catch up with the others.

Chaz waited for us. "Does anyone need to fill their waterskin, or are we good until Sary?"

We shook our heads; we had enough water for another decon or two. Sary was the end of the day for us. There would be warm food, soft beds, and stories. I tried to calm myself by thinking what fairy tale I would begin the night's storytelling. I wondered if any of them had heard a Matasi parable or West Islands Constellation tale. *I could tell some of those*, I thought.

But I couldn't do it. I couldn't cross the bridge. I slid off my horse and tried to think how I could explain to my new friends what had happened to me at Miya's thirteenth crossing. How could I tell them I had been a survivor of a massacre without telling them I had been traveling with Viklanders?

Solenn and Archie turned to watch me. I leaned my head against my horse and tried to convince myself to get back in the saddle and cross the bridge. Ria trotted up to them and told them I had eaten some spoiled meat, and they probably didn't want to get downwind of me. I heard laughter. Chaz called back and asked if I was going to recover, or if I needed to swim across to wash out my small clothes before I joined them.

I didn't have to cross the bridge! I sighed in relief. I lifted my head to joke that I would spare their senses and swim. I would meet them on the other side.

That's when I saw it. A glint of red-grey pottery that didn't belong among the stones of the bridge.

I yelled, "No!" My shout startled the horses. Solenn and Ria's horses wheeled about. Chaz looked at me, puzzled at my outburst. I jerked on my horse's reins to bring her back and she stepped forward in front of me. Archie's horse high-stepped backwards away from the others. Time slowed to forever as I watched his horse's hind leg

step

directly

on

the

pottery.

***

I realized I was lying on the ground. I coughed, but I couldn't hear it. There was a ringing in my ears like the gong Salik Oqina struck when the King's Standard was seen outside Manumina's gates. I felt rocks and stones beneath me and beside me. I coughed up more dust and wiped my arm across my face. It came away smeared with dirt and blood. A lot of blood.

I closed my eyes again and smelled all the ugliness of death. I thought if I just kept my eyes closed a little longer I could pretend that the great bloody lump laying between me and the damaged bridge was not my horse. I could pretend that although Solenn and Ria and Chaz had been all on the bridge, they would have managed to survive. If I just screwed my eyes tight enough, I would see that moment when Archie's horse stepped on the Viklander ghostfire pot, and I could rewind the moments until we were all laughing again. If I never opened my eyes again, this moment, this decon, this day would never have happened.

But Ngahuru always said, "If wishes were horses, we would all ride behind the King." I curled up into a ball, and pretended anyway.

***

I drifted awake and could feel the setting sun on my bare arms. I realized my shirt was shredded about me. The ringing in my ears had stopped, but the pain had not. I opened one eye and looked at the horse that had saved my life by stepping in front of me. I was sickened at the remains. I closed my eye and wondered how long it would take for someone to find me.

I heard the sounds of a horse coming from the west. It stopped a fair distance, or perhaps it merely felt that way. After a moment, or what seemed like it, I heard a voice urge the horse down the bank and into the shallow waters. The splashes were small, it was the Dry after all. The horse and rider scrambled up the other side. I thought I would wait for them to stop before

I called out for help, but there was no pause at all. The horse started galloping away.

I sighed. Oh well. It would have taken quite a lot of effort to call out. It was quiet again. I wondered when the pain would stop.

It was full dark when I heard horses again, and the thump thump of uneven wagon wheels. Nothing good ever came of travelers in the dark, I knew. I stayed as still as possible with my eyes squeezed tight, hoping the bandits would think we were too bloody to rob.

Someone threw a bucket of water over me. Caught unaware, I coughed in surprise and heard a voice say, "This one is alive." I felt footsteps and a lantern light flickered against my closed eyelids. Rough arms reached under me and someone else grabbed my feet. I was laid gently in the back of a wagon. No one searched me for my coin. No one took my Sailor's Curse. I didn't want to get my hopes up, but I wondered if I might live.

I was in bed for two handfuls of days. Rell told me the Sary Justice brought me to Manumina. Someone had told him there had been another battle at the bridge, and he had gone out with as many people as he could muster. He told Siba and Rygee I was the only Conrosan, but he knew we had farmhands. The Justice wondered if we had been out on business for him and asked Rygee to look in the wagon to see if any of the others were known to Manumina. Rygee had looked and said no, but after the Justice left, he had been sick to his stomach for a long time. Later, he told Siba and Rell the others were nothing more than body parts. Only the distance from the others and my horse standing between the blast and my body had saved me from dying of ghostfire.

CHAPTER 5

THE WAR ON OUR DOORSTEP

I laid my head on the open windowsill in my room and listened to the rains blowing through. It was a rare storm. I remembered them as more frequent in Kerek City, but I did not miss them. Sea storms that started far from the coast but barreled ashore with winds and heavy rains to wash away the dirt and dead in Lowertown and Dockside. Seldom did they come far enough inland for us to receive more than scattered rains through the night, leaving beat down plants, fallen fruit in the orchards, and broken sticks angling out of puddles that would disappear after the sun kissed them.

I liked listening to the rain drum on the side of the house because I was warm and dry. I felt my eyelids grow heavy as I was ready to drift off. I thought I should go back to bed when I realized there was a different sort of drumming underneath the rain. I recognized the gallop of more than one horse and hurried down the stairs. I pounded on Rell's bedroom door as I thumped past her landing, and before I could unbar the door, I could hear her window open and the thunk of her crossbow hitting the window sill.

I slipped outside in the dark, with the night lantern closed at my feet, and listened as the horses galloped closer. These did not race to the closed gates, but slowed and turned at an angle toward Rell and my house.

When I thought they could hear me over the rain, I called out in Keresh, "Welcome to Manumina—"

"Zren Janin? Thank the Lost God, I am Bima Ritwik! Can you help us?" he called out hoarsely.

I clanged open the night lantern and threw a circle of light reaching beyond the first step. There were three horses, but only Bima was sitting upright. Each horse had two bodies slung and tied over the saddle blankets on the back of the horses. I roared for Rell to come help me. Together, we carefully pulled the wounded and unconscious into our arms and inside our house. We laid them out on the benches, the table, and the old rope bed of Chul's in the corner.

I recognized Kern and Malik even though it had been so long since I had seen them both. Tyra, our Wren at Fortika, had her arm cocked at an odd angle. The fourth was a Viklander I didn't know. Rell took one look at Kern and her face drained of color. She ran out into the rain into the stockade to get Siba and supplies from the infirmary.

While she was gone, I pointed Bima to the soft chair and gave him a rough piece of cloth for him to dry himself and water to drink.

"I'm sorry I don't have anything stronger. We keep apple jack at the bakery and the infirmary. But Rell will be back with Siba and they will be able to help." As he was drying himself, I looked him over. He was thinner than when I last saw him. A deep purple bruise covered his arm from knuckles to elbow, and he moved with the effort of someone in deep pain.

Siba and Rygee let themselves in.

"Rell pounded on our door," Siba explained. "She's getting supplies from the infirmary, but I said I would come and get us started." She had Rygee draw and heat water, and sent me to Rell's bedroom for rags and her West Islands shears. She checked Bima's pupils and then sent Rygee back through the rain to bring apple jack and any other hard spirits he had in the bakery. Rell came back, and then Rygee. The only ones who spoke were Siba and Rell, giving commands, asking Rygee or me to turn someone, hold this, cut there.

Bima held his cup of apple jack, tears coursing silently down his cheeks.

Siba would go over and touch him gently on his shoulder, his hand, his cheek, reminding him, "You're safe now, you did your duty, now we will do ours. Rest." Finally, she was able to get him to lean back in his chair. He fell into exhausted sleep.

"We need to get them into the infirmary," Siba announced, "but they cannot walk and I am not willing to drag them so. I know it seems foolish in this rain, but Zren, can you hitch the horses and bring the wagon with a canvas top on it? We will need to use all your blankets to cushion them, I want them dry even for such a short journey."

I grabbed my cloak by the door, threw up my hood, and stepped outside on the porch. The lantern was still on the porch casting a feeble light into the night. The three horses stood there, heads drooping, reins trailing. I had forgotten all about them. I gathered the lantern and the reins together and took them in through the side door.

When I entered the stable leading the horses, I could hear movement above. Thank the Wester stars, Piffik was sleeping in Vigdis' rooms tonight instead of his house on the south wall. He came down the steps barelegged, dressed only in his long shirt.

"Piffik, I have three horses which have been standing in the rain too long. We have five injured at my house, and Siba wants to move them to the infirmary with a wagon and a canvas top. Can you help me?" I pleaded.

"Start with the horses first, Zren. I'll be down in a moment." He turned and ran quickly up the stairs to dress.

I wiped down the horses, fed, and watered them. Since Lou was out with the cheese cart and Tiju Tia was out on the rag and bone wagon, we slipped the horses easily into empty stalls. Then I pulled the willow braces we had used on Chul's wagon all those years ago and inserted them in the corners of one of our smaller wagons. Piffik took down the heavy oiled canvas and rolled it over the braces, and we secured it on each side. We turned the cart and he backed Old Dris into the traces. She was fidgety about the canvas, or maybe the late night, but at last Piffik got her to mind him. He grabbed his hooded cloak from a hook by the door, and we pulled out into the rain.

It took the rest of the night, but at last, all the patients were stretched out on beds in the infirmary. Rell and Siba had fed them the sleeping draughts and lit the sleeping incense, and Rell said she would sit up with them. Bima had stayed behind at my house, saying he was finally warm and dry, and he didn't want to go back out in the rain. He had stretched out on Chul's bed and was deeply asleep when I returned to my house and my own bed. I stood over him and watched his chest rise and fall. The tears had dried on his face, and I wondered what had caused them. The battle? Pain? The desperation of knowing he was the only one responsible for all of them? I closed the lantern and walked up the stairs to my room. After first meal, we could hear Bima's story.

***

The corner of the room where Bima was sleeping was quiet as I crept downstairs the next morning. I waited for a moment in case I had awakened him, but then went out to do the animal chores. I stopped at the infirmary, where Rygee had already brought food to the healers and soup to the patients. I asked if I should bring some to Bima, but Siba said to wait until he woke up on his own, since she had no idea how long he had been awake to bring everyone to safety.

I cleaned out the stables and then came around to see what Rygee was baking. I only got to the door of the bakery before he brought me a fetti for each hand, and then chased me away saying I stank too much from the stables to come inside. I went to see if Bima was awake and he could tell me what happened. I eased my head around the door, but he was lying still on Chul's bed. I knew better than to walk in the house with my stinky boots. Rell would make me wash the floor.

I was spreading fresh hay in the stables when Piffik came out to find me.

"Rell went back to your house a few moments ago to get her steel shears to cut more bandages."

I stopped pitching hay and wiped my face with the bottom of my shirt. "I'm quite sure I left them on the table."

He said gently, "Rell asked me to tell you Bima Ritwik is dead."

I stared open-mouthed at Piffik. I caught a glimpse of Piffik's startled face as I felt myself slide into his arms. And then I remember nothing at all.

***

It was a somber gathering. Rell and Siba were in the infirmary with Tyra, Kern, and Malik. The Viklander boy had died during the night without regaining consciousness. Malik had asked that he not be taken away, but only covered. She would explain while they talked.

Kern's long braid had been cut off close to her head and deep bruises circled her neck. Someone had very nearly succeeded in choking her to death. Malik's braid was also gone and she had a black eye that had faded to the greenish yellow of old hay and a fresh red burn across her jaw on the opposite of her face. Tyra was still asleep, her broken arm splinted and wrapped, her face nearly as pale as goat's milk.

Piffik and I slipped into the two chairs Rygee had put out for us. He stood behind Siba, his arms crossed, his face unreadable.

"We need to tell you what happened," Malik began in Keresh. "My group was fighting north by the Cold Mountains. We had heard of a farmer who was supplying the Kereki army encampment near Evensong with food, and we hoped to disrupt his supply wagons. We found them, disabled the drivers, and drove off the wagons and horses to our own troops. The farmer had his own militia and farmhands track us to the encampment. Our site is too well fortified for them to attack, so they must have waited and picked up our trail again and followed us as we went east toward Regno. We didn't know we were being tracked. I knew of an outbuilding that was supposed to be safe. We rested there for the night, and whether our sentries slept or whether the farmer knew the place well, we were surrounded and burned out. Juselly and I were the only survivors. Now horseless, we walked east to Fortika where we knew we could find help from the gamekeeper's daughter. Although we left messages, we could not find her. On the second day, a young boy came with a small bag of food and tied it to a tree branch above our rock message to Inezi. He left.

"The bag had bread, fruit and a message that said Inezi had taken Viklanders over to the border, but we should hide in the gamekeeper's cache where meat was hung to age. Someone would bring us more food at the end of the day. That 'someone' was your Wren, Tyra."

Kern continued, "I had been softfooting in the area trying to find out what happened to a patrol who had disappeared six days earlier. Anyway, I startled two men sleeping rough without the scent of a campfire. My skill is the crossbow, not good for hand-to-hand fighting. But I had a dagger of West Islands steel, and I was taller with longer reach than both of them." She gestured at her neck. "I won't say it was easy, but I walked out alive while they did not."

She paused a long time. "Tyra found me at dawn collapsed by the side of a path. She had a small basket of food and water. She asked if I knew my Conrosan folk tales, and said she was a friend of Zren Janin. If I could walk a little further, she could get a wagon to take me to Manumina and a Vik healer, or Inezi would come back to Fortika in a few days and take me over the border to Vikland."

Kern smiled at me. "Names have power. I found I could walk a little further after all. Tyra brought me to the shed where Malik and Juselly were hidden and gave them the basket."

Malik picked up the story again. "The next day the boy brought us more food and water, three short bongs, and Kereki clothes. He said he had a message Bima was in the area and someone would try to bring him that night to see us. He said Tiju Tia wasn't due for another six days, and it would be too long to hide us on Fortika lands. But he had a message traveling with a friend to get us some horses. We should rest as much as we could. If the Wren could get horses and a wagon, we would be leaving that night.

"It was just past deepest night when we heard our signal. Tyra brought in Bima and the Viklander soldier and the six of us made plans to leave. Tyra would take us to the stables at Fortika where a boy, Therin, would have horses waiting for us." Malik paused and Kern took up the story again.

"We had barely walked out of the shed when we were attacked. I don't know if they had followed Tyra or had tracked Bima and the soldier. Juselly had been the first one out of the shed and caught the first knife. We pulled our tahn bongs, but we were injured and there were more of them. When we didn't show up at the stables at the time we had planned, Therin knew we were in trouble and brought the four horses to us. The galloping horses scared our attackers and they fled. We would not be alive otherwise. Therin and Tyra got us on the horses. He told Tyra she had to go too. He had no news if we would be met with horses halfway. If we were not met, Tyra needed to take us and fall back to Nelo's holding. The boy said he could not find Nelo's home in the dark by himself." Kern stopped talking.

"Kern, Bima, and I rode singly. Tyra was too injured and the Viklander soldier took her with him. We took off southeast for Manumina." Malik fell silent for a long moment, "and that's all I remember until we woke up here to find out the Viklander boy is dead and we didn't even know his name."

"Rell?" Piffik raised an eyebrow.

"He's a lot younger than us. I don't know him either. I would say he was one of Bima's softfoots or someone still serving his military service," Rell said slowly.

"He certainly knew how to use a tahn bong," Malik added.

"He's not one of ours," Kern confirmed. "I know all of our softfoots." She paused. "If I ever get back to Vikland, I will never neglect my close weapons training again."

She looked out the window and spoke softly, "I can't believe Bima is dead. He was the one who kept us moving and on course through the backcountry. He said he could get us to the Northern Track and then I would need to take over for him to get us to Manumina."

She looked at me. "He said you had taught him to tell time and direction by the stars."

Rell cleared her throat. She explained how only three horses had arrived at Manumina in the remnants of the storm, and only Bima had been sitting upright and conscious. She described how he sat in a chair while she and Siba labored over the others on the tables and benches and bed, but he said nothing of his own injuries. There were cuts to clean, broken bones to set, bruises and burns to attend.

When the others were moved to the infirmary, he insisted he just wanted to rest where he was and not go out into the rain again. He had laid down, cautiously and stiffly, in the empty bed, but Rell and Siba had blamed it on sitting on a horse for so long. When Rell had checked on him the next day, it was clear he had died decons earlier, probably not too long after he had gotten them all to safety.

Rell apologized for tending to the ones in the infirmary and not going home that night, for not checking on him sooner, for not understanding how badly he was hurt, for not being enough to heal him.

We all cried then. For Bima, for the nameless boy, for Juselly and the rest of Malik's patrol, for all the wasted deaths in this stupid, stupid war.

CHAPTER 6

MAY HIS NAME LIVE ON

Malik and Kern had begged us to take the bodies to Vikland so the Viklander boy could be claimed by his family. It had already been a half day since he and Bima had died, so there could be no further delay. Piffik said he would do this, but only if Kern, Rell, and I accompanied him. Malik was too injured to travel, so she would stay behind with Siba and Rygee.

Piffik and I quickly finished two coffins adequate for traveling. Rell and Siba had already washed the bodies, but now wrapped them with herbs, myrrh, and winding cloths. We grabbed a few belongings. Rell reminded me to pack my Viklander clothes. I said she had never returned them when she and Piffik had gone to sell the horses, but then I found them in my chest exactly where they should be.

We had never dismantled the canvas from the wagon. Piffik said that would be the best one to take. The coffins would be protected, and Kern, Rell, and I could stay underneath out of the rain as well. The sun peeked out while we were loading the coffins. Some Dry season. That sun was the only moment of the trip when it wasn't raining. Siba filled our water flasks and Rygee gave us a bit of the morning baking with cheese and spiced meat. I loved fresh baked bread, but everyone was in a hurry so as soon as we finished midday, we were on our way.

All of us took turns crawling underneath the canvas with the coffins to escape the rain. I couldn't imagine what Kerek City would be like or the battlefields closer to the sea. Could they even fight when a sea storm was drowning them?

We reached the Ishes garrison—still held by Vikland— before sunset. Or I assumed it would have been before sunset, if the rain would have ever stopped. Piffik had insisted Rell and Kern be the ones to drive the wagon close enough to hail the fort. We were admitted into the garrison, they explained what happened, Piffik met with the quartermaster he knew, and I stood under dry eaves and watched everything about me.

Since we were carrying Vikland dead, the commander had everyone fall out. A richly painted caisson was pulled out of the livery by hand and the coffins were loaded on. Rell came and stood next to me so she could translate from Vik to Conrosan what was said.

The commander called out, "Bima Ritwik, a Son of Vikland," and every soldier called back in unison, "May his name live on." Then the commander had called out, "A soldier known only by his courage and his sacrifice," and every soldier called back, "May his name be known and his story retold." Then four heavy Vikland horses had been brought out and hitched to the caisson. Four soldiers in the fanciest uniforms I had ever seen on Viklanders came out of the barracks carrying bulging travel bags and tucked them in the caisson before the carved and gilded wooden cover was closed. Two took their seats on the wagon, and the other two soldiers mounted horses and took the honor guard positions. The gates were opened, and the procession moved out.

Another rider on a horse rode out quickly ahead of them. Rell told me the single rider would go ahead and let the other garrisons and stops know the procession was coming so they could be ready. The procession would change horses and soldiers along the way but the caisson would drive nearly continuously until they reached the palace at Juisiti. There would be formal ceremonies for each of the Viklanders once they reached the city attended by the highest ranking military leaders available. Rell said it was very important to Viklanders that those who made the decisions in war knew the blood cost of those decisions.

The commander ordered new horses to be hitched to our wagon and two soldiers to drive us. We would follow behind the caisson—a long way behind. The four of us huddled in the back under the canvas, dozed fitfully through the night and all the next day, then complained about our empty food sack until we reached the palace.

The honor guard must have reached the palace quite a while before we did. When we arrived, the soldiers drove directly to a side door where we were whisked inside to rooms with steaming tubs of water, fresh clothes, and hot food. The bath could wait I decided, the meal could not.

I was still pushing food in my mouth when there was a knock at the door. Without thinking, I called out "Come in" in Conrosan. While I was still trying to think of the Vik words, the door opened and Miyamoto Suki stood there. His beautiful long braid was now no longer than his shoulders, and there was a small scar high on his cheek, but I forgot everything except he was standing in front of me again.

"You're alive! And here!" I pushed myself up and hugged him tightly.

He laughed, awkwardly returned my embrace, and stepped quickly out of my arms. "Did you jump in the soaking tub with all your clothes on? You are wet through!"

"It rained the entire trip, but we didn't bring enough food in our haste to get here. So food first and bath after that." I cocked my head. "How did you know I was here?"

"The honor caisson came in decons ago. They said you were following. Kern had sent a message with them, if it would be possible to arrange for all of you to stay at the palace and to let her family know she was in Vikland." He paused. "She wishes to meet with the Diplo and First Soldier Joon as soon as possible about our armies in Kerek." His voice cooled, "She said Rell Huena is here."

"She is," I said slowly. "Miya, has Rell done something wrong? Other people, like Rani and Lomes, also were, mmmm, not happy when they saw Rell at Manumina. Why?"

"She did not return to her country and her position in the Diplo when she was asked if she had recovered from her wounds. She *should* be considered a deserter and her braid cut to show her disgrace. Rani says he needs her skills as a bowmaster, but Chul Swyler told First Soldier Joon he needs her at Manumina. So, because Manumina has agreed to be a way station for us and because of your help to Vikland, she is considered posted at Manumina until the war's end." He added darkly, "Then she must return, with or without her lover."

A lover? I knew there was a whole lot of something I didn't understand, and I didn't want to get Rell in trouble so I needed to tread carefully.

"Miya, Rell is our *only* defense at Manumina. If she leaves us, we fall."

He shrugged. "I regret you have no other warriors, but her duty is to Vikland. But as I said, she is posted there until we win the war."

When Rell and Piffik had come back from Vikland during the Dry, I remembered Rell saying she was on the rolls as serving as a translator and healer at Manumina. She had thought it was Miya who had listed her. After all, she had been traveling with him on his thirteenth crossing of Kerek when we had been attacked and she had been left behind. But Miya didn't sound at all like this was something he had done. So who? Obviously, I couldn't ask Miya.

I changed my questioning, "Any word on who the unknown soldier is?"

"From Kern's description, we have called any military leaders within the city to see if they will know him. Kern said he was a very strong tahn bong fighter. He and Bima put up a tremendous defense before the attackers fled."

I shivered. Miya mistook the reason and stood up quickly. "You're catching a chill. Take a bath, sleep, or wander about this wing, but no further. There are lots of plans being made and Bima's family has already been sent for. The celebration of his life and his victories will be at sunrise tomorrow."

"That's not nearly enough time for his family to travel so far." I blurted out, and then reconsidered my words. "Oh, was he finally able to bring them here?"

Miya gave me an odd look. "Of course, they are. His parents live just beyond Juisiti. His sister is in the West Islands. She won't come, of course, she never completed her military commitment." He made a face like he had smelled something unpleasant.

"No, I mean his wife and daughters. I think he said they live in Alenti. He met her in Matasi. Your messenger cannot even reach them by tomorrow."

"Truthfully? I had heard that about him, but I did not believe it was anything but a foolish boy caught in a bed not his own." Miya looked at me. "Where did you hear this?"

I hesitated.

Miya sensed my unease and shook his head. "It doesn't matter. Vikland has a warrior culture, Zren. The stories told at Bima's celebration are to celebrate his deeds and his bravery and remind his family of his sacrifice for Vikland. I do not believe *she* has ever been to Vikland, but I do not know that to be true, either. Perhaps his parents have never met her, and now would not be the proper time. And if she *is* from Matasi, it is best she is not there. There are families in Vikland who have an empty chair at their table because the Matasi Triune did not honor their promises." With that he slipped out the door, leaving me dumbstruck at his cruel words.

***

I am good at following directions. I nearly drowned myself in the tub by nodding off, so I crawled in the bed and slept deeply. I woke up at a knock at the door, and this time I remembered the Vik words for "please come in." Two people entered. One had another tray of food, and the other brought a pile of fresh clean clothes in the dark color and close fit all Viklanders seem to prefer. I held them up and they were in a much smaller size than the ones that had been initially waiting for me. I smiled and nodded. One asked—in Vik—to take away my wet clothes. At least I thought that was what she said. Rell had told me not to speak Keresh unless I had no other choice. It was in poor taste, she said, to speak the language of the enemy. She said it would be good practice for me to use my Wester, because everyone wanted to be posted to the West Islands, or no one would think anything of a Conrosan speaking Conrosan. So, I nodded again at the one holding my wet clothes and boots and hoped she didn't just offer to throw them away.

The boots left for me weren't as comfortable as my own Kereki leathers, but they were dry and sturdy and smelled like honey and something else. I wondered if it was the scent Arden's dog used to find lost Viklanders. I wondered if anyone in Vikland knew how the scent gave them away. I wondered why the Kereki army didn't use scent dogs. I ate again, a little, because I could, and decided to wander outside the room.

When I stepped out there was a man at the end of the hallway. He was handsomely built, broad-shouldered, but not as tall as most of the Viklanders. He had curly brown hair like mine. I couldn't see more than that. He turned my way and hurried down the hall to me.

"Piffik?" I was so surprised I said it again, "Piffik?"

I had always seen him in the baggy shapeless clothes of Kerek or the plain Conrosan trousers and long shirts. To see him in something that emphasized his body was as shocking as seeing him bare-chested. "You really need to wear Vik clothes more often. You look as handsome as these soldiers." I gave him a sly grin. "Has Rell seen you yet?"

He gave me a long-suffering look. "Have you seen Rell? We probably shouldn't be wandering about without someone who can speak Vik for us. I can't find her in this hall, and I don't want to wander where I shouldn't. I would hate to be mistaken for a softfoot."

"All I've done is eat and sleep," I admitted. "She's not in her room?"

"No. Kern's family has already come and picked her up. I don't know if Rell's family would do the same."

"Kern is gone?"

"Yes, but just for the day. I saw her off myself."

I knew that voice. I *knew* that voice, even after two years, I *knew* that voice. I laughed. I turned to greet Solkka Ulani and… froze.

His face, his beautiful face, had a scar along his jaw from below his ear to under his mouth. Someone had tried to slit his throat. Only tucking his chin, or something like that, had saved him. His braid had been hacked off close to the nape of his neck leaving too little hair to pull back into a braid or even a tail. Although his hair was black like a Viklander, without the braid to restrain it, his hair was even curlier than mine. For the first time, I recognized more than Viklander in his face.

The smile in his eyes died as he took in my horrified expression.

"Yes, well," he snapped. "I've changed a little since you saw me last." He turned away, and I could see the hurt in his posture.

I put my hand gently on his arm. "Solkka, I am beyond glad to see you again. I have written you a hundred letters in my head in Wester, in Keresh, in Vik. Okay, well, not Vik. I still cannot understand your language. But I couldn't write them down and send them because I did not know where you were. All I could do was look at the stars at night and ask all the West Islands constellations to keep you safe. Every time Tiju Tia and I would drop off food or supplies or coin to the Wrens, I imagined it would be used to make your life a little less dangerous, a little closer to coming back. I froze, not because of what I see in front of me, but because I came *that close* to losing you forever. I never once knew the danger you were in."

I turned my head to Piffik to have him reassure Solkka I was telling the truth, but he was gone and the corridor was empty except for the two of us. I moved in front of Solkka, and his eyes were bright with unshed tears.

"Solkka, please, Solkka, I don't want to think I ever hurt you."

He hugged me fiercely, and I could feel the pounding of his heart. Or maybe it was mine.

"*Ka rangona o kupu,*" he whispered, "*E arohaina ana to ngakau.*"

"Your words are heard," I repeated back to him. "Your heart is cherished." For two years I had wondered how he would greet me again. Had I messed up everything by not understanding his words at Manumina? Now, I felt he was saying he was willing to learn who I was. Living at Manumina made me feel safe, but this was something different, something better.

Too soon, I felt his arms loosen and he straightened. "Do you have time to walk and talk or has the Empress asked you to take tea with her?" At the shocked look on my face, he laughed. "That is a Vik joke. We say it when we have meetings here in the palace. Truly, this place is so large, you could live here for a year and never see the Empress or her daughters."

"Oh. I have time, I think." I rubbed the back of my head. "I don't know where I am supposed to be."

"Then let's go to your room and talk. If someone needs you, they will check there first," Solkka said decisively.

He followed me into my room and went straight to the tray with food. He stuffed a bun with cheese and grabbed a yellow fruit in his other hand.

"You were holding out on me, Zren."

"What are those?" I gestured to his hand with the fruit.

"Pears?" he offered. "They grow them in the east of Vikland. We don't export them so I understand why you don't know what they are." He took a bite and held it out to me. "Try a bite?" I put my hand over his and bit down. I looked up in his eyes as I tasted the juicy sweetness of the fruit.

"Zren, you are making this very hard," he said hoarsely. "I wanted to spend today just talking, so you could get to know me."

I stepped back. "Yes, well." I cast about for something to talk about that wouldn't remind me of how close he was and how good he smelled. "Do you know who listed Rell Huena as posted to Manumina?"

Solkka laughed. "Well, that's not quite what I had in mind, but sit down. It's a start." He took another bite of pear. "So tell me what you know."

I started from the time he and Bima Ritwik had left us almost two years ago. How the Council of Wisdom had told them 'no' and the two would be sent back to their Empress empty-handed. How the Kereki army had come, just as Solkka had predicted, and taken the livestock and burned the harvested fields—but the rains of the Wet had come early and saved Manumina. How after a winter of hunger, most of the Conrosans became refugees in Vikland. How a woman from Kerek City and her two handfuls of Wrens had joined our band at Manumina, and given us hope and help before fluttering their way across Kerek to help Vikland in the struggle for justice. How I had encountered Bima one time before this last time, and he had talked to me of the Matasi God, his family in Alenti, his daughters, and his duty to Vikland. By the time I finished, Solkka had sat down and eaten the rest of the food on the tray.

"Bima wanted to know who was running our softfoots. He wanted to know how the Wrens had come to the war already trained and unafraid," I finished. "He said it had Ngahuru's hand all over it. I was scared he would know Tiju Tia and Ngahuru were the same, and I didn't know what he would do with such knowledge, so I gave him our only Viklander, Rell Huena, as a *titiro mai ki ahau*. But Miya said Rell should be treated as a deserter because she didn't come back when you and Bima asked her to. I think you have something to do with it, but I don't know, and I don't know who to ask without getting Rell in trouble. Whatever happens, I don't want Rell in trouble. She is our only defense at Manumina."

I took a deep breath and added softly, "She says I am her little brother." I tipped my head to the side and grinned. "It's sorta talking about you."

Solkka looked at me gravely. "Tiju Tia and Ngahuru is a secret you and I share, Zren. If anyone learns otherwise, it will not come from me." He looked awkwardly at the ceiling and then looked sheepishly at me. "Do you know any Kereki Trickster tales, Zren?"

I looked at him in disgust. "They're terrible! I met a man who nearly lost his life because he had agreed to have his ship and his men freed..." Then I remembered no one should know the Spice Island sea captain was still alive. I hastily added, "Bima told me two on the way to Manumina once, one about Death and one about Greed. They were so tricksy, I made him tell me Parables of the Lost God for the rest of the journey!"

Solkka laughed so hard I thought he was going to fall off his chair. "Oh, Zren. There cannot be anyone like you in the entire rest of the world." He slowed his laughter to a chuckle. "Well, I knew it would catch up to me sooner or later, but I never thought it would be you."

He took a deep breath. "I suppose it goes without saying, tell no one, Zren. I would have my braid of honor cut off for this, if I had not lost it already. Only two people knew, and now Bima is dead. Do you understand how serious it is? What I am about to tell you?"

I nodded a little uncertainly, but Solkka told me anyway. He said the goodwill trip had not been as fruitful as they had hoped. They had found two Viklanders working on a farm just south of Regno who were beyond glad to come back to Vikland with them, but he was afraid the others lost on the crossings of the Northern Track were dead without the funeral pyre and a celebration to name their deeds. The Kerekis they encountered were friendly enough to take their coin, but they had found few, according to Bima, to trust to side with them if it came to war.

It came to war.

"I truly thought, Zren, when we parted at Manumina, I would come see you during the following Dry. Manumina is not so far from Vikland, and while I was getting posted about, you might want to follow, and we could travel together for a while." He gave a shy half smile.

"I knew when we left Manumina, we would be required to say whether Rell Huena was still healing or had she deserted. She knew so as well, and to her integrity, did not ask us to say she was still injured. I thought perhaps she needed a little more time. I told Bima we should say she is still healing, and when I came the following Dry, I would bring another Witness. We would talk to her about returning to Vikland and returning to her post in the Diplo, and then a hard decision could be made."

"Bima had another idea. If I agreed to say Manumina had thrown in with us, he would say Rell needed to stay there as our eyes and ears—to ensure Manumina stayed loyal and to help Viklanders if it came to war. He thought I might need to come often to meet with her, and then—you could get to know me." Solkka sighed. "I had not known until he said so, Bima could see my heart in my face. That was always Bima's greatest talent—to be able to see what our hearts most wanted—and trick us into giving away priceless jewels for his shiny baubles."

Solkka looked away from me. "He offered me a Trickster bargain. One in which he gained his heart's desire—Manumina as his conquest—and I was offered that which I already had, but didn't know I had—a chance to change your mind about me. I accepted and he listed Rell Huena as a healer and presented

Manumina as a gift to the Empress." He gave me a sly grin. "I don't think he counted on two hundred Conrosans showing up as refugees though."

"Bima Ritwik saved Rell?" I was incredulous.

"Zren, I have known Bima, I should say, I have been acquainted with Bima for nine years. I am younger than he is, and he had already been in the military for years when I served. Bima and Truth seldom sit at the same table, but the end result always benefits Vikland. He has crafted a perception which says otherwise, but he is a true son of Vikland."

"You mocked him for…"

"I did. And so did others. I had heard he had married in Matasi at an age when most of us were still learning to put our boots on the correct feet and find our way about the academies. But he never brought his wife to Vikland. So, I thought, as others did—I might add—he had married her in her country to appease her family, but he had no intention of honoring his marriage in Vikland.

"I did not know until you told me today his family lived in Alenti. But I do know, at the beginning of every Wet he stayed too long gathering secrets in Matasi until it was too late to come home to Vikland over the Silver Mountains."

He nodded slowly. "Quite clever, truthfully. We in Juisiti felt sorry for him trapped for the entire Wet in Matasi with all their ridiculous rules. He spent the season softfooting at the many embasados but tucked up with his family every night. A Trickster bargain for both Vikland and his wife."

"That's horrible," I sputtered.

"That was Bima," Solkka said gently. "Who is going to tell you their secrets? Someone you think is upright and serves Vikland as an honorable member of the Diplo? Or someone whom everyone says serves himself?

"He taught his softfoots through trickery and deceit, lessons that stuck more firmly than if he guided them with patience and forgiveness. He cast about a reputation of a man who served only himself in order to gather the information of dishonest men. He tolerated our jokes of his infidelity in order to find those who would whisper the secrets of others heard in bedrooms and on their pillows. He was a hard taskmaster to his softfoots, but until the war, he had never lost one to stupidity. *That* is how he became Vikland's finest Softfoot… and a man no one would trust."

CHAPTER 7

PLANS AND REPLANS

There was a knock at the door.

Miya stood in the doorway dressed in a full military uniform.

He smiled broadly, "Solkka Ulani, I thought I might find you here." He sobered quickly. "First Soldier Joon says they have a name for the unknown soldier. He is Malan Sala, second year military, his home is just beyond the Summer Plains. The Empress is sending her second daughter as Witness. You and I will be the honor guard." He paused. "I'm sorry, Solkka, First Soldier Joon said you knew him. But from where? He was too young to have served with us."

Solkka's face crumpled. "Malan Sala? I did know him. He was a friend and classmate of my younger brother, Tedros. At the Academy of Botanicals. He and I also served together under Ven Wila while she ran her hunt and hobble between Vingt and Balza. We were separated and lost him in the skirmish in which our healer was killed—during the Dry." He turned to me and explained, "That was just before we met Tiju Tia. That he survived in Kerek so long without help or assistance, until Bima found him, is a testament to his courage and his cunning. I am not sure I could have been so resourceful."

"May his name live on," Miya murmured.

"May his name live on," Solkka repeated. They were quiet for a moment and then Solkka cleared his throat. "I'll get my things. Where should I meet you?"

"Here is fine. We leave in less than a decon, and I have some things to say to Zren."

Solkka raised an eyebrow and stood. He waited for Miya to move in or out of the doorway, and I was struck by the difference between the two men. I knew I was slight of build, I was reminded so every time I stood next to anyone. But I always thought of Miya as more. To see Solkka who was taller and broader next to him made me realize Miya's presence which filled up the room was based on his command of power and not his size, just a hand taller than I was.

Miya finally stepped into the room and Solkka rolled his eyes. "I'll be back, Zren, as quickly as I can." I could hear him hurrying down the hall.

"Are you well? Did you rest?" I nodded as Miya shut the door to give us privacy.

"I am sorry for you too, Zren. But we will be back in four days if you can wait for us. The Empress said specifically Solkka Ulani needed to go as he knew Malan Sala and could talk to the stories of his life."

I startled. *The Empress knew Solkka Ulani personally?*

"Um, who is Solkka?"

"The son of a coffee farmer," Miya replied quickly. I waited, and he must have seen the skepticism on my face. He fidgeted awkwardly. "Solkka is my friend, my best friend. Anything more you must hear from him. But I did not come here to talk about others. I came to say, I'm sorry about what I said earlier."

He blew out a hard breath. "Bima Ritwik was a hard person to like, but I think he did that on purpose. Even so, the words I said were unkind." Miya gave me a wry grin. "You should know, Bima always said he liked you. At first, I thought he said it because he knew it would annoy me, but I believe it was true."

Miya paused, as if choosing his words carefully. "Bima had a way of giving a gift that always made me think there would be a price I would have to pay later. It made me less than kind to him many times when it was not deserved. But, Zren, he never held a grudge." And then, "I'm glad you brought him home."

I nodded. My own feelings toward Bima Ritwik were so complicated, I didn't know how to respond. My heart was still stinging over Solkka's earlier words: 'Bima's greatest talent was to know what we most wanted.' *Had he always only pretended to be a friend to me?*

I pushed the sadness away and listened to Miya as he continued talking.

"Our people in the field tell of the good work the Wrens are doing. I know they call each other Wrens, but when help is offered to us, they say they are a 'friend of Zren Janin' and ask if we know our Conrosan folktales. All of us have benefited from your information and your courage. You have helped countless Viklanders."

He grinned at me. "To think, to find a friend of Zren Janin means food, shelter, coin, horse, or a way to Vikland, just for the asking. I've studied the Conrosan fairy tales, Zren, and I've also traveled with you. I still can't put it all together. The network is too extensive for you to run so well. Tell me, is Padro Morto known to me? Tiju Tia? Who leads you?"

"I told Bima Ritwik it was Rell Huena." I looked Miya full in the face so he knew I was telling the truth. He laughed.

"You have learned to answer questions so your tongue and your face are in agreement." He shrugged. "I will not endanger Vikland just to satisfy my curiosity. I can honor your secrets." He grew serious. "Thank you for your letter, Zren, the one you sent with Chul Swyler so long ago. Once I read it with my head, and then again with my heart, I realized how cruel I had been at Manumina…and before. I had no idea."

He waved his arm about the room. "I grew up with this. All of this. My family has served as diplomats and advisors to the Empress's family for six generations. I spoke from a position of privilege without understanding the ground my words fell on. You have *nothing* to ask forgiveness for."

He paused. "I am glad from this moment forward; we will part as friends."

He saw me tip my head back, and so he swiftly turned toward the window and began talking of Chul's inventions—not only of ghostfire, but other inventions helping in the war against Kerek. When he saw me stiffen at the mention of ghostfire, he gave me a puzzled look, but swiftly changed to talk of Aajan's aptitude at the academies.

"I am beyond glad Chul recognized her talent. She continues to excel in her studies and in a few years you will hear the student has surpassed the master." He gave me a sly smile. "Piffik was a smart man to keep her unworthy suitors away."

We laughed at that, recounting how Piffik had found me in front of the butcher shop, an unknown Conrosan, and how, without knowing anything about me, had offered sanctuary to our group after the Battle at the Bridge.

He asked me about the others at Manumina he had met. I told him Rygee and Siba lived together and healed us all with food and friendship. How Rygee was listed as the Farm Manager of Manumina and kept the settlement's appearance as neutral in the war, while the work of the Wrens was hidden in the background. I said although Rygee and I were the same age, more or less, he had been raised to be a leader of others, and I continued to learn from him all the time.

"I misjudged him badly. I am glad he stayed and made a home for himself at Manumina. He would not have been treated so well here, much to my shame."

I thought about what he had said earlier about Bima's Matasian wife, but said nothing.

"Tell me more about Piffik."

I looked at him surprised. "He's *my* best friend." I explained how Piffik cared for his family until they scattered, Aajan to Vikland and the academies, his brother Zadah, a sailor on the seas. How his woodworking business kept Manumina in coin. How he drove a route of furniture and coffin deliveries to help the Wrens.

How he practiced non-violence as a way of life so completely he refused to carry a weapon against bandits on his wagon. How his tongue was so clever he could weave a story out of feathers and fairy dust—as Siba would say—to dance under the nose of the Kereki army. How he and Siba had been friends all of their lives, and together they had taught me how to live in a house, earn a wage, keep my word, and reach the other side of childhood.

"He is older than you, Miya, but not by much. He does what needs to be done. Why do you ask?"

"He is Rell's lover? The reason she won't return to Vikland?"

I was so astonished, I was speechless. Miya looked embarrassed. "Perhaps…perhaps, I made an assumption that was not true."

I put a stern look on my face. "Miya. Rell and I live together in the same house. I would know, and the answer is no." I looked sadly at the floor. "Piffik thinks she needs better friends than those of us at Manumina."

Miya reached out and put a hand on my shoulder. "I think she has exactly the right friends. I misspoke. It was wrong of me to assume something I knew nothing about. I, of all people, should know what it is like to have others say untruths because they claim to be an expert on my life."

There was one rap on the door and Solkka pushed it open. He was also in full military dress and carrying a traveling pack.

"They're pulling the carriage around. Jinhai's aide is ready for our belongings. She will place them in the carriage for us."

"I'll get Jewel," Miya headed to the door. "Don't keep us waiting."

"Who's Jewel?" I asked once he was gone.

"Jinhai, the Empress's daughter. Miya calls her Jewel as her byname."

"Miya uses a nickname for an Empress's daughter?" My eyes widened.

Solkka gave me such a warm laugh I thought my insides were melting. "You do know who you're mingling with, don't you? I mean, you called him the Prince of Vikland."

"I called you Prince of Vikland too," I protested.

"Yes. Well, in his case it's true." He pulled me into his arms. "But I missed my time with you because I thought we had days and days ahead of us." His kiss was sweet. Not tentative at all. He waited until I figured out how we fit together and then, oh my! How do you describe something that feels like liquid fire and tastes like the best pastry ever made? I let myself relax into him and heard a small sound. Was that me?

Solkka backed away from me with a soft look. His eyes were dark and his cheeks were flushed.

"Stars!" he said hoarsely, "You should have warned me!"

"Did I do something wrong?" I panicked. I just wanted him to kiss me again.

Solkka laughed. "No!" He straightened and said formally, "I have an Empress and First Soldier Joon waiting on me, but I wish I didn't have to go to the Summer Plains right now. I'll be back in four days, Zren, four days!"

He pulled open the door, grabbed his traveling pack, and ran down the hallway. I stepped outside the room and watched as he took the steps downstairs two at a time. I heard him say "Yes!" when he planted his feet hard at the base.

I walked over to the glassed in balcony just to see him, now without his pack, walk slowly and formally across the courtyard. He mounted his horse. Miya helped Jinhai into the Empress's carriage, and then mounted his own horse. The two men moved into the formal outrider positions. They cantered just far enough forward from the Empress's carriage, and then the heavy caisson with Malan Sala's coffin pulled into a straight line.

It looked like everyone in the palace was motionless in two lines on each side of the road. I saw a man step up on a wooden box and I heard a faint voice, "Malan Sala, a son of Vikland," and the crowd responded much louder, "May his name live on." Miya and Solkka looked at each other and then as one, their horses both stepped forward. The procession moved first between the lines of people and then beyond them. Not until the caisson was out of sight did First Soldier Joon bark a command and the lines quietly disbursed.

I turned around and saw Rell and Piffik standing behind me.

"Wow. That was impressive. What happens now?"

"It is, isn't it?" Rell nodded. "That's why it is so important to get as many of our soldiers back to Vikland as possible. I know it's hard for our Kereki friends to understand, they are risking their lives for a body, but this is part of who we are."

Rell went on to explain, tonight at sunset would be the family ceremony for Bima Ritwik. In Vikland, bodies were not buried like they were in Kerek, or set out to sea as they were in the Spice and West Islands. Here, the coffin would be placed on a funeral pyre and burned. It was why they used myrrh oil on the bodies. Only the family would be present. At sunrise, there would be a gathering for anyone who knew Bima. People would tell the stories of his exploits, his best softfooting, his final mission—Kern would tell this—and all of the great and good things he had done for Vikland.

She smiled at me. "At the end of each story, everyone says, 'May his name live on.' It's to give the family reassurances they have survived the worst night of their life—the death of a loved one—but with the dawn there are all these people who loved him and knew him and will remember him." Rell was quiet for a moment. "It's a beautiful tradition, but I didn't know Bima well enough to participate. We were both in the Diplo, that's true. But our roles were very different, and he was so much older than I was."

I was stunned. Rell was not considered a deserter in Vikland *only* because Bima had intervened. I opened my mouth to tell her what Solkka had said, but then I thought it over. Bima had offered Rell Huena redemption merely as a prize to Solkka to earn his compliance. Whether or not Bima believed in Rell's role wasn't important to him. *She had been something Bima could bargain away to get what he wanted. To lay Manumina at the Empress's feet.*

"If I don't participate, would we go back to Manumina?" I wondered how I could still be here in four days. I also wondered just how welcome I would be if I stayed to wait for Solkka, and there was no one to smooth my way or to speak Vik for me.

"Well, Axefield is half-day's ride southeast of here, and the refugee camp is another half day southwest of that. We can either make a zig zag progression south and then go over the Vikland border as far south as the shepherd's cottage, or come back to Juisiti and return through Ishes. Piffik has reminded me we have our horses at Ishes. Perhaps you can help me convince him to spend less time on a horse? Or you can stay here and wait for Solkka."

I stilled, wondering if she saw my struggle on my face. She gave me a sly look.

"What? You thought I couldn't remember why I spent a whole year of my life trying to teach you Wester? I was there, Zren!"

I thought it best to ignore Rell for the moment. "What are you going to do, Piffik?"

He blew out a sigh. "I should meet with the Council of Wisdom. And…I would like to visit with my mother."

"Me too," I decided quickly. "I would like to meet Rell's parents. And to tell her brothers they trained her to be the best sister I could ask her to be."

Rell barked out a laugh. "I would like to hear you tell them so, especially Dylis. You know I don't live in anything like this. Remember I'm just a hostler's daughter."

Piffik stared at her. "Truly?" He paused and I could see emotions flickering over his face. "I thought all of you in the diplomatic corps were sons and daughters of nobles or near royalty."

She gave him a worried look. "I thought you knew. I went to the Academy of Healing. And then I was accepted into the Diplo. Without that edge, I wouldn't have had a chance."

Piffik looked happier than I had seen him in …well, forever. "Well, come on. Zren, get packing, we have family to visit!"

CHAPTER 8

A PARABLE OF THE LOST GOD

We left just after midday. Rell had taken us out for street food, packed up our now clean and dry Kereki clothes—I felt sorry for whoever had cleaned my boots for me—and then she notified whoever needed to know the Conrosans were leaving with her. Piffik and I took the horses we had borrowed from the garrison at Ishes. Rell hired a spirited one for herself with the rigid Viklander saddle. I would have preferred a wagon and said so, but Rell said she didn't want to show up looking like a peddler.

Piffik pretended not to hear, but she quickly realized her words were offensive and was embarrassed.

"It's just a Vik saying, Piffik. We use it all the time. I didn't mean anything by it. But now I understand it is unkind, and I'm truly sorry. I will not say it again."

In Kerek, we had trails, tracks, and half-tracks. Only when Ngahuru, Koanga, and I had been fleeing down the Coast Road had I ever been on a paved road. On that journey, Ngahuru had said there was a legend the Coast Road had been made by giants of long ago. But now, even after we got out of Juisiti, the road we traveled was made of pavers.

I asked Rell about it and she explained how Vikland was such a large country, the dirt under our feet was dissimilar in different places.

"I have never been, Zren, but when I was in the military, I served with some who came from the area where they mine the clay, mix it with other ingredients, and then set it out during the Dry and finish it in kilns. I can't imagine what the kilns must look like, how big they must be, because most roads I know are made of this."

I was silent for a while, looking at the road, and the buildings around me. Even the trees were bigger here than they were in Kerek. Piffik was silent as well, taking in everything. Instead of open wagons or ones with canvas tops as they were in Kerek, we saw more carriages. When I asked Rell, she said almost anyone could afford a carriage. They were not just for royals and ambassadors like I knew from Kerek City. I liked to look at them. They were different sizes and some were brightly colored or had fancy decorations on them. Others were on horseback, like us. No one walked.

I watched Rell as we rode along as well. She sat regally in her saddle, her sleek black braid snaking down her back and right side. I looked over at Piffik sitting straight-backed and tall with a small smile about his lips. We were all wearing the closefitting dark Viklander pants and shirts.

Without thinking first, I blurted out my thoughts, "You should live in Vikland, Piffik. You are much handsomer here."

I thought Rell was going to fall off her horse from laughter. Piffik just looked down his nose at me, but the smile didn't leave his face.

"And how would a man who practices non-violence live in a land where the warrior is honored so?"

I thought he asked the question seriously so I considered it. "Viklanders defend the defenseless and fight for justice, Piffik. I saw those words in every language in both embasados in Matasi and Kerek." I squinted, thinking hard. "I think, I think Conrosans try to live so the world is just and fair, so violence is not needed."

"Well said, Zren!" Rell grinned. "If I knew you were going to be my champion, I would have had you move into Piffik's house ages ago and whisper these words in his ear every night." She threw a wicked grin at Piffik, and then pulled ahead of us so a small carriage could pass in the opposite direction.

When we were three abreast again, Rell asked for a story to pass the time. I asked her from what country would she like to hear one, and she oohed and ahhed what a man of the world I was to know so many from every country. I knew she was just teasing me. She was so happy today she was nearly giddy. I asked her to test me. Pick a country and I would tell her a tale.

She gave me a serious look and then said, "You have traveled with Ngahuru and her brother so you know West Islands Constellation stories, grew up in Kerek so you know the Trickster tales, lived at Manumina so you know the folktales of Conrosa, you have traveled with enough Viklanders so you have heard more than one Wisdom of the Warrior stories, or you should have anyway. Mmmm. I challenge you to tell me a parable from Matasi."

I smiled at her. I had heard a parable from one of our hosts in Matasi about a man built close to the ground who had ignored his pride and his false friends to climb a tree and meet a man of wisdom. I had heard parables from Bima to keep me awake on a long rescue from a death-filled cottage to Manumina. There was one he had told that night, which I had kept close to my heart. So close, I had been afraid to ask him questions afterwards. It may have been a parable, and Bima had assured me it was, but it was also the origin story for me, before I was Zren Janin, a Conrosan of Manumina. I looked at Rell and Piffik and realized these were two of the people I trusted most in the world. I could ask them my questions. So I began.

"In the writings of the Lost God, there is this parable. A traveler from faraway lands crossing through Kerek was set upon by thieves.

He was beaten and robbed of all he owned and was left naked and bleeding by the side of the road.

First, two Kereki women and their brother passed by. They quickly passed to the other side of the road because they knew robbers would pretend to be injured in order to prey upon the kindness of others.

Next, a Viklander passed by. He glanced at the wounded traveler but knew a strong man such as he was, well-trained in the tahn bong and the jeong bong, would have nothing to fear from a traveler so badly hurt. He walked on.

Finally, just as the sun was setting, a man and woman from Matasi passed by. They gave the injured man water to drink, dressed his wounds, and found clothes for him to wear from their traveling packs. This they did, not because they presumed the man was rich and would give them coin, nor because they thought him a prince who would grant them power and prestige, but because the Lost God demands we love each other as we love ourselves.

And thus ends the parable."

No one spoke for a while.

Finally, Rell asked, "Is that a real Matasi parable? Because I thought they were all about gaining land, and coin, and favors, to show how blessed you were by the Lost God." She turned back to me. "You know, the richer you are, the closer to the Lost God you are."

I shrugged. "I don't know. I told you that one because I wanted to ask you why so many of the parables have Kerek and Vikland and the Island countries in them as villains and victims. As if no one but Matasi can follow the Lost God and be rewarded by him."

We spent the next decons talking about it, and then somehow slid into the Viklander tales of courage and strength. Rell said the Wisdom of the Warrior tales are taught from very young so everyone works hard to have a strong body and a strong mind.

"Everyone wants to be the defender of the defenseless, not the one defended." She paused a long time. "It is why what happened to me was so terrible. In Vikland, when someone's mind breaks like mine did, they are locked away so they can do no harm to others…or themselves."

She smiled at us. "But in Manumina, you gave me time and space and a purpose. You tell me I am the *only one* to save you, and then act as if you completely believe it is true."

Piffik snorted. "You tried to teach Zren to shoot your crossbow; we weren't acting."

Rell looked thoughtfully at me. "I have thought about that for a long time. I have told you before, I thought it was not a lack of skill, but a lack of your eyesight. Sailors use a long glass to see great distances over the water. If it would be possible to make two of those for your eyes, Zren, I wonder if you could see as far as the rest of us see."

I remembered Raumati's long glass she had used back in Kerek City to check if a West Islands ship would be coming to rescue her. It had been the length of my forearm. I tried to imagine two long glasses attached to my head, maybe in a leather and wood contraption like Chul's leg braces. I squirmed in dismay.

"I think I see well enough to do my manabout chores and work in the woodshop with Piffik. I wouldn't want to wear those, I think."

Rell shrugged. "It was just a thought. I suppose if you can see the ground before you fall on it, you only have more time to think about how it will hurt." She laughed at her own joke, and Piffik and I just smiled. It was sort of funny, even though I knew I did not see so poorly as all that. I briefly wondered how Piffik saw the world. Were his eyes as keen as Rell's? Or like me, did he like woodworking because he could look as close as possible to see the perfect grain of the wood.

And then we turned at the bend of the road and saw the town. It was a cacophony of color and beauty, houses taller than those scattered about Kerek but not as tall as Manumina. There was a beautiful green near well-tended stables. Across the way, there was a huge building even larger than the great house of Evensong with gardens tucked into a courtyard between the two wings.

And that's how we rode into Axefield.

CHAPTER 9

A HOSTLER'S DAUGHTER

So Rell lied. She lied to me on the Northern Track. She lied when we lived together in a house in Manumina. She lied in Juisiti to Piffik and me when she said she was the hostler's daughter.

When her father was younger than Tiju Tia's Wrens, he was the man who looked after horses for others. He called himself a hostler. But Raul Huena was a man who believed hard work and ambition could accomplish anything. As we walked our horses through the courtyard of her family's inn, Rell pointed out the tree where she and her brothers would climb for stonefruit, the long pastures where she had learned to ride, the separate bakeries and kitchens where she would beg for pastries, "just like you do now, Zren. Only our baker wasn't as generous as Rygee. We only got one fingersweet for each hand, not as many as we could carry," she said archly.

We took our horses to the stables—barns so big they could have filled one wall of Manumina. One of the grooms did a second look when we walked our horses up, and said "Miss

Arrella?" in an uncertain voice. She gave a half smile and a nod. He called for a boy to send a message to the inn.

"No!" She said it again, softer, "No. We'll find our way. I don't want to bother anyone."

She walked us into the inn, and explained how there were two floors of rooms above a large number of rooms for eating, drinking, and socializing. When she had been sent to the West Islands with the Diplo, she had been delighted with the bathing rooms attached to the sleeping rooms. However, this inn was built with what the Viklanders knew and were comfortable with. The bathing rooms were at the end of the hall, sleeping rooms did not lock, but there was a hired man sitting or standing at the end of the hall ensuring everyone stayed in the room they were assigned, and no one was harmed or made to feel afraid.

I could see why Rell was so comfortable in Manumina. I felt as if I would much rather stay here than the palace again, or even the embasado, as fancy as those guest rooms had been. Once Rell had walked us through the place—"so you can find your way as you wish," she said casually—she took us back to the kitchens. There we found her mother presiding over the chaos with several cooks, servers, scrub boys, and under cooks all bustling about.

Rell stood in the doorway for a moment, inhaling deeply. "Let's come back later when Mutti is not so busy." She turned and walked away, but I took one last deep breath. How could someone who grew up with smells like this, cook as badly as Rell did? At least I had a reason for my failures, I grew up on the streets of Lowertown. I followed her back into the inn.

Her father saw her first. He was walking across the largest room, carrying a tray of cups. He looked, looked again, and then set the tray heavily on the table. He plopped into the chair next to it.

"Rell! I am much too old to have you walk in and out of my heart like so." He stood and opened his arms, and she walked into them, embracing him. After Rell hugged her father, she stepped aside and introduced Piffik and me with the formal Vik greetings she had taught me so long ago. Piffik and I both made the short bows. He smiled, and then turned to Rell.

"Have you found your mother yet? She is either overseeing the kitchens or in the storerooms taking inventory for our supplies."

"She was in the kitchen, but busy, so I thought I would find you first."

"Of course, because I am never busy," he laughed, "It has been too long, Rell, too long."

"I write every ten days!" Rell exclaimed. "Piffik," she pointed, "takes my letters to the Ishes garrison with the other dispatches and documents to be sent to Vikland, which is a day's ride there and back, mind you, and then it is up to Vikland to get them to you."

I jerked my head to Piffik. He saw me, smiled, and shrugged nonchalantly.

I narrowed my eyes and tried to think of what I was seeing and not seeing. Was this what Miya was talking about? I thought back to those nights when Rell and I could not bear the idea of each other's cooking, so we would bring food over to Rygee and Siba's house in exchange for a seat at their table. How often had we started walking across the village green just to see Piffik open the door to his woodshop, jokingly wave vegetables or fruit in the air as he joined us. Then enjoying the food and the company at Rygee and Siba's table, all of us laughing, eating, and cleaning up the meal together. All of us the best of friends.

When did it change for him? When did he look across the table and decide he wanted her as more than a friend? Then despaired because he thought he had nothing to offer one from a Viklander background of wealth and privilege. I tipped my head to the side and wondered. Or was I just making a story out of feathers and fairy dust? Piffik and Siba had been friends longer than I had been alive. Piffik knew how to have women as friends. What was I not seeing?

I came back to the conversation as Rell began to stand. The others followed, and I gave Piffik a desperate look.

He chuckled. "While you were counting the stars, Rell invited us to see the place with her and find our room for the night. Her father is going to call the family together. We will all gather and eat at sundown. It is late to eat, but this time of day is busy for them with all the travelers." I nodded and followed them out.

***

I tried to pester Piffik with questions that night in our room in the inn. He wouldn't say anything beyond, "Zren, the Huenas put you in this room with me because you are my chaperone for the night to ensure I stay here and I sleep alone. I spent more than twenty years with the old gossips of Manumina, you can ask all night and I will still keep my secrets."

I tried so many different ways of asking my questions I lost track. Still Piffik ignored me. Then, I remembered how we had traveled all night and all day to get to Juisiti, and after just a bath and a short nap we had saddled horses and ridden to Axefield. Suddenly, I was asleep.

I had thought we would just spend the night and then travel on to the Conrosans resettled at Rishka. But Piffik wanted Rell to spend time with her family. I noticed he was trying to get to know them as well, or rather, have them get to know him. We spent the second day at Axefield, Piffik talking with Rell's father, helping Rell's mother carry something or another, trailing Rell's brothers as they did their tasks, answering anything they wanted to ask about.

Finally, I complained to Rell, "Solkka will be coming back to Juisiti and will not find me there because I am here watching Piffik charm birds out of the sky." She just laughed at me and said I listened to so many stories, there was probably a Conrosan fairy tale about this too.

"Let it be, Zren. Piffik feels he needs to do this, and who am I to tell him otherwise? I promise you this: we will go to the Conrosans tomorrow, if I have to ask you to help me tie Piffik to his saddle." She saw me sneak a count on my fingers and knew what I was thinking.

"Zren, the Summer Plains are straight east of Juisiti, and even farther away than the Conrosan refugees at Rishka. If Solkka and Miya can actually make it back in four days, and you must remember they have the Empress's daughter and a military caisson to travel with, it would be so late, we will be asleep. Solkka Ulani has waited two years for you to decide how you feel about him. He can wake three days from now and see your charming face hovering over him when he opens his eyes. You do not need to be waiting at the gates of the palace."

***

Rell kept her promise. Early, the next morning we left for Rishka, the estate housing the Conrosan refugees. But now Rell rode the beautiful horse Tiju Tia and I had found with the wounded Kereki deserters. She was going to take us to Rishka, have midday with us, and then return to Axefield.

"All in one day?" I gulped. "On a Viklander saddle?"

"Don't you remember the Northern Track, Zren? Miyamoto Suki made us ride a lot longer days than this. I'm not dragging a heavy crossbow now." Rell gave me a wicked grin and threw back my old words at me. "This is nothing more than a pony ride."

***

Piffik and I stayed with his mother in her tiny room in the main house. He visited with every family, telling them what had been happening with the war, asking for instructions, or giving updates on their property. I noticed he chose his words carefully as he explained—truthfully—that we helped the Wrens, who were homeless children from Kerek City learning skills and earning coin to make their way in the world. We also cared for the Viklander soldiers, wounded or lost, who needed a helping hand to return to Vikland or recover from their injuries. The Conrosans heard what they wanted to, and nodded their heads and praised us for helping everyone and staying neutral in the war.

While Piffik met with the Council of Wisdom or anyone else who wanted his ear, I visited, ate, or played with the youth. For the first time, they could wander, walk, or ride anywhere in the countryside without coming across Kereki troublemakers. It made me realize that for a small group of people, living here communally in every available building, life as a refugee was still better than returning to Kerek and the life of fear they had before. I wondered how long the poison had festered in Kerek. How did the country never see that treating others differently meant a lesser life for everyone?

On the morning of the second day at the refugee settlement, I was desperate. Solkka could be arriving as early as tonight, and I was a full day's ride from Juisiti. And that was only if I could sit all day on a horse like Rell, which I knew I could not.

I pleaded with Piffik to go back, but he said he had more people to meet with and the earliest he could leave would be midday. If that was not acceptable to me, I could leave now. He knew I had observed the roads we had traveled, and he had confidence I could find my way to Rell's.

"Make sure you remember to change horses at Axefield. I want to return to the palace with the horses we borrowed from Ishes. They should be well rested if Rell's brothers didn't ride them to the Silver Mountains and back."

I agreed to wait until midday for Piffik. Rell knew Vikland and I trusted Rell. If she said Solkka would arrive so late he would just want to collapse into bed, then seeing him tomorrow would have to do.

At midday, Piffik found me waiting at the stables. I hadn't wanted him to waste time looking for me and risk getting a late start.

"Oh, Zren, my heart hurts to see you like this. There is no possible way I can leave before tomorrow."

I gasped in shock and anger, and he raised his hand as if to stop my words from reaching him. "I came to find you to tell you to leave without me. Ride to Axefield. If you leave now, you can eat with Rell's family tonight. Ask Rell what to do if you are not confident you can find the palace in Juisiti on your own. Perhaps someone will have a map for you, perhaps someone will be traveling to Juisiti and you can ride with them, perhaps Rell or her brothers will be able to take you, speak Vik for you, and help you find Solkka Ulani. You can do this. But I am discouraged my responsibilities to the Council of Wisdom and the people of Manumina, mean I cannot travel with you now."

He gave me a sly smile, "Perhaps Solkka Ulani likes to sleep as much as you do when there is not a watch to be set. Perhaps he can inspire you to wake before first meal."

Piffik helped me find a soft Kereki saddle in the stables at the estate and then saddled the gentlest horse we had from the garrison at Ishes. He had me repeat—more than once—that I would ride to Axefield, sleep at the Huenas, leave before first light tomorrow, and be in Juisiti before the day had reached midmorning. I wondered if he had second thoughts, but if he did, he kept them to himself.

I left almost immediately, and soon the excitement of seeing Solkka became uneasiness and then fear. I worried I would not know the breakaway from the main road to find Axefield, or someone would speak to me in Vik and I would not know how to answer.

But then I reminded myself I had traveled through Matasi, I had survived Bima and Lomes in Salisport. I had lived in Kerek City as a child, and Rell had said Juisiti was smaller than Kerek City, or even Salisport. Juisiti held only the Palace of the Empress and the Academies and the people who made their living from them, she said. If I asked for help and directions, Piffik said, everyone would know where it was I wanted to go.

So, I shook myself off, let my fears fall to the ground beneath the horse's hoofs and imagined them trampled into the dirt. I took an interest in everything around me. I made up stories and practiced telling them to myself. I thought about Tiju Tia and what she would think when she came home from caring for the Wrens to find all but Siba and Rygee gone. I wondered why

Lou stayed living out at the springhouse and running his own cheese cart so he could pretend not to know what we were doing rather than joining us. I questioned why Rell had chosen to stay at Manumina if she knew she would be considered a deserter and have her braid cut. I wondered if Tiju Tia would take Oro on a trip to talk to Arden and Linna. I wondered if Arden and Josef were still on their long journey and who had requested it of them. I practiced what I would say to Solkka if I did manage to get to his room before he woke in the morning. I marveled at my good fortune to have a day with no rain. I realized if I did not have someone to talk to, ask questions of, or beg for stories, a decon lasted as long as a day.

I sighed.

I reached the Huena inn at Axefield near sunset. One of the grooms recognized me and sent a message boy to find Rell or Dylis, her brother close to my age. Dylis came first and greeted me in Keresh. I breathed a sigh of relief. Rell may have said it was in bad taste to speak the language of the enemy, but truly I could not expect many to know Conrosan, and I had never learned more than a few words of Vik beyond the formal greetings.

Dylis said Rell was in one of the dining halls helping with the travelers. He would take me to the inn and arrange a room for me. Then he frowned.

"I am sorry, Zren, we did not know you would be coming today. The rooms left this late at night are not as nice as the one you stayed in with Piffik. We had a large number of travelers come in just two decons ago, and they have stretched us to our capacity."

I wondered if I knew him well enough to joke with him. "I'm glad it's you, Dylis. Rell would give me the same explanation, and then tell me that was why I was sleeping in the stable."

He laughed. "She would, wouldn't she?" He clapped me on the shoulder. "You can share my room with two younger brothers before I ask you to sleep in the stable. But first, let's find some food for you."

Even the least of the rooms had been let out before Dylis took me to find a space to sleep. Dylis took me to the room he shared with two younger brothers and assured me someone would come find me when it was time for the family to eat. I left my travel bag in the room and then wandered about. All the dining spaces were full, and I felt so underfoot and useless. I went back into the washery. I helped with the washing of the dishes.

Rell's father carried a tray of dirty dishes in and nearly dropped them when he saw me at the sinks with the other scrub boys.

"Zren, no! You are a guest of ours. This is not how it should be." Dylis came in behind him, looking equally shocked.

"Raul Huena," I said firmly, "this is something I know how to do. I came to you without coin and asked for food and a roof over my head. You did not make me sleep in a stable, you did not have me share a room with someone I didn't know in your inn. Instead, you invited me to come into your home, to eat with your family, and to share a room with your sons, even though I am nothing but a stranger to your house."

Rell's father looked flummoxed, and it was Dylis who spoke first. "More than once today, Zren, Rell has told me you are her favorite brother. Now I see why. Do all Conrosans have such a charmed tongue? For truly, you are as clever with words as Piffik."

"Oh no," I said solemnly. "Rell may call me her younger brother, but it is Piffik who taught me the words to survive such a dangerous role."

Dylis laughed, but Rell's father gave a huge sigh. "I am too busy to sort this out now. But truly, Zren, I thank you."

***

Later that night, during the family's end of day meal, I told the Huenas I needed to go to Juisiti. Rell explained to them, in words so sweet I could not believe she was talking about me, it would be best if there would be someone traveling in a wagon to the city who could take me as close to the palace as possible.

The family assured me this was not an unusual arrangement. Often merchants would take someone who could help unload the wagon once the city was reached. However, Rell suggested the family pay for my passage as I had important business at the palace, and I should not delay to unload someone else's goods. She asked her family if there was anyone leaving so early in the morning, the guests had made arrangements to be awakened by those who guarded the inn at night, rather than wait for first light.

The family did not know of anyone. Dylis offered to take me to the palace and do the family shopping while he was in Juisiti. This received such a resounding refusal, I knew there had to be a delicious story behind it. No one offered to share it with me however, so I sat silently while the family talked.

It was comforting. I loved the swirl of voices about me, teasing and serious, questioning and explaining. It reminded me of Manumina after most of the Conrosans had left, and it was just our little group left behind. We had made our own family of sorts, but it worked for us.

One of Rell's youngest brothers had been sent to find out from the stablemaster if any of the guests had given times they needed to have their horses and wagons ready. Rell's father had taken the list of names the boy had brought back and met with the ones he said he was acquainted with to find me a ride. Rell reassured me even students on the way to and from the academies traveled this way. I could entertain them with stories, and she would bring my Ishes horse back when she came with Piffik.

I asked how she would find me. She thought for a bit and then asked me to meet her and Piffik at Aajan's rooms at the academy—or send a message—with my plans the day after I arrived. From there, we all would decide together what to do once I had talked to Solkka. She said she did not know him so well to know why he had been in Juisiti, or how long he would stay. She did not think he was staying at the palace, but perhaps the barracks near there. Or perhaps somewhere else as she thought he might have an aunt who lived in the city.

"But wherever, Zren, once we meet at Aajan's, we can make our plans." There was nowhere else she had confidence I could find my way and stay safely out of trouble.

I went to bed with a plan and a light heart.

CHAPTER 10

CHUL SWYLER AND AAJAN QANAQ

The merchant who gave me a ride was a coffee broker. One who met with the farmers and bought the coffee beans in the middle east of Vikland under the foothills of the Cold Mountains. After the harvest, he told me, long wagon trains of coffee beans would come west to Juisiti and then disburse through Vikland and down to the Silver Mountains where they were packed in travel bags and carried over the Silver Mountains into Matasi. He had heard Vikland coffee was even drunk in the West Islands, although he did not know how that could be true, since to take the coffee over the Silver Mountains, all across Matasi, and then on a ship across the sea would make it so expensive, he thought only the King could pay the coin to drink it.

I told him I had met a Storyteller from the West Islands and had traveled with him through Matasi and heard his tales of the Great Constellations. The coffee broker was impressed and asked me to tell him one or more if I was so inclined. And so we entertained ourselves. The time went ever so much faster than yesterday's journey from Rishka to the Huena Inn at Axefield when I had only myself for company.

I reached the palace after midday. Rell had given me a small coin purse and had taught me the value of the Vikland coins before I had left Axefield. I had forgotten Ngahuru had told me every country had its own coin when she changed ours in Matasi. Rell had made me recite the coins and their value over and over.

"Pay attention, Zren," she had cautioned, "I don't want to come to Juisiti and find out you have bought a horse instead of a meal."

I had been shocked. "You are giving me so much coin?"

"No, Zren, it is a Vik joke parents tell their children before they go off to the academies. And I am not *giving* you this coin. I fully intend you should pay me back when we get to Manumina." She looked up to me. "I'm teasing, Zren. Heavens, you are so nervous about meeting Solkka again, you are even more thick-skulled than usual." She put her hand over mine. "It will be fine, Zren. It will be more than fine."

She paused and then gave me a sweet smile. "There is no one else in the world like you. Solkka Ulani knows this. I do not know him well, but I have never heard a discouraging word said against him. It will be fine. Now take this coin so you can find food to eat when you get there. You should not be dependent upon Solkka Ulani, Aajan Qanaq, or anyone else, Zren. You can do this."

I can do this, I reminded myself. *I can do this.* I found the same street vendor Rell had taken us to four days earlier. I pointed to the food I wanted and gave him the coins whose numbers matched those on the food cart. He smiled at me, gave me the food, and looked to the person behind me. I was so proud of myself I forgot to move out of the way. Someone cleared their throat, and I hastily moved to the side.

I ate my midday and then wandered around the palace grounds. Finally, I mustered up my courage and asked the guards for admittance. I spoke Conrosan first, certain they would not know it. And when they shrugged, I switched to Keresh. One of the soldiers scowled, but it was not the narrowed eyes I would have expected if I had started with Keresh.

It didn't help me. No one had known I was coming and so no one knew what to do with me. I wasn't on any list for admittance. And when I pointed out I had been a guest of the Empress four days ago, the guards had dutifully pulled the earlier roster. Yes, I had been a guest, because I and others had brought Vikland's fallen soldiers home to their families, but I had been checked out the same day and was thought to be back at Manumina.

I asked for the Secondo, only to be told there was no Secondo such as an embasado had. When I asked for a message to be given to Miyamoto Suki and Solkka Ulani, no one knew if they had left for the day or for the season, but they did know neither of them were in the palace now. First Soldier Joon was also gone, I was told when I asked for him.

I knew no one else in the palace. There was no help for it. I would go and ask Aajan what to do next. Or Chul.

What would I say to Chul? Would I tell him I saw his ghostfire explosions when Rell had fired it in the fields? Would he believe me if I said not all Kereki soldiers were bad, and his ghostfire had killed ones who saved me from bandits? Would I tell him what a man looks like after his horse steps on a piece of ghostfire pottery? Should I say I laid in bed for a handful of days until my hearing and my balance returned enough for me to do my manabout chores? How could a man who liked happy endings create ghostfire?

But then I wondered what would he say to me? He could not tell the Empress no. I thought this would be like one of Piffik's and Rell's never-ending conversations about non-violence and fighting for justice. Nothing I said would change the firemaster's course now.

I asked for directions to Chul's place.

"Chul who?"

I stood still, realizing I had lived and nearly died with the man—nearly died because of the man—and now I couldn't remember his family name.

"Um, he's a firemaster. He has labs by the Academy of Elements, or maybe it is another one, I am not sure, he never said. Very brilliant. Maybe the same age as Miyamoto Suki or a little older. Big man, big laugh." I searched my mind for more descriptions.

One of the other soldiers heard us. "He's talking about the Matasi cripple. The one that always shows up here with the foreign girl carrying all his papers and books."

My fear unguarded my tongue. "Stars! What's wrong with you? Chul has more brains than anyone I know, he has invented more things to make life better than you can imagine, he has saved my life and countless others, and all you can say is 'the Matasi cripple?'" I ran my hand through my hair. "This is the most messed up country I have ever had the misfortune to..."

I trailed off as I remembered where I had heard those words before. *Song.* Song and Nebs standing outside the greengrocer in Cloa, on the last morning of her life. I swallowed hard. Being afraid and angry would accomplish nothing. I blew out a sharp breath and started again.

"Forgive me." I made the soldiers a small bow of respect. "I am concerned for my friends who are not here at the palace and my fear made me unkind. You do know Chul and his… assistant." *Aajan would hit me with a wooden spoon if she heard me call her so.* "Do you know where he lives? Or works?"

A third soldier who had overheard my outburst came over and joined our conversation. "You are correct, his labs are by the Academy of Elements. Sometimes we are asked to send a pony cart for him when he is asked to meet with the Empress." He took the time to point me in the right direction and then gave me instructions on how to find Chul's workrooms. He did not know where the firemaster lived, but he assured me the building where Chul worked was no more than a half-decon walk away. I asked if I could leave a note for Solkka Ulani. The soldier raised an eyebrow, but he produced paper and graphite for me to write.

I wrote in Wester because I was sure the soldiers would try to read it as soon as my back was turned. I didn't know if Solkka could read Conrosan, but I had never learned to write Keresh. I smiled as I remembered the first time I had met Solkka Ulani at the embasado in Salisport. He had asked me how many languages I knew. Now I understood the value of his question.

I asked Solkka to meet me at Chul's workrooms no matter how late the night. If I left and traveled someplace else, I would leave another message telling him where he could find me. It was the best I could do.

I set out thinking what I would do if Chul was not there. Then I told myself I would just leave more messages and continue to try to find someone who could help me.

I should have known better. Lights were blazing in the windows when I reached the building the soldier had described. As I got close enough to turn up the walk, I could see Aajan pass before the lit window. I relaxed in relief. At last, I had found someone I knew in this city. I was no longer alone.

Aajan opened the door at my knock and stood there for a moment looking out at me. I licked my lips nervously.

"I don't speak Vik, but if I say hello in Conrosan will you shut the door in my face?"

Her face broke into a smile as she recognized me. "Zren Janin!" She opened the door wider. "Chul, look who is here! That poor Conrosan boy you had to drag all across Kerek." She pulled me in as I heard the click-slide click-slide of Chul's canes on the hard floor. "Come in, come in."

Aajan raised an eyebrow as I dropped my travel bag on the floor, but said nothing. Chul planted himself in front of me and then nearly knocked me off my feet in a hug.

"Zren! I heard you were in Juisiti, and I wondered if you would darken our doorstep."

"I visited Rishka. I just got back today," I explained. "I saw your mother, Aajan."

"Well, don't just stand there, come in and sit down. I bet Mother Qanaq gave you an earful," Chul laughed.

I followed him through his lab and then into a little living space with comfortable chairs. Aajan disappeared for a moment and then returned with two glasses of something cold.

"It's roux berry, Zren. They only have it in Vikland. Taste it, it's delicious!" She sat down in another chair. "So what did my mother have to say?"

I pinched my lips together and sat straight-backed as Aajan's mother did. "Chul is wonderful! Chul got Aajan into the Academy of Botanicals *and* the Elements. Chul escorts Aajan here and back so she doesn't have to travel alone or with Viklanders. Chul is so smart, he has done this and that for the Conrosans at Rishka." I relaxed from my impersonation and smiled gently at her. "She is also worried you speak Vik too much and will forget your mother tongue, you dress like a Viklander and will not remember how to wear a proper dress, and you will never leave Juisiti. Piffik reassured her that is exactly what they want you to do. Manumina is too poor and dusty for a clever girl like you."

"It is a hard place to be, Zren, between two worlds, two cultures. Each one thinks you are too much the other." She said nothing for a long moment.

"I should get us something to eat," she popped out of her chair, "Can you join us for the end of day meal? I'll be right back." And without waiting for an answer, she grabbed her cloak hanging by the door and slipped out into the night.

Chul was quiet while he drank his roux berry juice. Then, "I saw Miya a few days ago. He was passing through the city, wondering if it was dry enough to risk a transit through the Silver Mountains when he received word Bima Ritwik had died and some Conrosans were bringing him back to Juisiti. He told me he hoped it was you. He was headed to the palace to find out, but then I didn't see him at Bima's sunrise service. There were no Conrosans there either so I didn't know who had brought him home."

"Actually, it was Piffik. Rell Huena and I just came along because Piffik told us to, and Kern was one of those we rescued the night Malan Sala and Bima Ritwik died. Miya and Solkka Ulani were the honor guard for Malan Sala, that's why you did not see him."

"I heard Kern speak at Bima's celebration of life." He paused and shook his head mournfully. "Those are some nasty bruises around her neck."

"She said she was better off than those who attacked her. They're both dead." I gave him a sad half smile.

"That sounds like Kern. It didn't take her long to go back to softfooting. You had heard she had left the Diplo to travel and be a soldier's wife? When Ceri went to Kerek to fight, Kern said she wasn't going to sit around and let Ceri have all the fun and danger."

He paused. "I have heard from Rani, Rell Huena is running her own softfooting group out of Manumina. Who would have thought?" He waited for me to answer.

When I said nothing, he raised both eyebrows. "I was there, Zren. You came back from the Council of Wisdom meeting saying Manumina would be neutral in the conflict between Kerek and Vikland."

I shrugged, but dropped my eyes to the empty glass in my hand. Chul may not have known of the Trickster bargain Solkka had made, but he definitely knew Bima Ritwik had lied to the Empress. But Bima was dead, and I wasn't going to say anything about Solkka Ulani.

Chul let the silence stretch, but it wasn't all uncomfortable. "You don't have to say anything, Zren. I think you and I are starting to learn just how devious our finest Softfoot was in his defense of Vikland. To lie to an Empress? That is either very foolish or very brave."

He flexed his hands over the arms of his chair, and it dawned on me what I was seeing.

"Your hands! You can bend them again!"

Chul lifted a hand for my inspection. It was still shiny and oddly pink next to his olive-skinned forearms, but it looked very different from the thick mass of scar tissue he had when he left Manumina.

Chul told me of the toll the war had on Vikland's soldiers and fighters. He explained those sympathetic to Vikland would bring the damaged and the dead to Ishes or Nadon to be transported over the border. That some of the damaged soldiers had been burned out of barns and buildings and hayfields and anywhere else they had been fighting and hiding.

"Our Academy of…well, we call it the byname of 'the Academy of Pain and Misery' has been doing some interesting and difficult things with burn victims." Chul gave a wry grin. "I volunteered for some of them before they were tried on our more fragile wounded."

He went on to talk about debriding the scar tissue and Aajan's work in botanicals—unguents and ointments—to follow the work of the healers. He credited Aajan for his ability to move his hands at all. He was still praising her inventions when she returned with the end of day meal.

"Ah!" She laughed. "I left you two alone so you could talk about Zren Janin's amazing escapes from Kereki soldiers to help the brave sons and daughters of Vikland, only to be exceeded by Chul Swyler's daring experiments in fire and weapons to end the war sooner. Instead, I come back to false praise. You think I will bring your food to you so you do not need to leave your chairs?" She lifted her hand in mock distress and shook her head.

We spent the evening talking and laughing. I kept one ear to the door so I could hear Solkka's knock. If there was a lull in the conversation, I would listen for steps on the street outside which might be his.

But I enjoyed the company I was with as well. In the two years since I had seen her last, Aajan had grown from a shy girl—Piffik's little sister—to a woman to be reckoned with on her own. She was insightful, funny, and droll in her pronouncements about the academies. She reminded me so much of Piffik, I called her by his name. She laughed…thankfully.

"How is my brother?" she said gently. "I miss him."

"He is running Manumina and reports to the Council of Wisdom, he supports us all with his coin from woodworking, runs a delivery service as Padro Morto for lost Viklanders, and still has time to be my best friend."

Chul laughed his big laugh and Aajan grinned.

"That sounds like my brother." She put her hand on Chul's shoulder, "Can you imagine how miserable he would have made my life if you would not have taken me to Juisiti?"

"I noticed. But he was also the one who convinced your mother to let you go to the academies, so do not judge him too harshly."

We talked for a while of Manumina. Aajan would like to see it again, she said, but never return and live there. Chul asked about Siba and Rygee who had remained behind. I talked about Rygee's gift for hospitality and his love for Siba. How he knew how to live in Kerek, to run a settlement as big as Manumina, and how he taught me something new almost every day. Chul was glad to hear it. He thought the Farm Boys were better men who only had the misfortune to be conscripted and forced to travel with Bitterboots and Mouser.

At the academies, Chul had heard rumors a woman named Tiju Tia was able to whisk in and save entire troops of Viklanders. At first, when Aajan and Chul had heard the stories, they wondered if it was Piffik in disguise. But then they learned from those who had seen her, she was an old Kereki woman no taller than chest high to a Viklander.

Then, as the war went on, they had heard other names as well. '*Padro Morto.*' Chul had told Aajan it was a Mata name for Father Death.

"A rather good name for a coffin maker who is brave and knows half-tracks and hidden places all over Kerek. Wouldn't you say, Zren?"

I nodded at Chul's knowing smile.

All of the softfoots and Wrens were brave, he said. The Viklanders were forever returning from the war with stories of their resourcefulness.

"The Empress encourages those stories, Zren, as proof the Kerekis want the King of Kerek to be overthrown." He looked at Aajan. "What was the name of the girl who came back with Solkka Ulani? Do you remember?"

I stiffened as Aajan thought for a moment. "It was an unusual name, a Keresh name," she mused, "Jenny, it was Jenny."

I had never met Jenny, but I knew she was one of the youngest of Tiju Tia's Wrens and a favorite.

"Do you have news of her?" I asked. My mouth was dry with worry.

"Have you seen Solkka Ulani recently?" Chul asked. "He carries a scar on his face which reminds everyone who sees him he came a slash away from death. Jenny was in the battle with him, as tiny as she is. She turned the knife which would have killed him with her bare hand. He lived, but Jenny lost all but her thumb and her forefinger from the v of her fingers nearly to the wrist on her left hand."

I shuddered. Chul noticed, but continued on, "It is said, another Wren found them, and got them safely to a man called Padro Morto who drove nights and days to reach the garrison at Ishes. Someone there took them to the healers in Juisiti, who were able to save them both.

"Jenny lives with the Ulani family now. She is being tutored privately until she is ready to come to the academies. I have heard his family is raising her as a daughter equal to Solkka and his brothers in all things. It is not a replacement for her hand, it is said, but in gratitude and respect for her courage."

I licked my lips nervously.

"Is she far from here? I would like to see her. She is one of Tiju Tia's favorites, and I would like to send news of how Jenny is doing."

Chul and Aajan exchanged a look, and Chul spoke reluctantly, "She is, I'm afraid. Solkka Ulani is the son of a coffee farmer in the Keopi district. It is at the foot of the Cold Mountains and far beyond the Summer Plains. You are closer to Manumina from Juisiti than you are to the Keopi district." Chul cleared his throat. "And Solkka is not there. He and First Soldier Joon went to pull in some of Bima's softfoots and try to learn information. With Bima's death, no one knows if they were compromised, or if it was a random ambush."

My heart crashed into my stomach. "When?" I whispered hoarsely.

Chul raised an eyebrow to Aajan. "This morning. First Soldier Joon came last night to get some of my newest inventions, and he said he was just waiting for Solkka and Miya and Jinhai to return from the Summer Plains. Kern and Miya are to go over the Silver Mountains and meet with our ambassador at the embasado at Salisport. Joon didn't say what about."

"Why him? He just got back!" I whined.

"That is a question for First Soldier Joon. I just create what he asks and Aajan draws."

I bit back my next words. It wouldn't help to get upset with Chul. He had answered my questions with more information than I deserved. He had stopped everything to greet me and feed me as if I had last seen him two days ago and not two years past.

"Thank you for this news. Tiju Tia will be beyond glad to hear Jenny has survived and is no longer part of this war," I said wearily. "I thank you for your hospitality which I have abused by staying far into the night. I need to return to the palace."

Aajan smiled. "You said they did not expect you, and it's far too late to demand a bed now. You have no papers from another country, no one to speak for you and say you should rest there.

That is the home of the Empress after all. Come stay with us. We have a bed for you."

She stood gracefully and cleared away the dishes. Chul pulled himself up and balanced on his bastono.

"The General has spoken. I find it best just to do what she says. Our home is close."

I said nothing even though a lot of questions were running through my mind. I just stood up and followed Chul to the front door. As I picked up my travel pack where I had dropped it earlier, Aajan called out she would follow later after she had checked one of her experiments.

Chul and I walked in silence to the end of the street and turned right. Then Chul started with his big laugh and didn't stop.

"Oh, Zren, if you could have seen your face when Aajan said to stay with us. She's probably back there now, laughing so hard she had to sit down."

I scowled. "Well, you didn't give me any warning."

"Why should we? When I left Manumina, you and Rell shared a house and now here in Juisiti, Aajan and I share a house."

I squinted up at him. "Why do I think there is more to it than that?"

"Mmm, because you grew up in Kerek City?" He went on to explain how in Vikland people take the life debt very seriously. When he returned to Vikland from Manumina, he had talked to Miyamoto Suki. Miya had agreed to transfer his life debt from Chul Swyler to Aajan Qanaq to give her the opportunities she would never have gotten in Manumina. She received housing, free education, and very small coin until she could support herself—all paid for by the Suki family. Chul received nothing. "Which I knew. I knew I could resume my work at the Academy of Elements and find a place to live."

He went on to say Aajan had continued working with him as she learned and practiced the Vik language. Because of this, she had discovered he was sleeping in his workrooms at night. "You know Piffik—he's a general in disguise—well, his sister is no different. She found a house, and showed it to me. She said she needed to move out of the academy housing for women. She said it was no place for a poor girl from Manumina who didn't know the ways of Vikland. She badgered me until I said yes. It's a beautiful home, we each have our own spaces, and the country of Vikland gets two amazing inventors and creators for the price of one life debt." He laughed his big Chul laugh.

"It's what you both want?" I asked skeptically.

"It's what I want. You'll have to ask Aajan for Aajan's thoughts. But in Matasi where I was born, she would be pushed into a tiny box of marriage and children, and her dreams and all her talents would never see the light of day. In Kerek, she would need to live in her father's or brother's home just for her safety until she married a man who could cherish her and protect her. But it still would be a tiny box, Zren. Vikland doesn't care. She's here, she's contributing, and it's her life to live as she pleases. For now, that's enough for her. In twelve years, when she is the same age I am now? Maybe life will change and maybe not. But truthfully? I will worry about it when she changes the locks on the house. Here we are."

He stopped in front of a tidy house and slid the key easily into the lock.

CHAPTER 11

FAST HORSES AND GOOD NEWS

The next morning Aajan insisted on showing me around the academies.

"You can't leave Vikland without Piffik, and he wouldn't leave Vikland without seeing me. He'll find us, if not today, then tomorrow." She confidently tucked my arm in hers and led me around.

When I had told the Vikland ambassador in Salisport, Matasi all those years ago my price to travel with Miya across the Northern Track was a Vikland education and possible travel to Conrosa, I knew nothing of what I was demanding. To my amazement now, I was surprised no one had mocked me for my request.

Listening to Aajan talk about her classes, navigating the culture of the academies and the country, learning Vik as fast as she could, I realized with a sinking heart, I couldn't have succeeded here. Any boy from Lowertown in Kerek City could not have succeeded here.

Staying in Manumina where the entire village could teach me Conrosan by daily use, giving me manual labor jobs as a manabout to gain in confidence and grow in skills, living in a house to learn how to care for and work with others, was the only way I could have stumbled into adulthood. I blinked my eyes fast as the hardness of such knowledge hit me.

Aajan caught my expression. "What's wrong?"

I waved my hand about. "All this. However did you manage it? Manumina is such a small settlement…" I trailed off.

She gave my words serious consideration. "It's like riding fast horses. At first you're terrified, and then you realize you're freer than you ever have been in your life." She grinned at me. "I've always liked riding fast."

I remembered how we met, she and I. I had a wagonful of wounded after the Battle at the Bridge and in shock and fear I had hurried into Sary looking for help. Piffik had walked out of the butcher shop, looked at the state I was in, looked in the wagon, and had taken charge. He had requested my extra horses and sent Aajan ahead as fast as she could go. He asked his brother Zadah to guide me on the wagon, while he met the others to bring them to Manumina and safety. As she had wheeled about and galloped out of the town of Sary, Piffik had said, "She likes to ride fast. There's not much chance of that on the plow horses at the settlement."

I nodded. "Your brother knew this was a better life for you than Manumina. It's why he chased off your unworthy suitors."

She made a face. "I didn't think so at the time. I knew I wanted, but I didn't know *what* I wanted. Anyway, thank you for bringing Chul Swyler to Manumina. I wouldn't have known how to ask for this, how to navigate this, how to be *me* here without his experience."

She took a deep breath. "You should know this. He thinks I begged him to move into the house with me because…well, I don't know what he thinks, he never said. But I needed a place to retreat to, someone to ask questions of how things are done here without being mocked for it. The women's rooms at the academy—the other students—were as difficult as the academy classes themselves. I needed him, a Matasi who was not born to this, but had navigated it well, to help me understand it all. He's my best friend, Zren. I will always have other friends, but he is the one who helped me survive this."

I patted her hand. "You and I understand each other perfectly, Aajan. Your brother is the friend I cannot live without."

***

We wandered back into the labs in the afternoon. Chul was bent over some nasty smelling trays of stuff which made my eyes water. He waved us away, and Aajan led me to her greenhouse and labs on the floor above. I watched her as she mixed and measured, ground and bottled. It was such a comfortable silence.

Chul brought us the end of day meal, and we ate downstairs in the rooms off Chul's workrooms again. It was easy to see this was a routine for them: talking about the day's work, asking questions, listening to each other about what was accomplished, what was still ahead.

When the knock at the door sounded, Chul merely said, "That would be Piffik," as if Aajan's brother stopped by every night. Aajan slipped past him and ran lightly through the lab.

I stood up, and Chul murmured, "Let's give them some time. Tell me about your day."

I talked about the things I had seen about the academies and other students. He told me stories of when he had been a student years earlier.

"There were more Matasians, West and Spice Islanders, and Kerekis attending then. When the current King decided to be a fool instead of a ruler, everyone suffered, not just Kerek."

Piffik and Aajan came through the workroom to the sitting area then, and Piffik settled into the comfortable chair by the window. He talked of this and that, but said nothing of Rell.

I assumed she was staying with friends in Juisiti. He said he had arranged for us to sleep nearby—he didn't know Aajan had moved out of the women's dormitories.

"I can correctly assume Mother doesn't know either, Aajan?" his voice was tinged with concern.

Chul laughed but said nothing. Piffik just went on to say he had been away longer from Manumina than he had anticipated and wondered how everyone was getting along.

I was quiet the rest of the evening as I watched the three of them. Aajan told us stories to show Piffik his trust in her to succeed had not been misplaced. For all of her words earlier, Aajan was thrilled to spend time with her brother, and it showed.

I also watched the interaction between Chul and Piffik, and realized how much alike they were. While Miyamoto Suki walked into any room and pushed command into his posture and his actions until everyone in the room silently acknowledged him as the leader, Chul and Piffik were so comfortable with themselves, they just were. I knew I wasn't understanding something again, but I wondered if it was one of those things, I would spend days and days trying to puzzle out and then pester Piffik with questions until he told me what I needed to know.

I must have yawned once too often, for suddenly Piffik stood and said it was time to go; he didn't want to have to carry me asleep over his shoulder like he did his younger brother and sister when they were little and too tired to know when to go to bed.

Amid a flurry of goodbyes, we parted at the end of the street, Aajan and Chul to the right to their house, Piffik and I to the left to the inn where he had secured us a room for the night.

CHAPTER 12

LIFE WITHOUT RELL

I was still in bed admiring the sunlight streaming in through the windows and wondering if the Dry was as hot in Vikland as it was in Kerek and if I would be going home to Manumina and weeding, or harvesting, or fruit picking, or one of Rygee's other projects, when I heard Piffik's footsteps in the hallway and his rap at our door. I threw back the covers, pulled a shirt over my head and scowled. The Viklander style of shirts were not nearly so forgiving for a covering as the Kereki billowy long shirts, so I wrapped the blanket around me and trailed my bedding to the door and opened it.

As soon as Piffik walked in the room, he laughed. "My! As long as it took you to open the door, I thought you would be ready to go out to meet the Empress, not…" He waved his hand at me. "I don't even know what to call this."

"You wake me up? You get this," I replied archly.

"Well, I am going to need better than 'this.' Aajan's been called to the burn infirmary this morning with some of her latest inventions. Chul says that usually means she is gone all day and maybe into the night. I asked him what I should do, and he said if I needed to get back to Manumina, he could bring Aajan and my mother for a visit before the Wet begins…if our area remains quiet and removed from the fighting and the weather promises to be good."

I must have stood there with a blank look on my face.

"So I am saying, my friend, if we don't waste any more of the day, we can be to the border by nightfall of the day after tomorrow and home to Manumina the day after that."

"What about Rell?"

Piffik gave a deep sigh, and I saw how sad he was.

"Rell has been called to the war. She will not return with us." He held up his hand. "And before you ask another question, I cannot talk about it just yet. Could you give me that grace?"

I nodded slowly. Piffik didn't say anything, just gathered his pack and waited while I dressed in my Kereki clothes and tried to pack my belongings through my tears.

***

At Ishes, we gave up our fine Viklander horses for our own Conrosan plow horses, which had been growing fat on the Empress's oats for the last few days. The commander said the area was quiet, no one had come in or out we needed to concern ourselves with, and Oro had picked up and dropped off dispatches and messages the day before. If we were not too tired, we could attach ourselves to a patrol going out almost immediately, heading down past our road to Ahni. We could wake up in our own beds tomorrow.

I exchanged a look with Piffik. It was clear we were being pushed on, but I knew a military escort would be an advantage in the event there was trouble. We agreed. The commander looked relieved and within the decon we were on the way.

We reached Manumina at dawn, our horses in much better shape than we were. Lou was just stepping out of the stockade side door to check on his goats. We hailed the house, and he slipped back inside to open one of the big gates for us to drive through. He offered to put away our horses and the wagon, and we stumbled off to our beds. It was good to be home.

***

Malik was still at Manumina healing. We had told Lou she was Rell's cousin—here to be Manumina's healer while Rell was visiting her family in Vikland. He had narrowed his eyes at us as Piffik had told him the story. I knew he didn't believe us.

Then Piffik had made a reference to how Lou had been found by the side of the road because of bandits pretending to be Kereki soldiers. Lou had just garumpfed and walked out to his goats. I stared at Piffik in surprise.

"What was that about?"

Piffik just shrugged as I followed him out to the woodshop. "I reminded him he had told us a different story from the truth when we found him. We knew he had deserted. He may or may not tie the two together and think Malik is also a deserter and will be leaving soon." He looked at me. "That might be a good misconception for him to carry for a few days."

Everyone thought it best not to have Malik in the guest house where Tiju Tia needed to have a place to mix her pots of paint, practice disguises, and be herself. Siba thought it best to have her stay where other people were around. And so a few days later Malik moved into my house and into Rygee's old room above me. Nobody asked what I thought.

I missed Rell. I missed her stories about the Diplo, about growing up with her many younger brothers, what she had learned in the Academy of Healing, and in her Wisdom of the Warrior tales.

I never realized how many times I walked into my house and just started talking to her—until Rell wasn't there to hear me. Malik wasn't the same. Malik never told me a story about her brothers—explaining what I needed to do when I didn't know how to ask the question. Malik didn't know that if she scolded me for not remembering something, I would forget it again and something else besides, but if I was praised for my thoughtfulness, I looked around for other things to be thoughtful about. Malik didn't understand I told the same stories more than once because I wanted to tell it better the second time, or include details I thought I forgot, or because the story was so funny, I wanted to laugh again. Rell knew all those things about me and I missed her. I didn't miss her cooking, but I would have sat through a meal of her burnt offerings if it meant she was back, and we all were happy again.

Piffik only told the rest of us what the Huenas had told him. When Piffik had arrived in Axefield the next day, the Huenas had told him, "All bongmasters, bowmasters, soldiers, and softfoots in Vikland were recalled to Juisiti for active reassignment to Kerek."

A military rider had come to Axefield, just a decon or so after I had left for Juisiti. He had papers for a number of Viklanders in Axefield, including Rell and Dylis, to report to their previous military units in Juisiti. It was only luck and circumstance the military rider had found her at Axefield.

Dylis was to return to soldiering—he was being recalled— and Rell was told to report into the Diplo. She had been reassigned from Manumina effective immediately into a unit of elite bowmasters. All of us who remembered Rani's earlier visit knew exactly what that meant.

Piffik told us he didn't know if it had anything to do with Bima's death or the information Kern the softfoot had brought back to First Soldier Joon.

Piffik had not known what to do then, but Rell's parents had reassured him Rell would come back to Manumina as soon as possible—she still had all her things here. They had only the same information as anyone else. She was heading to the war. After my own experience with ghostfire, no one thought she would be safe from harm.

Piffik lamented, more than once, if only he hadn't asked her to travel to Vikland with him, the rider wouldn't have found her. Surely, they wouldn't have sent a rider all the way to Manumina to recall her.

When Malik said, "Yes, they would have." Piffik fell silent. But when he blamed himself again, nobody bothered to correct him. We knew our words had no meaning in his grief.

That's what he told us. He told Siba a lot more. I would see them walking and talking early in the morning coming back into the stockade. Sometimes I would find her sitting on his porch swing after the end of day meal if I was searching for him at his house.

One night while washing dishes, I complained to Rygee how much I missed talking to Piffik. Siba was taking all of his time and didn't that bother Rygee?

He shrugged as he put away some pots and pans. "Zren, those two have been friends longer than you and I have been alive. Can you understand that? He doesn't want to listen to me because I know nothing of the pain he is going through. He doesn't want to listen to you, because you never stop talking. He doesn't want to talk to Tiju Tia about the Wrens, or Lou about cheese, or Malik about Vikland. He just wants to sit quietly with his oldest friend in the world and grieve for lost chances. Let him be, Zren. He just needs time and space."

When I protested, he gave me a harsh look I had never seen before and said, "Let him be, Zren."

***

The work of Manumina continued. Lou had come back and left again almost immediately. He had some aged wheels of cheese he was going to take up to the great houses, Lou had told Siba. They would appreciate them the most. Oro teased me he thought Lou just wanted to be gone quickly so he didn't have to make an excuse of why I couldn't take the cheese cart out on its deliveries. Siba thought it might be because we were getting too careless around Lou. He wanted to pretend he still didn't know what the Conrosans at Manumina were doing.

While we had been in Vikland, Tiju Tia had left and told Siba and Rygee she would be gone for a while. She left Oro behind, saying he was needed at Manumina while so many were away in Vikland. She would visit Linna in Cloa, take coin, food, and clothes, and then see Nelo and check on the Wrens in the great houses—especially Tyra.

Tyra was still mending from the ambush which had killed Malan Sala and Bima Ritwik, but Rygee had returned her to her great house with a long, convoluted story about how she had been traveling to visit her family and had been injured by soldiers. He didn't say what side.

The housekeeper had looked Rygee up and down and asked Tyra who the man was standing next to her. Tyra said it was her uncle, her father's brother and the man of the house now that her father was dead. There had been another long slow sweep up and down and then the woman had told Tyra to stop dawdling, she may be one-handed for a little while longer but she still had work to be done.

Rygee told us this story and doubted he could ever be a parent. How could you understand the imagination of a child? He and Tyra had not rehearsed any explanations, and he was as surprised as the housekeeper to learn he was an uncle.

"She said it as casually as Zren would say he was hungry." He grinned at me. Then he looked grim and said he never knew people in service were treated so poorly. He would never treat a child the way he thought the Wrens were treated in the great houses.

Rygee decided after the harvest, we would start the planting for greens which grew during the Wet. He wanted to buy seeds and tubers, and get news from the Justices along the way. He would take the settler's wagon with the covered canvas. If there was any unexpected weather, Rygee didn't want the seeds and grain to get hot and sprout. He could carry on his business with the Justices and would finish up in Sary by telling the farmhands to return to Manumina for the harvest or report to the army. If Piffik's news got out and the Kerekis heard the Viklanders were planning a large offensive, Rygee was worried his contracts with the farmhands would be canceled, and he wouldn't have the men he needed to harvest the grains and plant the greens in the fields.

Oro took Malik to Ishes to be reassigned. Siba thought she should heal a little more, but with the farmhands coming back, we couldn't risk them catching sight of her. Her Keresh wasn't as strong as Rell's, and there was no way we could build a convincing story of why she should be there. Piffik loaded his wagon full of coffins and began his travels from Wren to Wren bringing the injured and dead and lost Viklanders to wherever they needed to go.

Until the farmhands arrived, Siba and I kept ourselves busy with all the work a settlement could offer, caring for animals, weeding and harvesting the house and medicinal gardens, and the never-ending laundry. I truly missed Rell.

CHAPTER 13

THE KEREK KING

The harvest began, and I felt like I wouldn't sleep until the hard rains of the Wet fell. The eight farmhands we had earlier in the season had worked on their own family's holdings when we had let them go earlier. Now they were all back and eager to show they were needed at Manumina, so we would not release them to the army. Some even brought their own scythes to cut the grain.

Lou came back from his travels with more stories and rumors to share with us. The King's son and heir, along with his good friend Primo Resoro, had gone out for a night of gambling and to flirt and dance with Trouble down in Lowertown. They may have been in disguise and thought themselves clever and daring, but any child over the age of six in the Sinner's District would have known them for rich fools. Maybe they found a gambling den, maybe not, but they definitely found a dance with Trouble. Their bodyguards had been knifed in the back. The prince and his friend robbed and slashed, royal blood dribbled out in the streets as easily as a street urchin's.

The King and Queen only heard of their son's death when an enterprising young gang of children loaded up the bodies in a hand cart and took them to the castle demanding a reward for the return of the Prince. No word on the likes of that, though Lou doubted it would have been a generous one.

With the Kereki army all in the field, the King had no way of knowing whether it was an attempted military coup within Kerek, an assassination from Vikland or Matasi, a private grudge with another, or Lowertown just being Lowertown. The King packed up his remaining family and all the gold and coin he could carry. He sailed for the Spice Island, the home country of his wife, because to him, a live King in exile was a far better choice than a dead King in Kerek City.

Within the day, Kerek City had claimed the castle for its own with looting and murder and chaos, Lou said with round eyes. As for the rest of the country? It was just a matter of who could get the armies there first to restore order and steal the throne.

We sat around Siba's table with our mouths hanging open. Kerek had fallen from within. All the years the various countries and ambassadors and softfoots had worked to bring the Kerek King to heel, and it only took a handful of thieves in the Sinner's District to murder the heir and frighten the King and his family off the throne.

I tried to think what we should be doing. Rygee and Tiju Tia were still on the road. I counted my fingers—Rygee was most likely near Balza if he started south and planned to return on the Northern Route. Piffik was traveling up his favorite half-track, and I guessed he was near Nelo's holding, possibly as far as Kid at Evensong. I had no idea where Tiju Tia was. None of them would be returning soon. It was the harvest end of the Dry, and I had no idea what to do next. Lou, Siba, and I just looked at each other.

Oro knocked on the door, and we called him to come in. He hadn't heard the news, and so Lou repeated the story he had heard in Sary.

"Well, that's good then!" Oro slapped his hands on his legs. "I will ride to Vikland to tell the Conrosan refugees at Rishka."

"What about Piffik? What about Rygee?" I worried aloud. "I don't even know where Tiju Tia is right now."

Oro leaned back in his chair. "Well, I don't mean any disrespect to those around the table, but Piffik is the smartest person I know. He doesn't need me to do his thinking for him. He'll hear the news just as Lou did and make his plans for that. And Tiju Tia..." He paused. "She's tricksy enough to have everyone home and tucked into their beds before Trouble knows she's missing."

I flicked my eyes in a panic to Lou and Oro stiffened. I could see him reliving his conversation in his head trying to think if he had said too much. We both relaxed at the same time.

"Well, then it looks like we all have our plans then." Siba smiled. "Oro to Vikland to tell the Conrosans at Rishka, Lou and Zren to finish up the harvest and oversee the farmhands, and I will begin cleaning out the common spaces we closed up when everyone left." She gave a deep sigh. "It will be nice to have everyone come back to Manumina and their homes."

CHAPTER 14

ANY CIRCUMSTANCES BUT THESE

I was shocked how little the lack of the King impacted our life at Manumina. Oro returned with the news the Council of Wisdom wouldn't return until the next Dry. They had their own harvest in Vikland to attend to. Piffik came and went. Rygee returned and helped us in the fields. No one heard from Tiju Tia. We all assumed she was helping the Wrens and that they were safe. Truly, we wouldn't know otherwise unless someone brought us the news.

The moon was full and the moonglow so bright, the houses and fences outside the stockade threw shadows. The nights were cooling; it was the end of the Dry after all. I pushed my head out further letting the breeze wash my face. I relaxed, watching everything and nothing on the distant Huntsman's Trail.

I noticed movement first, a dot off the track, but coming down the breakaway directly to Manumina. It was too late to be a casual visitor. It had to be one of ours. I grabbed my clothes and pulled them on in front of the window, wishing yet again Rell was here. Rell, who would have been able to pick out the driver's face while I was still waiting for the shape to decide if it was going to be a rider or wagon. Rell, who would have given her window a satisfying whoosh as she opened it, and let me hear the thunk of her crossbow on the sill to protect me. But she was either in Vikland or in battle, and this was something I had to face on my own.

By the time I reached my front porch, I recognized the coffin wagon and knew it had to be Piffik. I thought there was someone on the seat with him, but I hurried through the side door, and then opened the big gate so he could drive through. He drove straight through the green and up to the infirmary, calling out Siba's name. I closed the gates and ran to the wagon. I saw a blaze of light in the window above the infirmary. Siba and Rygee were now awake.

Piffik said, there were five of them—all injured. Piffik carried in Linna himself, Falan walked on her own. Rygee unlatched another coffin. He and I carried in Kid together. As we laid him down, Siba ordered me to the kitchen to pull and heat water, bring the boiled soap and as many soft rags as I could find.

The Wrens were bruised and bloody.

"Beaten not stabbed," Piffik said tersely as he and Rygee carried in a Viklander soldier. Rygee came to take my place in the kitchen and told me to go help Piffik. He was out in the night opening the clasps of the last coffin, the ones with breathing holes and false bottoms for smuggling Viklanders. Before I lifted the lid, Piffik put his hand on my arm.

"I am sorry, Zren, I would give a day of my life for you not to see this." He lifted the lid watching me rather than the body inside.

I looked at him and then at the person inside the coffin.

It was Solkka Ulani.

CHAPTER 15

SURVIVORS

We worked all night. Piffik left to take care of the horses and wash up so he could come back and help. Rygee and I washed away blood, cut away clothes, and did whatever Siba told us to do. She had Rygee mix the bowls with the sleeping draughts, and then teased him he made it so strong, it would drop all of us as well. I noticed she didn't tell him to weaken it however.

Piffik came back. Siba asked him if the unknown Viklander had ever been conscious? He said yes, the softfoot's name was Quan, and he had climbed into the coffin on his own to come to Manumina. He had the same type of battering and bruising as the others.

"Cudgels," Piffik said abruptly. "The news of the King's exile is making its way through the countryside. Without anyone to restore order or keep the peace, rumors are flying through the towns and settlements."

He sighed. "Those who understand Kerek has fallen are rallying mobs about them for raids and reprisals." He paused for a moment. "It is no different than Kerek before the King left for the Spice Island, except then it was violence against non-Kereki, now it is violence against anyone."

All of the Wrens' wrists or forearms were sprained or broken. Siba said by the location of the bruising, she would guess from fending off blows. As she examined each body, she would have us help her bind, splint, and wrap the damaged arms, shoulders, ribs, legs.

There was not a knife wound on anyone. Rygee said it only meant the mob was big enough they didn't need metal to inflict damage. Kid's and Quan's faces were badly bruised and Siba feared head injuries.

"Do we need any of them awake for questions? Otherwise, I would like them to sleep deeply and heal."

Piffik considered. "Let them all sleep. The damage is done, and I got them all out. They can wait to relive the nightmare, and I know most of the story from Falan. When she woke and found herself in a coffin, she panicked at the closeness and screamed. Thankfully we were already far from any settlements, and I was on my shortcut to Manumina. She sat with me for the last decon and talked of what had happened."

He came to stand by me where I was carefully washing Solkka's face. Siba had already bound and wrapped his wrists, forearms, and ribs. I knew he was too damaged for me to hug him, and so I gently washed his face over and over.

Piffik stopped my hand.

"Zren, look at this." He pointed to Solkka's knuckles scraped and swollen. "He either had a tahn bong, or something he used as one. The Wrens were huddled behind the two Viklanders. They protected Tiju Tia's Wrens as long as they were able."

I nodded as my eyes filled with tears. "Will he live?"

Piffik hunched up his shoulders as if to ward off my question. "It depends on what is damaged that we cannot see. It could be a bad beating, like those you described as given and received in Kerek City in your youth. It could be what happened to Bima Ritwik. Where something is badly damaged on the inside and we don't know." He saw my stricken face. "I'm sorry. I didn't want to give you false hope."

Siba came back in the room from filling her bowls with the incense to smoke the air.

"Zren, I will ask you to sit with them until dawn. Wake me then. Piffik, go to bed. I don't know how long you have been awake to get them here, but it has been too long."

Rygee looked at the sleeping patients. "What I don't understand is why these Wrens? This is Falan, am I not right? I know she is the one who lives with the widow in Balza. She passes information to and from Josef who lives north of her nearest the battlefields. But this is not Josef." He waved at Kid.

"No, it's Kid. He's the one Zren and I took back to Evensong when Nelo was taken by the crimpers," Siba offered.

"The other end of Tiju Tia's network in the far east and the far north. Is that not so?" Rygee said, "and this one?"

"Linna. She and Arden were the hub at Cloa. Tiju Tia said they worked well together," Piffik finished.

"This makes no sense to me. Why these three?" Rygee demanded of us.

Piffik breathed out heavily. "I will tell you what I know from Falan." He explained she had received a visit from Josef. He said her maskovesto was compromised, and she needed to leave Balza immediately. Men were coming to hunt for her. She told her Patron and the widow she lived with that her mother had passed, and she was needed at home. Josef arranged for her to travel with a Matasi missionary and her husband as far as Huk. Josef took the horse from Balza. Falan knew he was riding north to warn his contacts and friends. Balza had fallen and was now closed to them.

Once Falan reached Huk, she knew Ross and Callis could hide her until Tiju Tia or Padro Morto came. She stayed in their house while they decided if it was better for her to hide in Huk or at the settlement south of there where no one would see her, but she would be alone until a message could be sent to Padro Morto to pick her up and take her to Manumina.

A day later, Linna, wearing Arden's cloak and Kereki men's clothes, and the Viklander, Quan, arrived in Huk just before daybreak. They had walked all night east to west because Quan was traveling to Kerek City to confirm the Kerek King had fled with his family. While Quan was sleeping, the Wrens discussed whether Quan should join Falan and try to go south and then have Tiju Tia take them east, or whether Quan could travel better with a Kereki landowner Josef knew who was sympathetic to Vikland.

The Wrens asked Quan to wait another day so they could arrange safe passage north and try to make contact with Josef. When Callis and Falan were checking a hiding place north of Huk, they found Solkka. He had heard them call 'cio claro' to each other as they had searched the barn, and he had dropped from the loft where he had hidden himself. Without his braid and wearing Kereki clothes, they mistook his curly hair and darker skin for a Conrosan they had not met.

Thinking he was a friend of Padro Morto, Callis said they were friends of Zren Janin. He knew the name he said, but he could not help them because he was trying to slip through the country west to east without detection. Callis said they had a softfoot who needed to get to Kerek City. Could Solkka talk to the Viklander and tell him of a safe route to travel? Solkka agreed and came with them to Callis's house where he met with the softfoot.

Quan had been sent out because it had been too long since Solkka had been expected back and Vikland feared he had been lost or captured. With Solkka's confirmation that he had been in Kerek City, and the King and his family had indeed left the city for the Spice Island, it was no longer necessary for Quan to travel east.

Since Solkka had stained his skin and had been passing as other than a Viklander, he thought he could ride with Falan and hide Quan in a wagon to travel to Manumina or Ishes. The others agreed and the new plan was to have all four—Linna, Falan, Quan, and Solkka—travel back to Cloa. Linna suggested she could hide them there while she arranged for a small cart. They could use Manumina's horse stabled at Cloa to travel to Ishes.

"Where did they get caught?" Siba asked.

"Cloa," Piffik continued. When Linna returned to her house, Arden and Mother were gone, her cloak was on the hook, and Kid was sitting at her table. He said he had arrived the day before. Arden had let him in, fed him, and told him to sleep in his bed; he had to meet Josef to pick up Viklanders. This was even better, Linna had said. Kid could ride with Falan and both softfoots could be hidden on the way to Manumina and then over the border to Vikland.

While they were waiting for the stable to empty out of all the daily workers, Linna fed everyone. Then when she thought the stable was empty except for the feed boy, she took everyone to get the horse and cart. She left them hiding at the edge of the building and walked in alone. But the boy who had worked with Arden—and knew her as Arden's sister—was not there.

Instead, there were three unknown men who grabbed her. She whistled for the others to run away, but instead the Viklanders ran to her defense. There was so much noise in the fight, it drew the attention of the horsemaster nearby.

Piffik blew out a noisy breath. "I was driving into Cloa complaining to myself about the dust and slowness of a grain train ahead of me. It was coming from the port and stopped just beyond the stables. I wanted to feed and water my horse while I visited with Arden if he was in the stables or perhaps at his home. I grumbled at the inconvenience and then realized the Justice, the Patron and his crew, weren't there to meet the grain train and keep everyone away.

"Soon many people, including the horsemaster and everyone else, realized there were just a handful of guards on the train. They rushed the wagons in their attempt to steal food for their families.

I'm sure the troublemakers thought they could just return to the stable and finish off the five broken bodies later after they had finished looting. While they were busy fighting with the wagon train guards and stealing the grain, I drove my wagon into the stables. That's when I saw the bodies heaped in a stall.

"I scooped up the Wrens. Quan and Solkka were barely able to collapse into a coffin—I don't know what I would have done if they could not have stood on their own. I latched the coffins all down, and trotted out of there as quickly as I could. But it won't take the troublemakers long to figure out who took them. All of the Wrens and the Viklanders were too injured to crawl away."

Siba asked what was in my mind. "But why? Why now? The war is over and the King is gone. Kerek didn't win, but neither did Vikland."

"The Wrens are collaborators, traitors. They are seen as Kerekis actively aiding the enemy. It doesn't matter their country treats others so unfairly. It means nothing that Kerek refuses to acknowledge anyone without a voice of power and coin. Siba, this could happen to any of us at any time," Piffik said sorrowfully. "I never dreamed Vikland would lose. How could Justice fail? We need Kerek to be a safe place for anyone who chooses to live here."

Siba put her hand on Piffik's shoulder. "You saved them, now get some sleep. Zren and I can do the rest."

He smiled sadly but didn't say another word as he walked heavily out of the infirmary.

"Rygee, the farmhands tomorrow," Siba started.

"I've been thinking about it. I will tell them I will pay them for the day and send them home after the animal chores are done. I can explain I am securing more horses so we do not need to use our bodies to pull the wagons of harvested grain into the walls of Manumina. Piffik's team needs to rest for today. But I can ride out tomorrow to the Sary stables and send messages to have our horses from Balza, Huk, and Cloa returned to us. If Callis, Arden, and possibly Josef hear the news, I hope they will assume this also means they need to come to Manumina. I don't know how else to send word." Rygee hunched his shoulders and then let them drop. "We also need to let Arden and Josef know Falan and Linna are here safe. I don't want either of them worrying unnecessarily…or searching for them."

Siba checked all the patients one last time and then touched me.

"If you are very careful, you may lie down next to Solkka. He may respond better if he knows you are here." She put her hand under my chin and forced me to focus on her face. "Do you understand what I am saying, Zren? Let him know he has something to live for." She put the night shades down on the lantern and followed Rygee up the stairs to their rooms.

I crawled carefully onto Solkka's bed. He was lying on his back, arms bandaged and resting on pillows at his sides. At first, I did the same, shoulders touching, hips and thighs aligned. I bumped his arm by mistake and I heard him hiss in pain.

"I am sorry, Solkka, I'm sorry."

"Zren?" he struggled groggily.

"Yes. You are here at Manumina and safe. All of the others you protected are safe."

"Not dead then. It hurts too much to be dead." He groaned softly.

"Shhh. Sleep. The healer said you need to rest to heal. I'm here. I will always be here."

"No," Solkka said fighting his way to consciousness. "No, when this is over, you and I are going to sail to the West Islands. No more hiding in Manumina, never again to be trapped in Vikland. We will live in the West Islands where we can sail as we please, travel from island to island, eating, drinking, and listening to the Storytellers."

He groaned again. "I hurt everywhere."

I rolled to my side and feathered my fingers down his face. "Shhh. Sleep and heal." I drew my fingers along his jaw and down his throat. I switched to Wester and said, "Imagine we are living in the West Islands. The weather is perfect and we are happy." I trailed my fingers slowly down his arm, over his bandages, and gently dragged them over his battered and scraped knuckles, "Imagine we are at the Storyteller's hearth and these are the stories we will hear."

I started with one of the Smith's tales. How he and Mother Earth walked the land bringing good things to the people of the West Islands. I caressed his face. I trailed my fingers down his bare chest avoiding the bandages on his cracked and bruised ribs. I told stories of Gems and Grains, Mother Earth's daughters, and their goodness to those who showed Mother Earth kindness. I lightly palmed his hips and thighs and whispered tales of the Traveler.

He listened, he slept, he dreamed, he healed.

All through that long night, each time his eyelids would flutter awake, I would whisper, "You are loved, Solkka Ulani, you are loved."

CHAPTER 16

OUR JENNY

Siba came in shortly after sunrise bringing me a bowl of cooked oats and berries and honey. It smelled wonderful. I carefully sat up as to not wake Solkka. She walked around checking each of the sleeping patients while I ate.

"Well done, Zren! You kept them all alive." She stopped in front of Kid and frowned. I slipped out of bed and walked over to look at the Wren with her. His eyes were open, but he still looked groggy or maybe sleepy.

"How are you feeling today?" Siba crouched down closer to him and asked, "Do you know where you are?"

"Manumina?" he guessed.

"Yes! First meal for you then. Can you tell me how you came to be at Linna's house?"

He blinked. But said nothing.

Siba stood up and motioned me to follow her into the infirmary kitchen.

"I think the Wrens will be resting here for a while. We'll need to find them clothes for a few days while they mend." She looked at me. "Could you do the laundry today? Some mending too perhaps?"

I considered. "I'll have to tell Rygee I can't help the farmhands."

She agreed. "He's in the bakery working until they arrive. You can tell him I don't even have enough clothes for them to change out of the ones they were beaten in."

Rygee listened to my request as he fired the ovens. He nodded absently.

"She needs you more than I do today. It will just be the chores no one likes to do."

Once the farmhands arrived, Rygee had them repair all the fences, muck out the stables, clean the rabbit hatch, the goats' loafing shed, and the chicken coop. Piffik had a couple of them sand wood while he cleaned his tools. Siba helped me with the laundry until we had enough clean clothes for her to dress the Wrens and Viklanders.

Rygee was planning on leaving that afternoon to travel to the Northern Track and pick up our horses. He was going to try to leave messages to let the others know Falan, Kid, and Linna were safe and to find Tiju Tia. He said he needed to get our horses back from the delivery stables where they had served as exchanges for Piffik and the Wrens.

He talked his worries out loud to anyone who would listen. If he could not get a message to the Wrens, how would he find them if they were out softfooting or moving Viklanders from place to place? How did the Wrens leave messages in places where anyone could read them if no one could read anything but Keresh? And what about those Wrens who could not read even that? The only thing he knew for sure, he said, was that he would leave after he paid the farmhands.

After Rygee had inspected the farmhands' work, he had them help me empty the wash water over the gardens, paid them for the day's labor, and told them not to return for five days. At that time, he assured them he would have horses for them and the orchards would be ready for the first picking.

As he and I walked back into the stockade after saying goodbye to the farmhands, he thanked me for helping Siba with the laundry. Then he asked me to see if Piffik needed help and told me not to disturb him or Siba unless the stockade was burning down.

Happily, I went to the woodshop to help Piffik. He asked me to redo some of the sanding from the farmhands, "They'll never be as good as you are," which made me smile and we worked comfortably in silence while Piffik measured and cut.

Piffik said quietly, "You don't know this, but some of the best advice I ever heard came from Chul when he was here at Manumina healing after the attack at the bridge."

I looked up in surprise. *What made him think of that?*

He went on to tell how Chul had come to their house and told the Qanaqs how smart Aajan was. Not just in helping him with his experiments and inventions at Manumina, but truly brilliant with anything he tried to teach her. 'Would they consider sending her to the academies in Vikland?' he had asked.

Piffik replied she was the jewel in the family, smart, brave, and curious, but truthfully, there was no coin for the academies. His mother said she was too young; she had never been much beyond Manumina. A new country, a large city, different language and culture, the work in the academies, would overwhelm her no matter how smart she was.

But Chul thought Aajan had so much potential he wanted to be around for the end of the story. He told the Qanaqs he would take her and guide her, and listen to her.

"Not as a husband, or a guardian, or parent, but as a friend, he had said."

Piffik set down his tools. "And that is what I want, Zren. You came to Manumina with a nightmare of an upbringing I can't even begin to imagine. You are fierce, willing to do whatever is asked of you, and in spite of everything that has happened to you, your heart is wide open. I want to be around to see your story end. Not as a dusty old relic who talks about crops and weather, not as a lover who whispers to you of kisses, not as someone who offers you coin for your courage, but as a friend who resides in your heart just as you reside in mine."

He picked up a board and handed it to me. "You aren't meant for Manumina anymore than Aajan was. But I am beyond glad our paths crossed, no matter how long or short." He let the silence stretch.

It sounded like he was telling me something I wasn't quite understanding. So, I took the words exactly as I heard them, and I grinned.

"Me too."

We talked of this and that the rest of the day. I did most of the talking. Toward evening, the room started to darken, but rather than light the lamps, Piffik decided we were done for the day.

I rushed off to take a bath and visit Solkka in the infirmary. I got there just as Siba was handing out bowls of soup thick with vegetables and noodles. Her patients were all sitting around the table, moving very slowly and gently, but moving. Quan was trying to fold his swollen hands around the spoon without much luck. I unhooked one of the chairs from along the wall, and sat down between him and Solkka.

"Here, I'll help you tonight." I held up the spoon so he could take as much or as little as he wanted. "Too hot?"

He shook his head. "No, it's good. It's very good."

"I know." I shook my head in mock sorrow. "We have only two good cooks at Manumina and they happen to be married to each other. That's just wrong." I grinned cheekily at Siba as she came out with two more bowls. She set one in front of Linna and the last one in front of me.

"I thought Piffik probably forgot to feed you, and so I brought you one as well. If you are going to be here for a while, I'll take a bowl over to Piffik—I want to talk to him." I nodded. She went back in the kitchen, came out with two more bowls, and left out the door.

There was only the slurping of soup for a while. I kept my thigh pressed against Solkka's leg. He may have had pain from the contact against his bruises, but he returned the pressure. I cut a glance at him. He looked exhausted, dark circles under his eyes or maybe bruises, stubble along his chin and jaw everywhere except on that ugly scar. A scar for which Jenny gave up three fingers so he could be sitting next to me.

"Have you had word from Jenny?" I asked him. "Have you been home to see her and your brothers?"

The Wrens' heads popped up.

"You know our Jenny?" Linna asked.

"I do." Solkka cleared his throat. He drew his finger slowly along his scar from under his ear to his chin. "She gave me this," he paused and the Wrens' eyes widened, "instead of a coffin." He finished with a wicked grin. I watched them relax in relief.

"How is she then?" Linna asked. "The rest of us were able to keep in touch as we could through messages and glimpses as our Patrons took us or sent us to the next town, but Jenny nested with a Vik patrol west of Balza."

"It was a hunt and hobble unit," Solkka agreed. "I was in it." He pushed his bowl forward and continued, "You were all still in the cart headed to Manumina then. Our commander was Ven Wila. Jenny volunteered to stay with us and be the westernmost point in the network. A brave girl, your Jenny. She had a Sailor's Curse—I am beginning to think every person in Lowertown carries that nasty blade—and a pounded iron knife. Tiju Tia gave us West Islands steel, and we taught Jenny to throw riatas and use knives. We didn't have a crossbow light enough for her, and her reach was too short for the bongs, but she practiced with her knives every day."

Jenny was a gift from the West Islands Constellations, he went on to say. She cut off her hair and wore the Kereki clothes of a kitchen boy. She could be sent into the villages and settlements for news and food, and she would overhear of captures and losses, and tell the hunt and hobble soldiers where she heard the Kereki army was marching.

The Viklanders had worked as a sabotage unit. Wrecking wagons meant for the Kereki army, spoiling food—after they had helped themselves first—and interfering however they could. They were a defense unit only, too small to engage with the actual army unless there was no choice.

"We were hunters, not the hunted."

The Wrens all nodded in agreement. That had been their role as well.

"For an entire season, small groups like us inflicted losses from the Cold Mountains to just below the Northern Track. We were a vertical line that nothing from Kerek City was to pass until the Viklander army could march across the north of Kerek and join us."

Solkka continued his story, "The Matasi navy was supposed to sail ships full of soldiers into the Kerek City harbor and pinch the Kereki army in between us. But it didn't work that way. Our army was hindered by a thousand little skirmishes as they marched east, and our scouts in Kerek City looked out on an empty bay day after day."

Solkka blew out a breath. "Our hunt and hobbles were not meant to be a lengthy endeavor. Mostly on foot, we only had a few horses hidden around our territory. The Kerekis would learn where we struck and the news would be sent out in a sunburst pattern to try to find us. If our leader, Ven Wila, had not been so good, we would have been captured long ago."

They were headed to the north to hide for a while when they stumbled into a hunting party with dogs. The hunters were as surprised to see the Viklanders as the Viklanders were to see them.

"We ran and they released the dogs. Ven yelled for all of us to separate, and I took Jenny with me. We weren't the normal prey, but we gave them the thrill of the chase.

"Then some of the dogs caught the scent of whatever they had been meant to hunt and raced off to the sides. The hunters didn't know which ones to follow. Jenny and I dashed into the woods, and I heard footsteps pounding behind us. I tossed Jenny up into the trees. I told her to run for it across the branches, if she could, until she could find a place to hide and not to come down until the dogs were gone.

"I pulled my tahn bong and turned to fight. I knew I needed to live long enough to allow her to get away." There was a stiff inhale from everyone about the table. Even though Solkka was sitting next to me, I couldn't breathe.

"There were three of them. All had hunting knives, but they were not soldiers or militia. The bounty on our braids was already known. One of them said if I would cut off my braid and throw it to him, he would be happy to take his dogs and go." Solkka gave us all a wicked smile. "It was obvious he had never met a Viklander before."

Solkka leaned back carefully and sharply inhaled when his injured back touched the chair.

"Now the tahn bong and the jeong bong can fight many attackers if you have another partner skilled in its talents. I had only a tree behind me, neither friend nor foe. Still, I was able to keep them fighting to give Jenny time to hide. At least, until one of the hunters worked his way around the tree. When I stepped forward to knock one of the men in front of me to the ground, the one behind the tree grabbed me by my braid. He hacked at it with his long knife and pulled me off my feet." Solkka paused.

"I heard a thud and saw Jenny had not run across the branches after all, but had aimed one of her throwing knives at the man in front of me. It caught him in the belly and he went down on his knees. I rolled to my attacker to wrestle away his long knife. He grabbed my head to slit my throat as easily as one would butcher a goat, when Jenny threw herself from the tree and pushed out her left hand to turn the blade." He finished, "She saved my life, but the blade sliced through the hand from the v between her fingers diagonally almost to the wrist and the tip of it caught my face from ear to mouth."

He paused to take a drink of water. I looked about the table, jaws open, eyes wide, the others barely breathing as they listen to Solkka's tale, stunned by Jenny's bravery.

"My friends," Solkka grinned, "Have you heard the words that have fallen from my mouth? Your Jenny took *two* hunters to my *one*. Once she had disabled them, I ensured they did not suffer. Then I tore off the sleeves from my shirt and wrapped her hand and my face and we went to find the others."

He pulled the bowl towards himself again and began spooning in noodles. His left hand drifted below the table and rested lightly on my thigh. I shivered at the contact, but Solkka misunderstood. "It's all right, I am here before you now," he murmured.

"Did she live? Where is she now?" Falan asked.

"You can't just stop the story there," Linna added.

Solkka looked at Kid. "This is not the first time Kid and I have crossed paths." He nodded. "In fact, you have a history of rescuing me, not just the attack of two days ago, but also the one I have been telling. I think you should tell it from here. You and Jenny are the heroes after all, and my soup will get cold if I keep talking."

All our heads swiveled to Kid. He had barely said anything since he had been carried in. He still held himself unnaturally quiet, even here among friends. I thought Kid had found a position as an under-footman in the Kereki stronghold of Evensong. I remembered how recently Tiju Tia thought it was getting too dangerous for him to remain. I couldn't imagine any event which would have put Solkka and Kid in the same battlefields north of Balza.

Kid licked his lower lip and began, "Two Viklanders and I found them. Jenny had fainted from loss of blood and Solkka had carried her as far as he could. They were resting in a shallow grave behind a fallen tree. Although we had passed within a jeong bong length, we never would have found them except Solkka called to us." He looked to Solkka who nodded for him to continue.

"Jenny was badly hurt, and we knew she needed a healer immediately. The area we were in is north of Josef's range. He has often said there are no friends to Vikland there for him to use as allies."

He sighed. "We needed a healer, food, horses. All that took coin we didn't have. I knew a Viklander has their hair cut if they have been dishonest, or done something dishonorable. It is one of the reasons the Kereki army set up the braid bounty in the first place. It shames the Viklanders. I thought if I took a braid in with me and Jenny to the healer, I could collect the bounty and use it to pay the healer. It could also explain how Jenny was injured in the first place." Kid looked at us. "I had to ask the Viklanders to shame themselves to cut off a braid."

"Without Jenny's courage, I would have lost more than my braid," Solkka said simply.

"Solkka cut off his braid for me and hid in a shed we passed by. Jenny and I continued on with the braid to the healer in the settlement. I said she was my sister, and we had taken the life of the Viklander who had tried to take her hand. They believed us and paid the bounty. While Jenny was seen to by the healer, I went to the stable and hired two horses and enough food to get us to Huk, the next town. We took the horses back to the shed where Solkka was hiding and ate while we waited until dark to leave.

"We did not know the area around Huk well, but I knew Callis and Ross lived in a house north of the settlement. I recognized the rabbit hutches from Manumina and knocked on their door. Callis let us in and Ross took the horses to the Huk stable for me.

"Callis had her medicinals. She was able to help Solkka and checked on Jenny through the day. But she said Jenny's hand was far beyond her skill and we should not stay. That evening, Callis took us in a wagon to the house south of the Northern Track. She said Padro Morto would come through the next day on his way to Balza." Kid looked at Falan. "I did not know he checked the house every time he came to Balza.

"Piffik took us from the house, abandoned his deliveries, and drove straight to Ishes. He left me at Sary at my insistence. I walked all day to reach my home in Evensong. I told my master I had been separated and lost during the battle. I told him, not knowing what else to do, I found others from the Kereki army who allowed me to travel with them east. Then I walked home to Evensong. I looked tired and disheveled enough he believed me—that time."

I turned to Kid. "That was a long way from Evensong, days and days, why were you softfooting so far from home?"

"I wasn't. My master had brought his militia to fight, and I was forced to go along. We skirmished with a different group of Viklanders a few furloughs away. In the confusion of the fighting, I slipped away and found the two Viklanders. I told them I had plans and rosters of the militias in the area to give to their commander, and they got me to someone so I could turn them over. Once I had explained the maps to their leader, they took their knives from my throat.

"I said I could get them more documents in the future. That I was part of a group called the 'friends of Zren Janin,' hidden across Kerek to help Vikland. The Viklander had me searched. They took my boot knife, but never found my Sailor's Curse. Then he told the others to take me far enough south out of danger, I wouldn't be killed by the people I just tried to help."

Kid gave us all an earnest look. "My plan was always to give aid to the other side. It was fortuitous I had been given the musters and rosters of men and their locations. So much more than just the news in my head. When I returned to my own side, I told my fellow militiamen I got separated and lost during the battle. My plan was to look young and foolish and incapable of deceit. It was only chance I stumbled across Solkka and Jenny at all."

Solkka paled. "I am beyond glad I never knew that part of the story until now. Are you afraid of nothing?"

Kid looked at Solkka, his eyes unblinking, his face without emotion. "Kittens, I am afraid of kittens. They have these sharp pointy teeth and tiny little daggers for claws…"

We all stared at him, and he laughed. "I am not telling the truth, but by the looks on your faces, I must remember this joke to tell Tiju Tia when she returns." He paused. "Now Solkka, you must finish the tale. What happened after Padro Morto let us pick out a coffin as our home for three days?"

"It's a good thing I have finished my soup then. As you know, the top coffins on the wagon are real, but the bottom ones have false sides which allow us to turn a bit and small openings to see the road beneath us if we have eyes in our buttocks. Kid is right, from Huk to Ishes is a hard three-day ride, but Padro Morto kept switching out the horses at the stables along the way and we reached the garrison late on the second day. At Ishes, we took a fast horse, I took Jenny with me, and we reached Juisiti where the healers at the Academy of Healing were able to help her… and me," he added.

"Now Jenny lives in the Keopi district of Vikland. She has tutors to help her learn Vik and other studies she must know to enter the academies. She has her own horse to learn to ride well, and three older brothers to cherish her. Her new grandmother dotes on her much more than she ever did her grandsons, and she is safe from the rest of this war."

"A happy ending? For a child thrown away on the streets of Kerek City? I don't believe it," Falan sounded skeptical.

"My dear Falan, you weren't listening," Solkka teased. "I said she has to learn Vik, she has three big brothers to torment her, and the Keopi District is so far from the excitement of Juisiti you are closer to the festivals of the Empress here at Manumina than you would be if you were there."

Falan still didn't look convinced, but she didn't get a chance to say anything more as Siba and Piffik entered the room.

Piffik greeted us and added, "I know you are all still healing, but I think we need to move you to a safer spot."

"Safer than here?" Linna's eyes grew wide.

Piffik went on to describe a shepherd's cottage inside Vikland straight east of Manumina. It wasn't fancy, but it had been used before to move Viklanders and hide Conrosans during the Tax Collector visits. Most importantly, it was well within the borders of Vikland.

"Siba and I will go with you. She will stay and care for you until someone within Vikland can gather you up. I will need to go to the Council of Wisdom immediately and tell them Manumina may be in danger. Wrens, you most likely will not be going back to your homes, if you have any letters or requests of things you need or want, please write them down tonight. I will try to get them to any people you say can help you retrieve them.

"Linna and Falan, Rygee has gone to bring back our horses we have stabled along the Northern Track. He will let Callis, Josef, and Arden know you are safe, so they do not search for you. He will try to secure your wages if you have any due." He looked at Kid. "I assume you left Evensong to take Arden's position at the stables in Cloa. Do you have any reason why we should go back to Evensong?"

Kid shook his head. "Arden knew I had arrived in Cloa, he fed me and told me to stay at his home. I have nothing at Evensong. My master paid me my wages, but I could tell he was starting to have questions. It was a good time for me to leave." He thought for a moment. "Do you want me to travel back with you?"

Piffik looked to Siba, and she shook her head. "I am concerned enough I want to watch you for a few more days. I would not let you travel to Vikland, except Piffik tells me it must be so."

Piffik paused and then added gently, "We leave in the morning."

I looked at the table to hide my dismay. Siba told everyone to get their belongings packed and she wanted to look at everyone again after the meal. Solkka bumped my knee with his.

"Where do you sleep?" he whispered.

"Outside the stockade, facing the road to Ahni," I whispered back, "I will wait for you on the swing in the porch."

Siba came back in the room with a bundle of battered travel bags and the clothes I had spent most of the day washing and she and I had mended.

"Take everything you own out of the guesthouse and fill the rest of your packs with enough clothes from these to last you for a while. I don't know where you may end up, and we may not come back here first."

Piffik sighed. "Quan and Solkka, I will send a message to Ishes with our cheeseman to have horses sent to you at the cottage. He is not a part of us, but he has sold there before. I will need to have one of you write the message for your commander in Vik for me. I cannot take the chance Lou has learned to read Keresh. I need to have him return before he can be sent out again, but Siba wants you both to rest for a few more days before you sit a horse so long."

"I could wait here and heal," Solkka calmly looked at Piffik.

"No, you can't." Piffik blew out a breath. "I was the only one around when I drove into the stable and saw the five of you crumpled on the floor. I threw you in the cart and left immediately. I didn't make any deliveries, but raced back here to get you to Siba. Every person in that mob intent on doing you harm knows you didn't just crawl away. If people saw me drive my wagon into Cloa, but I didn't make any deliveries, they will begin to wonder why. I do not know who saw me or who did not and what they would do with the information. I expect it will take more than a few days for people to talk. It is possible the same Kereki men or similar will come here in a while when they ask about and follow my trail."

He gave a sad half smile. "All they will find at Manumina is a number of farmhands, Zren, and me. If they burn the fields, we can put it out. If they threaten to take the animals, we will stop them. I am hopeful they will know the farmhands as friends and neighbors and walk away once they search the settlement and realize no Viklanders are here. It is yet another reason, Siba must stay in Vikland at the cottage with you."

"And if they fight?" Solkka asked. "You are what, eight men, maybe ten? Against how many?"

Piffik stared back but said nothing.

"Look, Piffik. You are smart, you look ahead, you understand strategy. That's great, but you don't have any bong fighters. No archers, no firemasters. You can't fight with farmhands and pitchforks. I can understand sending away every one of us who was in that stable. I can see sending Siba away. But I don't understand, if it is so dangerous, why aren't you and Zren coming with us?"

"Because Tiju Tia, and Rygee, and Oro could be coming back any day. Because Lou could be driving into an empty stockade and alert the Justice in Sary who would search our buildings. Because a Wren could have ridden a day and a night for help—only to find no help is here. I am not going to walk out that gate and let any or all of them walk into a nightmare or a burned out shell. I am not going to let this place be looted and destroyed because there was no one here to talk sense to those who needed to hear it." Piffik ran his hand through his curly hair. "I'm open to ideas, Solkka, I truly am. But right now, I see nothing in front of me but the path I am following."

Solkka held his gaze for a long time. I could see the emotions play across his face. Then finally, he held out his palm.

"I misspoke. Your actions saved my life and those I was unable to protect. Your decision saved lives then, and your decision now will save more lives. I am sorry I questioned you. It shall be as you say."

CHAPTER 17

TO KNOW ME

I waited on the front porch on the swing until I saw Solkka limp slowly in the moonlight to my house. I didn't say a word, just took his hand, and led him upstairs to my bed. We had to pause on the landings, and even in between, for him to catch his breath. I realized how much pain he was still trying to hide from me.

"I won't be a lover tonight," he grimaced.

"Shush. *Pai ake te iti I te kore rawatu,*" I whispered in Wester, "Just let me be near you."

I had carried the idea of Solkka Ulani in my head for the better part of three years, but in all that time, we had only spent a few decons together. That night, he told me stories of who he was. Growing up on a coffee farm with two brothers, Kaede and Tedros, "one older, one younger, Zren, the best position in the family," and boarding at the academies at a younger age than most because home was so far away. His years of military service— "greatest thing to happen to me, I learned so much"— and the dawning realization three sons are too many to take over one family's coffee farm. At the academies, he learned he had a gift for languages, and with his family's blessing, he made the decision to enter the Diplo.

"My grandmother was so relieved, Zren. She thought I would drink coffee all day, have no profits on our coffee farm, and embarrass the Ulani name." He tried to laugh, and then coughed in pain. "I hope you meet her someday, Zren. She claims we grandsons are too beautiful to be useful and nothing but decorations around her table." He chuckled. "She loves us very much, Zren. You can hear it in her voice even when she pretends to scold us."

He told me of his worry for his brother Tedros who was in his second year of military service. No one had heard from him in ages. The last news Solkka had was Tedros had been at Earles before it had been fired.

"Escorting the body of Malan Sala to his home in the Summer Plains was hard, Zren. I knew Malan and Tedros had been in the academies and the military together. While he and I served under Ven Wila, Malan would tell me stories of my brother and ask me for others. He said he wanted me to tell the kind of stories to exhort enough coin from my brother to develop a gambling habit.

"Malan had the type of laugh to make you want to join in, and I could imagine him and my brother finding adventures wherever they looked." He paused, and I felt a shudder through his body. "They were good men. Now one is dead, and my little brother is lost in the wind."

He was quiet for a long time, wiped his face with the sleeve of his shirt, and then said, "Now, Zren Janin, please tell me who you are. Who is this sip of Trouble I wish to sail the West Islands with?"

I considered what he had told me, and I knew he deserved the truth. But Rell had told me once, the magic of growing up meant I could be whatever type of man I wanted to be. Siba had taught me Truth was Truth, but it could be cruel or kind depending on the grace of the storyteller.

"I would like to tell you a story, Solkka Ulani, Prince of Vikland. Would you permit me to do so?" I asked formally.

He carefully lay back on the bed. He blew out a hard breath as he briefly rested his weight on his injured forearms and then stretched out, his head on my pillow.

I smiled at him. "I'll take that as a 'yes,' then." And I told this story,

I am called Zren Janin. I grew up in Lowertown, a part of Kerek City near Dockside and the Sinner's District. I do not remember a

father or mother, but I know I was loved and cared for until one day when I was not.

I am a Conrosan by birth. I did not know that growing up. My skin is the hue of cinnamon, and my hair is brown and curly. My eyes are brown. My byname was 'Red.'

Like all children who have grown up in want, there was not always as much food as I would have liked. I am smaller than others, but strong enough, and faster than most. I speak castle Keresh and not the harsh dialect of the docks, although the Lost God knows I heard it often enough. But I never learned my letters, so I must have lost my protector, my parents, my one who kept me alive, after I learned to speak, but before I should have learned to read or write. Since I have come to Manumina, I have learned Wester and Conrosan. I can speak the formal greetings in Vik, and say kind words in Mata, enough to mislead people into thinking I have good manners.

My age is somewhere between nineteen and twenty two. Although so few people celebrate birthdays in Lowertown, you could argue any number of years and I would probably agree with you. For now, these are the years I have chosen.

I do not understand many things—sarcasm, tactfulness, jealousy, hiding sorrow, or how to tell a falsehood without my body warning you I am lying. But I know to work hard, keep my word, and to ask any number of questions of those I trust.

I love pastries and fingersweets, sleeping until the sun wakes me up, watching Rell Huena hit the center of a target I cannot even see the outlines of, working in Piffik Qanaq's woodshop, traveling with Ngahuru, and stories. I truly love stories.

Now I have heard the Great Constellation stories of the West Islands, the parables of the Lost God of Matasi, the Wisdom of the Warrior sagas from Vikland, and even the Trickster tales of Kerek, but the ones I like best are the folk tales and fairy tales of Conrosa. There we meet another Zren Janin, a changeling so in love with the humans, he decided to be their champion.

All the best folk tales have Zren Janin, who through his kindness, his cleverness, and his humor solves the ills of the Queen's Kingdom, but he doesn't always travel alone, oh no! Zren is but a part of the Legion of Heroes and though they do not come at his beck and call, they always have his back.

What? You do not know these heroes? How can such a thing be? There is the Wizard, the Warrior, and the Wit. You know this much is true, for Zren Janin could never stand against so many without Ngahuru, a Wizard of Trickery and Disguise, Rell Huena, a Warrior of Courage and Strength, and Piffik Qanaq, a Wit whose gifted tongue could talk them out of any danger. Zren Janin also has a True Friend, a knight of such honor and many talents, he won the heart of Our Lady of Healing, a noblewoman of such grace and wisdom she took a feral child, sheltered him, and taught him until he could find his way to be a man."

Solkka made a soft chuckle, but he did not open his eyes.

"Now all heroes must go on a quest—for how can they be heroes if they do not prevail over a foe? And so it was with Zren Janin and his Legion of Heroes. Their enemy was not the winged monsters of Vikland for those had been vanquished ages before, nor the immortal fae of Conrosa for a veil of peace hung between the two realms. They did not look for the gifts of the West Islands Constellations, or the Lost God in the face of every person they met.

No. They stood firm against the corrupt King of Kerek. He had taken the treaties of his father and grandfather and crushed those words of honor under his heel. He had heard the cries of those who had been injured and murdered and stopped up his ears. And when the men and women had stood before him and said they were preyed upon and dying for the color of their skin and their Viklander blood, he had laughed and told them to run like rabbits.

And the House of Nations stood firm and Zren Janin drew his magic Sword of Courage…"

I blew out a breath, "and yes, well, it was pretty much Rygee who started our little rebellion, but I am telling this story so I get to be the hero."

I felt a movement, and I looked down on the white blankets. Solkka's eyes were still closed, but he had opened his hand to find me. I took his hand between both of mine. His palm was much larger than mine, and his fingertips callused from bow strings.

"Solkka, do you shoot a short bow or a crossbow?" I asked. "Your fingertips are more like Ngahuru's than Rell's."

He stiffened, so slight I thought it might have been from pain. "I shoot both, but I prefer the bongs. I had lots of practice with my brothers."

I slid my hand up to his wrist and tried to circle it with my fingers. Solkka's skin was lighter than my own—it reminded me of the late season honey the beekeepers would harvest from the ground bees east of Manumina. He lightly squeezed my hand.

"Did you forget you were telling me a story? Your story? Go on."

I scrunched up my nose. "Actually, that's about as far as I am. I started making it up when I was riding horse from Rishka to the Huenas in Axefield." I folded my body over myself. "Solkka, I had nobody to talk to for almost the whole day! I *had* to make up stories."

Solkka started to laugh, and grabbed his ribs. "Remind me never to put you on all night sentry duty. You'd invite the enemy to sit down for a long chat." He paused. "Your story is beautiful as far as it is. But you are more than Kerek City, I have known so since I first met you.

"So tell me more, Zren Janin, what would you like me to know so you can say, 'he sees me, he knows me.' For those are not little words. We must be seen and heard for who we are, Zren, and not dismissed by the words and thoughts of others. I want you to know me from the inside out, just as I am learning to know you. You whose face cannot tell a lie understands this. Your heart and mind and body are already aligned with Truth."

I dropped his hand on the blankets and crossed my arms over my chest. I turned my face away so he could not see the pain his words caused. What if I didn't want to be who I had been?

I told him I didn't know my name—any name but those others had given me. Everyone in Lowertown had called me 'Red' until Ngahuru had given me the name 'Zren Janin' when she introduced me to Miya. I *liked* the name Zren Janin, I said. Ngahuru had read a book of folk and fairy tales and said he was the hero. I wanted to be like Zren Janin. I wanted to be a hero.

I liked learning things, I said. I liked how Piffik could teach me without making me feel small for not knowing what all the other apprentices had already known. I liked how Rygee could seem to do anything—and didn't mock me when he needed to show me more than once how to do all the many things to run a farm. I liked how Rell made my world bigger by talking about all the things she had seen and done and taught me how a family cared for each other. I told him I knew so little of kindness, affection, friendship, and love, I thought Miya and Ngahuru were to be a couple when they crossed paths in Ribelo, Matasi.

Solkka bit back a laugh. "Miyamoto Suki has only had eyes for Jinhai, and she for him, since they were both about four years old."

"I know that now." I scowled.

He smiled and reached for my hand again. "What else do you know now that you didn't know before?"

"I know I could not survive in Vikland," I said sadly. I described my visit to Chul Swyler and Aajan Qanaq. Even with all of her intelligence and love of adventure and her bravery, Aajan still would have struggled without Chul as her best friend and one who had navigated it before her to explain what must be done and how to do it.

"The city of Juisiti and the academies are not all of Vikland," Solkka reminded me. "But I agree, they are difficult to navigate. Most of us from the wop-wops—that is what the students call the far away districts—struggle when we first come to the academies. Some never do fit in, and go early into their military service, some leave for other countries, or go back home. I did well, only because my older brother Kaede had taught me what to do and to expect, and most importantly, how to ask for help.

"Even so, I have no desire to stay in Vikland. The more I know of the West Islands and learn their beautiful language, I know it is there I want to live out my days. In the Diplo if possible, a day laborer if nothing else can be found."

He paused. "When I was on the ship from Matasi to the West Islands, with Ngahuru and Koanga, she said you had negotiated to take Miya through Kerek on the Northern Track in exchange for passage to Conrosa. Is that still your dream? To find your family perhaps?" He let his voice drift away, "Or is it you wanted to travel with Miyamoto Suki, a Prince of Vikland from a family of diplomats, and live the life of one with the power and coin of an Empress to express and enforce her wishes in a foreign land?"

I laughed and kissed his battered knuckles. "I wanted to go to Conrosa, it's true, but after living at Manumina, I have learned it would be next to impossible to find my people. That's a very long way to go to be disappointed, when I could stay here and feel the same."

Solkka burst out laughing, and then groaned again. "Please, Zren, don't make me laugh, it hurts so much. I have no idea how Siba thinks I am going to ride a horse within a few days."

He breathed deeply and coughed, and then rolled away from me. "Sorry, I am going to need to sit up for a bit." He carefully positioned himself with his back against the wall. He winced.

"I would like you to tell me a story, Zren. One I heard, but not from your lips." He picked at the bedclothes. "Kern told me and Bima her version, but Kern can tell a story that sounds like a festival of the Empress out of nothing more than watching grass grow. It is one of her gifts as a *titiro mai ke ahau*. Do you know the meaning of these Wester words?"

I nodded. "A 'look at me.' Ngahuru tells me that is why she stopped to save my life on the road to Aldi. She thought I would make an interesting distraction. She thought she needed more than Koanga if they were to survive through Kerek and Matasi." I smiled at Solkka and patted his hand. "I know she is telling a joke. Koanga said West Islanders would never leave a person to die alone by the side of the road."

"I hope you think that of Viklanders as well. No one, Zren, should allow another to suffer if it is within their means to help another. No country's border takes away our humanity." Solkka blew out a hard breath.

"But the story I want you to tell me, is the truth as you see it. Kern's version did not serve me well." He looked me in the eye. "I would like you to tell me about Bitterboots."

I sighed and sat cross-legged facing him. I noticed neither one of us was touching the other anymore. I wondered if that was significant.

"When I was growing up in Kerek City," I began, "there was a pirate. No one knew where he came from, but he had coin, and he walked with demons. Everyone called him Mouser. He would catch the little ones, boys or girls, and drag them into the alleys and doorways of Lowertown. Sometimes he would just beat you with his cane, and take your coin or your food. Sometimes, if you were running messages from the docks, he would take your messages and sell them to the rival owners, and you would get a beating from those who paid us to be dockrunners. And sometimes," I licked my dry lips, "he would hurt the children and call it pleasure. No one stepped in to help us."

Solkka sat so still, I thought he had stopped breathing. "Solkka?" I stirred uneasily.

"I'm listening."

"When we met our Kereki soldiers, Bitterboots—Kern named him—was the leader. The kind of soldier that has been in the army too long, but doesn't know how to do anything else. Nebs and Rygee, the two Farm Boys, they were all right. The fourth one—he was Mouser all over again. The way he looked at Song and Rell and Kern, I knew if he thought they were weak and young and no one would step in to help them, all of us would be watching for a knife in our back the entire trip."

I paused, wondering what Solkka was thinking. "So, one night, the first night, I thought to prove my worth to Miya. I borrowed Rell's traveling cloak because it was a pretty red color and could not be mistaken for anyone else's, and I pranced about the fire making enough noise to wake the whole camp. Only… only instead of Mouser falling into my trap, Bitterboots grabbed me. I had West Islands steel and a Sailor's Curse, and he was dead before he hit the ground."

Solkka didn't say anything for a while, and then, "So why didn't you go after Mouser a second time?"

"Men like that only prey on the weak. Later, he asked me if the girls could fight, and I said they were warriors who could beat me with any weapon of their choice any time they wanted. He looked at me a long time and said he believed me. I thought that meant, if I was the weakest in the group, and I could commit Kereki metal poisoning without remorse, he was no longer interested in harming any of us."

I looked at Solkka lying on the bed with his eyes closed. "But Solkka, I was wrong. The evening of the day we had found the massacred settlers, he went looking for Song Yao while she was practicing with her jeong bong by the river. Rygee and I ran to find them, but Song had already faced him. When Miya and Rell came with weapons, Mouser was already knocked senseless on the ground. Miya said it was only Song's mercy that he lived." I paused. "Miya also said Viklander women do not wait to be rescued. He told the Kereki soldiers, all of them, Song and Rell and Kern were the better fighters. He told the truth. I killed Bitterboots because he was a threat, and I did not know the strength of the others, but any of the Viklanders could have done the same."

"Hmmm."

"What does that mean?"

"The only two people alive who witnessed the entire action were you and Chul Swyler. He says you lured an old man into a dance with your knife. That your reasoning was sound, but it was still planned and not an accident. Kern, who did not see it from the beginning, said you murdered a man you *thought* might hurt them. And…you murdered the wrong man."

"Anyone else?"

"Miya says you protect those who need protecting, and he will travel with you anywhere and never watch his back."

I tried to pretend it didn't matter, although it mattered very much. I made my voice as carefree and light as possible, "What does Solkka Ulani, Prince of Vikland, say?"

He smiled sadly and reached for me. "I think I never would have survived your childhood."

***

We did sleep some that night. If we both drifted awake at the same time, we told each other stories, lighthearted funny stories that would have us falling back to sleep with a smile on our lips. I asked him if Jenny liked having a family, and he said he didn't know; he had returned to the war as soon as his face had healed well enough to travel.

I said I loved having Rell as a sister. She said I was her favorite little brother— "and she has a lot of them, Solkka"—so I thought he would like having Jenny as a sister. He just murmured sleepily we had probably saved each other, Rell and I, and to remind him to thank her when he saw her next. I asked him if he knew where she was, and he said all bowmasters had been sent as a perimeter to restore Viklander shipments and soldiers on the Northern Track.

I hesitated. I knew Solkka was a soldier, but I thought he had been softfooting—I knew he had—and I wondered how much he would tell me about Rell's whereabouts if he knew more.

So, I told him I had gone with Rell when Rani the softfoot was testing the distance the bowmasters could shoot at ghostfire and survive. I told him I had been traveling home to Manumina from a trip to Cloa and some Kereki soldiers had asked me to ride with them to protect me against bandits. They had been kind to me as fellow travelers, but all four of them had died when one of their horses stepped on a ghostfire pot planted on a bridge. I said the only reason I had survived was because when I had shouted to warn the others, my startled horse stepped in front of me and took the blast. I asked if there were times bowmasters shot at ghostfire and it injured or killed the Viklanders, or if there were times it didn't go off at all and the bowmasters were found and killed by the Kereki soldiers or wagonmasters.

Solkka opened his eyes and looked at me. "I will not lie to you, Zren. You know in your heart and your head the answers to all of the questions you just asked me. I am beyond sorry to hear I nearly lost you to a Viklander weapon, but the price of Justice is not trivial. I know and you know, Rell Huena is a bowmaster known for her eyesight and her endurance. I will only tell you this. I know she is in Kerek, but I don't know where."

He said he was thankful she had practiced every day she could at Manumina.

"She'll come back, Zren. She's the kind of soldier who comes back even if they have to crawl the entire way." He kissed me gently on the head.

I knew I would have to be content with that. I decided I would spend every night asking the West Islands constellations to light her path to safety and the Wisdom of the Warrior tales to remind her how to be strong. I didn't know if the Lost God of Matasi looked after Viklanders but I thought I would ask him too. That was all I could do for the moment.

I asked Solkka if he got his beautiful face from his mother. He quirked a half smile and said his beauty came from his father and his cupful of wisdom came from his mother, and truthfully, that was the best possible outcome. His older brother had wisely married a woman smarter than he was. Eventually, if Jenny wished, she could marry or not, but the coffee farm would always be her home. He didn't mention Tedros and I thought the hole in his heart might be too big to talk of his missing little brother.

I touched him with my fingertips or with the back of my hand. He shifted many times during the night, but he never pulled away when my arm would drape over his waist, rest on his chest, or wrap lightly about his bicep. I had no idea when we would see each other again. When I asked Solkka, he said the war was all but over. There were Viklander troops at the Ring Road outside of Kerek City. It would be soon—very soon, he said.

My heart was at peace.

***

It was barely dawn when Siba shook me awake.

"How did you get in here?" I asked sleepily.

"You left your house unbarred, I guess you had other things on your mind." She smiled at Solkka curled up away from me, still sleeping. "I thought I would get you two up first. Piffik needs your help. I was going to ask Solkka to let me check his ribs again and the bruising across his back before he travels. Go on now, I'll make sure you have plenty of time to say goodbye."

I pulled on a long shirt and scooted out of bed. Siba was focused on checking Solkka's bandages on his forearms, and his fever.

I had already pulled on my pants, linings, and boots and headed for the door when I heard, "Zren?"

"I'm right here, Solkka. Piffik needs me to help him. I should have warned you what a hard taskmaster he is." I smiled so Solkka would know I was teasing.

He gave me a sleepy smile. "We can sleep late in the West Islands."

I gave him my biggest grin. "Yes, we will."

CHAPTER 18

THE END OF THE WORLD

I stepped off my porch and rounded the corner to enter the side door to the stockade. The sunrise this morning was a soft pink and apricot sky, but far to the west the sky was a dark ominous green. The air felt sticky, not like a normal day at the end of the Dry at all. I found Piffik in the stables trying to put our last two horses into the traces. They were fractious, and Piffik, usually so even tempered, was not having any of it. I took the second horse and muscled her in place, and soon they had both resigned themselves to a journey.

"What has them so riled up?" I asked.

"The weather most likely. At first, I thought it was a distant fire, but the air smells all wrong for it. It must be another sea storm coming too far inland. Take care of the livestock today. Until Rygee gets back with the horses, there won't be any farmhands coming to give you help. I should be back in two, three days. Lou should be coming from the great houses soon, maybe today.

I have no idea when to expect Tiju Tia, or even Rygee. Tell them where we are, so no one worries."

I could tell his mind was on other things, and I tried to calm him.

"It'll be fine. It's probably just an early rain blowing through. I'll be here, and how much trouble can I get into by myself?"

He smiled at me. "I don't even want to imagine."

We took the wagon out of the stable. Siba had everyone ready on the village green. She had three large baskets of food, and I looked at her in mock dismay.

"I'll starve! You've left nothing but dried fruit and old bread for me."

Siba smiled. "There's food in the cold room and in the infirmary kitchen. You won't starve."

I greeted the three Wrens in the formal Vik manner. "Falan, Linna, and Kid. You are brave, you are resourceful, and as you cross the border into Vikland, know that your new home has the hardest language to learn in all the known world." I heard Quan laugh beside me. I shot him a sly look before turning back to the Wrens. "I shall bring Tiju Tia to you as soon as I can. She should hear of your adventures and tell you stories in which you are the hero." Falan just rolled her eyes at me. Linna gave me a knowing smile. I suddenly wondered what had ever happened to the boy called Pike. I would ask her later I decided.

I made Quan the short formal Vikland bow. "Thank you for all you have done to protect Tiju Tia's Wrens. I am beyond glad they had you to defend them at the stable in Cloa."

I stopped in front of Solkka and made the short bow.

"Oh no, you don't." He smiled and pulled me in close. I bumped his ribs and he sucked in a hard breath. "We'll see each other soon. Practice your Wester, soon it will be the only language we will ever need to speak."

He released me and slipped into the back of the wagon where the others were already sitting. Although the land from Manumina to the Vikland border was currently under Vikland's command, Piffik and Siba were still taking precautions with hay and many quilts in the back to hide and rest in. I saw a short bow and two tahn bongs, half hidden as well. Even now, the Wrens and Conrosans would not be unprotected. Although I wondered how Quan and Solkka thought they would be able to put up much of a defense as damaged as they were.

I opened the big stockade gates. They drove through in a chorus of goodbyes, and I was left alone.

***

Rabbits, chickens, goats. When I had first come to Manumina, I had detested the animal chores. Now there were only smaller animals, and Lou took care of his own goats when he was about, so it wasn't quite so bad. I still thought chickens were ugly. I stopped midday and cooked three eggs for myself and found the biscuits in the infirmary kitchen Siba had left for me. They reminded me of the biscuits I had eaten at Linna and Arden's house a short time ago. I wondered again whatever happened to the little boy called Pike. I wondered what would happen to those who had put their confidence in Vikland's army. Would Matasi be a friend to them?

I wondered what Arden would think when he came back and found Kid and Linna gone. I wondered if Josef had returned to Balza and lurked about trying to learn if Falan had gotten out in time. I wondered how the Wrens knew the difference when someone was in trouble, or just softfooting for a long time, or hiding away trying to save someone's life. I wondered if Josef's and Nelo's houses looked like Arden's. Arden had said Linna had grown up in a proper house. I wondered if Linna was glad the war was over for her.

After I ate, I was so tired, I just wanted to go back to my house and take a nap. Instead, I went back out to clean the stables. I thought it would be easier without any horses in them, and it was something I could do half asleep.

I filled the muck cart and pulled it out the side door to dump it on the gardens. The western sky was a sheet of ominous grey. We were in for a pounding rain. I wondered if that meant the Wet would come early. I wondered how much of the crops we would lose. The breeze had freshened to a stiff wind, immediately chilling the sweat on my body. I was glad I was working inside the stockade even if it was cleaning the stables.

I turned back to the muck cart and saw a familiar shape in the distance. It was the cheese cart with Old Dris pulling. Lou was back! There were nearly a dozen horses and riders loosely bunched about the cart. I laughed to myself, *who had Lou brought home?* I squinted hard to see if I could pick out the Wrens. Were those our other horses? Was Rygee with them?

Still smiling, I went inside to wash the muck off myself and clean up. I found a fresh shirt in the infirmary and finger combed my wet hair. Then I went to open up the big gate so Lou and the riders would be able to drive straight in to the stables before the rain began. I had taken longer than I had thought to wash up and Lou hadn't hailed the house, but I figured he had seen me at the cart and knew I was coming to open the gates.

I walked the big door open, peeked around the corner to hail Lou, and stilled.

The cheese cart and horse were driverless, and the horses and riders surrounding the cart were all Kereki soldiers. Not real soldiers, not like Chaz, and Solenn, Ria, and Archie, the kind with polished boots and clean uniforms. These were bedraggled men, unkempt, not one wearing a complete uniform. The one in front spurred his horse forward.

"This is where you say, 'Welcome to Manumina, come inside, come inside and help yourselves to anything we have.'"

I said nothing. How could I have been such a fool to open the gates without waiting for Lou to hail the house? Was I truly so addlebrained from lack of sleep I would make such a stupid mistake?

"Well? Who are you? Or did the Viklanders cut out your tongue so you couldn't tell all their secrets?"

"Where's Lou?" I stammered out.

"Lou," the leader snarled. "I am assuming you are talking about the Kereki traitor we found wandering about south of Evensong." He looked at two riders by the back of the cart. "Boys, throw him down."

Two men on horseback pulled on a rope at the end of the cart and kneed their horses back. Lou's body crumpled into the dirt. I started forward and a horsewhip snapped in front of me.

"Now, now, a smart boy like you would know there is nothing more you can do for him." He leaned down from his saddle. "But there *is* something you can do for me. Who were you working with? Those who knew Lou said he wasn't smart enough to run a smuggler house, so he had to have help. They whisked traitors and Viklanders out of the stables in Cloa under the nose of the militia. Where are they?"

The wind was keening and I could hardly keep my feet. It had gotten colder. The clouds were still the ominous greyish green, but now they were billowing up furloughs and furloughs high. I could smell the crackle of the coming storm.

"You simple, boy?" he menaced. "…Or just need help remembering?"

I snapped my eyes back to him, but I couldn't form a coherent thought. This was why I hadn't been a Wren like the others. This is why I was seldom out alone on a horse and wagon to resupply the others. When I was afraid—and right now, I was very afraid—I couldn't speak, think, or act.

"You know what we do to traitors? Well, if they want to be like Viklanders, we just let them die like Viklanders." He turned to the others. "Light him up."

Two poured lamp oil, then I smelled alcohol, and then someone touched a flame to Lou's clothes which whooshed into a fire almost as tall as I was. The gusting wind whipped the flames around and the horses shied away. The horse on Lou's cart bolted for the stable and I went to grab her. The whip snaked about my ankles, and I fell to the ground. Sand and sticks and burning clothes blew about my feet. The riders were having a hard time keeping their seats as the horses smelled the stink of the fire and the smell of the storm on the rising wind.

"Who are they? Where are they?" The leader pushed his horse closer to me. "You see what we do to traitors. Tell us who they are and where they are and we let you live. You do not talk?" He shrugged. "You do not live."

The leader looked about the stockade and shouted, "Hiding, huh? It's easy to betray your King when you sneak about the countryside, but now? When faced with justice, you all hide under your beds!" He turned to shout to the others over the wind, "Burn them out! We'll let them die like Viklanders!"

I remembered the Battle at the Bridge. I was only one person, but I could still fight. I slid the West Islands steel from my boot, my Sailor's Curse that never left my side even now. I pushed myself to my feet, and ran towards their horses, waving my arms, slashing at men's legs, slapping at horses' flanks. Horses reared and wheeled about as the men fought to get their horses back under control. I turned and saw a cudgel come towards me.

The world went white.

INTERREGNUM

The storm hit with a vengeance. The riders couldn't keep the fires lit, the horses were spooked by the wind and driving rains. A few riders dismounted and searched the buildings closest to the green, but they were empty or nearly so, and the riders soon gave up in disgust. They had promised themselves horses, and braid bounties, and stores of hoarded Vikland goods. Instead, it had been a long ride to Manumina and there was nothing here. The stories they had heard of unguarded Vikland gold, West Islands steel, and wagon trains of Matasi grains had been just that—stories. They would be going back to Sary and Evensong with no stolen goods, no food, and no Viklanders or traitors to push before them or drag along. No one and nothing to earn them fame or coin at the Kereki encampment.

The leader looked about the shabby stockade. If he and his followers could be fooled into chasing dust over the Kerek scrubland, others could too. Now? All he wanted to do was to return to the warm dry tavern where they could boast about getting rid of the treasonous vipers. Their story could grow in the telling. After all, who would look for the remains of Manumina?

He took one last look at the two bodies lying motionless on the ground, threw up the hood of his traveling cloak, and trotted his horse out of the stockade. The others followed silently. A strike of lightening lit up the area, throwing the hooded figures in stark relief against the storm-dark skies. But there was no one there to see their faces and know their names.

The rain continued all night melting the churned up hoofprints into puddles of mud.

The dawn sky filtered weakly into the stockade. The village green glistened with the remnants of the storm while tiny rivers of water and mud coursed through the beaten paths.

The mare, tired of standing all night and hungry for her manger, stamped impatiently and then pulled the empty wagon to the green where she could at least reach grass and water.

At midday, a light breeze from the east blew away the acrid scent of smoke and charred flesh. It danced around the courtyard drying puddles and pushing scraps of burnt fabric like butterflies on the wing.

By the golden end of day, the chickens were clucking to be fed, and the goats were bleating to be milked. Only the rabbits were silent in their hutches watching the empty track.

Sunset was throwing the last splashes of color across the sky when a settler's wagon with a team of two horses and three mounted outriders clomped down the road to Manumina. The driver pulled back on the reins when he saw the stockade gates wide open into the gathering darkness. Tiju Tia, hunched and bunched into her old woman disguise, sat beside Rygee on the wagon seat.

"I don't see any movement," she said quietly.

Rygee said slowly, "No one knew we were coming today. Abandoned? Or taken?"

"Let's have the Wrens pull their steel." She waved the outriders over. "Callis, Josef, Ross. It could be trickery; it could be abandoned. I will light the night lantern and walk inside. Once the shadows cover you, slip in the perimeter and check the buildings. Siba and the others could be hiding, call your names or hers."

The riders silently slid from their horses, and pulled their daggers, their knives, their Sailor's Curses. Tiju Tia waited until they were near the edges of the stockade and then lit her lamp with the three night shades down. Rygee pulled Oro's short bow out of the wagon. He stood at the open gates, and nocked an arrow as Tiju Tia walked into the middle of the courtyard so the Wrens could slip undetected down the sides.

The beam of light from the lantern picked out two bodies lying crumpled on the ground. Tiju Tia pulled a dagger and hurried over.

Behind her, the first of the Wrens—Ross—called out, "Cio claro!" and soon the all clear signal echoed across the green. Tiju Tia pulled the night shades up and light flooded the ground in front of them.

"Lou," Rygee said abruptly, pointing his bow at the pale hand and forearm just within the circle of light.

Ngahuru lifted the lantern higher and saw the partially burned body.

"By the stars!" she turned away. Now she recognized the acrid scent of burnt flesh and fought to contain her nausea. She set down the lantern spilling the light on the other body crumpled carelessly in the mud.

"Zren!" She dropped to her knees and turned him over in her lap.

"He's alive!"

SCATTERED

My face was sunburned on one side and covered with mud on the other. Parts of me felt like I was on fire and other parts frozen. I could hear Tiju Tia and Rygee talking, but I couldn't form words to answer them. I couldn't make my arm move to touch her. I couldn't even force my eyes open. I hurt everywhere.

"Rygee, do you see a knife wound? He's neither burned nor trampled."

I felt the light shift as Rygee lifted the lantern higher. "Look at the angle of his arm and shoulder. He was either thrown from a horse or was hit with something. That looks like a broken collarbone, and look here, a knot the size of a goose egg." He gingerly touched the tender spot on the back of my head, and I promptly vomited on his boots.

"Welcome back to the land of the living," I could hear a smile in his voice. I heard the rasp of fabric as he wiped his hands on his pants. Then carefully he opened up one of my eyelids and then the other. "His eyes are blown wide open and mismatched. I've seen this on the men who break the horses on the farm where I grew up. He's got his brain rattled." He bent down close to me. "Where's Siba?" He paused. "Zren, can you tell me where everyone is? Where's my wife?"

I forced my eyes open and tried to pay attention to his face but it just blurred in and out.

Exasperated, he tried again, "Zren, blink your eyes if Siba is safe."

I slowly blinked—and realized my body was going to be mine again—someday, but not immediately. I was so tired, and so tired of having my body battered about.

"Is she here?"

I couldn't make my lips move but I wanted to say, "Who? Who is here?"

Rygee huffed in frustration. "Blink again if Siba and the others left for the shepherd's cottage before this happened."

Oh. Siba. I blinked again, and then closed my eyes against the pain. I could hear Rygee's sigh.

I could hear Tiju Tia scuffling about near my head, and I cracked open my eyes again to see Rygee look around slowly. "Tiju Tia, I hear the sounds of a farm untended for a while. Give me your Wrens to help get Zren to the infirmary, then put Josef and Callis to take care of the horses, feed the animals, gather eggs, and milk the goats. I'll take Ross to help me bury Lou. Pull the stockade gates shut and bar the gates and the side door, we'll all sleep inside tonight. Once it is light tomorrow morning, I'll search the buildings and try to figure out what happened. Siba isn't here, but I don't know if that means they are still at the shepherd's cottage in Vikland or at Rishka." He blew out a noisy breath. "I guess we are on our own for one more night."

Tiju Tia called the Wrens, and Rygee pulled some blankets from the wagon. The three helped him carry me in a body sling into the infirmary. After a little while, Tiju Tia came in, washed her hands back in the kitchen, put the pot on to boil, and brought me a cold cup of water to drink. I swallowed about half and then threw up on the blankets. She didn't say anything, just stripped the blankets, and filled a basin with heated water, and with soft rags began washing my face, my hair, my body. She looked at my swollen shoulder and reached for my fingers.

"Can you bend them?"

I looked at my fingers, but couldn't remember how to make them bend. I looked at her and she saw the anxiety in my face.

"It's all right, Zren. I'm familiar with rescuing you. Do you remember the first time? On the road to Aldi?" She smiled gently.

I looked at her and opened my mouth to respond and couldn't. Finally, I nodded once. The room swam, and I closed my eyes quickly so she wouldn't need to change the blankets again.

"See? You are already better than you were then. A day or two of rest and Rygee's cooking and you will be back as Manumina's manabout."

"Oro," I croaked. I meant to say Oro was the manabout now.

"We left Oro near Nelo's." She sat down gently on the bed next to me. "I've closed the network, Zren. The Matasi army and navy have taken over Kerek City, and the King is in exile. There will be a few more skirmishes, and Matasi and Vikland have a lot to talk about. But for me and mine? The war is over. I want the Wrens out of the way of those who are only looking for a dance with Trouble."

She went on to explain how she had found Oro near Sary. She had thought he was at Ishes. But he had been traveling the Northern Track instead of Piffik's shortcut and she suspected he was traveling to Cloa to see Linna. He had agreed to travel with her to Huk to pick up Ross and Callis. When they arrived in Cloa, the house was empty, Arden, Mother, and Linna were all gone. She wasn't sure Nelo could read well enough for her to leave a message for him saying Balza and Huk were closed, and the Wrens were at Manumina. Oro had volunteered to remain behind in Cloa, and let Nelo and Linna know the war was over. Tiju Tia's mission was done, and it was time to fall back to Manumina.

"The others?" I rasped out.

"They have learned well." Tiju Tia nodded. "They are closing the network properly." She told me Josef had the horse from Balza and had left to let his allies know. He had said he would find the travelers again, either on the way, or rejoin them at Manumina. He told them Falan's secrets were known, he didn't know how, but no one should return to Balza. He thought she had escaped in time. Then when Tiju Tia had reached Huk, Callis had told her Falan had gone to Cloa with Linna and two Viklanders. Tiju Tia decided then the west was now closed to the Wrens.

When they reached Cloa, the door had been unbarred and they were able to enter Linna and Arden's house. They could see five people had been there, but no one was there now. At the stables, the Manumina horse was there, but the boy feeding the horses said Arden no longer worked there, and no one new had replaced him. Without more information, Tiju Tia thought either Arden or Linna was out on a rescue. They tidied the house, and left a written message for them. Arden or Oro would help Nelo pull in Dica and Tyra and Kid. Tiju Tia was confident someone would bring Linna home to Manumina so she would not travel alone.

I cringed at Tiju Tia's words. So much of her information was wrong. The Wrens were scattered about and I wasn't sure how they would all find each other.

Tiju Tia went on to explain how she, Ross, and Callis, had met Rygee just outside of Sary. He told them what had happened at the stables in Cloa and why he was pulling in the horses. They told him Josef had one horse and Linna would need the other, and they had the one from Huk, and so his journey was done.

"Frankly, Zren, I was glad to have him join us. I would have sacrificed a horse or two to have that happen." She patted my hand absently and continued. Rygee had told them Linna and Kid and Falan were at the shepherd's cottage, or were supposed to leave the day after he had left. Callis offered to ride back to Cloa, a day's ride each way, to let the others know.

"I disagreed, Zren. I thought if Arden wasn't the fifth one at the table, then he would still know what had happened. I had underestimated Linna earlier, but I knew the two worked well together. I didn't want people chasing down those who were already safe, Zren. Callis protested, but I insisted, and she came along with all of us. Josef caught up and found us at the road to Manumina."

I tried to follow along with her explanation of who was where, but my head hurt and I decided if she was confident everyone would come home, then I didn't need to worry on her behalf. I still thought so much of her information was wrong, but I couldn't string together the words to tell her so—or why. She must have seen my confusion.

"There. That's enough. Rest now. I am going to find Rygee. He may be the best baker I've ever known, but he's still a farm boy in his boots, and if he has seen your injuries before on the horsebreakers, he'll know better how to treat you than I will. I'll check on my Wrens as well." She patted my good shoulder. *"Kia okioki inaiaei. Ka pai koe. Moe atu ra."*

I was too tired to disagree. I was safe now. I closed my eyes and slept.

***

It was full dark outside when Rygee came in and woke me. He had washed up and was carrying a plate of cooked grains tossed with vegetables and cheese.

Sitting carefully at the edge of my bed, he asked, "Do you want me to feed you, or do you want to try it yourself?"

I popped my mouth open like a baby bird in response. He faked a huge sigh.

"I was joking, Zren."

After a few spoonfuls, I reached for a cup of water. I took two swallows, checked my reaction, and tried a little more, then leaned back against the head of the bed and closed my eyes. He had lit the room with only a night lantern, but I still felt the dim light was too bright.

"I hate to badger you, Zren, but I need to know. Do you know—for certain—where Siba is?"

"Vikland." I nodded tentatively and felt a shooting pain through my head. "They are safe in Vikland. I was here alone."

He shuddered out a long sigh. "Thank you, Zren." Rygee pushed the plate towards me, and I promptly opened my mouth again. He spooned in more and then, "Do you want to talk about what happened, or eat?"

"Eat." I took the spoon in my good hand and let him hold the plate. He wasn't shoveling it in fast enough. "It was a mistake. I thought it was Lou and the Wrens. When I opened the gates from the inside, they were Kereki, but not soldiers, and there was no one I knew."

"Was Lou…" He left his words unfinished, but I knew what he was asking.

"He was dead when they brought him home. They said they

stopped him south of Evensong. I'm glad Kid left when he did. It could have been both of them."

"I think we are abandoning Manumina. Tiju Tia and I think we should, but this is not our home. We will wait to talk to Piffik and maybe Siba, if they come back before the rest of the Wrens arrive."

"Why?" I was confused. "Why leave?"

Rygee shrugged. "Which reason do you want? The war is over. Rumors from the west say the Matasi army arrived in full force on Matasi navy ships and took over Kerek City and all the roads leading to the port. The Kereki army is going to feel the squeeze between Vikland and Matasi. I think there are too few to defend Manumina. I think the mob that killed Lou is going to be the first of many coming to Manumina. Not to mention it was truly stupid to build the houses on the *outside* of the stockade."

"You think more like Piffik every day," I groused.

"Why, Zren, that's the nicest thing you have ever said to me." He gave me a teasing smile, then sobered. "Is Piffik coming back?"

"Yes. Tomorrow or maybe today. How long was I…?"

"When did the raiders come?" He knew what I was trying to say.

"With the storm. The day after you left. Piffik and Siba had already taken the Wrens and the Viklanders to the shepherd's cottage. The soldiers were going to burn everything down because they thought people were hiding in the buildings. But the storm came just before they did, and their horses were frightened. They hit me. I don't remember anything else." I looked at him mournfully.

"You were out on the green for a night and a day, then." Rygee took the empty plate and stood up abruptly. "I've tired you enough and we can talk more tomorrow. Do you want someone to sit up with you? I know Siba would, but she's a better person than I am."

I shook my head. He took the lantern and left me in the dark.

I slept.

CHAPTER 20

MISSING

By the time Tiju Tia brought my first meal late the next morning, I had accomplished three things. I reached the chain commode without falling over and dying, I washed my hands and face, and drank a cup of water from the infirmary kitchen. By the time I collapsed back on to the bed, my head was pounding and my neck and shoulder were on fire.

I grimaced at her standing in the doorway, and she looked down at her clothes—dressed as a Kereki street boy down to the Kereki ties about her ankles and calves—and then at the bowl in her hand.

"Oh, don't worry. I didn't cook it. Rygee was up decons ago making this stew. He said he can't sleep for worrying about Siba, so he might as well be useful." She paused. "How are you feeling?"

"Like my brain and my body are strangers in the same room. I hurt everywhere," I whined.

She put her hand gently on mine. "I am sorry. I am sorrier still for Lou. He was a good dairy man, and he was honest because he couldn't be anything else. I know he knew more then he pretended to, but he moved out to live at the springhouse and the shed, so he could say nothing. He was the right man to conceal our actions. He deserved better than what he got."

"The raiders said they knew it wasn't Lou. The villagers had told them it wasn't him. They weren't soldiers, I don't think, or at least, not soldiers anymore. They were just looking for a dance with Trouble."

"Well, they'll get it soon enough. Did Rygee tell you Matasi troops have taken Kerek City? The Matasi navy has blocked the harbor and taken over the docks. No Kerek, West Islands, or Spice Island ships can enter or leave. That's what we heard in the settlements and towns anyway."

I reached for the bowl of stew. "Rygee told me. Why now? Years ago, Miya said Vikland and Matasi were going to attack together."

"Ah, but the Matasi diplomats will say they honored their agreement to attack Kerek. It is their army in the streets, their navy in the harbor. The Viklanders took the losses and kept Kerek looking eastward. The delay was only…three years," Tiju Tia sneered.

"What will you do now?"

"Look for my lost Wren," Tiju Tia answered promptly. "Rygee told me Falan, Linna, and Kid are at the shepherd's cottage, and I have Josef, Callis, and Ross with me. If Oro finds Nelo, and if Arden reads our message, they will bring in Tyra and Dica. Only Jenny needs to be returned to me." She sighed. "But I am afraid she is so far away, and the hunt and hobble groups are so elusive, it will be harder than it sounds to bring her home."

I cocked my head to the side. "Jenny? The one with Ven Wila north of Balza?" When Tiju Tia nodded to my question, I grinned. "She is also safe in Vikland. She is living with the Ulani family. She and Kid saved Solkka Ulani's life, and Solkka took her back to Vikland to heal." I leaned back against the wall and smiled. "So all your Wrens are found."

Tiju Tia tipped her head back and away from me, but I could still see the tears coursing silently down her face.

After a moment, she blew out a breath. "Thank you, Zren. Now as soon as the others come in, we can leave for Vikland. I have an Empress who owes them dearly for the part they played in deposing a King."

Josef stuck his head in the door. "I knew it wasn't true. Rygee said I needed to do the animal chores again this morning because you had a broken collarbone and a head injury. But I said to him, 'This is our Zren you are talking about. If there was a head injury, how would you know?'" He laughed at his own joke and came in. "Tiju Tia, if you wish to eat with the others, I will sit with Zren for a moment and be sure he doesn't drown in the soup."

Tiju Tia nodded. "Thank you. If we are to abandon Manumina, there are other things I must do." She stood up and without another word left the room.

Josef glanced after her and then back at me. "Those looked like tear tracks on her face. I didn't think anything could upset her. What did you do?"

"I told her Jenny was safe in Vikland. I think Tiju Tia finally believes she is going to meet the Empress of Vikland with all of her Wrens alive and ready to receive their reward." I grinned at him. "What do you think it will be? Bags of gold? Castles and palaces?"

Josef grimaced. "I wish I was so confident. Were you ever at Linna's house in Cloa?"

I felt the smile leave my face as I remembered how neat and well-kept the house had been. How proud Arden was he lived in a place—a proper home, he called it—like Linna had grown up in. His clever hooks in the ceilings and the pole he used to hang the lantern so the house was light and bright even after sunset. The comfortable chairs he had built and the battered books on a small table. I nodded, but my face must have shown my unease.

Josef agreed. "Exactly. They kept that house well; it was Arden's proudest possession. Whatever Linna wanted, or remembered from her childhood, she only had to ask Arden, and he was clever enough to make it or build it. Their house was the center of our network, Zren. All of us were welcomed there. They left the house unbarred when they were not there—they had Mother to protect it—so we could move in and out as we needed." He grinned. "Well, as long as we remembered to use Linna's soap on our boots to keep Mother from eating us alive."

Josef paused and then gave a deep sigh. "Arden and Linna did not risk written messages that anyone who entered their house could read. They used a code of the pottery and the clothes at their house. Differently colored shawls and Kereki ties on various pieces of furniture said whether the Wren was moving east or west, contacting Nelo, or meeting with me. Pottery on the table—cups and bowls, right side up or upside down—said how many Viklanders and how many Wrens were traveling with horses or on foot, how many days they expected to be away. Everything had something in the house Linna or Arden or Nelo would immediately know the meaning of. They communicated with each other and with Nelo without ever writing words on paper that could be intercepted by strangers." He looked at me waiting to understand. I shook my head.

"Zren, I had already left to tell my friends at the encampment. I also wanted to dig up coins and maps in the properties I used—

'to pull up my tracks' as Tiju Tia calls it. When I reached the road to Manumina and found the others again, I heard how Oro and Callis had 'tidied up the house' while they waited for either Arden or Linna to come home. Then Callis left with Tiju Tia, and Oro left for Nelo's hiding places to tell him to bring in Dica and Tyra."

He nodded at my growing comprehension. "*Now* you understand. Linna had placed five cups and bowls on the table. Tiju Tia remarked on it. Rygee said there were three Wrens and two Viklanders who came to Manumina. I *think* Linna had left Arden a message saying where she was planning on going, who she was traveling with, and when she had left. If Arden comes back from softfooting and does not find Linna or Kid, and no message where they were or are going, he is going to search for them."

"How do we let him know they are safe?" I asked.

"If it was anyone else, I say we send Mother after him. But the dog is already with Arden, so I have no idea. I had hoped you could go with me back to Cloa to try to find him."

I folded over myself. "When I can stand for more than a moment without toppling over, I will help you hunt for him, but today, Josef, I can't." I let my sorrow show. "I can't."

He nodded sadly. "I see that now. You may be able to stay upright on a bed as wide as you are tall, but I doubt you could sit a horse that long. My plan was to have one of us take Piffik's short cut and one of us take the Northern Track. We would meet at Arden's, one of us would find him surely, and the three of us return. But now, after seeing you and your injuries, I will need to wait for Nelo. He should be here today or soon depending on where Oro finds him. He knows the signals so we can travel, in circles if we must, to bring us all home."

"Piffik should be back tomorrow." A memory tugged at me. "Oh, Piffik shouldn't go back to Cloa. He's the one who rescued them." I paused. "Callis and Ross?"

He blew out a noisy breath. "Callis would go if I asked her, Ross would refuse to go if I asked him." He gave me a wry grin. "So I do not ask." He saw the questions on my face. "Do not ask, Zren. The beating Ross received at the hands of Viklander soldiers could have happened to any of us. But we needed him in Huk and he understood that. I do not know what it cost him to stay and help us. I do not know if he believed he could not walk away. But I do know what it is to feel trapped in a life that is nearly unbearable to live. All the Wrens do. And so, Ross pushed out messages, fed us with his rabbits, covered for Callis so she could softfoot in the dark, and more than that we did not ask it of him."

CHAPTER 21

LOST AND FOUND

Ross took over the animal chores. Callis and Josef cleaned out the houses of Manumina with all the professionalism of Lowertown thieves. They would write down the house description and any coin or valuables found. Rygee carefully packed up Piffik's tools, Siba's medicines, and the seeds and tubers not yet planted to grow during the Wet. He took cuttings from all the trees in the orchard, and told Ross they were his responsibility to keep alive. Tiju Tia walked around the stockade with a small spade and her book. She would carefully count off steps and dig, remove wood spindles, and homemade brick blocks, unearthing small bags of coins, and the travel papers she had held in safekeeping for her Wrens. Rygee and Josef checked the wagons and the horse tack. We were abandoning Manumina.

I slept.

Piffik was now overdue from the refugee camp at Rishka. We assumed Siba was still at the shepherd's cottage. We had no word from Oro, Nelo, Dica, Tyra, or Arden. Everyone was anxious to be gone from Manumina where a Kereki mob could descend on us at any time but hesitant to leave without the rest of the Wrens.

Callis was the most optimistic.

"They were trained by Tiju Tia, and none of them are fools. If they cannot make their way here for any reason, they will go to the garrison at Ishes where Oro is known, or hide within Rani's network at Fortika until Inezi can get them over the border where they will ask directions to the place with two hundred Conrosans. Manumina, or Rishka, or the shepherd's cottage are just some of *many* places where they will be safe. When we finally arrive all together, they will be cooking sausages over a fire and smiling and joking how we took so long to join them." She said this so frequently and with so many variations, we began to believe her.

Rygee went in to Sary to the Justice to release the conscripted farmhands. The Justice had no news on those who had murdered Lou and made it clear he wasn't planning on asking a lot of questions. He had commented on the company Rygee seemed to be keeping and wondered why. He asked why we were releasing the farmhands. He knew the harvest was over for nearly everyone, but he could not imagine we could have already planted all the greens to grow over the Wet. Rygee told us he hadn't answered him. Just turned and walked out the door.

But the conversation unsettled Rygee enough, he announced we were leaving the next day, with or without me. I told him he didn't need to waste a horse on me, I'd be happy to sleep in a wagon all the way to Juisiti. Rygee left immediately for the farm west of Manumina.

When he returned, he told me he had told the two boys who had worked in the traces with me to harvest everything still in the field and keep it for themselves. He then walked about Manumina and noted the food from the bakery, cold rooms, and springhouses to go with us. It would be packed last in the morning. He checked my shoulder and eyes again. He did not know how to make Siba's potions to take the pain away, he said, but he thought if I could sleep, it would have to be enough.

***

I drifted awake with the sounds of a large commotion. I heard the drag of the stockade gates and the shouting of others. With no one in my room to help me, I swung my legs over the side of the bed, grabbed the headboard, and slowly pulled myself up. Spots danced in front of my eyes, and I huffed quickly to keep the nausea away. Rygee had called it 'brain rattled' but truthfully, it felt like someone had taken my brain out, stomped on it, and stuffed it in sideways and upside down.

I made it to the entry and leaned against the doorway so I could look out. Two wagons with the flat canvas backs like the Matasi missionaries used were in the center of the village green. There were two people, dark haired and olive skinned, dressed in the bright colors I remembered from Matasi, on each wagon. I thought the Kaumpfts had fled their settlement and had come to Manumina for safety.

I squinted, but I was too far away to make out faces. As the settlers jumped down from the wagon seats, and others slipped out the back of the wagons, I couldn't imagine Tiju Tia or Josef hugging near strangers, and the strangers enthusiastically giving them back.

Rygee saw me propped up against the door and quickly came toward me.

"Can you walk? I'll help you, and then I better start working on feeding this bunch. This crowd is going to be hungry tonight." He took my arm and slowly led me down the step and across the yard.

It was Tiju Tia's pots of paint, of course. Nelo had stained his fair eyebrows and white-blond hair to dark brown. His face was the olive shade of a Matasi farm worker, far darker than what we had seen on the way to Salisport, but it hid his scar and emphasized his green eyes.

Inezi—I remembered her from Rani the softfoot's rescue—sat beside him with no paint or dye at all, but with her Matasi features and sun-dark skin, she would have blended in with a casual dismissal of a missionary wagon.

Arden and Dica were the two on the second wagon. Dica was tall and slender and her dark brown hair was twisted back into a married woman's knot. She no longer looked fourteen, but she also didn't look old enough to be a wife. Tyra and Oro had slipped out of the back of Nelo's wagon. Arden's dog, Mother, and a small boy about nine or ten jumped down out of the back of the other wagon.

Up close I could see Oro's shirt was torn and he had a black eye. A bruise blossomed on the opposite side of his face along the jawline. He came over to me, took my hand in his, and I could see scraped knuckles—a fight then, not a beating.

"When we passed through Sary, we heard there had been trouble at Manumina," he began quickly. "We weren't sure what we would find when we arrived. But Ross was outside caring for the goats and he waved at us. Our disguises must not have been very good."

"They are good enough. You are here. You can ask him how he knew you." I paused. "We have no healer here, and I see you are injured. Are there others who need a healer as well?"

He shook his head. "My injuries came after I found Nelo, and before Arden found me. No one else is hurt. We are all hungry, tired, and ready for a bath."

"That we can do. Rygee has already left to begin finding and making food for end of day meal. Tiju Tia can help you with the rest." I wobbled a little. "I'm for my bed." I grinned at him. "It is so good to have you back. Wake me up before the food is gone?"

CHAPTER 22

THE LAST NIGHT IN MANUMINA

The meal that night was a glorious affair. We all ate in the guesthouse as even the infirmary kitchen was too small for all of us. Rygee had killed three chickens and had made a fricassee with vegetables. The table was full with fresh baked biscuits and butter, stone fruit preserves from last fall, cheese, pickles, and odds and ends of things from the cold room he didn't want to take with us the next day.

All the Wrens were telling their adventures: Viklanders they had met, messages to pass on, places they had been. The small boy was called Therin. He had been a part of Rani the softfoot's group at Fortika and a friend of Tyra's. Inezi nodded to everyone, but I noticed she stayed close to Nelo. Now that everyone had been accounted for, the room was loud and happy with the joy of survival. I sat back on a chair near the kitchen with Rygee and Tiju Tia.

"How old are you, Zren?" Rygee asked casually.

"I don't know, Rygee, a little younger than you? Twenty? Twenty two? Not a lot of birthdays are celebrated in Lowertown."

"I am twenty four, but I look at all these Wrens and I feel like an old, old man."

Tiju Tia sighed. "When I first came to Kerek City, my first street runner was nine years old, more or less. Like Zren said, not a lot of birthdays celebrated in Lowertown. Now five years later, all my Wrens are between twelve and nineteen—or whatever age Oro claims to be. Yet they risked their lives to save strangers, soldiers, and softfoots, just for a promise I made them their new lives would be better than what they had in Kerek City."

She paused. "And now what is that promise worth?"

She shared what she had been struggling with all day. She knew there was nothing for her Wrens in Kerek City, but she wasn't sure about resettling them in Vikland where the color of their skin would remind Viklanders of those lost at Kereki hands. In the beginning, she had thought they could stay at Manumina, the settlement wasn't rich, but the Conrosans would embrace them, teach them, and value them. However, if the Conrosans didn't come back, it would not do to stay.

Rygee waved his hand about the stockade. "Tiju Tia, the Conrosans had been here for three generations and this is all they have. Houses crowded up the outside of the stockade, limited businesses in the inside. They hadn't assimilated; they didn't feel safe beyond the walls. If Vikland can give them more than that, why come back to a war-ravaged country?"

He paused. "I think it is also best we are in Vikland before the Matasi army gets this far. Piffik said this was an abandoned Matasi fort when his grandparents came. I can't imagine the Matasi army coming this far and not taking this one back and using it as a garrison. It would be easy to defend from Kereki troublemakers, and we are too few to protest."

He continued, "Also, if we leave tomorrow as planned, we can go slowly and take all the animals and our belongings we have stockpiled. If we wait until we are forced out with either pikes or pitchforks, we may not even have water for the journey."

Tiju Tia nodded. "I don't disagree with your decision, Rygee. I just have been thinking about my choices. We leave tomorrow as planned. The new horses should be rested enough. We will go to the shepherd's cottage and send messengers to Juisiti, the Conrosan refugees at Rishka, and perhaps the Huena family at Axefield. Once we have heard from them, we can discuss what is to be done."

Tiju Tia fell silent. We watched and listened to the Wrens. They cleared away the plates and food, did the dishes, and swept the floor, still talking. They joked about sharing a room three deep after they had experienced the luxury of sleeping alone and knowing they were safe. I saw Nelo place his hand on Arden's arm and lean in close to whisper. Arden raised both eyebrows, but nodded without saying anything. I saw him twist back to Mother who had contentedly lay against the far wall during the meal and was now enjoying food of her own. He commanded her to stay and then went out of the house. He came back a little later with his travel bag and Mother's blanket and walked up the stairs without stopping. I waited for him to return to ask what was happening. Then Oro broke away and asked to walk me back to the infirmary. I wanted to sleep in my bed instead, and so we walked together out the side door and to the porch swing on my house.

"Are you sure you want to sleep out here? You're the only one outside the stockade," he offered.

"I'm sure. The stars are brighter out here." I snuck in a sideways glance to see if he would smile. He did. "So I was sleeping when you and the others told your stories, can you bear to repeat them?" I settled into the swing, and he sat beside me.

He was quiet. Finally, "Rygee is right. We have to leave. There were rumors in Sary: Matasi troops were taking over Manumina, and the Kerekis know about 'a ring of traitors.' Tiju Tia and Rygee barely got the Wrens out in time, and if Piffik had not been in Cloa that day, we would have lost three of ours. The entire country has collapsed without anyone in charge."

He looked up at the sky and began his story at the beginning. Two days before Piffik's rescue, Arden had heard a militia group ride through Cloa talking about their raids. Falan had been betrayed in Balza, perhaps by the widow she lived with or the shop where she worked.

"I think they planned on taking her first and getting her to give up the other Wrens." Oro grimaced. "So Arden had taken a horse and left for Balza to get Falan out. He got there and she was gone, as you know, because Josef had warned her first. She had fled to Callis and Ross in Huk. Arden then went south to see if she was hiding in the settlement where you had picked up Bima Ritwik and the three other Viklanders. That is how he missed the others at Huk. He swung back north to Cloa and he said parts of Linna's message were still intact. He knew she and some others were safe, but the rest of her unwritten message had been destroyed. He found Tiju Tia's message to go to Manumina, but thought if it was written down, Nelo wouldn't know. Since Arden didn't think they would be returning, he had packed his and Linna's things and took the horse and the Manumina wagon from the stable and headed north to find Nelo. At that time, Arden thought only he and Nelo still needed to fly home.

"Instead, he found me at Nelo's holding. The two came so closely behind one another, Arden and Nelo, I thought at first they had traveled together. But Nelo had come from Evensong and said the Kereki army knew they had a traitor in the great house and they were questioning all the servants. Nelo had been looking for Kid. That's when Arden told Nelo, Kid was already gone from Evensong. I said Tiju Tia's message was to roll up the network and go to Manumina immediately. Not until I told them, did they know Linna had Viklanders with her and it had started as a rescue. Nelo and Arden wanted to warn Bima's softfoots and helpers. I knew this would take more time, and I wasn't sure how much time we could risk helping others. They both insisted this was bigger than just the Wrens. Arden came up with a plan to make it work.

"We three decided I would get Dica from Regno. Nelo would pull Tyra from Fortika and tell Therin and Inezi what was happening. Arden would warn the Kaumpft settlement. Both of them thought the Kaumpfts were an important part of Rani the softfoot's network and more than just a way station. Both Arden and Nelo said there was a Viklander called Lomes who drove a Matasi missionary wagon about, but they weren't sure where to find the softfoot. We decided we would meet at Nelo's holding in three days. If we could not be there in three days for any reason, we should head straight for Manumina. Without Viklanders with us, we had no chance to cross the Vikland border."

Oro snorted. "I'm too Vik for Kerek, and too Kereki for Vikland."

I nodded sadly, but said nothing.

"I lingered in the woods at Regno until I saw Dica go out for a morning walk. She was not expecting me and I nearly got a knife in the belly for my trouble. I explained to her all of our plans, and the concern Evensong may cast a wider net looking for traitors. Dica thought they might be going after a footman who liked to talk a lot about the things he saw and heard. But she couldn't be sure it was *not* Kid. She was glad he had left to take Arden's position at the Cloa stables."

Oro looked at me and shook his head. "I should not have told her then, but I said according to the feed boy at the Cloa stables, he had never arrived. I did not know until today; he was one of the ones Piffik had rescued."

He continued, "Dica had tipped her head away and said she needed to go back to the house and get her things. She had two fortnights' worth of wages she hadn't turned over to Tiju Tia for safekeeping and didn't want to leave behind. I told her we needed to leave now for Nelo's, or we would be walking all the way to Manumina, and did she really want to be seen in the woods with a man who looked half Vik? She retorted she definitely needed to go back and get her West Islands steel if she was going to have to protect me for a handful of nights. She told me of a place to sleep and wait for her. She would work some of the day and pack her things as she was able. She huffed and said since I failed to carry any food, she would have to steal food for us as well. But she would do all that, she said, and bring her things long before sunset. We would walk all night."

He shook his head. "I do not know where Tiju Tia found so many Wrens who like to tell me what to do. Only Linna is sweet. Dica and the rest all think they are made of sparks and steel."

I raised my eyebrows at that. "Only Linna grew up in a shopkeeper's home. Even Falan and Callis who *had* parents in Kerek City grew up in gambling halls and taverns where they had to watch for a dance with Trouble as soon as they could walk. Dica, Jenny, and Tyra were Lost Girls and then pickpockets, and you can't tell me they were coddled with lullabies and sweets." I realized what he was trying to say. "You didn't stay where Dica told you to, did you?"

Oro blew out a noisy breath. "She told me of a thicket of rhododendrons, a circular opening where I could lay on the ground, have no fire, and animals crawling about me while I tried to sleep. As I found the overgrown path and realized I would have to push through brambles, I saw a shepherd's cottage just a bit farther. I'm not a fool, Zren, I checked the place thoroughly. It had been empty since the last Dry most likely. The bed was dusty but soft, there was wood for a small fire, and I recognized Rygee's preserves on the shelf. Obviously, Dica or Inezi used this cottage, but she had told me to sleep in the woods. I thought she had done it out of malice."

I groaned. I missed a lot of what went on about me, but I was smart enough to trust the instructions of those who knew better than I did. It was a lesson Oro still needed to learn.

"How many and when did they show up?" I sighed.

Oro gave me a mulish look. "Three, just after midday. I had unbarred the door and let the latch out so we could be ready to go as soon as Dica arrived. There is no window on that side of the house, and I couldn't see down the path. I thought she might bring a horse since she had already worked all morning. I could not imagine her walking all night.

"I heard horses and I thought, 'Ah good, we will each have our own mount.' I reached down and grabbed my travel pack. When I turned, there they were, crowded into the doorway. I threw my pack at the first one, pulled my boot knife, and stuck the second one. I got a few punches in before they recovered from their surprise and fought back. The first one said 'Don't kill him, he's a Viklander—there's a bounty.' The other said the bounty was only for the braid. Since I had already given mine up, he'd take me to the Kereki army encampment at Evensong for coin. A live Viklander is so much more entertaining than a dead one, he said to me.

"They pulled me out of the cottage and tied me to the dead man's horse. We wheeled about and headed back towards the road to Evensong. As we passed the rhododendrons, I saw Dica pressed up tight, hiding in the thicket. I said, 'I would rather go to Fortika than Evensong.' The others were oblivious to our surroundings. They ignored me and didn't see Dica. I had no way of knowing if Dica understood my message."

"You're here, so obviously, she did." I smiled.

He gave me a long look. "She was on foot. Fortika is a half-day's walk. Nelo was most likely already gone with Tyra. She thought Kid was dead, and we were all fleeing for our lives. No, Zren. She did exactly what any Kerek City street runner would do. She left me to fend for myself."

We rocked in silence for a while. I could feel Oro's hurt at Dica's abandonment. But I knew it was because neither of them knew each other. Oro was quick to dismiss Dica without understanding his own behavior had caused his trouble. If he had been hiding in the thicket, he would not have been found. It had been designed to hide Viklanders for a while. I knew because I had been there for a rescue—it was where I saw the softfoot Lomes again. The cottage was just a landmark, a supply stop. Oro didn't understand that when Dica did see him, he had been captured and traveling with two Kereki on horseback. He was tied and couldn't help her, and she was on foot, without a short bow, and the smallest of all of them. She knew those were odds she could not win at that moment.

I waited for the rest of the story.

Oro grunted. "We were down past Evensong. Not long before the cutoff for the encampment, a team of horses and wagon came into view. It was one of those wide Matasi wagons with the flat canvas tops and the person driving it had a traveler's cloak with the hood up. I could not see his face. He slowed as he came up to us, but did not move over from the center of the road, and my captors were forced to the side. They jeered at him, but he calmly said something in Mata and nodded as he went past. As soon as we regained the road, I heard two quick snaps and a whoosh. The men who captured me couldn't keep their seats and fell off their horses." Oro smirked. "Of course, that could have been the arrows blooming out of their lower backs. I turned my horse just to watch in amazement as Arden threw back the hood of his traveler's cloak and jumped down from the Matasi wagon. He nodded to me and then ensured the Kerekis were dead. He untied me. I told him about Dica in the thicket doing nothing when she saw me tied behind the Kereki horses."

Oro looked at me. "Do you know what he said? 'What did you expect from a fourteen-year-old girl?'" Oro paused for a long moment. "At first, I thought he was agreeing with me."

I hid my face. I knew Arden's humor from all those days I stayed with him when he was mending from a beating. He didn't talk much—at least not to me—but when he did, his words could hide a bite as easily as a smile. He was telling Oro he should not have expected to be rescued by a someone without a horse or weapons at her command.

"Let me guess the rest," I offered. "Arden sent his dog Mother after Dica, while you and he buried the bodies. Then he changed the appearance of the Kerekis' horses enough for you to string them and bring them behind the wagon."

Oro stared at me. "This is true! Dica and Mother showed up over a decon, maybe two decons later. She said she had been trailing our horses, but since she was on foot she had been falling farther behind. When she and Mother reached the wagon, she gave Arden a hard hug, but said nothing more—no words of gratitude to him or an apology to me. Just crawled in the back with the dog and went to sleep. Arden pulled a skirt out of Dica's traveling pack, told me to tie it on and wear his traveling cloak with the hood up. He walked into the woods a little ways and came out rubbing a root on his face and his hands. It darkened them. Then he dropped his braid between his collar and his neck and climbed back on the wagon. And that's how we trotted into Nelo's holding."

I closed one eye and squinted at him.

"That's how you tell a story?" I snorted. "You need to go to the West Islands to learn how to properly tell an adventure tale."

Oro leaned back and smiled. "I'd like that. I've been trying to think what I would do now that Kerek has fallen. I do not want to return to my family in Kerek City. I am not sure I would want to live in either Vikland or Matasi. I'm not enough of a sailor to sail to the Spice Island or Conrosa. That leaves the West Islands. I know I was born there. More than that, only the Orphan Master of Kerek City knows."

We rocked in silence, and I could see he was struggling to say something.

Finally, he sighed and began, "I am sorry I told Dica, Kid had not arrived at the stables. I did not know he had been brought to Manumina with the others." He was quiet. "I did not realize until she hugged Arden how alone and frightened I had made her feel." Another pause. "I did not understand until I told you my story, you and Arden both knew Dica would be following us to see where the Kerekis would take me, so she could bring help. Arden knew he could send Mother to follow the scent of the horses' tracks—my tracks—and the dog would find Dica."

"You told the truth." I thought a little more. "You told the truth like a softfoot would. Sideways, so people hear your words but think something else. It is how Tiju Tia talks and Bima Ritwik did. I never learned the trick of it. It was one of the many reasons I could not be a Wren. As for the Wrens? They hear our words, but listen for Truth between the sounds of our voices."

Finally, I was ready to talk. "My story is like yours. Piffik and Siba had just left with the three Wrens: Falan, Linna, and Kid, and two Viklanders to the shepherd's cottage across the border when a mob of Kereki troublemakers came with Lou and the dairy wagon."

I paused a long time before I confessed, "Oro, I do not see as far as you and the others. So I make many guesses. This time, I recognized the wagon, and so I thought the riders about the wagon must be the Wrens and Rygee. I knew he had planned to bring back Manumina's horses that we had at the stables along the Northern Track. So I opened the gate without waiting for Lou to hail the house. I guessed wrong," I said sorrowfully.

"Lou was already dead when they dumped him out of the dairy wagon. They broke my collarbone, rattled my brain, and left me to drown or burn, I don't think they cared which. Only the storm kept them from burning Manumina to the ground."

I blew out a breath. "I guess I know we have to leave, it is just this is the only place I have ever felt safe. I know that sounds stupid…"

"No, that's exactly why I want to stay. I knew you would understand," Oro agreed. "But…" He paused. "It will be good to see Linna and the others tomorrow. To be together."

We rocked on into the night, content in a home soon to be no longer ours.

CHAPTER 23

EXODUS

After Oro had left to sleep inside the guest house with the other Wrens, I began packing. Too restless to sleep, I had gone through Rell's room and found her traveling bag of coin from Miya, her Kereki clothes and boots, her traveling bag still half full of Vik clothes and books and quarrels from her previous trip to Axefield. I added things I found about her room I thought might have meaning for her. I wondered how she would find out that Manumina was abandoned. Would she hear it as casual talk among the bowmasters? Would she grieve for us? Or would she know we were all safe at the shepherd's cottage?

I missed Rell so much. I wondered if this is what all families felt when there was someone gone without warning. Is this what Solkka felt with his brother Tedros? Piffik and Aajan with their brother Zadah? How could anyone bear to leave if there would be such an emptiness left behind?

It was easier to pack for myself. Nearly everything I owned fit into the small wooden chest Piffik had made for me when I first came to Manumina. But I put my knives and daggers in the traveling bag I had used on the Northern Track. I knew I wouldn't be defending anything on this journey. Still, it made me feel better to know my weapons would just be at my feet.

The next morning the sun was high in the sky when I found one of Chul's old canes and used it to help me wobble my way to the village green. Every wagon we had—the settler's wagon, the rag and bone wagon, the two missionary wagons, and the dairy cart had been taken out, cleaned, extra props removed, and repacked with Piffik's tools, Siba's medicines, the valuables Callis and Josef had found, the food from the springhouses and the cold rooms, the last of Lou's cheeses, Chul's inventions, Rygee's bakery tools and ingredients, tack room supplies, short bows, the Wrens' traveling bags, and crates and cages of rabbits and chickens hooked on the outside. I was thankful I had slept outside the stockade and missed Rygee getting everyone up at first light to work.

Tyra came over, shoved a pastry into my hands and hurried back to help pack.

"Wait," I called after her. "Only one?"

"You were too slow," she called back. "I needed a hand free to help the others."

At last we were ready. Oro went to my house and easily carried Rell's and my belongings back and placed it all into the rag and bone wagon. There was no room for ride alongs; those who did not drive the wagons would be herding the goats.

Rygee had planned to have me drive one of the wagons. But then he looked closely at me, and said I would drive the wagon off a cliff even if there was none around. He told me to ride with Tyra while he drove mine.

We sorted out weapons and drivers, hitched the horses to the five wagons, belled the wether goat and hoped the kids, does, and billy goat would follow it. Rygee climbed on the lead wagon, snapped the reins, and we moved off.

Two of the Wrens, Josef and Ross, stood by the gates as we all pulled through. They closed the gates and barred them from the inside and slipped through the side door. The goats spent a long time trying to figure out what we wanted them to do, and the Wrens tried to figure out how to get them to move forward together.

I spent a long time looking back at Rell's window where so many nights she had protected me with her crossbow while I greeted strangers and Wrens to Manumina. My eyes filled and spilled tears down my cheeks, and I stared backwards until I could no longer see my house, the stockade, the wild plum trees on the east side, the valley itself. Then I turned forward and looked toward Vikland.

I had lost my home.

***

Tyra was quiet and I watched her as she struggled with holding the reins too tight. The horses were getting irritated.

"You don't know how to drive a team," I blurted out.

She hunched her shoulders defensively. "Give me time, I'll figure it out."

"No, that's not what I meant. Here, let me teach you." I put my hands over hers and had her loosen her grip. "If you need to change direction, just a little tug, never haul back on the lines. Rell Huena used to tell me horses were smarter than people, we just had to give them a hint and they could take it from there. See? They like you better already."

A small smile played about Tyra's face and I took my opportunity. "I heard how Dica came to Manumina yesterday, but I did not hear how you came to rescue Inezi and Nelo." I waved my hand at the Kerek landscape. "We have a lot of time. Now the horses know you want to follow the others, they can drive themselves." I casually stretched my legs out.

She shot me a look. "I did not rescue Nelo."

"No?" I leaned back against the wagon seat, closed my eyes, and tilted my face to the sun. "Well, you are telling the story so you can rescue everyone and the Empress of Vikland in your tale. How would I know differently?"

She barked out a sharp laugh. I waited with my eyes closed, and soon I could hear her shuffling about. I hid my smile.

"Matasi troops were at Regno. Did you know that, Zren? They pulled in the master of Regno and said his life would be spared because he had been working with the Viklanders, but they took all of his fine horses. Once the troops left with all of the maps of the area and the numbers of the Kereki encampment, the master starting hunting for those who had betrayed the Kereki cause in his household. Dica did not tell you this yesterday, did she?"

I scowled but kept my eyes closed so she did not see my surprise. "No. She did not. Does *no one* know how to tell a proper story? All of you Wrens keep out the best parts."

She snorted and I felt her relax beside me. "The footman at Evensong who likes to talk too much had come over and was telling Cook and anyone who would listen about the Matasi army and the upcoming battle at the encampment south of Evensong. You may remember, Zren, Fortika is owned by a retired Matasi general. We knew we were not in danger, but I wanted to get word to Nelo or

Inezi that we needed to get Kid out of Evensong and Dica out of Regno right away. I told Cook I needed to go to my room for a moment, ran up the stairs and threw all of my clothes and my coin in my travel bag. Then I went back downstairs and tried to work.

"When I could get a moment alone with Therin, I explained we needed to get Dica out of Regno. I was packed and could leave as soon as I could get my travel bag down the stairs with no one watching. He told me to throw my bag and traveler's cloak out my window. He would pick them up, hide them in the stables, and go find Inezi. No one else in the house would know."

She paused. "Later that day, I looked out the window in the room I passed, and I saw a row of pale rocks in an arrow on the lawn. It was one of Inezi's signals. It meant Nelo was in the woods and would stay until he talked to me. I stopped what I was doing, and ran out the door. I don't know what anyone else thought. I was scared and I knew I was never coming back. I ran a long way into the woods, and when I couldn't find the others, I thought they had not been able to wait for me. I thought maybe Inezi had put the arrow down in the morning, and I didn't see it before they had been forced to leave.

"I was sitting on a rock waiting for the sun to use me as a compass so I could find east by my shadow and start walking to Vikland. Inezi found me then. She took me back to the others—Nelo and Therin.

"They had four horses saddled and ready to go. My travel bag tied to one of them. They were not my master's fastest horses, so I knew we were all leaving Fortika for good. Nelo handed me a pair of Kereki pants and a shirt so I could change out of my work dress. Then we mounted up and Inezi led us east and around the edge of the Fortika lands.

"We stopped at every building and hideaway they had for Viklanders, some I knew about, and most I didn't. Inezi had us help her dig up wooden boxes or move rocks to retrieve maps, clothes, coins, and food. She said we wanted to leave nothing behind if the battle between Matasi and Kerek below Evensong did not go in our favor."

"Well done," I nodded. "Tiju Tia would be proud to know how well you kept our secrets. So when did you find out Dica and Kid were safe?"

Tyra explained once they had left Fortika land, Nelo had ridden close to her and told her Kid had left Evensong days earlier. Arden had sheltered him in Cloa. They—Nelo and Arden— believed Kid was safe in Manumina with Linna, Falan, Callis, Josef, and Ross, as Linna had left a message she was traveling with five people, and what other five could they be? Nelo had said Oro was to pick up Dica from Regno, but they had made those plans before they learned the Matasi army had been so close.

At the Kaumpfts, Arden had learned the settlement had been visited by a Matasi patrol. Arden warned them Bima's softfoots and Tiju Tia's Wrens may be betrayed and in danger, and the Wrens were falling back to Manumina. Arden traded all of the coin in his purse and the Manumina horse and empty cart at Kaumpfts for a team of horses and one of their sturdy wagons and then drove north to see if he could meet Dica and Oro along the way. Tyra fell silent.

I opened my eyes when I felt Tyra shuddering beside me. She was red-faced with trying to cry without a sound. I didn't say anything, just reached down in my travel bag and took out one of those small squares of linen I used to protect my best knives. She gave me a fierce look, but I just glanced off into the distance. I felt her snatch it out of my hand and give me the reins.

I pretended to be very interested in the scenery, the wagons ahead of us, and the Wrens trying to herd the goats beside us. I saw Arden walking, but not his dog, and finally located Mother riding on the wagon seat beside Dica. I watched as Josef and Nelo walked and talked together. I looked for Therin, the little kitchen boy from Fortika, and found him on Tiju Tia's wagon. I smiled just thinking about all of the secrets she was learning as he told his stories. Ross and Inezi were trailing behind, using skinny sticks to keep the goats moving along.

I twisted and looked ahead of me at Rygee driving the largest settler wagon, and I realized he had horses I didn't recognize. I turned back to Tyra and made my eyes as large and round as possible.

"Tyra, are we horse thieves?"

She choked back a sound, mopped her face one last time, and replied, "Of course, we are. Once we all met back at Nelo's, we stopped to eat the food Dica had taken from Regno. We decided we should have another wagon for everything we needed to take to Manumina. That's when Nelo said we should go back to the Kaumpfts, trade their horses back for our wagon, and use the four Fortika horses to take us to Manumina. He told us he and Arden would ride out with a second string. Inezi and Mother would protect us while they were gone. The rest of us should sleep as much as we could. He told Dica to go through the wooden box under his bed for costumes and pots of paint and to pack them very carefully as they would be traveling with us."

She cocked her head to the side. "I think Nelo was very sad to leave his little house. While Arden was out getting the horses ready, he touched every piece of furniture in the place."

I nodded. Of course he had. Just as Manumina was my place of safety, Nelo had found a place where he belonged. He had decided it fit him very well.

Oro had taken Nelo's bed and napped. Tyra, Therin, and Dica curled up on the floor next to the pile of belongings Arden had unloaded from the wagon before they had traded it the first time to the Kaumpfts. Dica had pulled out some thick blankets from the heap. They had slept, but not until Dica had told Tyra how Oro had gotten captured, and Tyra had told her how she had panicked thinking she had been left behind at Fortika. Dica had reassured her, the one thing she knew as much as the sun would rise every day, is Nelo would not leave anyone behind as long as he had breath in his body.

Tyra was quiet, and I was content that she would either finish her story or let me puzzle it out for myself. Not that there was much left to figure out. Sometime along the ride between Nelo's holding and the Kaumpft settlement, Arden and Nelo had created the new plan to travel as Matasi missionaries. It made sense. If they came across any Matasi or Vikland patrols they would be treated kindly. If they ran into the Kereki militia or other settlers, they would be left unmolested, or if there was trouble, they would be able to trade on a moment's confusion before all of the Wrens fired their short bows. I knew now Arden spoke Mata, and I wondered if Nelo had been able to pick up a few words as well. I was glad both Nelo and Arden had known the Kaumpfts before this journey. The best time to make friends is before you need them.

CHAPTER 24

THE SHEPHERD'S COTTAGE

I had never been to the shepherd's cottage although I knew Tiju Tia, Piffik, Rygee, and Oro had used it to slip Viklanders out of Kerek. It was half a day's ride on a fast horse and a day's walk to the Conrosan refugees at Rishka. But for the returning soldiers it was only a half day's walk in any direction where the Viklanders could find an estate where someone could take them to any of the nearby villages or towns to get a horse, an inn, a way to the nearby garrison or Juisiti.

Siba was standing out at the sandpoint well, pumping cold water. Rygee barely braked the wagon before he was off and had scooped her up in his arms. He held her so tightly she finally had to pat him on the back to get him to put her down. The rest of the wagons slowly pulled in.

We knew we would have to put up some type of shed and fencing before the walkers driving the goats arrived. Once he had finally released Siba, Rygee showed us how to fix the fence.

We wrapped our hands and arms in leather and canvas strips and twisted brambles together tightly to form a third wall. With the shade from the cottage, we had enough to keep the goats protected from the sun and from wandering off.

Siba and Tiju Tia started cooking before anything else was done. As we all sat down and filled our bellies, Siba told us Piffik had gone to the Conrosans two days ago. He had sent back a messenger with two extra horses for Kid and Linna to ride to Axefield and tell the Huenas Manumina may be in future danger, and he had two Viklanders at the shepherd's cottage too damaged to sit a horse.

One of Rell's youngest brothers had come with a wagon the same day, and after staying overnight, had taken Solkka and Quan to Juisiti very early that morning.

She looked at me as she said, "I'm sorry, Zren. No one had any idea you were coming today. I had said they should rest one more day, but they said the ribs were not broken, and their wrists were merely sprained. To travel now would only be discomfort, and not deadly. Both said their news was too important to Vikland to wait upon their well-being."

I looked down at my plate to hide my sorrow. Siba asked Nelo for the names of his friends.

"This is Therin. He worked as needed in the kitchens at Fortika, and she is Inezi, the gamekeeper's daughter. They were part of the Viklander helpers, and we worked closely together. I had heard Bima the Softfoot was dead, but not who took his place, so I offered them sanctuary with us until we reached Juisiti, or we can find Lomes or Kern."

"I'm sorry," Tiju Tia asked Inezi. "Your parents, are they…"

"My father was Kereki. My mother was from Matasi. How she ended up in the back of beyond in Kerek, I do not know. She died before I could ask her." Inezi bit out.

I recoiled at the venom in her voice. Tiju Tia, however, continued as if Inezi had spoken of a lovely day.

"Actually, I was going to ask you if your parents will be concerned you are not there. Will they think you ran away or came to ill-harm?"

Inezi looked skeptical but she answered, "I'm sorry, I am asked so often who I am. As if I do not deserve consideration until someone has passed judgment on my parentage."

Tiju Tia waved her hand. "You do not need to apologize to me. I am delighted to meet you, but I do not want your father to grieve."

Inezi gave Nelo a long look. His face was hard and stony; it was Inezi's story to tell.

Finally, Inezi looked at Tiju Tia and sighed. "No one will care that I am gone."

After we ate, I went inside and laid down on the floor of the cottage to try to stop the pain from my aching head. It was cool and dry, and someone must have cleaned it sometime before we arrived. It felt good to close my eyes. I dreamed Siba came to check on me and waved incense under my nose. The pain of the last few days finally faded away.

I awoke several decons later to find everything had changed yet again. The area outside the cottage looked like a robber's camp. The canvas coverings over the wagons and been converted into lean-tos. Traveler's cloaks, blankets, and clothing were laid out into beds. Wood had been gathered for cooking fires. I still needed Chul's cane to keep my balance, so I sat down carefully on the front step and looked about me. Tiju Tia and Inezi were bending over maps on a makeshift table of wood and a wagon side. Tiju Tia was using her finger on the paper as Inezi explained to Tiju Tia without ever looking at the maps. I thought I remembered Nelo say she could not read words on paper, but she could read the land, and track soldiers, hunt wild game, and ride Fortika's notoriously high-strung horses. I wondered how she would fit in with the softfoots of Vikland. Would they respect her as Nelo did? Make a place for her talents?

Callis was standing over a chair with steel shears in her hand. Josef's blond hair lay wet and scattered down over his shoulders and spread out in Callis' hand as she prepared to cut it. Falan was sitting cross-legged on the ground in front of them, a verbal looking glass. If it turned out well, I mused, I might have her cut mine. Nelo and Arden both wore their hair tied back with a leather strip, Nelo in a tail and Arden in a braid, but I was ready to cut mine as short as Falan wore hers.

Oro and Nelo were northeast of the cottage away from the others, walking back and forth and talking. Nelo's shoulders were nearly even with Oro's lanky frame, and I thought about how much all of the Wrens had grown since they left Kerek City. None of them were more than twenty or so by Tiju Tia's reckoning, but they all showed the promise of who they would become. They were all far more resourceful and stronger than I had been when I came to Manumina. I wondered about that. Why do some troubles hollow us out and others do not?

Ross was over by his rabbit crates, feeding and caring for them. Arden had a few of the goats out and with the help of Therin, Dica, and Tyra, was trying to teach his dog to herd goats. It wasn't going well. Mother was more than happy to track them all over the yard, but she didn't seem interested in herding them anywhere in particular.

I remembered Arden had told me once, the dog was a scent hound, a Dunker, a rich man's breed he had thieved as a pup from a litter. I wondered if there was such a thing as a dog that herded goats or other animals and what that dog might look like. I laughed as I wondered if Arden had finally reached the dog's limit on what she could learn or do.

Now Oro and Nelo were walking back to the cottage and Nelo flicked his eyes to me. I used Chul's old cane to pull myself up and went to join them. Nelo started talking as soon as I got close enough to hear.

"Tiju Tia wants Oro, Inezi, Kid, and me to go to Juisiti and see if we can get someone to listen to us about what we heard and saw at Evensong, and the Matasi visits to Regno and the Kaumpfts. We will leave now on horseback and get as far as Axefield. Hopefully, Kid and Linna are still there and not on the way to the Conrosans. It will be late when we get to the Huenas, but they run an inn and are perhaps used to travelers at all decons. We'll need coin, and none of us have Vikland style clothes if we are to go to the palace. Tiju Tia said you have been there before. What do we need? What do we do to be sure we are heard?"

I considered carefully. "I have the clothes, but none to fit you. Ask Tiju Tia for coin to buy clothes and boots as well as the stay at the inn and food for your journey. Ask the Huenas if they can send a son with you to speak Vik and show you what to do. Have the son teach you the formal greetings on the way. They are very important to Viklanders, and it will make your way much smoother if you know them and use them. Rell told me not to use Keresh as a first language when asking for help, it is considered rude to use the language of the enemy. This is why it is so important to have a Vik speaker along." I paused, trying to think ahead.

"If Kern, or Lomes, or Rani are not at the palace to speak to, ask the guards for directions to the working rooms of Chul Swyler, a firemaster. He is well known and well liked at the palace and a friend to Manumina. He may help our information reach the right people."

Nelo nodded gravely. "If the Huenas do not have a son to travel with us? Should we go directly to Chul Swyler for assistance? I cannot imagine our Kereki faces would be allowed to wander freely in the palace looking for Viklander softfoots."

I agreed. "Chul shares his working rooms with Aajan Qanaq, who is Piffik's sister. She has a clever mind, but her humor has a bite. Do not take offense at her greetings. Piffik says she uses harsh words to pretend she does not miss us. She will know what to do if Chul is not available. She will help us as far as she is able, though she will act as if it is a great hardship."

"Another one like Falan." Oro rolled his eyes as I described Aajan.

Nelo gave him a sharp look, and then glanced over at Josef still getting his hair cut. "I was going to ask Josef to pick out the best horses for us to ride to reach there without exhausting them." He grinned. "But, he looks a little busy." He looked at

Oro. "Guess you'll need to do so before we go. You can tell Tiju Tia what we agreed."

Oro gave Nelo a long look, and at first, I thought he might refuse. But then, Oro walked stiffly over to Tiju Tia. I drifted over to a wagon so I could lean back and prop myself up. Nelo came over and easily draped his elbows over the top of the wagon box. I just scowled and kept my arms crossed in front of me. We watched as Callis used her fingers to brush out the loose strands still floating about Josef as he shook his head. Tousled blond curls now framed his cherubic face. He looked like the prettiest girl I had ever met. I wondered what the gamblers had thought of him as he had pranced and cooed about the tables at the Red Cup. I decided Callis would not be cutting my hair after all.

"I need to take Josef to Matasi," Nelo said drily. "All those old ladies singing the beauty of the Lost God would fall over themselves. They would swoop him up and he would never breathe on his own again. It would be worth all the trouble he'd cause me on the way."

"You want to go to Matasi? I mean, after all this is over?" I cocked an eyebrow.

He looked at me. "Zren, it *is* over. The King is gone. Matasi runs Kerek City and the port and therefore the rest of the country. Vikland is still boxed in the mountains. Manumina is gone. Tomorrow you are going to drive a wagon of other people's belongings to go beg *refugees* for a place to live."

I stared at him. "Well, when you put it that way, I wonder how I will be able to drag myself there."

He blew out a noisy breath. "You'll be fine. Tiju Tia will sail to the West islands, and the Wrens will all just fly away."

Ah, now I understood. "You have more choices than you think, Nelo. Tiju Tia has never hidden the news she is going to ask the Empress of Vikland to pay a life debt for the Wrens' help in the war. I'm not sure what that means, but you have many more choices in front of you than you did in Kerek City."

I heard the bitterness in his voice. "Maybe if I looked like Josef or Kid. Or could tell them I worked in a shop like Falan and Linna. Or could read or write…"

"But…" I slyly smiled. "I look at those big strong muscles, and I think, there's a manly farmhand, and I will never need to empty a muck cart again."

He laughed in spite of himself. "Only you, Zren, could say that to me and live to see tomorrow. Only you."

Tiju Tia and Oro came up then and Nelo left to talk to Josef about the horses and what would be needed. Inezi showed up a few moments later with a travel bag and some maps rolled under her arms. I wondered if she had a mapcase since I hadn't seen her with them earlier.

I didn't know what to make of Inezi. It was clear she had feelings for Nelo, her eyes would track him nearly everywhere he went. He treated her kindly, but as if he didn't notice her interest. I tried telling myself it was none of my business. I must have been staring a little too long, however, because Tiju Tia came over to stand by me as the three went to saddle their horses. Together we watched them mount, and in a chorus of goodbyes, they turned their horses northeast.

"You look like you found a puzzle, and you are not going to let it go until you've reached the bottom of it."

I squinted one eye and looked down at her. "We're talking about Inezi, right?"

She quirked a half smile. "Inezi and Nelo… and perhaps Red and Koanga on the Coast Road to Salisport."

I sighed. "Please, don't tell me I looked so lonely and lost every time I looked at your brother." I paused. "So are you telling me Nelo is not blind to her?"

"No, he is only allowing her to keep her dignity. She has not been shown much care and affection. She has the skills to survive but has not been given a chance to learn to thrive. Once she lands in her new home, she will be able to forget this."

I thought about what Nelo had said earlier. "You are still planning on asking the Empress for a home for the Wrens, are you not?"

"I am. If she does not acknowledge the life debt owed to them, then I will go to Miyamoto Suki and ask for coin for passage to the West Islands and take them all with me. The King of the West Islands will give them a home and repay my debt to Miya. Someday Miya and I will meet again—perhaps in Conrosa. We both desire to serve our countries in their court."

She went on to explain how it had been many years since the King of the West Islands had news from Conrosa, but with the world changing so dramatically, all the countries needed to reopen their embasado there soon.

"History is written by those who tell the story first and best. Conrosa needs to hear this story from us and not from Matasi or Kerek."

It was an easy evening. Someone built a campfire, others milked the goats. Since there wasn't a way to transport the milking, Rygee made a creamy soup with greens, and grains, and spices. We had the last of the baking, and Therin brought us all some late berries he said were good to eat.

I turned in early, sharing a canvas lean-to with Ross. I knew we would have an early start the next morning and with the goats, it was going to take a while.

***

Of course, Piffik wasn't around the next day to see me awake while the sun was still sleeping. I grumbled to myself wondering why I didn't notch a wagon side to show all my early mornings. I could show them to him later as evidence I wasn't the layabout he thought I was.

Instead, I took one of the well-rested horses and attached her to the smallest cart for Siba and Rygee. While the night was still cool, they would be hurrying with the perishable foods to the Conrosan refugees. The rest of us would plod along with the goats and the heavy wagons later. Siba came out with two baskets with steel flasks freshly filled with cold water from the well. I watched her silently as she nestled those about in blankets.

This morning, she wore her brown wavy hair loosely twisted on top of her head, and changed to a dress like the other Conrosan women wore. I had gotten used to the loose braid and Kereki baggy pants and shirts she and Rell had worn when there were so few of us at Manumina. She looked older somehow when she dressed in the Conrosan style. She was kind and smart, as witty as Aajan without the bite of Aajan's humor. But after watching

Rygee the last three days grow increasingly frantic to be reunited with her, I wondered what I didn't know.

I missed Solkka, and I thought the future of sailing through the West Islands would be incredible. But I never felt the anxiety I had witnessed in Rygee.

So, I asked her about it. "Each day Rygee was back at Manumina and he didn't know for sure you were here and safe, he grew more worried and concerned for you. But I don't feel that way about Solkka Ulani and I wonder if I should?"

"Oh, Zren." She smiled and squeezed my good shoulder. "Don't measure your feelings for someone by anyone else's standards. You two will know what's best for the both of you."

Rygee came out from the cottage with two stacked wooden crates and a blanket over his arm. He raised an eyebrow at Siba standing there with an arm about my shoulders.

"It's going to be fine, Zren. You'll see me again very soon, and there will be food for you." He set the wooden crates in the back of the cart and covered everything with another blanket to keep the chill in.

He smiled at Siba with such a big goofy grin, I couldn't resist, "The past three days, you've been so grumpy I feared for my life, and now you are all soft mushy Rygee."

He lightly cuffed me on my good arm. "Yes, well, you'll figure it out someday."

Siba had already settled herself in the cart and had picked up the reins. Rygee jumped up easily beside her and released the brake. I waved until the dark swallowed them up. They would arrive at Rishka before we even got started.

I shivered in the early morning chill as I passed by the tents where the Wrens had camped with those who made them feel the safest. Dica and Tyra in the first tent, no surprise there—they had worked at neighboring estates and knew each other best.

The second tent had Josef on the outside but the traveling cloak over him wasn't his. Mmm. I walked around to the top of his tent. I heard my name.

"Zren Janin, I know you can softfoot better than that. Which leads me to believe you want to wake me up on this morning that isn't even a morning for another two decons." Josef sighed and rolled over on his back. "What do you need?"

"Just wondering whose traveler's cloak you stole."

He snorted. "You woke me up for that?" He poked the person next to him. "Wake up. Zren is practicing his softfooting by trying to figure out why you are in my tent."

"It's the middle of the night." I heard her voice grow louder as she pushed down the cloak, "But if you must know, most of the cloaks and blankets were packed too deeply into the wagons to take out just for one night. Josef gave his cloak to Dica and Tyra to share, and Arden is sharing his with Therin. I was not going to sleep with Arden's dog. Josef agreed to share his tent with Falan and me if we would share our cloaks. Now can I go back to sleep?" Callis pulled the cloak over her head.

I felt sheepish and Josef must have sensed it. "If it makes you feel better, Zren, I'm nothing but their *titiro mai ki ahau.*" He laughed out loud at the startled look on my face, and I hurried away to my lean-to with Ross.

CHAPTER 25

A WORLD NOT FAR FROM THIS ONE

When I woke again, the sun was up a good hand's width in the eastern sky. I could hear people carrying things out of the cottage, smell Vikland coffee over the fire, and happy voices ready for a journey. I lay on my back, eyes closed, just listening to all the sounds of rough camping, when suddenly, "Hey, don't eat all the mush, Zren hasn't eaten yet." I rolled to my feet and hobbled around the corner of the cottage. Everyone was standing facing me, and Josef was holding the porridge pot. They burst out laughing, and I knew I had been played.

"I suppose this was your idea," I groused as I grabbed the pot out of Josef's hands.

"Just because you woke me in the middle of the night?" Josef started laughing again.

I spooned in the porridge and looked about. My tent was the only one still up and as I watched, Ross and Falan came around the corner with it, and Callis was carrying my travel bag and traveler's cloak.

"What's left?" I slowly scanned the area and realized they had let me sleep to the last possible moment.

"The goats," Josef said promptly. "Tiju Tia said those who rode yesterday walk today. We're down the wagon and horse Rygee and Siba have, and the three horses that Oro, Inezi, and Nelo took yesterday, so we are leaving the settler wagon and the rag and bone cart for now, and bringing only the missionary wagons."

I handed the now empty pot back to Josef. "Guess I'm a walker, then."

Either Vikland scrub tastes much better than Kerek scrubland or the goats had worked up an appetite. They wanted to wander everywhere. None of the Wrens had any idea what to do, and Ross and Therin were at the age of boys where they found all of our efforts hilarious. I watched in pleasure as they laughed and joked and acted like children.

Everyone treated this as a stroll through a market fair rather than a march of exile. I wondered if it was because no one had to look over their shoulder for danger, or because Tiju Tia had promised us all a new life. I walked with Arden for a while and asked him of his travels since I had been Linna's cousin. I thought he would avoid my questions or say nothing at all.

But he grinned at me, and said Mother had taken him on some incredible adventures.

He told me stories of how he would quietly untether Kereki patrol horses at night from their hobbles or their tie out lines and then once he was far enough away, Mother would go back and stalk the horses until they spooked and ran in the opposite direction. How the two of them could walk through a crowded encampment or shop or gathering of any size and Mother would stay quietly by his side. He could watch and learn which traveling bags had maps and dispatches. How he could spill just a little meat broth on the bag as they walked by. Later, Mother would be able to go back when the soldiers were sleeping or playing dice while on sentry duty and carefully steal the marked bag— always the right bag. How Mother had saved his life when he had received a message to pick up an injured Viklander at a settlement far north of Cloa. When they reached the barn, Mother stiffened and refused to go forward. Arden had stopped and waited to see what she had smelled or heard. She didn't relax, so he didn't either. In a while, Kereki soldiers had come out grumbling about a wasted night. Coincidence or trap, he didn't know, but he knew he was alive because she had sensed trouble.

Arden reminded me how Linna had carefully given all the Wrens a small piece of fancy soap she had bought and told them to rub their boots and the hem of their clothes with it every time so Mother would recognize the scent and be able to track them if they were hurt or injured or know them if they crossed paths. The scent of the soap also allowed the Wrens to enter Arden and Linna's house through the front door whenever they needed without harm from Mother.

He said it was a lesson the boy called Pike took to heart. Even after Arden and Mother had left with Josef, the boy had taken more baths with the fancy soap than Linna had thought possible for a child who had to haul his own water. The boy had replied, of course he was not afraid of the dog. But since Mother had been trained to know that scent, it was important, the boy said, that Mother knew Pike was a friend and not someone to be bitten.

Arden gave me a sly smile. "When Josef finally returned me and took the boy back to his family, Pike told Linna he was ready to marry and set up house. He knew how to make biscuits, he said, and Linna's Patron had told him many times he was the most responsible of all the men the Patron had known of Linna's family. So, Zren, what should we say to such a boy as that?"

I was saved from answering as a shout went up from the Wrens. Arden's dog, Mother, was truly smarter than all of us. She had been watching us try to herd the goats for the past two decons and once she figured out what we were trying to accomplish— we didn't need her to track them, only herd them—she began barking and nipping at them when they strayed, and kept them close together and moving along with us. She and the billy goat had a few tense moments as they determined whose herd it was anyway. We finally just tied a rope around the billy and took turns hauling him along so he would let Mother do her new job.

We arrived at Rishka after midday. It had been ages since I had been there last, and the place had not improved since then. Piffik was there—looking tired and defeated in his drab Kereki clothes. He walked up to me, reached for my injured shoulder, and then dropped his hand by his side.

"I am sorry, Zren, I am beyond sorry. Rygee told me what happened at Manumina. If I thought they would have found me so soon, I would never have left you alone. How can you ever forgive me?"

"I never thought it was your fault. I never once blamed you," I said surprised. "These weren't Kereki soldiers, just troublemakers. If anyone else would have been there, it could have been worse. The storm put out the fires, and I ended up with this sunburn on half my face."

"Rygee said you have a broken collarbone and had your brain rattled. Siba called it something else, but I forgot what the word was," he said sadly. "She is concerned, because this has happened to you before, and each time it is harder for you to recover."

"Truly, Piffik. I am well." I patted his arm. "It is my turn to be sorry. There wasn't room on the wagon for all of your wood, but we brought all of the woodworking tools we could load in the wagons. Tiju Tia and I looked everywhere in your shop and in your house and in the stables and we couldn't find your secret stash of coin any place. I do not think we can go back for it, the Matasi army has Manumina now."

He gave me a confused smile. "Zren, I didn't hide anything. All the coin I made went to food and supplies for Manumina, the Wrens and their needs, or I brought it here for the refugees. I own my tools and my clothes." He looked me in the eye. "And I am very, very glad about my tools. Thank you for your kindness, Zren."

In the time between Siba's arrival this morning and our arrival after midday, she had met with the Council of Wisdom to arrange for places for the Wrens and the rest of us. All of the housing available was very nearly full, so they split up the Wrens into various households. The rabbits, the chickens, and the goats were added to the livestock already there, and the horses unhitched and cared for in the large stables. Someone would go back for the remaining wagons at the shepherd's cottage, the day after, or soon.

The Wrens and I just sat and watched as Piffik directed the unloading of the wagons. We probably weren't making a warm impression, but I was starting to hurt all over and I didn't care what people thought. I saw Tiju Tia talking to Salik Oqina and

Piffik, and I thought I would go over there and learn what would happen to all of us.

I pushed myself to my feet and stood up shakily. Seriously, was I that tired? I caught Josef's eye as he headed for Tiju Tia. And then, I felt a wave of dizziness.

I don't even remember hitting the ground.

***

The room was dark and cool. I heard Siba's voice and then nothing more.

***

It was later. I felt someone sitting at the edge of the bed.

"Hey, Zren." It was Rygee. "If you are going to faint from hunger, next time do it nearer the kitchens, eh?" A metal spool forced its way in between my teeth, and I tasted hot meaty broth with some spice. I moaned in pleasure. I heard Piffik's throaty laugh in the background.

"Can you open your eyes, Zren? Siba wants to look at you." I opened my mouth instead and Rygee spooned in more broth. There was a cool dry hand on my forehead—Siba. I could smell the medicinals on her skin. Well good then, Piffik, Rygee, and

Siba were here. I had nothing to worry about. I let myself sink into nothingness.

***

I drifted awake. Oh, my bladder was uncomfortably full. I should get up and take care of it, I thought. Maybe later. I drifted off.

***

Gentle hands rolled me to the side and then the other. Someone was changing the sheets under me. I thought to reach for the blanket and realized I was naked. I tried to think of the word for shirt but my head hurt too much. "Sh-h-h-h-h."

"That's right, shh-h-h-h-h." Hands cupped the back of my head and I felt a shirt eased over gently. "Rest, Zren. I want you to do nothing but rest, eat, and call me the next time you need to use the chamber pot." Siba laughed drily.

I blushed. Or I would have if my head would not have hurt so much.

"I'm just teasing you. You gave us all quite a scare." A pause. "Now I want you to take a big drink of this," she held a cup to my lips, "and a deep sniff of this," some smoky thing under my nose, "and then sleep as long as you can. Someone will always be here with you, all right?"

***

I smelled food. Chicken stew. I felt someone sitting on the edge of the bed and I popped open my mouth. Tiju Tia laughed, and I snapped my mouth shut and scowled.

"Zren, can you open your eyes for a moment?"

I tried, I truly tried. But the light in the room was too bright and I squinted, then closed them again.

"No." I repeated, "No."

"That's fine. Siba was just hoping to get a look at your eyes." Another pause. "I brought some stew, can you eat?"

"Did you cook it?" I whispered.

Tiju Tia laughed again. "You're a survivor. No. Rygee made it but Siba put something in it to help you heal. Let us prop you up and you can try to eat something."

I felt large hands around my ribs strong arming me into an upright position. *That wasn't Tiju Tia.*

"Yazza! Why haven't they been feeding you? I could throw you over my shoulder and toss you out for chicken scraps."

I pulled an eye open. "Josef?"

"No, I'm Nelo. Of course, it is Josef, who else is this pretty?"

I cracked my lips for a smile and Tiju Tia shoved a spoonful in. I grimaced. It didn't taste like Rygee's cooking.

"That's the medicine," Siba said apologetically. "I need you to eat the entire bowlful."

I wanted to tell her I grew up in Lowertown with never enough food, of course I was going to eat the entire bowlful. But then I forgot the words, and then I forgot to open my mouth, and then I forgot to stay awake.

***

I slept for a long, long time. Sometimes I would hear movement around me changing the sheets but most of the time I just sensed light and dark across my closed eyelids. Once I woke up, it was night, and I needed the chain commode. I pushed my legs to the side of the bed and used the headboard to pull myself to my feet. I was woozy, but I could almost see where I needed to go. I took three steps and crashed to the floor. Strong arms picked me up under my shoulders.

"Solkka?" I choked out.

"It's just Piffik. I'm sorry, I fell asleep. What do you need, Zren?"

I realized I could never walk to the chain commode. "Chamber pot."

After Piffik had shoved it back under the bed, he washed his hands and brought me a cup of water.

"What's wrong with me?" I croaked out.

"Siba's aunt, the healer, do you remember her? She said your brain has swollen from your fight at Manumina, and they need to keep you very still and quiet until it heals."

"But I was fine yesterday. I walked from the shepherd's cottage," I explained.

There was a long pause. "Actually, Zren, you have been out of it for eleven days. We feed you when we can, but you are barely staying with us long enough to swallow the medicine. You get any thinner, and Solkka is not going to be able to find you in your bed."

"Eleven days? I've lost eleven days?" I whispered.

"Tiju Tia says this is not the first time you have had your brain rattled so badly. If it is like the horsebreakers, Rygee says, the more this happens, the worse each one gets. It is why everyone is so careful now to keep you quiet and still so you can heal as much as you can."

"But eleven days?" I repeated.

"If it's any consolation, you haven't missed much." Piffik explained how the goats had escaped twice. How most of the Wrens rejected their new homes because they felt they were being treated like little children. "Siba tried to explain to the Conrosans, that to grow up in Kerek City means your childhood is stolen and the Wrens had lived as adults, but…"

He went on to say someone, he wasn't sure who, but he suspected Falan, emptied out a storage shed. Nelo and Arden had scavenged about for wood in the stables and other sheds and built beds for all the Wrens. Callis and Linna had pieced together blankets and quilts. Now they were staying in the shed together and eating at Rygee's kitchen.

"The Wrens do as they please for now, Zren, and most of them sleep as much as you do. I think they finally feel safe enough."

Piffik went on to say how one day he had been setting up his new workshop in one of the extra tackrooms in the stables when Rell and her brother Dylis had come to visit. But she had been only home in Vikland for four days and then had to go back to Kerek. She was currently assigned to Evensong as a member of the Vikland Diplo with the Matasi occupiers and Kereki owners. It was a safer job than it sounded, much safer than her role as a bowmaster, but she wouldn't be able to leave Kerek for a while.

"We tried to wake you, but you weren't having any of it. She was riding that fine Viklander horse you found for her. She calls her horse, 'Wishes.' She said to tell you she is only a pony ride away and to let her know when you are well enough so she can teach you how to sit a horse properly."

He paused a long time, and I thought there was something else he should be telling me but I couldn't remember what it was. Then he started talking about the Council of Wisdom and how they were going to send a group to the Empress to ask for more land and building supplies, except they were worried she would tell them to go back to Kerek. Then what would they do?

He finished by telling me Nelo and Inezi were back from Juisiti where some clerk helped them find the Viklander softfoot, Rani. In turn, Rani confirmed the rumor the Wrens had heard in Sary. The Matasi army had taken over Manumina and fortified it as a garrison. "Nelo tried to leave Inezi with Rani. Nelo said he would bring him Therin as well, but Rani didn't understand the real issue—we have no life to offer them—and said they were free to join us if they wished."

"I thought you said nothing happened." I tipped my head to the side and the room spun. "Who has been taking care of me?"

"You don't need much. But the Wrens have been sitting with you every night so Siba or her aunt can go home and take care of themselves."

"Tiju Tia was going to Juisiti. I was going to go with her." I remembered.

"She did. Rell needed to travel back to Juisiti. We talked it over and Tiju Tia and I went with her so Rell could serve as our interpreter and our guide. Rell took us to the councilor we needed to see. She taught me how to act and what to say so we would be heard as friends of the empire and not as supplicants." He paused. "We must wait two fortnights for both of us to beg for help from the Empress. It will be the beginning of the Wet, so we will almost certainly be stuck here for another year." He shrugged. "But we'll use the Wet to build what we need. Whether we stay or go, we'll need to prepare."

Piffik leaned in to look at me. "I think I've talked enough. You need to go back to sleep. I've missed you. We all have. Come back to us when you are ready, but come back to us."

I smiled. I was going to tell him how much I missed him too, but I was already drifting off to sleep. *I'll tell him in the morning,* I promised myself.

CHAPTER 26

ATTEMPTED MURDER

I dreamed someone sat gently on the edge of the bed. I thought I should wake up and roll over on to my back, but it felt better to lie still. Soon, I felt long legs tuck in carefully behind me and an arm curve gently over my waist. I smiled to myself and snuggled tight against the bare chest behind me. Solkka was here. He would watch over me. I was safe. This was a wonderful dream.

Tiju Tia brought the first meal. I still felt woozy, but I thought it was more from the medicine than feeling like my brain was going to fall out of my head.

"Can you talk or do you want to listen?" she began.

"Listen," I said promptly and reached for the food.

"So I went to Juisiti with Piffik and Rell. I am sorry I could not wait for you. We have our meetings scheduled to be heard before the Empress and her Witnesses. In two fortnights, the Council of Wisdom will petition the Empress for a bigger home for the refugees. I have asked to have Ngahuru, a diplomat of the King of the West Islands, be heard on the same day for a repayment of the life debt for help and assistance during the war. It will be to settle a future on the Wrens. Neither Piffik nor I spoke for you. I believe you have not yet decided, and neither of us will presume to know what is best for you." She waited for me to speak, but I kept eating.

She gave an exasperated grin. "Piffik and Rell are going to marry."

I swallowed hastily. "Well, that's about time! Wait! Is Rell here? For good?"

Tiju Tia shook her head. "Rell is still in Kerek, serving at the whim of the Empress. But the Viklanders look at marriage differently than the Conrosans do. Zren, you should know Piffik is penniless. He was never wealthy in Manumina but the war and my Wrens have cost him all his coin. He felt he couldn't offer her enough." She bit her lower lip pensively. "However, Rell's father is also a man who made his own way and he has offered Piffik an opportunity."

I put my bowl down. "I'm not going to like this, am I?"

"I don't know." She bobbed her head. "The Huena family has more business than they can manage. Their inn is situated in a very good location between Juisiti and the entire southwest district. Rell's father says he grew up as the son of a hostler and has learned to be an innkeeper—he knows little of building. So the

Huenas would like to have a second inn and put Piffik in charge of building it. In addition, they want to build the inn in the West Islands style with wet rooms attached to the sleeping rooms and not at the end of the hall as they are in most of Vikland. Piffik would be in charge of those doing the building, ordering supplies, inspecting the workings, and keeping everyone busy as they earn the Huena coin."

"Piffik would leave here."

"Yes."

"He would be good at this." I thought carefully. "He has already said yes, hasn't he?"

"He has. He is taking my oldest Wrens with him so they can earn wages while they are waiting to hear from the Empress. Callis will stay here to learn to be a healer from Siba and Bett. Arden will stay to be a manabout for the Conrosans. Therin is too young and is staying here. As well as Inezi. They will stay with me and learn to read and write. I will practice my Conrosan in preparation for a future posting by my King."

"I could find Solkka," I said abruptly.

"You could. But you might want to heal a bit more first."

"You know where he is." It wasn't a question.

"I do. When Piffik, Rell, and I went to Juisiti we asked after Quan and Solkka. Quan is a Vikland softfoot and Solkka in the Diplo, so they would not tell us of their whereabouts. But Rell was able to learn from friends, Solkka is on leave to heal at his family's coffee farm."

I fell forward with a groan on to the blankets. "Solkka has said that's seven days' ride from Juisiti and Juisiti is another day from here. I could never sit a horse so long!"

"Ah, Zren, how you tug on my heart. Well, it is no secret I wish to see Jenny again." She stood up and reached for my empty bowl. "You continue to get better, and I will formally write the Ulani family and request permission to visit."

I thought I would be too excited to sleep after that, but Siba must have put better tasting medicine in the soup. I was asleep before Tiju Tia ever left the room.

***

Later, Siba brought my soup and medicine separately. For a change she didn't have to wake me and she smiled.

"This looks promising."

"I talked to Tiju Tia earlier. She said all the Wrens except for Callis and Arden are moving to Axefield with Piffik." I reached out for the bowl. *Mmm, noodles. My favorite.*

Siba talked while I ate. She told me of the plans for the new inn. How Piffik was excited, and she was pleased for him, but she would miss him. How well Rell looked when she was here. How Siba had doused me with a strong dose of sleeping medicine not half a decon before Rell and her brother arrived and they could not wake me. But Rell had said it was just an opportunity to come back again. How the Wrens seemed so much older than the Conrosans the same age and it caused hard feelings. The Wrens wanted to be treated as men and women and had the experiences of men and women, but…

"My fellow Conrosans weren't as welcoming to the Wrens as I wish they would have been. Sometimes it is hard to explain what the right thing to do is when it is right in front of you."

I handed her the empty soup bowl.

"Goodness, Zren, did you even see the noodles before you swallowed them?"

"I'm catching up. I heard you didn't feed me for eleven days." I put a little whine in my voice to see if Siba would look guilty. She didn't.

"You worried us." Siba nodded. "The Wrens would come out in the morning saying you did not move all night. Callis would bring in her looking glass so she could see your breath on it." She put down the empty bowl and gave me a small cup. "We fed you enough to keep you alive. Broth mainly. Here's the medicine. Or do you think you will sleep without it?"

"Without it. I think that's the stuff making me woozy. It gives me good dreams though."

She smiled. "Good. Let's try a night without the medicine. Tomorrow, we will get you up for a little bit and see how you feel. But if you cannot sleep because of pain or a headache, just send your Wren to find me."

Siba was just leaving the room when Arden and Mother stopped by.

"Hey, I'm the one that gets to lose a night's sleep by watching you tonight. But Inezi just told me Piffik needs to see me right away. I'll be back, but you'll probably be asleep first."

"I usually am," I agreed cheerfully. I pushed myself down into the bedclothes and let myself relax.

***

I started to slide towards wakefulness when I felt a knee on the bed, but then just let myself sink deeper into sleep. *It's a dream, a very nice dream*, I told myself. Warmth and softness covered my head. Through a fog of sleep I felt a weight on my chest and pressure on my face. The pressure deepened and soon I was suffocating. I fought myself awake. My arms were pinned by my sides in the bedclothes and the pillow was pressing down harder. My healing collarbone sent jolts of pain through me, and I roared in pain and frustration at my inability to fight back. Fabric pushed in my open mouth and I bucked my hips to try to dislodge the body sitting on my chest. I struggled to breathe. Sparks flashed behind my eyelids.

I heard a growl.

"Bite and roll!" Arden's voice. A cry of pain as dog and a body rolled off the bed and on to the floor.

I shoved the pillow off my face and panted in fresh air. "I hurt, I hurt, I hurt."

Arden was standing over someone with his dagger pulled. His dog stood stiff-legged, a low throaty growl rolling out softly.

"Call it off." I didn't recognize the harsh voice.

"She. Mother is a lovely bitch, which I cannot say the same for you. Why were you trying to murder Zren?" Arden spoke so casually, the hateful words sounded even nastier.

Nothing.

"I've seen Mother eat the face off a Kereki soldier when we couldn't find food for four days. I could see if it's a skill she still remembers." Arden sounded nonchalant. I couldn't tell if he was truthful. I hoped not.

Nothing.

Arden gave a soft chirp and Mother crouched, nearly quivering with anticipation.

"Stop!" Inezi scrambled back against the wall and into my field of vision. "I wasn't trying to murder Zren. It was supposed to look like he died in his sleep. He's been so close to death, no one would question it."

Arden held his palm level to the floor and whispered softly. Mother stretched out beside him, still alert but lying flat. He pointed his dagger at Inezi.

"You sent me all over this place looking for Piffik so no one would be in here. You thought Zren would be so drugged, he couldn't fight back."

The silence went on and on. Finally, Arden blew out an exasperated breath. "Go. Just go. You're a bigger fool than I imagined, but you will have to live with the shame of this."

He paused. "I will not say anything to Nelo until midday tomorrow. Zren, once his body is talking to his brain again, may have another idea, but for now, this is the grace I can give you."

I rolled over to my side now that my neck and shoulder had stopped throbbing. Through my haze of pain, I could see Inezi sitting on the floor against the wall. She was dressed in the shapeless baggy men's clothes of Kerek, her hair twisted back.

Even without my injuries, she would have been stronger and taller than I was, and I couldn't think for a moment of what I had ever done to her to deserve to die at her hands. But the look on her face was not shame, or sorrow, or soft misery. It was hatred and desperation muddied into fury. If I was Arden? I would be sleeping with one eye open for a very long time.

Inezi pushed herself to her feet and Mother rose as well, stiff-legged and watchful. No one else moved or spoke until Inezi had crossed the room and walked out the door.

Arden stood facing the wall where she had been, head tilted down as we listened to her continue to walk down the hall and out of the infirmary. When the door slammed, Mother flopped to the floor and put her head on her paws.

"Thank you," I croaked out.

"Well, don't thank me yet." He sheathed his knife and turned to face me. "I think you need to know what I have done. You played a part for us without your consent or knowledge and it nearly killed you." He paused. "Is this a story you wish to hear now? Or do you wish to sleep and Nelo and I will come tell you together tomorrow?"

I lightly touched my aching collarbone. "I hurt too much to sleep." I patted the bed beside me. "Come tell me a story."

Arden rolled his eyes but sat down on the bed next to me.

"You know Inezi had feelings for Nelo? Of course, you did. Everyone knew," he responded drily. "We knew, I mean, the Wrens, Nelo wasn't interested in Inezi, and he was kindly waiting for it to pass. This in itself are the first two miracles of the Lost God," he flashed his odd smile so I knew he was telling me a joke, "First, that anyone could see beyond Nelo's hard unhandsome face, and second, Nelo, our Nelo, could respond with kindness." He sobered and blew out a hard breath.

"But Inezi didn't understand the difference between kindness and affection. Her actions only grew worse. Nelo has described the ride from here to Axefield as the worst day of his life." Arden looked at me. "Including the time during the war when he was trapped in a hayloft with Viklander maps and plans. There were Kereki soldiers who came into the barn after him to get out of the rain and then stayed down below for decons playing dice."

Nelo had explained to her on the ride to Axefield, he had no feelings for her beyond respect for her woodsman skills and as a fellow softfoot. She in turn, told him ever more ominous stories of her talents with knife and bow.

"Now Nelo knew Trouble was not only trailing Inezi, but Oro and Linna as well. Nelo knew Oro had feelings for Linna. It was why Tiju Tia replaced him with you for a time or two on the rag and bone cart, Zren. Oro would talk with Linna in her shop and with his Viklander face, Tiju Tia thought it put the Wrens in danger." Arden shrugged.

"No one thought it was more than that—even though she had brought him with her when we left Kerek City. We only thought each Wren had passed along a message of hope and escape for the next one. Ones we knew and trusted. Nothing more, nothing less. But then the group reached Juisiti. After Nelo and the others met with Rani the softfoot and shared our information, Oro and Linna stated they were in Juisiti to register their marriage."

I gasped. "Oro and Linna? But they're children!"

"According to the Vikland court of records, Oro is twenty-one and Linna is nineteen, which makes both of them older than I am, Zren," Arden said drily. "Nelo and Kid served as not so willing witnesses." He let out a long breath. "But this is not the story I meant to tell tonight."

"Go on." I flopped my wrist at him.

"When they all returned, Nelo told Josef and me everything which happened at Juisiti. He also told us of his concern that Inezi had grown too fond of killing during the war. His rejection of her had drawn such an odd response he felt she would cause trouble. In the time since then and now, her behavior has grown so strange, Tiju Tia has talked with her. Others too—from the Council of Wisdom—about their way of non-violence and if she wishes to remain, she must abide by it. But Nelo would not let them send her away because he said we did not understand the horror of her life."

Arden gave me a long look. "We all grew up in Kerek City, Zren. We do not know horror?" He huffed. "Nelo is my friend, if he says he is not worried, then I must believe one of two things. Either he is not worried, or I am not a friend he can trust with the truth." He sounded like he was trying to convince himself.

Arden continued, "One night Nelo was asleep in his bed in the bunkhouse when he heard someone enter the room. It was Inezi, carrying a knife. He did not wait to find out what she would do but climbed out the open window and stayed the night with me and Mother in the loft above the stables. We knew she was afraid of Mother—all dogs—and would not bother him the rest of the night. I told him he could stay with me and whatever he needed to say, I would agree it was true. But he knew I loved another," Arden gave me a pointed look, "the *child* that I am—and said he did not wish to waste our friendship on a lie. So we planned another way, but one without your permission."

He sighed and looked at the wall for the next part. "Callis said you did not respond to anything during the night. So Nelo started to sleep with you in your bed. Then we had the Wrens who had the watch of you carry tales to Inezi. They said she would also casually pass by late at night, which was what we wanted, to see you and Nelo in bed asleep. But we never imagined she would try to murder you in her mistaken belief that Nelo would turn to her in his grief and sorrow." He fell silent.

"And now she hates you," I said gently. "I saw the look she gave you."

"She has hated me for a long while. I am not sure why or what I have done. Three times I have found poisoned meat by the trails where Mother and I walk early in the mornings. Thankfully, my dog has learned from her earliest days in Kerek City only to eat food that comes from my hand. It has saved her life more than a handful of times."

"Now what happens?" I asked.

"Tomorrow I will tell Nelo what has happened to you. But not until midday as I promised. Inezi will either confess her foolishness to him, which I do not believe, or she will take a horse and leave before I speak to Nelo.

"She has no future here at Rishka. None of us do. She is half Matasi. Whether she goes to Manumina, which is now a Matasi garrison, and finds work as a scout, or to Juisiti and finds something there, she will have more of a life than she will here. Nelo will leave in a few days to work with Piffik at Axefield, and I will remain here to care for the animals."

I pleated the edges of the blanket between my fingers. "Why *are* you staying here? I've seen the things you built at your house in Cloa. Linna says you can do whatever you set your mind to. Piffik could use a good carpenter like you, and you would be with all the rest of the Wrens at Axefield."

He looked at me sadly. "Ah, Zren." He stood up from the bed and tossed his brown braid over his shoulder. "I only promised to tell you one story tonight." He paused. "Again I ask for your forgiveness. We never meant to put your life in danger. Though we knew Inezi was no longer in her right mind, and I should have thought it through more carefully." He gave me a wry smile, "Try to sleep. Mother and I will watch over you."

Perhaps I had been close to death too many times.

Perhaps I could... Suddenly, I realized Arden was finally sharing that he was so much more than a thick-skulled thief from

Kerek City. I smiled to myself at his trust in me. In return, I could trust Arden and Mother with my life.

I slept.

MYSTERIES OF THE HEART

Arden and Mother were gone when I woke up. Dica was in the chair curled up, watching me.

"Good morning." I yawned. "Or did I sleep until after midday?"

Her grave face broke into a shy smile. "It's still morning and your first meal will be coming soon."

"So, I went to sleep with Mother watching me and wake up to you watching me." I tried to make her smile again. "I much rather wake up to your face." It worked. The smile was bigger and accompanied by a yawn.

"Josef came by my bed in the night and said I could either help gather goats in the dark, or I could take Arden's watch over you and he and that miracle dog of his could herd them all in and none of the Wrens would need to trip over a tree root in the dark. So here I am."

"Ah. Wise choice. I am much easier to care for than a herd of goats. I smell better too." Her smile grew wider. "So tell me, Dica. What's been going on in the world since I have been stuck in this room with only one wall of windows and no one to tell me stories?"

"I know better," she said archly. "All you do is eat and talk according to Rygee."

"Are you working in the kitchens now? How do you like that?"

She shrugged. "I was a maid at Regno during the war. The work is different, but everyone still tells me what to do. I want to learn to read and write in Vik and count their coin so I can get a position in a shop like Falan or Linna had as their maskovesto in Kerek."

We were interrupted by Rygee carrying in a plate of greens and scrambled eggs. He lifted a brow at Dica.

"So now I know why you didn't show yourself in the kitchens this morning. And on the day I am teaching fingersweets." He shook his head in mock sadness. "I know how much you like sampling our efforts."

Dica had a concerned look on her face. Rygee laughed. "Go ahead, I'll feed Zren and you can catch up to the others. They are still only mixing their doughs."

Dica left in a hurry, calling back over her shoulder, "Bye, Zren!"

Rygee handed me the plate. "So even in the infirmary, you cause the Wrens trouble."

I jerked up my head. "You heard?"

He stood looking at me. "No, but now you have me curious. What happened?"

I thought over the night's events as I started eating and realized I had not promised silence on anything. And it was my story to tell after all. I had been the one nearly killed by my pillow. I started with Nelo and Inezi, talked right through Arden and Mother saving my life, and then Dica taking Arden's place so the goats could be gathered and returned to their pasture.

"The goats were never out, Zren." He held up his hand. "At least not to my knowledge."

Rygee kept talking and I thought about his words. Suddenly I wondered if Arden's words hadn't been meant for Inezi at all, but for me. Arden wanted *me* to believe he would do nothing. He wanted *me* to think Inezi would confess and leave and build a life somewhere else. While in reality, Arden never intended for her to leave on her own. I remembered the look she had given him as she had skulked out of the room at the point of his knife. He had even noted she had hated him for a while now but claimed he didn't know why. I wondered how long Arden had been looking over his shoulder, trying to avoid trouble. Rygee didn't grow up in Lowertown. He didn't understand as Arden and I and the rest of the Wrens did, you get rid of the threat before it sneaks up on you unaware. What was Arden planning to do?

I had to get up and out of there before Arden did something that would follow him the rest of his life. I had made a mistake with Bitterboots. He did not need to make a mistake with Inezi. I shoveled in the eggs as fast as I could. Rygee saw me.

"Slow down, Zren. You'll choke on your food."

"Rygee, can you get me Chul's cane from across the room?" He did so and I finished the eggs. I slid my legs over the side of the bed and pulled myself up. The room spun, but I was on my feet. I reached for my pants on the chair near the bed.

"I know Siba said she was going to have you get up today, but are you sure you want to do this now?"

"I am. It's really important, Rygee. Do you know where Arden is?" I begged.

"I haven't seen him, but I am up before most people to start the bakery ovens."

"I need to get to the stables. Can you help?" I threw a shirt over my head and it nearly swallowed me. "Great stars, Rygee, did Siba put your laundry in here for me?" I groused.

He put his arm around me as we moved slowly to the door. "That's your own shirt you're wearing, so that's how weak and frail you have become. But I just want you to know, Zren, if Siba or her aunt comes by, I am going to swear you threatened me with my life to help you. You'll need to look better than you do now to make it convincing."

"I agree." And then I couldn't talk anymore because all my effort was in standing upright and moving forward. By the time we reached the stables, I was a sweaty mess. But my eyes were still focusing clearly, and my collarbone only ached and not throbbed. I didn't recognize any of the stablehands. I wondered whatever happened to Vigdis.

"Say, have any of you seen the Wrens this morning?" They looked at each other and shook their heads. I looked down the row of horse stalls. "Are you missing any horses?" *Please say no,* I begged silently. Rygee said nothing, just stood quietly watching me.

"One. Old Dris. But we don't worry about her. She comes to find her oats every night. Sometimes the goatherds use her when the goats are out. She's calm that way."

I blew out a breath. Where else could I look? Maybe I should find Tiju Tia, I thought absently. I lurched out into the sunlight and saw Piffik walking across the courtyard.

"Piffik!" I called and then stood still and swayed a bit. He hurried over.

Rygee looked at me. "I need to get back to the Wrens before they burn up my kitchens. Should I send someone to you?" I shook my head, and he gave me one last considering look before he nodded to Piffik and walked away.

"Zren! It's great to see you out! How are you feeling?" He gave me a wide grin.

"I'm fine. Where's Nelo? Where's Josef? Where's Arden and that dog of his?" I wanted to cry in frustration.

Piffik pulled back in surprise. "Nelo is working with me in the woodworking shop." He paused to consider. "I am not sure where the others are, although I heard the goats got out of their fencing again during the night. You could check there, or the beds in the Wrens' nest if the boys were up half the night chasing the goats home."

Nelo was with Piffik. Of course, he was. And if I went to the Wrens' bunkhouse, I would find Josef asleep or visiting with the others. I leaned on Chul's cane as I stood on my wobbly legs and breathed deeply. *I am a fool,* I told myself. I immediately assumed the worst. "I'm sorry I overreacted. I'll come see what you are working on in the workshop."

As we slowly made our way across, Piffik asked, "Are you sure you are ready for this?"

"I'll find out soon enough. But I need to get out of bed or I will forget how to walk and then how will I learn what is going on in the world? The Wrens sit with me at night, but none of them know how to tell a proper story—they leave out all the best parts." I waited a long moment. "Just like you do. You spent an entire night with me and never said a word about you marrying Rell. I had to hear it from Tiju Tia."

He laughed easily. "That's because I haven't married her yet. I am only being given the chance to prove I am worthy," he paused, "to gaze in her direction." He cast his eyes sideways at me to catch my reaction. He laughed at my expression.

"You aren't upset about it?"

Piffik stopped. "If her parents asked me to fight a Vikland warrior and win, or sail to the West Islands and forge a dagger that could never dull, or cross the Silver Mountains and discuss wisdom and parables from the Matasi God? Then yes, I would be worried I am asked to do more than I am capable of.

"But running a crew to build an inn which is nothing more than an oversized house, sorting out people and materials to come together at the right time? That is no different than building and maintaining Manumina, or keeping the Wrens alive when they throw themselves in danger every day. Or teaching the apprentices and journeymen and other youth I know to grow into men, including my brother Zadah, before he sailed the great seas, and my friend Zren Janin, who is still an unworthy suitor for my sister." He grinned. "This is nothing more than a Conrosan fairy tale come to life."

We entered the woodshop where several youths were working in the various areas. Piffik had wasted no time in retrieving the wagons we had left behind at the shepherd's cottage and rebuilding his workshop here. He walked through easily and slowly, looking at each person's work, praising one, pointing out an opportunity to another. Most of these girls and boys were the same ages as the youngest Wrens, only two of them were as old as Nelo.

I hobbled over to Nelo and watched him work.

"Do you like this?" I asked. "I always found it relaxing, and I liked the feeling of seeing something beautiful I had made."

Nelo grimaced. "I do like it. But I am not yet at the stage where I see something beautiful." He looked at me thoughtfully. "You did not crawl from your bed to come admire my woodworking skills." He put down his tools and defensively crossed his arms over his chest.

"Do you know where Arden and Josef are?"

"Yes." He seemed surprised. "The goats got out during the night. They are using Mother to chase down some strays and said they would go rabbit hunting if there was time. I asked if they needed me to go with them. Josef said I may need to be your nursemaid tonight if they get back too late."

"Horses?"

"They were on foot as far as I know." He shrugged. "It makes it easier to track the goats."

"There's one horse missing—Old Dris." I watched him carefully to see his reaction.

Nelo cocked an eyebrow. "I'm standing in front of you, Zren, I'm not riding her."

I scowled. "Do you know where Inezi is?"

"No." He looked me steadily in the face. "And for that, I am heartily glad. I plan to ride to Juisiti soon and beg Kern or Rani or whoever is in charge of Vikland's softfoots now, to come take her away. She is Vikland's responsibility and not ours. I only did her the kindness because of what would happen to her if we had stolen horses and she was left behind to be punished."

A small smile curved at the edge of his mouth. "I have told the other Wrens countless times, kindness only comes back to haunt us, and see? I am living evidence. This should have happened to Josef. He is always promising kindness and more to pretty girls."

I snorted and ducked my head to hide my face. Nelo picked up his tools again, and I listened to the soft rasp, rasp, rasp, of the plane against the wood.

I pushed my luck further. "I heard you stood as Witness to Oro and Linna's wedding."

A look of hurt and sadness filled his face. "I did, and I am full sorry for it. I like Oro, don't get me wrong. He has proved himself to be a friend to the Wrens even when his Viklander face could do him harm. He is tall and handsome and sets the moon in the sky for Linna. He is older and grew up in a proper house and knows the pretty words to say so she will smile." He put down his tools and looked at me. "But there was another who also wanted to do the same for her, or would have if she asked. And the other, I count closer than a brother." He paused a long time as if he was trying to decide something.

He blew out a noisy breath. "Before I agreed to stand Witness for her, I took her aside and asked if she was sure. If she knew of another who loved her, would she wait a year or a while longer to listen to *his* heart and be sure of her feelings?"

I looked at him surprised. This was a Nelo I did not know. "What did she say?"

"She said she knew I was talking of Arden. She admired him as brave and clever. She was astonished at how easily he learned things if he was given the tools and the teachers, and could make things just by her descriptions, and could figure out an answer to any dilemma. She said she felt blessed to call him a friend and she would trust him with her life. She said she had never known him as a child thief in Kerek City, and so from the very beginning she had thought of him as a man and not as one younger. But she told me she knew the difference. She had loved Oro since her days in Kerek City and wanted to spend her life with him."

He lifted his shoulders and dropped them. "What else could I say? I knew Arden would think I betrayed him, but she said she knew the difference between her feelings for Oro and those for Arden."

I rocked back and grabbed the edge of the table for balance. "So *that's* why he is staying here and not moving with the rest of you to Axefield? He doesn't want to see Linna every day with Oro?"

"Well, it's not because he likes the smell of goats," Nelo replied sarcastically.

"Ah, there's the Nelo I know." I pushed myself up. I needed to go back to the infirmary. My head was spinning with too much information. Now I finally understood what Siba Namikk had been telling me a season ago when she saw Arden and Linna and Oro colliding as they discovered and grew into their feelings. I needed a nap to sort it all through. "When Arden returns from rabbit hunting or stray goat chasing, will you ask him to come visit me?"

Nelo shot me a hard look. "You won't say anything."

"Of course not, I just want to ask him if he was successful enough I could bother Rygee into making me a rabbit pie."

Nelo laughed. "It is good to have you back with us. We—I have missed you."

"It is good to be missed," I said solemnly.

I was dragging my decrepit body across the yard looking forward to a long nap and a good gossip with anyone who would stop by when I heard Mother bark. Around the corner came Josef leading two does on short ropes, a quiver over his shoulder, and a short bow in his other hand. Beside him, Arden had four fat rabbits dangling from his left hand, and the billy goat following in a harness in his right. Mother was dancing between them keeping the billy on his own four feet away from the does.

"Zren!" Arden called cheerfully. "And here we have the third miracle of the Lost God today. First, we find the billy who has led these two lovely does astray with his wicked ways, then we find enough rabbits for Rygee to make a stew for us, and the greatest miracle is you are up and standing like the King in his court!"

Both men walked up to me with huge grins.

"Truly, it is good to see you on your feet." Josef smiled. "How do you feel?"

"Rough, but glad to be alive."

Josef cocked his head, "You look roughly alive."

I grimaced. "I will walk with you if you go slowly enough. I need to remember what it was like before I decided to live as a princess in her bed looking at life through a window."

We ambled over to the goat enclosure, the two chattering about the goats, discovering the stray was the billy goat.

"To be truthful, if it would have been one doe, I might have given her up as lost. But with no billy, there are no kids, and with no kids, there is no milk and cheese, and with no milk or cheese, well, you understand better than most, Zren." Arden shot me a sly look.

I held the gate while Arden kneed him in and took off the harness. The billy frisked about in the pasture while we examined the fencing. It was intact all around. I was as puzzled as the others as we tried to figure out how the escape could have happened. Josef walked the does over to the other area and slipped them in their field. They rejoined their sisters in the shade of the loafing shed, and the three of us leaned on the fence and watched them for a while.

Arden pushed himself off the gate. "I'll take these rabbits to Rygee and stay to skin them for him." He looked at me. "Truly, it is good to see you up and out again."

I watched him as he walked away, trying to see him as Linna had seen him. His long brown hair in a loose braid swinging between his shoulder blades. His shirt belted easily about his lean waist. I smiled and turned to Josef who grinned back at me.

"You would do anything for Nelo, wouldn't you?" I cut him off from making a smart remark.

His grin fell. "What happened to Nelo?"

"Nothing. But there is a horse and a girl missing."

Josef laughed. "Zren, I have spent half the night chasing goats and all morning hunting rabbits. I am going to wash the stink of the day off and then sleep for a day and a night. If you wish, wake me for Rygee's stew. Otherwise, I will see you tomorrow." He waved at me and headed off to the storage shed which the Wrens had turned into their home.

I was tired as well. I may have been standing like a king in my court as Arden had said, but all was not well in my kingdom. I headed back to the infirmary for a long nap and a hard think.

Old Dris came home alone at sunset for her oats. No saddle, no bridle, no leading rope. Just as if she had wandered out of her stall before daylight and then wandered home again.

CHAPTER 28

BACK TO A DIFFERENT BEGINNING

Inezi missing from the refugee camp seemed to be a puzzle only to me. The more questions I asked, the less people were willing to talk to me about it. The Conrosans accepted the missing travel bag and bedroll as a woman who didn't like the refugee camp and walked her way to a better life somewhere else.

The Wrens would give me a blank look and say, "She's gone. She was unhappy and she's gone."

Even Tiju Tia, before she left for Axefield, would change the subject when I brought it up. "Zren, you didn't give her a moment of your time while she was here, why all the attention now?"

And maybe, maybe it wasn't only Inezi. Maybe it was because I wanted to know *how* they did it. This wasn't like my clumsy efforts to remove Mouser from being a threat to us on the Northern Track. This was finesse and skill and a disappearance under the noses of hundreds of people without a drop of blood in sight. Was this how Arden, or Arden and Josef, or Arden and Josef and Nelo had survived the war? I couldn't even figure out how many or which ones were involved! I decided tussling with this mystery was the best way to get me out of the infirmary and back into the world.

I started with the attack on me. Inezi had been escalating in her trauma and the others had known her to be a harm to others and possibly to herself. The Wrens, well truthfully, Falan, had refused to let Inezi move into the shed the Wrens had converted into a bunkhouse. Falan said there was no room. The Wrens had put truth behind their words as Arden and Mother lived in the storage area above the stables. When Oro and Linna had returned after their marriage, the couple gathered their belongings without staying even one night, and moved to Axefield. I wasn't sure where Inezi had been sleeping. When I asked, I received shrugs of indifference.

I hadn't taken the sleeping medicine the night she tried to suffocate me, even though I knew it gave me such good dreams. And if I *had* taken the potion that night, I would have just thought Inezi suffocating me with a pillow was a dream right up until I was dead. But Inezi didn't know I hadn't taken the medicine.

Inezi did know it was Arden on watch that night because she sent him chasing after Piffik. All the Wrens looked up to Piffik as much as I did, and if he said he needed them, they would search all night. Did she deliberately choose to hurt me on the night Arden was on watch because of Mother? She could say later everyone knew she was afraid of dogs.

I made a plan. If Inezi had suffered Kereki metal poisoning, I would find out how they did it. I mapped out the estate and started with the hilliest sides first. Using Chul's old cane, I walked to the top of the highest point I could manage. Gasping and sweaty, I nearly crawled to the top, an easy walk for someone else. From the summit, I turned in every direction looking for something out of place: an area grazed short, stakes for the goats, a cage or net proving the rabbits were not wild. I tried different angles and times of day, trying to catch a glimpse of metal from a half buried bridle, an iron ring on a leading rope, disturbed earth from a shallow grave.

When that was unsuccessful, I tried to imagine how far the murderers would have been able to go if they had been able to leave earlier in the night. What if Dica had been wrong about the time Josef woke her to take Arden's place? What if it had been closer to dusk than dawn and she could have slept most of the night in the chair?

I borrowed Bess, the plow horse with such a gentle gait it was like riding on a bed. I packed a midday and ambled further away looking in hidden ravines, kicking at dirt mounds—and usually falling over—and searching for tracks that didn't belong.

I realized hunting for a grave was too random. Whoever had killed Inezi would not have been so careless. So I tried to imagine how they did it. Did Nelo give her the sleeping potion meant for me? Did Josef whisper pretty words in her ear and then tap her on the head? I tried to imagine Old Dris loaded with Inezi and a cage with four rabbits. Josef carrying a bow and a quiver full of arrows, and Arden leading two does and a billy into the hills so they could come back a half day later and say it couldn't possibly have been them. I pestered the manabouts and goatherds with questions.

But I knew how contrary the billy goat could be, and I couldn't imagine a scenario where it would have been an easy three decon walk out, a murder and a burial, and an easy three decon walk back, killing the rabbits on the way.

Could Nelo have taken part? Could all of them have ridden out and dug the grave and then Nelo returned with the horses and showed up in Piffik's shop all before the first meal of the day? No. That didn't work either. Nelo had not been able to hide his surprise when I asked him if he knew where Josef and Arden were. He didn't smell like horse, and he didn't look like he had been up all night. And why bring back the horses but leave Old Dris to find her way home alone?

I knew Nelo remembered Mouser. He had said so when we were stripping the bodies at the burned out Earles garrison. Josef and Arden may have been too young, but they had grown up in

Lowertown or nearby. They had all the knowledge to do this, but so did I. I should be able to figure out what had happened.

I needed information I didn't have. I knew Tiju Tia was still at Axefield, and Piffik was too busy with setting up his plans for the second Huena Inn. I didn't know who else to go to, so I looked for one of the older Wrens. I wanted Callis—she was nicer to me—but I found Falan sweeping out the Wrens' bunkhouse. I collapsed into one of the chairs she had moved outside to make it easier for her to work. She didn't say anything at first, just gave me a long look.

Then, "I suppose you want me to stop what I am doing and bring you a cup of cold water."

"Oh, Falan! That would be wonderful!" I gave her what I thought was my most charming smile. "Thank you!"

She huffed. "You know I grew up with Josef, you are going to have to be much better at flattery than that." But she left and in a moment returned with a cup of water for each of us. She sat down in the chair beside me. "So who are you looking for? Because I don't think you planned to show up half dead on our doorstep just to talk to me."

I finished my water and put the still cold cup against my forehead to cool me.

"Actually, I did, Falan. You are the only Wren who knows enough about Tiju Tia's workings on the Northern Track to answer my questions."

For a moment, her face flashed that hunted look I had first noticed when she arrived at Manumina. Then she waved her hand.

"Well, then ask away. Unlike some people I know, I actually have things to do today and sitting in the sun like an old man is not one of them."

"Falan, when people were first training at Manumina, Tiju Tia had different ideas for the Wrens then how they ended up in the field. There were also a lot of things all of you did which didn't get back to Tiju Tia. I think Nelo's exact words were, 'Tiju Tia doesn't know everything.' How did the Wrens know to make changes? How did all of you know when you needed help and when you were away softfooting? When did you contact Bima's softfoots? How did you make it work?"

She leaned back in her chair and just looked at me. I waited. Actually, I rested. I knew Falan was just trying to make me feel stupid for asking, so I would apologize for bothering her and leave. I waited some more.

"At Manumina, how did you think the Wrens were going to work? Seriously, Zren. I want to know."

"I thought…" I paused. "I thought you would give Viklanders food and maps and have your positions in town where you earned your coin, and lived in houses, and pretended to be good Kerekis. When you needed to move people, you would give them directions, or take them in a wagon close enough to the nearest Vikland garrisons or encampments that they could walk for help.

"Like when I drove the cheese cart. You were the faces Piffik and Tiju Tia and I could give coin and clothes and maps. Then you would hide them in your secret places if we didn't get there often enough. I knew Tiju Tia planned Huk as the hub, and Callis and Ross would be the center of the Wrens. That's why Callis's maskovesto was a tailor with only a few decons at the toggery, and Ross raised rabbits. They barely worked for someone else, so they could move the most freely. And Huk was the friendliest to the Viklander cause."

I stopped and considered. "But it didn't feel like it worked that way."

Falan smirked. "What did it *feel* like to you at Manumina— safe and secure behind those big stockade gates?"

I answered slowly, "There was the Balza encampment where Josef was known, but it sounded like the Viklanders there relied on him to bring them news and dispatches. Because he could travel freely in the countryside. Kid was an under footman at Evensong, a critical Kereki army stronghold in the north, but Bima didn't have a single softfoot in the house or on the grounds nearby. Kid provided messages to Therin, an eight-year-old child who had a half day's walk to and from Fortika. A child—a child, Falan—to pass along critical plans and maps and news to the softfoots, Rani and Kern, when they were in the area.

"Ross was beaten by some soldiers and refused to help you anymore. But we didn't know at Manumina because you and Callis and others just added on Ross's work to your own. There were no prisoner exchanges like Tiju Tia talked about, and we paid bribes to free Viklanders at some of the settlement jails.

"The Viklander field infirmaries were too far apart and too small for all of the injured. The soldiers we would get for Siba and Rell to heal, we never planned to have them come so far south. But Tiju Tia and Piffik had nowhere else to bring them."

I considered my next words carefully. "I knew Linna had you rub a scented soap on your clothes and boots, so Mother could find any of you by smell if you were hurt or dead or taken on foot. We heard stories Jenny and Josef and Arden took the lives of others to protect Viklanders and Wrens. But there was no one to protect them." I cleared my throat. "There was no one to protect any of you." I waited a long time before I answered, "It felt like Lowertown."

Falan looked away. "It was better and worse than Lowertown. Josef would joke and tease it was about time he could protect me after all those years of me standing between him and my father's greed." She paused. "Dica said she knew as long as Nelo was safe, she was safe. But when she heard he had been taken by the crimpers, she cried every night until the day she saw him in the woods again on her half day and he hugged her. *He* hugged her. Those of us in the west leaned on each other, the strongholds had Nelo, and Arden and Linna were the knot keeping us all together. They tied us to the Matasi missionaries and Bima's softfoots. We knew no matter how bad our news or situation was, Linna and Arden could think a way clear for us. *They* were the center of the network. Not Tiju Tia, not Piffik, and certainly not any Viklanders we were only supposed to be *helping*." Falan turned and gave me a fierce look. "Are you hearing the words falling from my mouth, Zren Janin?"

I nodded but said nothing. She was still so angry, and I knew she had more to say.

"Well, good. If you have truly heard what I said, you will stop your foolish wandering about and decide what you want your life to be. Tiju Tia tells us we have just a fortnight or two to decide where we want to live, what we want to do, and what price our lives are worth." She raised an eyebrow. "And you cannot tell me we were not just bought and sold to help Tiju Tia achieve her revenge against the Kerek King." She was nearly quivering with indignation.

A long shadow appeared to my left and soon Josef stood beside us.

"My dear Falan, are you entertaining? Are there fingersweets and Vikland coffee to be had?" He touched her lightly on the shoulder to calm her and looked at me. "Checking on our whereabouts next, Zren? Did you tire of digging up rubbish mounds?" He gave me a cheeky grin, so I thought he was joking.

"Falan offered me a cold drink and a moment's conversation while I rested in the sun like an old man." I handed her back the cup. "She has assured me, Josef, whatever moment in time I am questioning your whereabouts, she and Callis will swear you were with the both of them." I pushed myself to my feet with the cane. "Therefore my work is done. Gossip like this is a coin so great, I will be invited to eat at any table I choose for the sake of my stories alone."

Josef laughed. "Falan, Falan. Isn't it enough I have to live with this pretty face? How will I ever convince one of these lovely Conrosan daughters to walk out with me if you tell such tales to Zren?"

Falan snorted. "You flirt with any woman on this side of the ground, Josef. Your own actions condemn you, not anything I could say or do." She stood up and stretched. "As long as both of you are here, you can carry in these chairs for me again. No one will thank me for doing today's housework if I leave half the house outdoors." Josef gave her a short Vikland bow and had all the rest of the chairs back in and under the table in the time I had dragged one to the threshold.

CHAPTER 29

AN INVITATION

While I had spent my days hunting about and my nights dreaming of different ways Inezi's murder could have happened, Piffik was preparing to move to Axefield. He wanted the shell of the building up before the Wet season began, so teams of people could be working inside where it was dry and safe while the rains poured.

The night before Piffik left for Axefield, he and I walked back to the main house together after end of day meal at Rygee and Siba's. Piffik was temporarily staying in his mother's room, as small as it was. I had been left in the infirmary, because frankly, there was nowhere else to put me.

"You've been riding horse quite a bit lately," Piffik started off. "Since that is not your favorite method of traveling about, I'm assuming you're planning to go find Solkka soon."

I wasn't fooled by his casual tone. "Has Tiju Tia heard news? Did she send a message?"

"She has. But you're gone at first light and not home until dark, so no one has been able to find you to tell you." He waited.

"Piffik!"

"It's not good news, or maybe it is. Your elusive Solkka is no longer at the Ulani farm. He sent a letter written in Wester, saying the Empress is sending him to the embasado at Salisport, Matasi. He also said to tell you the first opportunity he gets he will travel to Alenti and take care of some unfinished business 'so his daughters will know.' I assume those words mean something to you."

I nodded. Solkka Ulani would do what Miyamoto Suki would not, tell Bima's Matasian wife and daughters, Bima Ritwik, a son of Vikland, had died in the war saving the lives of others. How ironic Solkka was the one missing his Viklander braid of honor.

Piffik was still talking, "However, Solkka was enclosing his mother's invitation, also written in Wester, for Tiju Tia and you to travel to his family home in the Keopi district, visit with Jenny who misses all of you, meet his family, and they can meet you. He says his mother is proficient in Wester and his father speaks Keresh as well as Vik, so you will be able to tell your stories and listen to theirs without the awkwardness of the lack of a common language."

"And he sent this to Tiju Tia and not me," I snapped.

"Yes. The letter came to her at Axefield. A messenger brought her letter to me when he couldn't find you," Piffik answered calmly.

I blew out a breath. "I can read, Piffik. Solkka knows I can read. Well, not in Vik, but I can read Wester. Why would Solkka do this?"

"Zren, how much time have you spent with Solkka? I don't mean thinking of him or sleeping next to him, but actual time where you are talking getting to know each other?"

"Well, in case you didn't notice, there was a war going on."

"Mmmm." Piffik was non-committal.

"What's that supposed to mean?" I scowled.

"I've noticed, maybe from personal experience, Viklanders don't have casual relationships. They have their families involved and there isn't a rush to move things along quickly. It's not something you and I have experience with in Kerek or at Manumina."

He paused. "I'm saying, Zren, you aren't a boy from Kerek City anymore. Solkka wants his family to meet you because he wants you to be important to him. If there is a proper way to do this, and I am guessing there is, I know you will be smart enough to pay attention to what is going on around you to make him glad to know you."

I considered his words.

Piffik continued, "And if that means having Tiju Tia along as a chaperone, well, I can't imagine having a diplomat and softfoot, familiar with all kinds of cultures and able to read and write many languages, would be a bad person to have along… if you pay attention."

We stood at the doors to the main house.

"I miss the porch swings at Manumina," I said suddenly.

"I was just thinking the same thing." He smiled in the dark.

"I can't imagine anyone who could possibly be a better friend than you." I meant every word of it.

"Ah, Zren, we just need to spend every day thinking of the good in people." He paused a long time. "Remember when we were scrambling to bring all the Wrens home? When Arden overheard a Kereki militia say Falan's maskovesto was known? He spent four days on horseback to Balza, the settlement south of the Northern Track, and then back to Cloa looking for her. Remember when Nelo was taken by the crimpers and Arden walked to Nelo's holding to learn if the Wrens were also in danger, then he walked to Evensong to get more information from Kid, and then drove you and Siba during the night, so you could get some sleep? Remember when he rode all evening and all night to Manumina to tell us of the rescue we needed to make at Regno? There were eight Viklanders and your friend Lomes. Arden ate first meal with us and then got back on a different horse and rode back to Cloa, so he could be at the stables and Linna would not have to lie for him for more than one day. And you have heard, how when Oro was captured at that same spot in Regno, Arden freed him from his captors and gathered in Dica."

Piffik waited until I nodded before he went on. "Think on this, Zren. Oro told me Arden knew of his interest in Linna since the time Oro tried to slip in their house. It wasn't until later, much later, Oro came to understand Arden cared for Linna as well. When Oro was captured, it would have been easy for Arden to pass those Kerekis and have Oro taken to the military camp never to be seen by any of us again. No one was with Arden. Oro didn't even recognize Arden. Any Wren will tell you Oro brought his trouble on himself by not listening to Dica who knew the area best. But Arden didn't. He rescued Oro and Dica and brought them home."

He let those words soak in.

"I think I know what you are doing every day you are out riding. But ask yourself this, 'What if Inezi let the goats out and took Old Dris early in the morning so no one saw her. And then after she had traveled on horseback for three or four decons, she stripped the horse of its saddle and bridle, sent it on its way home, and continued walking to her destination. Remember, she was a softfoot for Bima and Rani. She is now gone without a trace and even Arden's dog Mother would not be able to track someone whose feet never touched the ground. Worse, she would have raised a cloud of suspicion over Arden whom she hated. Maybe she felt it would have been enough to convict him before a Vikland Justice. Maybe she was content to destroy two friends by casting mistrust Nelo never could overcome."

Piffik looked at the stars, and then looked at me. "If you forget the good in Arden—then she has won—just by leaving."

I tilted my head back, pretending to look at the stars. Piffik wasn't fooled, but rather than let me make an idiot of myself, he just put his hand on my shoulder and walked up the stairs into his house.

CHAPTER 30

TRANSLATIONS

I slept in the next morning. When the sun was nearly overhead, I dressed and made my way out of the infirmary. The courtyard was deserted. Usually there were people milling about, some going to the garden plots, children playing, others heading to their apprenticeships. But today, nothing. I took a deep breath and swallowed the quiet.

I had spent the night dreaming of a long wagon train running from Kerek City to Ishes filled with food, supplies, and everything missing from our lives while the war was fought. But my dreams had been nothing more than absorbing the sound of Piffik loading the traveling village, tools, and teams relocating to Axefield to build the Huena's second inn.

Last night, Piffik had talked about Vikland culture, but now I wondered if the Huena family understood Conrosa as more than just a distant land in their geography lessons. Did they grasp the concept of communal living, of holding livestock, and tools, and wagons, and work in common? Yes, the Huenas had made their contract with Piffik Qanaq to be the lead builder—the man in charge—something he was well suited for, but he would bring his own people, people he had known his whole life, people who could help him talk through the problems, and listen to his ideas as he listened to theirs. Women and men together would work on the building, hunt and grow food, and build a village of laundry, ironworks, infirmary, and cookhouse. Only the wood, iron, and steel for the building would come from Vikland and the West Islands.

The very old, the very young, those assigned to take care of them, and the livestock remained behind. No one wanted to admit to being too old to work so even those were few in number. I had been left behind because Piffik didn't want me to get dizzy and fall off a roof, he said. Callis was training with Siba for a few more days and then she would move to Axefield and help Bett in the new infirmary. Siba remained behind while her latest batch of medicines finished brewing and to keep an eye on me, then she would join Rygee in Axefield as well. The cheesemaker who had taken over Lou's work would still need someone to make the occasional trip between here and Axefield to deliver her cheeses to the community kitchens. I planned to be the one to travel back and forth to check up on my friends.

I smiled at the quiet and wondered what I would do today. I was done with Inezi's disappearance. As Piffik explained what he thought had happened, I could feel the rightness of it. I had seen the murderous look on her face as Arden had sent her away. I didn't know Arden as well as I knew Oro, but the Wrens had scornfully let me stumble my way through my mystery without intervening because they knew the three men—Arden, Nelo, and Josef—better than I did. Now I knew too.

Siba, accompanied by Mother, came out of the great house with a basket on her arm.

"At last, the giant awakes!" she exclaimed. "I asked to borrow Arden's dog because I thought we might have to drag you from your bed. Are you up for berry picking? I want to make some fruit tarts for tonight."

I tried to keep a straight face. I loved fruit tarts.

"Did you bring food? I need to work on a full stomach."

She laughed and handed me a cloth napkin. It was still warm.

"First meal was decons ago, but I made these for us to eat while we gather. Arden said he will do the animal chores and then take his ease, while you climb every hill and crawl through the briars to help me."

I sighed. "I wished he would have gone with Piffik. I have seen the furniture he has made, Siba. He is a good carpenter.

And he has no fear of heights. Callis says it is because he spent his childhood climbing on the roofs and through the windows of rich men's houses."

Siba looked sad. "He has a fear of Linna. Even misguided kindness can hurt." She looked at the dog at her heels. "He also doesn't want to worry about Mother getting in the way."

"Pah! That dog is smarter than most of us. Teach it to hold a hammer, and it will have one wall built before Piffik has unrolled his plans." I ate my biscuits and jam as Siba led the way south to the berry patches.

Decons later, my hands were stained and scratched, my basket was full and so was my belly. Siba had chatted easily about everything and nothing, and I felt guilty for having such an enjoyable day when I knew the others working under Piffik would have spent the morning traveling, then setting up their village, and preparing to start work on the inn the next day.

Mother trotted in just a few feet ahead of us as we walked back to the estate. There were three saddled horses in the main yard. I recognized Tiju Tia by size and shape as she was pointing out various buildings to the tall well-built man dressed in Viklander clothes beside her. He had no braid, but curly black hair and broad shoulders. As we got closer, he turned and I saw the edge of his face. *Solkka! He must have decided to stop here on his way to the Silver Mountain passes!* I shoved the basket into Siba's hands and ran across the courtyard. He turned to me just as I threw myself into his arms.

"You're here! You're here! You're truly here!" I laughed, squeezed him hard, and leaned back to cup his face.

He wasn't Solkka. I quickly stepped away, dropped my eyes to the ground, and crossed my arms over my chest. I could feel my face flame in embarrassment.

He laughed, and it was Solkka's same joyful laugh. The beautiful face was so similar. Even the missing Vikland braid and unrestrained curls. He was Solkka—without the scar.

He replied in Keresh, "Hello! Even my mother is not so glad to see me!" He folded his hands together for the short Vikland bow. "I am Tedros Ulani, third son of Devi and Hilanna Ulani." He tried to hide a grin and failed. "I am the favorite brother of Solkka, Jenny, and Kaede Ulani. Your escort to our coffee farm."

"I am sorry. You look just like him." I tried to hide my confusion and embarrassment with apologies. "I am so very sorry," I whispered.

His smile turned sweet. "Do not apologize, Zren Janin. At least I hope you are Zren Janin, or my brother has some explaining to do. I am glad to know my brother is so cherished. I am sorry though, he is not able to escort you himself. The summons for him to report to Matasi with all haste was not welcome news in my parents' home." He gave a chagrined look. "You do not speak Vik? I only ask because my Keresh is so poor and my tongue has an accent. I do not have the gift of languages as my mother and my brother do."

Both Tiju Tia and I shook our heads at his request. "Ah well, I apologize in advance for abusing your poor ears. I will place blame by saying, I was born on the far side of Vikland. The Keopi district is too far from Juisiti to attract the artists, teachers, and amusements which would have curbed my rough ways, but Solkka has told you all this already—I hope." Even his eyes smiled, and I was immediately reminded of Josef and Kern. This one also flirted as easily as breathing.

Siba walked up to us, and Tiju Tia introduced her to Tedros. He explained his plans to escort us to his family's home beginning the next day, as he had only a short leave before returning to his military assignment. Siba invited him to the end of day meal and asked if she could offer her aunt's home as an overnight stay. He agreed immediately. Siba nodded and excused herself to prepare her aunt's room. She called to Mother to have the dog follow her.

"Wait!" Tedros called after her. "Is this your dog?"

"No. She belongs to another who is here," Siba replied.

Tedros thought for a moment. "I met a black dog in the war—far north of the Northern Track. She belonged to the Matasi missionaries who saved my commander and two others with me. It was such an odd name for a dog, I remembered it." He looked at the dog and called softly, "Mother?"

The dog cocked an ear and gave a slow uncertain tail wag.

"It is you!" Tedros laughed and turned to Siba. "Will the missionaries be joining us for the evening meal? I would like to see them again and tell them of our adventures after they rescued us."

Tiju Tia interjected smoothly, "One of them will be at end of day meal tonight, the other I am sad to report is working a half day's journey away from here."

I looked from face to face. Siba was as confused as I was and Tiju Tia was not giving any information away. I couldn't wait to find Arden.

But first I helped Tedros take the three saddled horses to the stables, rub them down, water and feed them. He told me his mother had written a letter to him to escort us home when he was on leave. He had immediately sent a letter to us—in Vik and Keresh—telling us of his plans. I said we hadn't gotten it. He nodded, Tiju Tia had said the same. But he had stopped at the Huena's inn for food and drink on the way from Juisiti and had been amazed to see nearly an entire village arrive shortly after him. He had watched as tents and fences bloomed into a city before his eyes. Someone had told him the Huenas were building an even larger second inn and these were the workers.

Then a woman approached him and questioned, "Solkka Ulani?" It had been Tiju Tia. She had made the same mistake I had.

Tedros gave me a flirtatious grin again, "I don't know how this happens, Zren, I am ever so much handsomer than my big brother." He and Tiju Tia had made plans to gather me and then take another road to the Keopi district, "It is mostly half-tracks and small roads, Zren, but it will eliminate two days of travel." He chuckled. "I understand horseback is not your favorite way to travel."

I wrinkled my nose. "It was not something I learned until lately."

He raised an eyebrow, but said nothing more on the subject. He talked about his upcoming leave and how he was sorry to miss Solkka's visit at home. He mentioned he had served in the war mostly in the very far north just under the Cold Mountains.

"There is a reason they call them the Cold Mountains, Zren. I would have to count my fingers and toes every morning to make sure none had frozen off during the night!"

He told me Solkka had written him a letter telling him of the death of Malan Sala and how it had been his honor to escort him home to the Summer Plains and to speak to his courage and resourcefulness.

"Malan and I had met at the academies and then served our first year in the military together. He was smart, Zren, so very smart. If only he could have found another unit sooner, I'd be having a cold drink with him today." He stopped and leaned his face against his horse and I busied myself in the tack room to give him a moment.

Later, I took him outside and up on the hills so he could see all of the surrounding land about the Rishka estate. I explained how Conrosans lived in community and shared all things. They practiced non-violence and had their disagreements and grievances heard by the Council of Wisdom.

Tedros looked sadly at me. "They must hate Vikland. We cost you your home."

I considered his words carefully. "No. Kerek's deceit in no longer providing you safe passage to the sea gave you no other option. War is not noble. But Rell taught me your warrior culture does not train you to burn and kill because you can or have the ability to." I thought of ghostfire then and how it would be years before every pot had been found and destroyed. I wondered how many people would die long after the war was over.

"No," Tedros interrupted. "Our culture teaches us to defend those under our protection and to stand up for what's right no matter the cost."

I nodded. "And there were those of us Conrosans and Kereki who chose to help Tiju Tia and her Wrens as they fought alongside you, helped you with maps, and softfooted where your faces would give you away."

I thought to myself, and then I said it out loud. "We are not so different from you. We live a life to our values and protect our friends."

Tedros turned his eyes from the horizon and looked at me. "My brother described you as an original thinker and completely without guile. He did not mention you were also wise. I hope you are not wasted on him."

I squinted at him. "I am not sure what that means, but the only way Solkka could be any more perfect is if he cooked well and considered feeding me his life's calling."

Tedros laughed, and we headed down the hill.

When we reached the bottom of the hill, Siba was there waiting to take Tedros to her aunt's room for a bath and a rest before the end of day meal. Tiju Tia walked with me to the infirmary for a cold water wash and an immediate lesson on Vik behavior at the end of day meal.

I remembered what Piffik had said last night about paying attention and how there was a right way to do things.

"Why did you wait until now? You could have been scrubbing off Lowertown for ages already," I groused as I heated water. I was *not* taking a cold water wash.

"I have been," she replied. "And thank the Traveler, you learn fast. But there's so much to learn!" She walked into my room. "Do you have any Vikland style pants and shirts to wear?"

"I did. They were in my chest Piffik made for me. But I never saw it come off the wagon when we arrived here. I have no idea where to go looking for it now," I grumbled at her.

I heard Ngahuru mutter under her breath, and then I was left alone to take my bath in peace.

***

I had wrapped a sheet around myself and was finger-combing my hair, when she returned with her hands full of clothes.

"Here, try these on," she said. "I have several different sizes. You'll have to wear your own boots. You weren't cleaning out the muck wagon before we got here today, were you?"

"No," I scowled. I found a pair of pants and slipped a shirt over my head. I took a sniff just to make sure, but it smelled of sunlight and soap. I pulled it down over my body. I added clean boot linings and pulled on my leather boots. Tiju Tia's satisfied smile had me trying to catch my reflection in the darkening windows.

"You look fine, Zren. You look better than fine." She bit her lower lip. "Braid your hair like Arden does—don't wear it loose. I'm going to dress and meet you at the dining hall."

***

There were five of us for the evening meal. I don't know what Siba and Tiju Tia had done with the others, Siba only said Callis had flatly declined. Siba was in the kitchen and Arden was helping her. Arden was freshly scrubbed and also dressed in Viklander clothes; however, *he* had found a black pair of Viklander boots to fit. His long brown hair was washed and braided.

Siba was wearing her Conrosan best. A skirt with many colors and layers and a brightly colored blouse. Her brown hair was twisted up in the crown of a married woman. After she had me set the table, we stepped back to see what still needed to be done. At that moment, Tiju Tia and Tedros entered the dining room. I watched Arden's face. His eyes widened, but otherwise not a flicker of movement gave him away. Tedros came over, folded his hands formally, gave the short Vikland bow, and introduced himself to Arden.

Arden gave a half smile. "My friend, I did not know your name before this evening, but I am beyond glad the Lost God, who protects us from our enemies and lights the way of the brave, has given me the gift of seeing you again, and with no more harm than a lost braid."

Tedros grinned as he finally recognized Arden.

"Yes, some Kereki is riding a very fine horse on the bounty of my braid. But you, my friend, you have lost much more. I did not recognize you until you spoke. You have lost your Matasi skin. Have you lost your Matasi wife and God as well?"

"My 'wife' was Kerek-born and my good friend Josef who seems to be able to play any role we ask of him. But I have followed the Lost God and his teachings since I was a child, and I shall do so until the end of my days."

"And did you travel as missionaries through the entire war?" Tedros asked. "Truly, I am without speech. We Viklanders traveled with you for four days until you could get us to the border. I never once suspected—and I know the others did not either—you were anything but the missionaries you claimed to be."

"We were taught by Tiju Tia," Arden said simply. "We wore many disguises throughout the war both together and separately."

"If not for your dog, Mother, I still would find it difficult to believe. Why such an unusual name? It's how I remembered her, you see."

Arden gave his odd smile, and I knew he was telling a joke. "Mother has many talents—more than just finding Viklanders. If I had to give her quiet commands, I needed a name someone might mutter in their sleep."

I didn't understand where there was a joke, but I heard Tiju Tia choke back a sound. She covered it by inviting us all to take a chair. Siba brought out the food and we ate and talked.

Tedros told of his adventures before and after his rescue. Arden had such a peculiar way of telling stories he made it sound as if Viklanders had always rescued themselves, and he had just shown up in time to note it.

Tedros asked questions about the Conrosans. He confessed he remembered studying the country in the academies, but had never planned on traveling so far, or dreamed he would meet any in his life. Siba patiently answered his questions, even the personal ones, as when he asked if she was married. She said she was, she had married a man of Kerek, but they had married in the

Conrosan way which meant they went to the Council of Wisdom and said they were a couple, and then moved in together.

Tedros laughed so hard, I thought he would choke.

"Oh, Zren," he said, wiping his eyes, "If this is what you have planned for my brother, I am not so sure my father will thank me for bringing you home."

I started to scowl, and I felt a sharp pressure against my leg from Tiju Tia.

"Zren and I are looking forward to meeting your parents and eager to see Jenny again. We are beyond glad you are willing to bring us to your family home."

Tedros' smile slowly faded as he reconsidered his words. "I am sorry, Zren and Siba. I did not mean to make light of your cultural traditions." He cleared his throat and added stiffly, "It's very different from Vikland."

He asked me what a manabout did. I described what I had done at Manumina and what Arden and I were responsible for at Rishka. I described the goats and how we had gotten them in the first place because Lou had been a cheesemaker in south Kerek.

"Lou was from south Kerek? He was not Conrosan?"

So, I told how Piffik and I found Lou—a deserter from the Kereki army in the scrubland. How Rell, our Viklander healer, had mended him. Then Lou had asked to stay and work with us in getting our dairy running again.

Tedros raised an eyebrow. "A Viklander healed him? We are not usually so kind to our enemies."

I told Tedros how Rell and I had met on Miyamoto Suki's thirteenth crossing. I explained how she had stayed behind with me at Manumina as her legs had not worked right after the battle of Sary because of so many knife wounds. How she and Piffik had fallen in love and now Piffik would build an inn for the Huena family to prove he was as capable as Rell and worthy of her.

"It's a Conrosan fairy tale," I repeated Piffik's words. And then I added, "Just like in the fairy tales, it's okay to trick the fae to win the bargain. Piffik agreed because he is a woodworker of renown, but also because he knew all the Conrosans would help him and earn coin for the year ahead. He builds the inn, the Conrosans earn the coin we need, and he can marry Rell."

Tedros was quiet, but I saw a muscle jump in his jaw. Siba quickly asked me to help her carry in the coffee and fingersweets. We cleared the plates and she directed me into the kitchen.

"I know that look, Siba." I sighed. "I've seen you give it to Rygee. What did I do wrong? Why did you ask me to help you and not Arden?"

She stopped and gave me her full attention. "Zren, you are one of my favorite people, but it might not be in your best interest to say it is good to trick Viklanders, when you are talking to your Solkka's brother."

I stood stricken as I realized what she was telling me. "How could you let me do this?"

"That's why you are in here with me, and Tiju Tia is out there explaining what you really meant to say. Just put these on a platter and give her another moment."

When we no longer heard Tiju Tia's voice, Siba carried in the tray of coffee in the tiny cups, and I carried the platter of fingersweets. Tedros gave me a small smile and I smiled back. It was a start anyway.

We talked a little more, but Tiju Tia said she needed to prepare and pack if we were going to be gone for a while. Siba offered to walk Tedros back to her aunt's room, and he gave us all a formal goodnight.

Tiju Tia helped Arden and I clean up, and then she left to pack while Arden and I did the dishes. I looked at my hands in the hot soapy water and avoided his gaze. He was silent, but it didn't feel uncomfortable. Much.

I took a deep breath. "Arden, I owe you an apology."

He put down the drying linen and the pottery. "I am listening."

I looked at him. "After Inezi left, I did a lot of walking and riding and looking about."

"I noticed… and so did everyone else," he said drily.

"I thought…" I faltered. "I thought you may have harmed Inezi so she would never be a threat to Nelo or you or Mother again. You said she hated you. You and I had both grown up in Kerek City, and we were taught to get rid of the threat before the threat gets rid of you. So I thought that you, or maybe you and Nelo had…"

"Given Inezi Kereki metal poisoning?" He folded his arms across his chest.

He saved me from fumbling for a word that wasn't murder. "Yes."

"Is your search over? Because today you went out berry picking with Siba."

"It is." I pulled my hands out of the soapy water. "I looked at the wrong end of it. I had dismissed Inezi as unable to plan this, that she could not do this." I looked at Arden. "That she was not capable. As Tiju Tia would say, 'that was my fatal mistake.' Inezi was a gamekeeper's daughter and one of Kern's and Bima's softfoots and scouts. She was good at what she did. She stayed alive through the war and helped many others. I think Inezi let out the goats to cover her escape and then rode Old Dris far enough away so Mother couldn't track her. Then she walked away knowing the stink of her disappearance would stick to you like the scent of a muck cart."

He gave me a half smile. "Pretty good description."

I blew out a breath. "I could see where you would be angry with me. Yet today you did everything you could to make Tedros Ulani welcome and his stay pleasant, knowing how important this is to me."

"He's an easy person to be pleasant to. Although when Tiju Tia told me what she needed of me, I did not know he and I had met before. We called all of our rescues, 'soldier' and we had asked them to call us 'man' or 'missy' or 'Wren.' We didn't use bynames or our family names in our rescues. We didn't want to know their names in case… well, it was safer for everyone that way."

My curiosity won out. "When you said you follow the Lost God, was this true?"

"Yes."

"Why?"

He tipped his head to the side and considered me. "As you said, I had grown up in Kerek City. One day, when I was very young, I was fleeing a man who claimed I had stolen his purse, when a woman stepped between us and ordered him away. He laughed at her and said a fresh boy like me was worth more coin than she had in her pocket. Then her husband came out with a large cudgel and the book of the Lost God's teachings. I don't know which was more effective, but he left. The woman explained to me they were missionaries and asked if I was hungry." He smiled. "What child in Kerek City is not hungry? They brought out food and fed me."

He paused. "Whenever I saw them, they asked if I was hungry, and then they fed me. If I wanted to stay and listen to stories, they were happy, but they never stopped feeding me, or hiding me when I was fleeing from those who would do me harm. And in the three years they were in Kerek City, I heard a lot of stories."

"Are there stories about forgiveness?" I asked in a small voice.

"There are…and about grace and mercy." Arden turned and picked up the drying linen. "You should know, I was never angry with you. I knew I had done nothing wrong. Well, with Inezi anyway, and I knew you would soon know that too. It was also good to see you taking an interest in life again." He shrugged. "I think Piffik was frustrated with you more than anyone."

I stuck my hands back in the soapy water. "Yes, well, I think that's a permanent state with him. I never seem to be as smart as he thinks I should be."

Arden chuckled. "That was brave of you at the meal tonight calling Piffik's work for the Huenas a Conrosan fairy tale. It took every bit of Tedros' self-control to say nothing."

I groaned. "Siba already told me. When she had me help her bring the coffee and fingersweets. Please tell me Tiju Tia made it better."

"She did." He smiled. "Something along the words that your first language *may* be Conrosan and his first language is Vik and sometime ideas don't translate well into Keresh if it is a second language for both."

I laughed. "If only I could think so fast. Well, just so you don't misunderstand," I turned and faced him. "I am heartily sorry I forgot the good in you and thought you harmed Inezi."

"Thank you." He dried several more platters, and then, "Zren, does Tedros truly look like your Solkka?"

"Yes." I thought of how I greeted him in the courtyard. "So much so, it is like Callis's looking glass."

"Hmmm." He laughed at my quizzical look. "I will remember to tell Josef I have seen Tedros Ulani again. He will be glad to know another of our rescues survived the war."

I laughed with him and we finished the washing up.

CHAPTER 31

SECRETS REVEALED

The next morning, Tiju Tia appeared at first meal, dyed as a rich almond-hued West Islander with black curls twisted tight and two working hands. She only said she had been in disguise when she had approached him at Axefield, and she appreciated his confidence since her actions had nothing to do with Vikland. She would not harm her host country.

After Tedros' initial speechlessness, he had immediately adopted a graceful and elegant manner with her. "My mother's letter said, you would offer a name to me. Do you still wish me to call you Tiju Tia?"

"Until we arrive at your home." Tiju Tia responded and nothing more was said. I wondered if there had been more to Tiju Tia's letter than she had confided. I know *I* would never have stopped asking questions if any person had changed so completely in front of me.

I remembered we had all just gone through a war where appearances were not what they seemed to be. The Wrens had not been the only ones: there were the Kerekis Josef had used as allies, and Matasi missionaries, or those who dressed as them, who had helped Viklanders all through Kerek. I wondered if *not* asking questions was a critical part of staying alive. Once again, the war reminded me of Lowertown—no wonder the Wrens had survived so well.

***

It was five days on horseback to the Ulani farm using the small roads Tedros told us about. He was an entertaining traveling guide. He told us stories of growing up in "the wop-wops"—as he called them—and describing the beauty around us, land and mountains and trees far different than anything I had seen in Kerek or Matasi. Vikland was a wilder country, richer and more bountiful. Sometimes he would shyly ask Tiju Tia for a story of her softfooting. I was right. He knew she was not just any West Islander.

Tedros was as beautiful as Solkka. With his braid cut, his hair curled softly about his face and a thick mop would occasionally flop in his eyes which he would impatiently push away. Sometimes, when he would turn back to look at us and smile, he could look so much like Solkka my voice would catch on whatever I was saying. He must have known this because he would quickly turn back and allow me to pull myself together before continuing my story.

Tiju Tia noticed it as well, and on the third time, she casually asked Tedros, "So how is it, so much beauty rests in the men of the family Ulani?"

Tedros burst out laughing, and his entire face lit with the same joy Solkka always seemed to convey as he turned to answer her.

"Tiju Tia, you must meet my grandmother, my father's mother, who has a house at the next coffee farm. She is almost as wise as my mother and has an opinion on every idea that flourishes under the sun. She calls my mother her greatest treasure, but she says she despairs of her grandsons, each of them born more beautiful than the last. She has said the gods stored all of the family wisdom into one goblet and the gods poured so generously for the first one there was nothing but droplets for me."

He smiled. "She is greatly pleased with your Jenny."

We came to yet another gate, and Tedros nimbly jumped off his horse and then closed it after we all passed through.

Tiju Tia smiled. "I had hoped our Jenny was not seen as an obligation to be borne."

Tedros whipped his head around, shocked. "She is a treasure in her own right! She is the daughter my mother yearned for and the wit my grandmother delights in. She is the gift I give thanks for every day." He remounted and his horse moved forward. "Obligation, pah!"

Tiju Tia and I exchanged incredulous looks.

"It will be interesting if she feels the same way. My offer to take her to the West Islands may not be as welcome as I first thought," Tiju Tia said quietly.

We fell silent, and I admired the deep green coffee shrubs marching up and down the hills. In the far distance to our left were just a few of the Cold Mountains sparkling with tiny white caps of snow and ice. Most however, hunched like old men with grey and green traveling cloaks pulled about their shoulders.

We came to another gate, and as I followed Tedros' riderless horse through, I asked, "Are the Silver Mountains like those?" I pointed to the left.

"Yes and no." He swung himself back in the saddle. "The Silver Mountains are older mountains, more worn down, none of them have snow at any time of the year. There are Matasi farmers who terrace their sides of the mountains and grow food, but on the Vikland side? There are mostly goat or sheep farmers and small orchards."

He sighed. "The mountains are beautiful but deadly. I have gone over the Silver Mountains twice. The paths are sometimes no wider than your boots—if you have small feet. It is easy to take the wrong path and find yourself unable to move forward or inch your way back.

"It is why we pay to be guided by those who walk those paths every day. There are also hermits who live in caves on the mountains. They say it is so they can better hear the Lost God." He paused. "It is not an easy life. Not one I would want."

We came to another gate. "Not much further now. Just another decon. If the hills were not in the way, you could see the house in the distance from here."

I looked around. "What are the fences for? I don't see any animals to get into the coffee bushes."

"Not so much. It mainly divides the fields. Each field is named and numbered and when the coffee pickers come from all over Vikland they are assigned a field. They set their camps and pick the same fields every ten days to get only the ripest berries."

"Where does your farm start?" Tiju Tia pushed herself up in her stirrups to get a better look.

Tedros smiled widely. "Why, Tiju Tia, you have been riding on Ulani land for the last two decons. The first fence we opened was to our westernmost fields."

I gave Tedros an incredulous look and protested, "But Solkka said the farm wasn't large enough for all three of you. I thought that meant you had small holdings like they do in Kerek."

"No, it only means Solkka has the same wanderlust as my mother. She traveled halfway around the world to attend the academies, then met my father, and asked to settle here in

Vikland. Solkka joined the Diplo so he could live anywhere but here." Tedros shrugged. "My brother Kaede and I think he must have been dropped on his head. This is paradise to me. Once I finish my military service, anyone who wants to find me will only need to come here."

I said nothing but gave Tiju Tia an anxious look. Solkka had said he was the son of a farmer. What did I know? I had never seen a coffee farm before. I had imagined Solkka growing up like our farmhands. I had told him I was a manabout because I thought he would nod, and we would laugh and tell stories of what we had done. I immediately felt sympathy for Piffik when he loved Rell but believed her to be of a noble family or a princess and thought she was out of reach. I promised to find him and apologize. I knew *nothing* of Vikland.

We finally rode into a dooryard with a tall foursquare house. It looked like it had less stories than a Conrosan house but it was as wide as three of them together. There were long barns to the left—"the coffee sheds," Tedros said—and stables to the right. The house was the smallest of all the buildings. The boy who ran out to take our horses was greeted by name. He told Tedros his mother was in the gardens.

Tedros gave us a shy smile. "I know you haven't had a moment to freshen up, but we are very informal here. Come meet my mother and she will have a plan for you to rest and refresh yourselves. My father and older brother will be in the fields now. We will see them this evening. My brother's family and my grandmother eat with us at night. Come."

He walked around the house and into a brightly colored garden. A West Islander no taller than I was stood up and dusted off her hands.

"Tedros! It is good to see you. We only received your letter yesterday." She gave him a long hug and turned to face us.

Tiju Tia immediately swept into a deep curtsy and murmured, "*Rangatira* Ulani, it is my greatest pleasure to meet you."

Tedros' mother laughed. "Well, I haven't heard that title in years. No, my friend, I am not a princess of the West Islands any more. I am just Hilanna Ulani, mother to three beautiful boys and a daughter who brings me joy like no other." She paused. "I do not think you are just any West Islander, Tiju Tia, and I asked my boys to treat you with the respect of one who has the ear of my brother, the King."

Ngahuru straightened. "I have now traveled with two of your sons. They do you credit. I confess I did not know who I was traveling with when your son Solkka was my honor guard after Vikland helped me home. I am Ngahuru of the West Islands, daughter to the tailor of the King and sister to Storyteller Koanga who has his own hearth and home."

"Welcome, Ngahuru. I am beyond glad to meet you. My brother wrote and told me of your cleverness and bravery in ensuring our niece and nephew made it alive out of Kerek City when the ambassador and my sister were murdered. We will not talk of it today, but another time I would like to know how the children are doing."

"Certainly." Ngahuru curtsied again, but not as deeply.

Hilanna Ulani took my hands in hers. "You also need no introduction, Zren Janin. My son has written of you in his letters as a man whose slight frame can hardly hold his wide-open heart and courage. Welcome to my hearth and home. Please call me Mother Ulani. It is the name I am known by in the Keopi district." She paused. "It has always been safer for my sons not to be widely known as the nephews of the King of the West Islands. Especially now, when they are soldiers."

I answered her in Wester, "I am beyond glad to meet the mother who taught my friend all of his wisdom and grace." I didn't know if I should bow or what, so I just stood there stupidly.

"Such pretty words." She laughed gently, and I heard the same joyfulness Tedros and Solkka had in their laugh. "See Tedros? This is how it is done."

She tucked her hand in her son's arm. "Come. You are tired and dusty from the road. I wish you could see Jenny, but she is at her grandmother's house and won't be here until this evening's meal. This afternoon, please refresh yourselves and rest. Tonight, when I am surrounded by those I love, we will share stories."

She hesitated. "I have no news of Solkka. We have not yet heard if he has safely reached Salisport." She hugged Tedros again. "But this one, this one was lost to us for nearly a year before he turned up dirty and sick and begging to be fed. I can only hope the Traveler will guide Solkka's way safely."

"Of course, he will, Mutti. He's just collecting stories along the way." Tedros patted his mother's hand on his arm.

The room I was shown to be mine was filled with natural light. The bathing room was next door and shared with another bedroom. Tedros assured me Ngahuru would be elsewhere, sharing a floor with Jenny.

"We three boys had this top floor to ourselves once our tutors left. You have Kaede's room, but he's been married so long, there's nothing of his left. Take a bath. Mutti will send food up, and then you can sleep. I'll wake you when my father arrives."

I've always been good at doing what I am told when a hot bath is involved. I let my sore muscles soak until I felt I could move without wincing. Whoever decided horseback was an acceptable means to get from one place to another anyway?

CHAPTER 32

MEETING OUR JENNY AND THE FAMILY ULANI

I had dressed in clean Vikland clothes, but I only had my Kereki boots. My hair was finally dry and curling everywhere, and I was just going to tie it back when Tedros tapped on my door to take me down to end of day meal. I opened the door. He looked at me, smiled, and gently asked if I could braid my hair.

"Unbound hair is…" and he trailed off. I remembered back to my first night at Manumina. Miya had scowled at Kern when she had her long black hair drying like a curtain across her shoulders while we ate.

"Too personal?" I offered. He gave me a relieved smile.

"Exactly." I clumsily braided my hair, tied off the end and followed him downstairs.

Devi Ulani, Solkka's father, filled the room with his presence. He was taller than Tedros and Kaede with a black braid to his slim hips. While his sons had their mother's West Islander features to soften their faces, darken their skins, and curl their hair, Devi Ulani looked like he could have stepped out of any of the tapestries and paintings I had seen at the embasados. He greeted me formally, and I remembered my formal greetings in Vik as well. He looked me over carefully, but I didn't feel any scorn or condescension, just curiosity.

"You speak Vik?" he raised an eyebrow.

Mother Ulani quickly translated into Keresh for me.

"No, only the formal greetings." I grimaced. "I cannot seem to learn your alphabet and without that, the words and meanings will never follow." I didn't want him to think I was stupid, however, so I offered, "I do speak Conrosan and Wester, if you wish, as well as Keresh."

"Ah, well, I am only a coffee farmer—so I speak Vik because I had to have some language to pester my parents on how to grow coffee and a little Keresh left from my military days forty years ago." Devi shrugged. "The country is fallen, and that is the only export they ever had—their language." We settled on Keresh as the language of the table as Tedros and his grandmother claimed their Wester was so poor it brought tears to Mother Ulani's eyes.

Solkka's grandmother was my height. Her Vikland braid was moonlit silver, and she wore a deep blue dress down to her ankles.

I realized the only other time I had known a Viklander woman in a dress was the ambassador at the Kerek City embasado. I greeted her formally, but I didn't know the Vik word for 'grandmother' and so I substituted 'Empress.'

She smiled broadly at that, patted me on my hands, and told the room, "Now this boy, I like. We need to feed him, but for now, it is good I can look at him without looking up and seeing the stars behind him." She turned back to me, "So you speak Wester as well as Conrosan and Keresh. I thought it might have been just a few words to flatter us, but now I see who your friends are," she nodded at Ngahuru, "and I am well pleased."

Jenny had blossomed. Ngahuru had faltered for a moment when she had first walked in the room and Jenny had turned to greet her. Surprised and confused, Ngahuru's first words had been, "Oh my Jenny, you grew!"

Good food, fresh air, and family had conspired to turn Jenny into a young woman. I knew she was just as young as Dica and Tyra, but there the similarities ended. Jenny had seasons of peace, healing, and comfort while the other Wrens had been softfooting, hiding, and working as servants in a war-torn country. It showed. They hugged tightly, and I knew it wasn't just the Softfoot who had missed her Wren.

"Zren Janin," Jenny made me the small Vikland bow. "I was forced to hear so many stories of you from Solkka which he said *he* had heard from his friend, Miyamoto Suki, about your journey through Kerek and Matasi." She leaned in close and whispered, "You made me a braver person."

Instead of a tense meal with everyone staring at me, it was as much fun as one of Rygee's 'Fourth nights.' There was laughter and stories and such good food. The Ulani family asked questions of me, but nothing to make me cringe. They were especially interested in Manumina.

Mother Ulani thought she remembered Conrosans at the academies when she was a student, but when she asked her husband, he replied he only had eyes for her—the smartest person in the Academy of Botanicals. She shook her head gently, but a smile curved her lips.

When I said my best friend's sister, Aajan Qanaq, was a student at the Academy of Botanicals and had developed unguents for burn victims, they asked thoughtful questions on how the process worked. I explained how Chul had volunteered before the soldiers and now had use of his hands again. Then I explained how Chul had taken Aajan back to Vikland to be educated because Manumina had offered sanctuary to us on Miya's thirteenth crossing.

"Miya?" Kaede lifted a brow. A look of disapproval flashed across his face.

"Miyamoto Suki. I traveled with him on the Northern Track…"

Kaede's wife, Lark, laughed. "You know Miyamoto Suki so well you can call him a byname?" she teased as she fanned herself with her hand. "I feel like I should be in the serving kitchen, not sitting at this table with such exalted guests." I realized she was teaching me like Rell did. That I should not refer so casually to Miya when he was not there to acknowledge his friendship with me.

She continued more seriously, "I went to the academies with Miyamoto Suki. However, then he was still trying to grow into his name. Now we hear the stories and the news that travels from the palace and all report he is worthy of the trust put in him by the Empress."

Mother Ulani asked, "Is 'Kid' one of yours, Ngahuru? I would like to meet him someday. I understand he has saved my Solkka's life twice."

Ngahuru nodded, but it was Kaede who spoke.

"My brother needs rescuing often, you see," Kaede said to me with a smile. "I hope you know how much work he is."

"My grandsons are beautiful—" his grandmother began.

"Here we go again," Tedros laughed easily.

"—but it is up to those who love them to keep my grandsons safe from day to day," his grandmother finished soberly.

Tedros nodded in agreement. "Grandmother, you will be pleased to know I met again the Matasi missionaries, well, one of them anyway, who saved my life and those of my commander and two others."

Tedros recounted how he and the others had been survivors of the firing of the Earles garrison. They had been hunted to the caves in the Cold Mountains, and trapped for a long time, barely risking a fire to cook the meager food they could gather without detection.

Finally, the Kereki soldiers stopped the searches and they had watched in relief as the horses and army wagons and soldiers had all moved out. The Viklanders had left the foothills the next day heading west hoping to rejoin other units closer to the battles and the Northern Track.

A few days later, they had felt they were being followed and slid off into the woods to hide. It took a little while and then a very tall Kereki woman came walking alone down the path singing a Vik song of "The Battle of the Harpies and the Crossbow." She stood in the middle of the road, put her hands on her hips and offered help and aid to the trees or anyone else that was listening. She asked to have one who spoke Keresh come say hello to a friend of Zren Janin.

Tedros smiled at me. "We had already been told by our own Vikland softfoots and others to trust a friend of Zren Janin, but I thought it was only a fairy tale or a code word, I did not know you were real." He chuckled. "Trust my brother to invite you home as casually as he would a friend from the academy." He gave his father a sly look and continued with his story.

Their commander had gone out to talk with the woman in the road. The Kereki— "she was very pretty, Mutti"—brought them to a house and fed them. Then she brought out a basket of Kereki clothes and told them to find some to wear. She would travel to get another person to help her move so many Viklanders, she said, but they should not leave the house while she was gone. She pointed to a huge copper tub and suggested with a smile that they heat water and wash their clothes and themselves. If she still had not returned in seven days, it meant she had been captured or killed, and they were to shift for themselves. Then she washed her face paint off, unpinned her hair and twisted it into a tail. She dropped her skirt in front of them to reveal Kereki pants and changed into a flowing Kereki shirt and tunic. She laughed at them and their shocked expressions.

"What?" he had said, "Had they never seen such a pretty boy before?" He told them to sleep as much as they could, eat well while he was gone, and not to unbar the door unless it was a Conrosan driving a coffin wagon, a Matasi missionary, or Tiju Tia herself.

"Five days later, two Matasi missionaries drove one of their settler wagons to the door and asked to speak with our commander. They called him out by name, so we unbarred the door and they came in. They brought a black-haired dog they both called 'Mother.' The man had five rabbits he had killed. While he made a stew, we packed food and our Vik clothes in the extra traveling bags they gave us.

"The woman never looked us in the face but told us there were no units that we could be safely taken to west of us. The fighting was too hazardous, and the exchange of lands too frequent to know where to put us safely and ensure they would be able to leave alive as well.

"They offered us another plan—to skirt the large Kereki encampment around Evensong and take us to the border where we could connect with a full unit and supply train which would have the soldiers necessary to move through Kerek. Until the Viklanders found a replacement for the garrison at Earles there was no closer or better spot for us or for them to survive. We agreed and then learned we were northeast of Huk and it would take four days."

Tedros gave his mother a sweet smile. "I am sorry I caused you such heartache for the seasons I was missing, for truly that was the worst time of the war for me, except for those four days. The missionaries took us to buildings and barns and game sheds for each night's shelter. Each night before we were allowed to crawl out of the wagon, Mother would sniff all around the building and the tracks leading to and from. We had shelter and hot food every night, and hot oats or barley and broth every morning. They had short bows and a Vik crossbow at their feet in the wagon to protect us. We lay sleeping under the canvas during the day and took turns taking watch while they slept at night. They prayed in Mata with us each morning for safe travels. Never once did any of us suspect them to be anything but what they said to be—a young married couple from Matasi fulfilling their missionary service north of the Northern Track."

Tedros smiled. "Can you can imagine my delight, when I arrive at the Conrosan settlement and meet the dog, 'Mother,' again? Only now her owner is not a Matasi missionary, but a lean Spice Islander younger than I am with braided brown hair who claims no wife. I tell you true, the entire four days across Kerek, our Matasi couple were two young men trained by Ngahuru to be whatever they needed to be to help Viklanders. And not one of us ever suspected!" He leaned back in his chair and lifted his cup to Ngahuru. "Thank you."

Everyone lifted their cup to Ngahuru then, and repeated, "Thank you."

When the fingersweets and coffee were brought out at the end of the meal, I stiffened. How do you sit at a coffee farmer's table and tell him you cannot tolerate the taste? Tedros saw my dilemma.

"Father, you will be happy to know Zren will not drink up all your profits from this year's crop. He will make sure all of his cups make it to market. I, on the other hand, plan to drink you into the poorhouse until I have to go back to Juisiti."

"My grandsons..." Grandmother Ulani began, and everybody laughed.

JENNY CLAIMS A HOME

The next day I caught glimpses of Ngahuru and Mother Ulani walking side by side in the gardens. I could hear snatches of Wester. I realized they were talking of people and places I had no knowledge of and I assumed they wanted to be alone with each other. Jenny spent the morning with her grandmother, but then came home at midday and spent the afternoon walking me around the coffee barns and the nearest fields.

Jenny asked about all the Wrens, and if I could remember any of their adventures. I told her I would start as far west as Balza and tell a tale of each Wren if she would tell me of the person they had been in Kerek City. She gave me a quizzical look and wondered aloud why I would want to know. Then she shrugged her shoulders and agreed.

I began with Falan and Josef and the soldiers at the southern settlement and how Falan had 'rescued' Bima, the best softfoot in Vikland. How Falan lived with a widow in defiance of

Kereki custom, and would dress as a man to move Viklanders, documents, and messages between Josef and Callis.

"She would steal the boots of dead scouts to make those soldiers who came behind afraid their lives were worth so little; they would be murdered for their boots."

I paused. "At first I didn't like her, Jenny. She is always so cruel to me, but Josef thinks the world of her and so I try to see her from his eyes." I blew out a breath. "I think it is how she survives. She thinks she always has to fight for something or against someone."

I looked at Jenny. "Tedros told you last night of one of Josef's adventures. I do not know them all, but I know of others. Josef told me once he dressed as a woman so much because Kereki metal poisoning does not come easily to him. He needs that extra moment of his enemy's condescending scorn to be able to think of every other option before murder."

Jenny nodded. "They were part of Tiju Tia's network in Kerek City. Although then we called her Ngahuru. Falan and Josef heard gossip and helped gamblers lose their coin. They passed secrets and news of losses to Ngahuru, so she could find a weakness to twist to her advantage. She would approach the clerks and officials who had lost coin they could not afford, and offer to buy documents and news from them which would help the West Islanders.

"I was not surprised to see Josef in the wagon when we left Kerek City. He can be anyone he wants to be with clothes and face paint, but I was not expecting Falan until I realized he would not go without her." She looked at me. "They are not a couple," she hastily explained. "But if one is gone, the other would be desolate."

I agreed and went on to talk of Callis and Ross at Huk. I explained how Tiju Tia had wanted the center of the network to be in Huk because it was the friendliest to Vikland, and so neither of them had positions which required them to be present every day. How Ross had been taken away and tormented by some soldiers and refused to leave Huk again, raising rabbits to feed the Wrens but letting the others take on his work. How the others hid this from Tiju Tia so she didn't know and couldn't make changes.

"Of course not, Zren," Jenny said scornfully, "The Wrens thought, as I do, if we did not do as Ngahuru told us to, she would just drop us and find someone else who could do what she needed. It is what happened in Kerek City. When a street runner disappeared or a secret gatherer suffered metal poisoning, no one cried over it. Those with power and coin just found new street runners, secret gatherers, pickpockets, and other children to fit their needs.

"Even as we left the city, Zren, Ngahuru did not look for us. She found Dica and told her to spread the word that Ngahuru was in town and ready to rescue us, but *only* if we were in the embasado street the next day at midday. As soon as we heard, we ran to find as many as possible, even as the night grew late and we risked ourselves. We knew there were no second chances. Ross knew this, and so he kept his secret and the others did as well."

I gave her a long look. "You describe Ngahuru so very differently than I know her."

She shrugged. "She needed you to play a different part." She waited a moment. "What about the others? I know of Kid, and of Arden, you do not need to tell me of them. Did you know he has had that dog since it was a pup in Kerek City?"

"I know Tiju Tia said Arden had a puppy when she first met him," I replied.

"It is the same one. The dog went everywhere with him, and it could have been recognized when he used it to scent trouble. He was a thief in the Flower District, not in Lowertown. A very good one from a family of thieves. He called it the family business." She tilted her head to the side. "I thought I had heard his sister was a softfoot." She looked at me. "Do the Spice Islanders have an embasado in Kerek City?"

I shrugged. If they did, it was not on Embasado Street. I wondered about that.

"When Callis asked him why he was in the wagon with us—a thief as successful as he was—he just laughed and said in that odd way of his that it was time for a change of scenery. I think, I think he may have had a close call." She gave me a puzzled look. "That does not feel right, but I don't know what else it could be." She looked at me. "And Dica and Tyra?"

I told her how Dica had been able to use her master's long absences at Regno to hide Viklanders until Inezi or Nelo could get them away. How Dica and Tyra fed information to Therin who passed it along to Inezi. Fortika was the stronghold where the Viklander softfoots and Tiju Tia's Wrens worked the most closely together.

I told about Nelo being taken by the crimpers and how after his beating he went back to softfooting. I told her how Nelo had gone to bring Tyra back to Manumina when the King had sailed away from Kerek and the network was uncovered. How he brought Therin and Inezi along because they would have been blamed for the theft of the horses.

"Nelo did this?" she exclaimed. "Nelo?"

I gave her a look. "Nelo was one of Tiju Tia's best Wrens. He took tremendous risks to report troop movements and get plans to the garrison at Earles, or to Inezi to give to Kern, one of Vikland's softfoots. When the garrison at Earles burned, Nelo and others had to move the Viklanders many days to get them to the border or to safety. Why does this surprise you?"

She bit her lower lip. "Nelo was…not kind in Kerek City. I was dismayed he traveled with us in Tiju Tia's wagon."

I replied slowly, "He didn't just run Lost Girls and rob people in Kerek City, did he? He made sure they wouldn't be able to say it was him." When she nodded, I continued, "Ngahuru must have known he was capable of hard choices. She placed him as a traveler between some of the most unfriendly territory— Evensong and Cloa. He had to do some difficult things to keep Kid and Dica and Tyra safe."

She looked away and then back at me. "I left the others too soon. I only know them from Kerek City and not what they became." She huffed. "It doesn't matter. We were never friends. At the most we looked out for each other."

I stopped on the path and turned to face her. "Jenny, I am just a foolish man who grew up in Lowertown. I feel you are trying to tell me something important, but I am too blind and deaf to understand what you are saying. Tell me plain and if you need my help you have it."

She wrapped her arms about her waist and refused to look me in the eye.

"Zren, I am now fourteen. The Ulani family wants to send me away to the Keopi district school so I can be ready to go to the academies at Juisiti the year after. I don't want to go. But if I say 'no,' I am scared they will send me away, and I don't remember the Wrens or know how they changed to know where else I could find a home."

I considered her words for a long moment. "I think I hear what you are not saying. You think you must be exactly what they want you to be, or like Kerek City, they will just find another Wren—maybe Josef or Arden because they saved Tedros' life, or Kid, because he saved Solkka's life twice."

I watched her face, but she said nothing more.

"Jenny, I can only repeat what words have fallen from the mouths of others. Solkka told your story to the Wrens at Manumina—Falan, Linna, and Kid—and he says his parents treat you as his equal in all things not as an exchange for the loss of your hand," I gestured at the lace glove and wooden fingers she wore on her left hand, "but in gratitude for Solkka's life." I tipped my head up quickly, *where did those tears come from?*

Once I thought I could talk clearly again, I continued, "To me, that does not sound like a Trickster's bargain. I do not believe they will have a change of heart just because you do not curtsy at their suggestions. Have you talked to Mother Ulani about this? Or Grandmother?"

She turned back to me slowly. "I have. But Mother Ulani doesn't understand. She loved her time at the academies, and she thinks the Keopi district school will be the same—only with younger students. Lark and Kaede and their cousins all had tutors at home so they cannot tell me what it would truly be like. But Mother Ulani was a princess—a princess! —and she is so smart. She was treated very differently than I would be at the academies. I don't want to disappoint them." She waved her hand over the green hills of coffee bushes. "I don't want to leave this."

I scratched my ear with my fingertip. "Is it Tedros?"

If Jenny could have cast fire with her look, I would have been cinders on the wind.

"Tedros?" She snorted. "Tedros is my *brother*. As is Solkka, as is Kaede." Her looked turned sober. "I am part of a *family*, Zren. I don't want to do anything that will push me out. Don't you want a place that's yours? This is mine, and I don't want to leave."

I remembered the conversation Oro and I had the last night of Manumina. Both of us had finally found a place we could call home.

"I understand. I really do. Actually, I think Mother Ulani will understand as well. She hasn't returned to the West Islands and she could, so she may understand more than you think she will. Perhaps they can have tutors come here to teach you what you need to know, instead of sending you to the teachers. And if not," I shrugged and looked around, "you could probably hide out here and camp rough until they forget your name."

She gave a half smile then. "Thank you." She pulled her brightly colored wrap a little closer around her. It looked odd next to her dark Vikland pants and shirt. I wondered if Grandmother made it for her.

"What is your life like here?" I looked at her. "Truly, I want to know."

She squinted at me. "Mother Ulani and I have breakfast together. We speak pleasantries in Wester so I can learn it, and she talks about her day ahead. She makes plans for what she will do and shares them with me. Cook comes in and the three of us plan for the evening meal and next day.

"Then I ride over to Grandmother's house. She and I spend the time talking in Vik. We may talk about running a coffee farm, or stories of Vikland, books I should read or am reading with her, or her family, or Juisiti. The entire time we talk in Vik. If I do not know a word, she gives me other Vik words until I understand. She says the best way to learn a language is to drown in it." Jenny gave me a half smile. "I'm not sure she is wrong, but I always enjoy my ride home where I can take as long as I want to clear my head."

She continued, "After the midday meal with Grandmother, my afternoons are mine. I can ride horse, walk the hills, read in the gardens, even go down and watch Cook so I can learn to feed myself when I go to the academies. Every other day, Mother Ulani teaches me how to do the account books and the ordering for the coffee farm and the household. She calls it 'learning the skills of the Right Hand.'"

She paused. "I am so safe here, Zren Janin. I can truly do anything I want and fear nothing. Have you ever had such a feeling? For the end of day meal, Kaede and his family and Grandmother come over. We speak Keresh because Devi Ulani says, at this moment, it is the language which gives me the greatest voice, and he wants to hear what I have to say."

She squared her shoulders. "Zren, I know you have heard the Ulani family laugh—Solkka, Tedros, his mother—have you ever heard such joy in a laugh before? It is the joy of growing up here. Of having this be the place where you are known." She looked at me with unshed tears. "This is why I cannot make myself leave, even if it is Mother Ulani's desire."

"What about Tiju Tia? She would take you to the West Islands."

She smiled at me sadly. "I want to see the Wrens again. But we fought different wars. I was a soldier until I lost most of my hand. Since then, I have become a Viklander. And now, if they came here and saw my good fortune? Which of Tiju Tia's Wrens would be glad for me?"

"Why, they all would!"

She gave me a withering look and led me back to the gardens.

CHAPTER 34

THE PRICE OF AN ULANI NAME

The next day I invited myself along to the coffee fields. Jenny and Ngahuru were spending the day with Grandmother, and Mother Ulani said she needed to shut herself in her office and work on the business accounts. She wanted to take advantage of our return to Juisiti to send along documents and orders instead of hiring a separate messenger. Devi and Tedros seemed surprised at my request to accompany them, but I assured them I was capable of manual labor and learning on my feet as long as animals weren't involved.

They apologized for walking rather than riding, saying the horses were too big and rough to go between the coffee bushes. First they tried to make lighthearted talk, but soon the work ahead of them took over. They examined the health of the coffee bushes, checked the ground in various places for moisture, sniffed the berries, and rolled a few through their fingers. They taught me what to look for and we three moved quickly down the fields, Devi recording our notes in a tiny book of pressed papers.

"Did you learn all of this," I waved my hand over the fields, "at the academies?"

Devi Ulani smiled. "Here at my father's side. My grandfather was the first Ulani to plant coffee as a young man. He had great success and when he passed, the farm was given to his two daughters and one son. One of those daughters was my mother.

"She loved another coffee farmer, a second son without his own property. Before she agreed to marry him, she asked him to allow their children to bear the name Ulani. He agreed. Together, they increased the wealth of the land until they bought out his own family fields from his older brother. When my father passed, far too young, my mother divided the lands between her two sons, saying families should not work together, it brings disagreements to the heart as well as to the purse. She built a small house between our two farms. My younger brother, Gayo, and his family—he has two girls and two boys—now farm the lands to the east of us. My sons—and Jenny—will inherit after I am gone and I want to leave good records for them."

He paused. "I am not quite the beautiful fool my mother sometimes thinks, but I do not learn from books, only from touching with my hands. I am a good coffee farmer and steward of this land because there are others, mostly Hilanna, who do the book and coin part."

He smiled to himself and then told me the story of how he had asked *Rangatira* Hilanna to his home over the harvest holidays because it was too far for her to sail home, and he could not bear to think of her staying alone at the academies. He had been surprised she had accepted. She was a princess, the fifth and youngest daughter of the Queen and her husband of the West Islands, but even royalty need friends.

They had spent the holidays talking about everything, riding through the hills, visiting with family and neighbors. His parents had been respectful, but not in awe, and Princess Hilanna had been kind. As they prepared to leave at the end of the holiday to go back to the academies, Princess Hilanna had said she hoped she could come again, this was the happiest place on earth.

Tedros had obviously heard this story many times for he warned me, "Here comes the sad part, Zren. Get ready to wipe the dust from your sleeve."

Devi Ulani gave a look of mock reproach and then shrugged. "It's true. The Queen and her husband caught a fever sickness and died even though they were not old, and Hilanna's oldest sibling, a brother, ascended to the throne of the West Islands. He was married at the time but had no children. He is a good King and only wanted what was best for his family."

Devi went on to say he finished his studies at the academies, and went on to complete his three years of military service. "Ah, Zren, because the Vikland military has such a sense of humor, I served my three years in Matasi, the Spice Island, and Kerek City. Such cruelty for a man who thought he was in love with a West Islander. But times were peaceful and I spent a lot of time writing *Rangatira* Hilanna."

After he completed his service, he was invited to visit her family. The visit did not go well, however, because he did not speak Wester or Mata and the King did not speak Vik or Keresh. With no language in common, Hilanna or strangers within the court had to be a part of every conversation, and so people did not speak freely.

"Her brother felt my face was my fortune and refused to consider Hilanna's desires," he said drily, "as if Hilanna has ever been swayed by something so shallow." Devi had returned to Vikland discouraged that the West Islanders thought him nothing more than a beautiful fool.

The King had children of his own and Hilanna's older sisters married and settled into their royal duties within the islands and as ambassadors. The throne was secure. Still unmarried, Hilanna wrote and asked if Devi had forgotten her and loved another. If not, would he wish to sail to the West Islands, and escort her to her new home in the Keopi District as his wife?

Devi left the coffee farm the same day he received the letter and took fast horses all the way across the Northern Track.

Once he arrived in the West Islands, in front of the royal family, *Rangatira* Hilanna, youngest sister to the King, gave up her title and her right to the throne, distant as it was. They were married the next day.

Devi looked at me. "This is why she says she prefers to be called Mother Ulani by everyone. She says she gave up one title for a better one."

I was speechless. Tedros leaned forward and took in my expression.

"Ah, Zren, have you truly heard the words that have fallen from my father's mouth? My grandfather gave up his family name to marry my grandmother, and my mother gave up a crown to marry my father. This is the talk my father has with anyone who smiles at his beautiful sons. Consider yourself warned." He laughed, saw the new expression on my face, and laughed even harder.

Devi Ulani's face crinkled into a broad smile. "I wish Solkka could be here to see your expression. Never mind, Tedros and I will perfect it until we can show him ourselves." He clapped me on my shoulder. "You're a fine man." He glanced at the sun and the shadows behind us on the coffee bushes. "Come. We should get back before the day gets away from us."

***

The rest of the time passed quickly. Ngahuru would spend the day with Jenny or Mother Ulani, and I would learn more about coffee farming and the Ulani family by trailing Devi or Tedros or Kaede around and doing whatever task they set before me. Kaede was much quieter than the other two men, but he answered my questions cheerfully. He also took the time to explain why he needed me to do whatever task a certain way. I appreciated his patience. I realized he talked to me like he did his six-year-old son, but since I thought we had about the same amount of coffee knowledge, his son and I, it wasn't so bad.

Devi was the storyteller. He could make the decons fly with his tales as the father of three boisterous boys who spent every free moment practicing their short bongs on each other, or so it seemed. He also talked of the joy of having Jenny enter their household.

"She feels very blessed to be here," I started. "So much so, she doesn't want to go to the academy nor the district schools."

Devi had been gently pruning a broken branch, but he paused and looked at me.

"She has said this to me as well, but I think she is worried about the cost."

"No," I chose my words carefully. "She learns as you do, not from books, and now she has found the place she wishes to call home. She wants to stay and learn at your side. She is very fond of your mother," I added.

"My family and I were worried you would take her with you." He looked at me critically.

"If she would have desired it, Ngahuru would have talked it over with you. But Jenny has told us she is home, and you are her family. She has been happy to see us these seven days, but she wishes to remain here when we leave."

Devi Ulani visibly relaxed. "That is good." He repeated, "That is good. She would have taken part of my heart with her." He looked closely at my face. "Your Ngahuru will be sad."

"Yes. But she wants all of her Wrens to be happy wherever they choose to land."

I waited a moment. "Tedros said we must leave for Juisiti tomorrow. He said he must take care of some business for you in Juisiti before he rejoins his unit."

"Yes, we had hoped a messenger would deliver a letter from Solkka saying he had arrived safely in Salisport, but all of us along this road are dependent on those who travel back and forth for our news. A letter may be already in Juisiti and only waiting on someone to travel this way to deliver it to us. If there is a letter waiting, Tedros will read it and send it on so all of us, you as well, know he has arrived safely."

"I will let you know if I receive news. I am living for the moment at Rishka, the place of Conrosan refugees in Vikland. Our settlement, Manumina, was taken over by Matasi soldiers as a garrison in eastern Kerek. I am told this happened the day or the day after we abandoned it."

"I am sorry you have lost your home." Devi looked at me gently. I felt for a moment he truly understood what it meant to give up the place you had first felt a sense of home. I wondered how a man who walked the same fields his father and his grandfather had walked could know of such a thing. I wondered if Hilanna, a princess of the West Islands, had been able to teach him what it meant to find a home, or was it his understanding that drew her to him in the first place? It was a question I didn't know how to ask, or if I should.

"Thank you. You have been gracious and kind, and I have been beyond glad Ngahuru and I were able to travel to meet you."

We finished our work and walked easily back to the house to clean up before the end of day meal.

CHAPTER 35

EXPECTATIONS

I never realized how easily the rest of the world traveled. I hadn't understood what Devi Ulani had meant on how dependent the Keopi district was on travelers for news. Since we were now traveling on the main road to Juisiti, Tedros stopped at all the large farms and settlements along the way to gather letters, documents to be delivered to the administration clerks and the courts, even a large bag of coins to be taken to the central bank for taxes.

All of the Ulani boys were known, and Tedros referred to the landowners by name. A couple of them asked after his sister, Jenny; one asked how his grandmother was coping with four of her grandchildren as soldiers in the war; a shy man asked after Tedros's cousin Lissil and if Tedros knew where she was fighting; another commented on Solkka's new scar as the only way he could tell the brothers apart, "although I'm sure he could have found a less dramatic way to help us." Tedros laughed at that, and said they could not even determine who had lost their braid in battle first, it was so hard to compete with each other.

I had never seen the like. Even Ngahuru said the West Islands did not have such a level of social trust in one another, and they had Traveler tales as their example. Tedros shrugged when we questioned him.

"It is like this everywhere in the wop-wops, I think. If we do not work and stand together, we all fail." He paused. "Also, everyone knows my mother or my grandmother. They think if we boys do wrong, they will only need to tell either of them." He grinned mischievously. "They are not mistaken."

Once we arrived at the academies, we split up. Tedros was going to go to the city offices and take care of all the items he had been entrusted with, Ngahuru wanted to go to the West Islands embasado and meet with the ambassador there, and I wanted to visit Chul and Aajan. I took my traveling bag and gratefully slid off my horse at the end of the street where they worked. Tedros offered one more time to leave it with me, but I just shook my head. I was glad to be on foot. Ngahuru waved goodbye, and I walked alone to Chul Swyler and Aajan Qanaq's labs.

Aajan opened the door.

"Chul?" she called over her shoulder. "Are we taking in strays today? This one looks like he needs food and conversation." She looked at me. "Still not fluent in Vik?" She rolled her eyes at the shake of my head. "And Chul refuses to learn Conrosan. Truly, I am the only civilized one around here. Please come in, Zren. We've been hoping you'd stop by for a good gossip—even if it has to be in Keresh." She stepped aside with a sad smile.

She walked me back to Chul's lab and then offered to get food and drink, "since I don't have anything more important to do."

She gave me a quick pat on the cheek as she grabbed her carry all bag and her coin purse and slipped by me. I heard Chul coming down the hall with his tell-tale click-slide, click-slide and soon he filled the doorway.

"My favorite stray. Please come in and sit down."

I twisted my head to look at the front door. "Is Aajan all right? Her humor is always sharp, but today I felt more bite than usual."

He gave a heartfelt sigh. "She believes she has been treated unjustly. Politics at the academy and politics at the palace. She'll weather them both, but that is her story to tell. Come in, come in."

We chatted about my journey out to the Keopi district. Chul had never been so far east and was interested in the differences in climate and geography. I had not known until he told me, coffee could only be grown in that specific area of Vikland, and how brave the first coffee growers had been when they didn't know how successful they would be.

I mentioned one of Tiju Tia's Wrens was making a permanent home out there with the Ulani family, and oh by the way, had he happened to hear or see anything of Solkka Ulani?

Chul laughed. "You, my friend, are such a joy. Your face is as wide open as your heart. And to reassure such a sad and hopeful face, I heard just yesterday from Lomes, all three of those crossing the Silver Mountains, including Solkka Ulani, arrived safely in Salisport. He is alive and well and stuck there at the whim of the Empress for the foreseeable future. More than that I cannot say because I do not know."

I heard the door open and close and Aajan's voice, "What? The great and wonderful, Chul Swyler, firemaster of Vikland, does not know something or someone?" She stepped into the doorway of our room. "I could have sworn I saw the sun rise in the east today. Zren, did you see the sun rise in the east?" Without waiting for an answer, she turned and went through into the workroom.

I looked at Chul. He wasn't smiling anymore.

"It's not my story to tell," he repeated.

We sat listening to Aajan mutter as she gathered cups and plates and carried it all in to us. Her face wore an expression I had seen on Piffik's face a hundred times. The one which said 'I am not happy about this turn of events, but I am going to make them bend to my will and come out victorious on the other side.' We ate silently. It wasn't uncomfortable, more like everyone was waiting for me to say something.

I felt my way forward cautiously. "Thank you, Aajan. There are no two people in Juisiti I enjoy seeing more than you and Chul. I thank the stars you are always willing to open the door to me. No matter what my home: Manumina, a refugee camp, or the battlefield in Kerek, you have always invited me in, fed me, and made me feel welcome."

She looked at me closely. "You believe that. You are not mocking me."

"I do believe it. You are so interesting, there are many who want to see the rest of your story. I am beyond glad each time you reach a goal, that you don't lose all of your old friends."

She snorted. "You should have stopped at 'I do believe.' Beyond that, and you remind me of those silly first year students who offer to walk me home."

I leaned back in my chair and let the hurt creep into my voice. "Don't mock my feelings. You are better than that." I changed the subject. "Now I have bored Chul with everything I learned about growing coffee, and he is still sitting here and has not fallen asleep. What can you tell me of Juisiti so I may become clever and witty?"

Aajan gave Chul a long stare. He matched her gaze with a quiet smile.

"It's your story to tell. You have fresh ears to hear what you want to say."

She turned to me. "Nothing. Nothing ever happens." I could hear sorrow in her voice.

"Do you want it to?" I asked carefully.

Her words fell out in a torrent. The academies were recognizing superior work, and she had entered her unguents used in the burn units. She was excited to be competing against much older students, and she had helped people, she said. Lots of people. She had provided samples and references and confidently gone to her meeting with those who made the decisions and then, and then. She was so angry she stopped speaking, and I looked fearfully at Chul.

He shook his head, and so I said nothing.

"I lost, Zren. I lost so badly my work wasn't even mentioned. All the prizes went to final year Viklanders, and they are the ones with the attention and the awards. I wanted to show my family what I could do and I didn't even get a single notice. Not one!" She was up and pacing now and I let her vent for a while. Finally, she threw her braid back over her shoulder and said, "Well, aren't you going to say anything?"

"What would I say?" I offered meekly.

"Oh, Aajan," she started out bitterly. "You're only a first year student. You must consider you've made lives better for all those soldiers—that's a reward in itself!" Then she dropped her voice as if she was mocking an old teacher, "My dear girl, there is always next year. Don't worry so much about it, nobody remembers the award winners from one year to the next." Then she pinched her face into a sour scowl, "You are doing such interesting things, you'll have lots of awards later on." She cocked an eyebrow at me and waited.

"Huh," I grunted. "None of those came to mind."

"They didn't?" She gave me a wary look.

"No, first thing I thought was I would never have even thought to enter. I would have assumed everyone else was smarter, older, Viklander, and people like me need not apply. You're running on an entirely different level, Aajan. You have demanded to be seen and heard and already proven you are a force to be acknowledged. This year you have put everyone on notice, someone with true talent is coming up. Whether or not you win next year depends on if anyone was paying attention. That's what went through my mind."

"Oh." This time the pause was hers. "That's not all of it," she said chagrined. She walked over to the table by Chul's chair and picked up a heavy square of cream-colored paper. "This came by palace messenger yesterday."

I took the card from her hands and tried to read it, but it was in Vik. I handed it back to her.

"I'm sorry, what does it say?"

Chul interjected smoothly, "Miyamoto Suki and Jinhai, second daughter of the Empress, are getting married. My guess is the Empress wants something cheerful to turn everyone's eyes from the Matasi takeover of Kerek City right now. There are a lot of people who think she mishandled the war."

"This is good though, right?" I questioned. "I mean, Miya has been planning to marry Jinhai forever, I thought."

"That's not the problem," Aajan said stiffly. "The invitation came addressed like so," she handed me another folded paper of the same heavy cream color, this one with a broken wax seal. As I flipped it over, Anjan said, "It reads 'Chul Swyler.'" She paused. "Only Chul Swyler."

I thought about what Chul had said earlier as I handed both papers back to her.

"I understand a little of your hurt at not receiving an invitation. After all you are here in Vikland because of a life debt owed. Miyamoto Suki, a Prince of Vikland, came to Manumina and gifted you a horse, a gift so extravagant in your settlement, even one of your 'unworthy suitors' as your brother called them could not have matched such generosity as a bride gift. He asked you to call him his byname of 'Miya' something he reserved for his friends. His family is paying for your education and your home, and he stays involved enough he knows how well you are doing in your classes and in your life. He is a worthy friend, Aajan, and a wealthy one.

"But if the Empress is having the wedding now, then perhaps the Empress is deciding who may attend. If you saw Miya tomorrow on the street in front of your house, and he crossed the street to avoid talking to you, then you could be hurt, and I would be hurt with you. But that?" I pointed to the cards in her hands. "That is nothing more than politics and has nothing to do with the understanding we carry in our hearts of who we call our friends."

The room was silent.

"It still hurts," she sniffed.

"Of course, it does. We all want to believe we are important to one another. But you are important to me, Aajan. And I am telling you this now, so you never forget it, no matter how far I travel away from Juisiti and the wisdom I find in your home."

We sat quietly. Chul barely moving in his chair. Aajan almost visibly mending her broken heart in front of us. At last, she stood.

"I'm sorry, Zren. I need to work on an experiment before I leave the lab tonight. Please stay as a guest in our home." She flashed a little of her old Aajan smile. "Unless the Empress is waiting for you to return to the palace?"

I folded my hands in the formal Vikland bow. "You are the first and last place I plan to visit here in Juisiti, Aajan Qanaq. I gratefully accept your offer."

She went over to Chul sitting in his chair and gently laid her cheek on the top of his hair. "Zren's words would not have taken root tonight, if you would not have sown the ideas earlier. You are more than I deserve, my friend. I am beyond glad you have not yet discovered this to be true." Neither of us said a word as she left and walked up the stairs to her own working rooms.

We were in no hurry to leave. Chul and I talked about the wedding and he wondered if this meant the newly married pair would take a tour of all the embasados before leaving to take up residence in Conrosa and reopening the embasado there.

"It's no secret Miyamoto Suki has been training to reopen that posting for years," Chul added. "And now we need it open. Quickly."

I wondered what it would take to run an embasado. I asked Chul if he had heard if the embasados in Kerek City had reopened. Did he know if they ever would?

"As far as I know, Kerek is still under martial law by the Matasi army. They are exacting masters, but the Kereki people don't seem to have any stomach for rebellion. I can't imagine other countries are going to rush to reopen their embasado if the future is still so uncertain."

He grinned at me. "Make no mistake there is a lot of talking and posturing going on, but it is all behind closed doors and in front of the Triune in Alenti."

I tried to understand, but finally just asked Chul, "So I thought the whole point of this war was Matasi and Vikland would work together to recover free passage along the Northern Track—along all the tracks. The war lasted three years and Vikland still has no port. So what am I not understanding, Chul?"

Chul considered my question carefully. "I have heard a foreign occupation is expensive. Matasi is looking forward to having the trails and tracks from Vikland's border to Kerek City and down to Matasi open for business as soon as possible. Vikland is the largest of the three countries with the most raw materials.

It would be far cheaper and faster for Matasi if our goods could travel through Vikland, cut diagonally across the south of Kerek and cross just beyond the foothills of the Silver Mountains.

"In exchange, perhaps Matasi could clear the corridor along all the tracks, or charge a toll or tax which would actually grant safe passage. This, I believe, is why Solkka Ulani is in Salisport. He and the others he traveled with are presenting the Empress's wants and needs to the Ambassador who will travel to Alenti to meet with the Triune." Chul considered. "If the Empress wants to keep Miya in Vikland until the wedding, Solkka will probably go along as window dressing to Alenti as well." Chul smiled at me. "Our Empress may not always use every opportunity wisely, but she is quick to see them when they grow up strong and beautiful and are related to the King of the West Islands."

I opened my mouth to ask what he meant, when there was a knock at the door.

"That will be Piffik," Chul said to my surprised look, "we were expecting him." I rushed to the door to open it so Chul wouldn't have to struggle to his feet.

"It is you!" I exclaimed. "What are you doing here?" we both said together. I stepped back to let him inside. He had a large traveling bag he set down just inside the door.

Piffik greeted Chul. Aajan must have heard his voice because she called down the stairs, "I am so glad you are here, let me finish one tiny step and I will be down for good."

Piffik took the chair by the window.

"I thought you were at the Ulani coffee farm?" Piffik asked me.

"We got back today. Tedros Ulani escorted us. Ngahuru has her meeting with the Empress tomorrow to talk about the Wrens and what Vikland owes them," I said.

"I also have been invited to see the Empress regarding the Conrosan refugees. Our Council of Wisdom was surprised the Empress felt free to demand I be part of the group to be heard, but they are staying nearby while I asked to stay here."

Chul gave a wry grin. "Remind her of how much two Conrosans, you and Siba, out of two hundred, helped her cause?"

Piffik shrugged. "There were many of us, more than just Conrosans, who used Manumina as a base. No matter the reason, we have lost our home to the Matasi. I don't mean to be ungrateful, but the Empress needs to know the estate where we are now is too small for all of us. We need land where we can be self-sufficient."

He paused as he looked at Chul. "This is where I need your help, my friend. I have a plan to give Vikland her own port in her own lands. But this is the farthest I have ever been from Manumina. Do you have maps and books about the rest of Vikland?

"The Huenas have many friends and they have helped me talk through what I need and for what I must ask. While we have been building the Huena's second inn, I have searched the libraries of all of the Huena's friends in Axefield.

"Chul, I have never seen a river except for the Huk. I know the different woods I get from sawmills in Kerek and Vikland, but I have never seen the forests that grow them. I do not know what a mountain looks like—either Silver or Cold—but I know blasting through them with ghostfire is important to my plan of finding a sheltered bay and building a harbor. I don't want to bargain away my people's future because I was too stiff-necked to admit I don't know anything about the land I want to live in."

Chul leaned back smiling. "I can help. I am beyond glad to hear ghostfire will have a purpose beyond bloodshed. But I will need your help to get my maps and books down."

We spent the rest of the afternoon and evening learning Vikland geography and geology, imports, exports, population, culture, and politics. Chul believed the Empress would offer the Conrosans several estates which, because of the war, no longer had heirs.

"If she can split you up among several different estates, especially those at a distance, you will be forced to assimilate faster. The quicker you lose your language and your culture, the quicker you become Viklanders, in her opinion."

"It was the same at Manumina. Some of the young would go to your academies or to the nearby towns and villages in Kerek to earn wages of their own. Once they left, they never returned. My brother, Zadah, was one of them." He sighed. "Is all the land near the Cold Mountains considered valuable? It is better for us to build from the roots up, than to take over a Vikland estate, I am thinking."

"With what? You have no coin," Chul countered. "What will your Council of Wisdom say if the Empress demands your youth serve three years in the military? If she says your district schools cannot be taught in Conrosan, but must be in Vik so your children are prepared for the academies here in Juisiti?

"You believe you can build a deep-water harbor through the Cold Mountains. Four years ago, I would have shaken my head and said you were misguided. But with the war, we have made ghostfire dance to our music and I think it can be done. Not easily, and at great risk, but it can be done. I think you and I can best decide *where* you want to live and build this. But it is up to you and your Council of Wisdom *how* you are willing to live in Vikland."

"I know." Piffik nodded grimly. "I've been thinking about this a lot. That's when I knew I needed your help in more than just formulas and demonstrations of how we could blast through a mountain. I need to understand what Vikland wants and what Vikland needs."

Chul just smiled and opened another map for us to learn.

Aajan joined us and Chul went out to bring our end of day meal back so "you can talk amongst yourselves." After he left, Piffik went to his traveling bag and pulled out his drawings and blank papers. He explained his dream of carving a path through the mountains and asked Aajan to make new drawings to match what we had talked about. Piffik asked us what we thought Conrosans could live on.

We asked Aajan about food in Vikland, what was common, what was inexpensive, what was imported, and what no one would eat. We talked about West Islands steel, the wood that made the bongs—both short and long—and the ingredients Chul needed for his liquid ghostfire. We talked about the riots in Kerek City and how I suspected Chul had blown up those warehouses years ago. How he refined his invention and made ghostfire. We all thought he already knew how to make ghostfire strong enough to blast through mountains of rock.

We talked about the coffee fields of east Vikland and how the exports would be cheaper and profits higher if the farmers could sail coffee on a Vikland ship from a port in their district. We talked about where the sea and the mountains would conspire to make the best crossing and the best harbor. We looked at Chul's map of Vikland and marveled at the size of the country—far larger than we had imagined. Matasi had taken Ngahuru and me eight days to walk just to the closest port. Kerek only took eight to ten days to walk top to toe and port to border, but the Vikland maps showed the Keopi district—a journey on horseback seven long days from Juisiti—as barely halfway across the country.

"Tell me more about the mountains. Do we live on them? Farm them? I know Viklanders say they cross the Silver Mountains to go into Matasi, but I don't understand what that means." Piffik looked at me patiently.

"The Cold Mountains are not as worn down as the Silver Mountains according to Tedros, and he has seen both. I remember Tedros saying something about Matasi farmers terracing the hillside and farming food crops." I shrugged. "But I did not ask him what kind of crops, or if it was a successful plan or one of desperation."

Chul came back with the food, and we moved to another table to eat. We visited about Juisiti, and Piffik asked a lot of questions of other larger cities farther east in the interior of Vikland. Piffik went on to ask about ghostfire.

Chul gave a long explanation of how unstable ghostfire was and pointed to his leg. He had been working on longer burn times, more stable compounds, but it was still not something he could use in a long-range explosive farther than a bowmaster could shoot.

"So invent something more. Aajan, you're a student at the Academy of Elements. Dream this up so I can build it." Piffik wiped his hands on a cloth and stood up. "Show me a place on a map where the mountains are the lowest or have the widest gaps or whatever I need to break through to the sea."

Chul pulled himself up and we all looked at the maps again. Chul had to check some of his books to understand the geography and topography, but finally selected a portion of Vikland more than a day's ride from even the easternmost coffee farm. The bay was wide and sheltered, the sea maps claimed it was deep with no dangerous reefs.

"But if you do this, you will be far from the population centers of Vikland," he warned.

Piffik considered. "But close to the raw materials Vikland could export. Close to the coffee farmers, close to the orchards you showed me pictures of earlier. Populations move. Right now everyone is crowded against the border because it is the shortest distance to move goods. I want to build better."

Chul gave him a thoughtful look. "I cannot promise you I can invent everything you may need." Then he grinned. "But it would be fun to try."

"I know, my friend, I know. But it is a plan I can present to the Empress tomorrow and believe in. If I am wrong, then I have selected a spot where we can live in peace far from the eye of Vikland's rulers."

"But if you are right, Piffik," Aajan said slowly. "You will move the financial center of the country to here." She pointed to the map, "and you will have the richest land in the country."

"It could take two generations, maybe more." He nodded. "By then the Empress will have abdicated in favor of her eldest daughter, and Miya and his princess will have been a part of Conrosan society for decades. We can sell our holdings and sail for Conrosa if we need to."

I looked up shocked. "That's your plan?" I squeaked.

"That's one of my plans," Piffik said gently. "I want to be prepared for many things. I have a lot of time to think with all this traveling about. All I do is make plans."

"Huh," I grunted. "I just usually think about what I want to eat for my next meal."

CHAPTER 36

NGAHURU AND THE EMPRESS

Piffik had agreed to meet Ngahuru before her audience with the Empress and accompany her to the palace. While we were still eating first meal with Aajan and Chul, a messenger from the West Islands embasado arrived with new Vikland clothes for us and shiny black boots. Aajan cut Piffik's hair back to his neck because he didn't want the Empress to wonder why he refused to put it in a braid. The result had even Aajan saying nice things about her brother.

Once we were dressed, Chul ordered us a small pony cart to deliver us to the West Islands embasado where we would meet Ngahuru. When Piffik complained he was sure we could find the place if Chul just gave us directions, Chul merely replied that wasn't the point. Today we were meeting Ambassadors and the Empress. We needed to act like it.

Under Piffik's arms were new drawings, maps, and written plans for buildings and works and costs for everything. He must have stayed up half the night after I had gone to bed. He told me the Council of Wisdom would be coming later and meet us there, closer to their own summoning time.

When we arrived at the West Islands embasado, Ngahuru was waiting for us, wearing a beautiful West Islands dress, brightly colored to contrast with her freshly dyed black hair and dark skin. Her glove was off, and she stretched and folded her hands many times in anticipation.

While we were in the reception room, a graceful older woman who looked like Mother Ulani came in to meet us. Ngahuru introduced us to the Ambassador from the West Islands, an older sister to *Rangatira* Hilanna. I made the Vikland bow—a deep one because I didn't know what else to do. I reminded myself to ask Solkka how to greet people in the West Islands *before* we sailed there.

The Ambassador thanked me—in Wester—for the bag of letters and gifts Ngahuru had carried for Mother Ulani to deliver to her sister. I just smiled, made a deeper bow, and said it was my pleasure. Ngahuru had her reasons for saying it was me and holding the conversation in Wester, I wasn't going to stumble through and disrupt her careful plans.

The ambassador called her carriage for us. This time Piffik was more gracious and thanked the Ambassador for her thoughtfulness. I smiled. It seemed we all could learn how to live in Vikland and speak with royalty.

At the palace, we three were escorted into a large antechamber for waiting. The Master at Arms told us Ngahuru would be announced and escorted in. She would be seated at a table with the Empress, Yong-ji - the Empress to be, Jinhai - the second daughter, and her intended husband, Miyamoto Suki. Ngahuru would then be offered a small cup of coffee, she was to accept one cup and one cup only, even if offered a second. She would make her request to the Empress. The others would serve as Witnesses. After she had answered their questions, a clerk would be summoned to document what had been decided. She would be escorted out. She was to curtsy both before stepping on the platform and then again as she was leaving the room. Did she have any questions?

"No questions. I understand. It is the same in the West Islands when I visit with the King," she said quietly. The Master at Arms looked at her thoughtfully but said nothing more.

Once she was announced, the Master at Arms pointed Piffik and me to another door in the opposite direction.

"You can't hear anything, of course, but if you go in there, you can sit *very* quietly and see everything that goes on. Your diplomat will be in your sight at all times."

The room was about the size of Aajan's sitting room at her lab. There were two handfuls of chairs scattered about the room, but no one else was inside. We looked through a small opening no taller than a hand, but the width of the room.

The Empress, her two daughters, and Miya were sitting around an ornate table at the far end of the hall. After Ngahuru deeply curtsied, Miya stood up, came around the table, took her hands in both of his and escorted her to her chair to sit. Someone brought in fingersweets and coffee, and one of the daughters served. I wondered which one was Jinhai. Miya was watching Ngahuru, and I wondered if he thought she was Tiju Tia during the war and how she had done it. I chuckled to myself at the mystery he couldn't solve.

The meeting lasted two decons. I was beginning to think Ngahuru was retelling each adventure of the Wrens one by one as she bargained for their future. Finally another person joined them and wrote out a series of pages. He laid each document out on the table and the Empress and her two daughters signed them and then they were passed to Ngahuru who signed them as well. When they finished, Miya stood first, then Ngahuru. She dipped deeply into another curtsy to the Empress.

Miya walked her to the door which swung open. Piffik and I slipped out into the corridor to meet her.

Ngahuru was beaming.

"That went well," she said without preamble. "Each Wren will have coin and the choice to stay in Vikland or travel to the West Islands. There will be sufficient coin for them for the upcoming Wet—a soldier's pay—but they are resourceful, it will only help their own earnings. The academies are out of reach for them. They are clever enough, but not in the knowledge measured in the academies." She let out a sigh. "I am very pleased, Piffik. I hope your session goes as well after midday."

We walked out into the sunshine. There were two of the Council of Wisdom members waiting where Piffik had told them to gather. I looked at Ngahuru's sumptuous dress and the patched and frayed clothes of the Conrosans and had a sudden sinking feeling.

But I knew Miya would be there, Vikland took the life debt seriously, and the Empress was a very proud woman who still did not have a path to the seas. It would have to be enough.

We walked Ngahuru down to where her ambassador's carriage waited.

"Thank you for serving as my honor guard. I am going to go back to my embasado and sometime tomorrow travel to the Huena Inn. I'll send someone to Rishka to bring Callis, Arden, and Siba to Axefield and we can share our news with all the Wrens. Is this agreeable to you?"

Piffik agreed and handed her into the carriage. He stepped back, nodded to the driver, and we watched as the carriage and horses stepped down the street.

We took the Council of Wisdom members to a nearby coffee salon. Once I knew its location well enough to return or give directions, I went back to the steps of the palace where I would wait for the others and send them on to Piffik. He would need all of this time and more to discuss his plans, his numbers, and what we learned this morning of how the meeting would go with the Council. I blessed Ngahuru and Chul again for teaching us what we needed to know without ever making us feel foolish and awkward. I did not know what I had done to deserve such friends, but I knew enough to be very grateful for them.

The Council members came in singles and pairs. I answered their questions as best I could and sent them on to the coffee salon to talk with Piffik. I knew some of them wanted to stay where they were at Rishka, while others wanted to go back to Manumina without understanding the Matasi army now called it home. Piffik needed to convince *them* as well as the Empress his plan was sound and not to accept the leavings they had already been given.

I remembered what Piffik had told me this morning at first meal. "Change is hard, Zren. But if we don't grab our chance now, we may not get another. Once Miya sails away with his new bride, we have lost our known voice in front of the Empress."

For the next decon, I shepherded Conrosans to the coffee salon. I wished I would have counted them to know if I had them all or not. I was just ready to walk away when a young woman from the palace called out, "Conrosan!" I winced as I turned and she approached. "You are one of the guards of Ngahuru of the West Islands?"

I fumbled for a moment. "Ah, yes?"

She gave me an odd look, but handed me a cream-colored folded paper sealed with purple wax. I wasn't sure if it was for me or Ngahuru, so I opened it as soon as the woman walked away. I relaxed as I saw the familiar Conrosan script inside. Miya had simply written, "Piffik, Zren, if at all possible, let us meet at Chul's and Aajan's working rooms tonight. I ask as a friend and not as a diplomat. Thank you for your consideration of my request. – Miya."

I hurried to the coffee salon to share the news with Piffik.

CHAPTER 37

A HOMELAND FOR CONROSANS

The first indication the Council of Wisdom were not going to be treated as well as Ngahuru, came at the hands of the Master at Arms. He looked everyone up and down and then said only three of them would be permitted to enter. No one understood his Vik except Piffik. As Piffik started translating to Conrosan, the Master at Arms repeated himself in Keresh with a sour look. Only then did I realize he had spoken Wester to Ngahuru and I and Piffik earlier. I wondered why Piffik had not said anything. I knew he didn't understand Wester.

The Council debated briefly and selected three people, but not Piffik. Unhappily, Piffik started to hand over his maps, when suddenly the Master at Arms said to Piffik, "You have to be one of the three. You are the only one dressed appropriately to meet the Empress." There were grumblings and side looks at Piffik's Viklander dress, but he had a relieved smile as he recollected his drawings and documents.

Their instructions were also different from what we had heard this morning. No mention of food or coffee, only to bow before and after they presented their request. Then Salik Oqina, Piffik Qanaq, and one other were announced and permitted to enter.

I started to walk down the hallway to the same viewing room, but the Master at Arms stopped me.

"No one is permitted."

"But I was in there earlier—to watch Ngahuru," I protested.

"I thought you were her honor guards, her attendants," he clarified.

I thought fast, "We are, Piffik and I, but we are also Conrosans with a stake in our future."

He waved me away. "No one is permitted," he repeated.

There were soldiers who escorted the rest of us out of the building. I guess milling about in the hallway wasn't permitted either. We retreated to the outside steps where we had first met to wait. No one had enough coin to go back to the coffee salon, and I didn't feel comfortable enough in Aajan's friendship to take them all to her place while she should be working. So we stood or sat on the benches around the small pocket gardens of flowers and grass in front of the palace like the homeless and destitute. Which, I considered to myself, we actually were.

I estimated we barely waited a decon, and I was going to wander off and buy some stonebread to quiet my stomach, when I saw Piffik and the other two walk slowly down the steps. Piffik's arms were empty and I wondered where all of Chul's maps and the drawings had gone. Piffik's mouth was in a pinched tight line and Salik Oqina was talking sharply.

"You ask too much, Piffik, you cannot stand in front of the Empress of Vikland and say to her you have a better idea than anyone she or any of her advisors have known."

"You're the one who refused to bow," Piffik bit out.

"I was only showing her and her daughters we Conrosans have our own Queen to honor."

"No. You were being disrespectful!" Piffik sighed. "It's over. Let's gather the wagons and head back. Miyamoto Suki promised all the papers and maps would be returned to Chul Swyler. I don't have the stomach to stay here for another moment."

"But…" I started, and Piffik shot me a hard glance. I swallowed the rest of my words. As he herded the council members out of the flower gardens, he whispered to me, "Go to Aajan's. I'll meet you there in a little while."

I realized Piffik hadn't forgotten Miya's note, he just wanted the council gone before we met at Aajan's working rooms. It was impossible not to notice Piffik's frustration. He had noted how Ngahuru had been treated—as an esteemed guest from the West Islands. I finally understood why Ngahuru had worn such an elaborate West Islands dress, dyed her hair and skin, and asked Piffik and me to dress in Viklander clothes and serve as her honor guard. Maybe Piffik had understood as well, and that is why he said nothing when the conversations were in Wester that morning. However, the Council of Wisdom had not, and they had been treated as supplicants, and not as the respected recipients of a past due favor.

I took my time, buying a noodle bowl and enjoying the sunshine. Finally, I wandered down the academy streets and delivered myself to Aajan's and Chul's working rooms.

She opened the door at my knock, gave a startled, "Oh! Chul's not home," and stepped back to let me in. "Can you run up with me? I am in the middle of something." I followed her quickly as she ran up the stairs and when I started to speak, she shushed me as she stirred a pot over her flame and pushed others about, measuring and sifting. I sat quietly and when I heard a knock downstairs, jumped up to get it so she would not be disturbed a second time.

It was Piffik. I briefly told him Chul wasn't here and Aajan was in the middle of an experiment, so we quietly waited downstairs.

At last she called down, "Almost done, be there in a moment!"

Suddenly, the air filled with a sharp acrid scent and my eyes watered.

"Whew!" I coughed. "That's what Chul has to endure?" I waved my hand in front of my face as Aajan appeared in the doorway.

"Yes, well," she said drily, "my brother wants me to blow up the side of the mountain, so of course there are going to be some side effects."

I jumped up. "Are we going to be safe here?"

"Of course, only Chul gets to add the part that goes 'boom,' and he just got called away to the palace." She looked at her brother closely. "You wouldn't have anything to do with that, would you? They sent a two-wheeled carry cart and a cute little pony for him to come quickly. They didn't even make him find one of his own."

Piffik lifted up his hands, then dropped them. "I don't know. That's what I wanted to talk to all of you about." He ran his hand through his short brown hair. "That and to tell you Miya is coming here tonight—as a friend."

Aajan wheeled on me. "You didn't tell him, did you?"

"Of course not, I didn't even get close to talk to him. Only Ngahuru and Piffik are worthy enough for that." I grinned at Piffik.

While we waited for Chul, Piffik started talking and didn't stop. He discussed the differences between the Conrosans meeting from the one Ngahuru had. He repeated all the questions the two daughters had asked and his responses. He debated with us what he could have said differently, how he could have respectfully kept the Council of Wisdom members from speaking, and the words they had said at cross purposes to his own.

The Empress had said nothing, had offered no questions. Piffik thought she had been offended when Salik Oqina had refused to bow. Piffik had said the formal Vik greetings as Rell had taught him, but he had been the only one, and he berated himself again for his thick accent.

He had tried to redeem himself by offering to hold the conversation in Vik, Conrosan, or Keresh, but the other two Conrosans had insisted on Keresh and the Empress had consented. One of the daughters had frowned at that.

Miya had asked the Empress's indulgence to ask questions, and Piffik gratefully acknowledged Miya had asked very good questions, but he could tell Miya was being cautious in front of the Empress, and Piffik knew it wasn't Miya's role to speak to the

Conrosans' cause. He debated with us what else he could have said to better assure the Viklanders his plan had merit.

I had never seen Piffik like this. He was always so self-confident and assured. I began to get an uneasy feeling the future was not going to go well for my friends.

CHAPTER 38

THE FUTURE AHEAD OF US

Chul and Miya came in the same little two-wheeled carry cart about three decons later. As Chul opened the door, Miya walked in carrying a wooden crate with freshly cooked food.

"Since I invited myself over, I thought I should at least bring the end of day meal." He set it down on the table and gave short bows to Aajan, me, and Piffik. "My friends, it is so good to see you again."

We offered him congratulations on his upcoming marriage and he grinned. "She finally said yes!"

"Jinhai?" I was confused.

"No, her mother. Jinhai said yes when we were eight years old. Now we have been wearing down her mother for the last twenty years." He sobered. "The Empress wanted Yong-ji to be married first since she will take over the crown and the empire and her consort matters."

He shrugged. "But we need to reopen our embasados with Conrosa, and other countries to the north. We need to tell our side of the war, and Jinhai said she would not do that without me by her side." He took in our astonished looks. "It doesn't matter to me why she said yes, just that she did. I am happy, my friends, I am very happy!"

I gave him a quick hug. "And I am happy for you."

Miya turned to look at Piffik. "I need to say I am sorry. The Master at Arms said you had observed Ngahuru's meeting this morning. There is protocol for everything. We cannot allow more supplicants than Witnesses for the Empress's safety. That is why only three of you could enter. Food and drink are only offered to those of equal status. Ngahuru holds the same status to her King as I do to my Empress. Or we think she does, the West Islands are very different than Vikland."

Piffik held up a hand to prevent Miya from saying more. "I understand this, and I was not offended. But I do apologize for the stiff-necked stubbornness of my countrymen."

"Trust me, we have seen worse. Princess Yong-ji was subjected for years to the unwanted attentions of one of the Kerek King's sons. They were truly..." Miya gave a wicked smile, "...unworthy suitors. She is probably happier than most the Kerek King and his family have sailed for the Spice Island. An exiled prince would never be in consideration."

He waved his hand at the basket of food. "Let's eat. I have been in meetings all day and coffee and fingersweets are not going to keep me alive."

We fell on the food and laughed, told stories, and enjoyed each other's company. It had been ages since I had seen him—briefly before Bima's funeral—and even longer for Piffik. Yet Miya was relaxed and acting as if it had been just a few days since we had all been together. I wondered if this was what living in Vikland was like, or being a part of a royal family—so much was demanded of Miyamoto Suki, he came to visit with us to be someone else for a few decons.

The food was gone and the night was late, when Miya went out to the carry cart and brought in Viklander mapcases, Chul's books and papers, and a travel bag of Piffik's drawings, cost reports, and other documents.

"I had only planned to say hello to my friends tonight, but Piffik's meeting gave me another purpose. I have returned these as I promised. Thank you, Chul, for dropping all of the things demanding your attention to come to the palace and answer our questions. Piffik's scientific mind is far beyond what the Empress and I could comprehend, and you were able to enlighten us. Yong-ji appreciated your succinct summaries of her explanations. She grasps inventions, designs, and new ideas quickly. She will make a good Empress someday." He gave Chul a deep Vikland bow and Chul smiled, pleased with the acknowledgement of his time and knowledge. Miya smiled and turned to Piffik.

"Piffik, your drawings and plans showed us our solution is to the east and within our own borders. We need not be dependent on Kerek or Matasi." He pulled a thick sheaf of papers from the travel bag. "The court administrator turned pale with fear when I asked to deliver these to you in person. But the Empress agreed." He carefully handed them to Piffik with both hands. "You have a home."

He paused. "But I am warning you, it is a long way from Juisiti—eight days ride, longer with your wagons. It is to the east of the middle of the country, but we believe the best deep water harbor will be there. There will be many more meetings between you and the Empress's advisors between now and when you begin. I would not be surprised to hear if Yong-ji wishes to take part or even head this project. Having our own port would be a significant accomplishment for her before she begins her rule as Empress. But for now, you can tell your people, they have land holdings so great it will take all day to walk across from east to west and from the mountains to the south.

"We also agreed to your request that your youth shall serve their military service in building the path through the mountains, the port, and the roads surrounding for one generation. We agreed to you educating your own children, but the best of them must try to attend the academies.

"In return, you agreed to this: We will need a census, records of your births and deaths, and the generation who are serving their military service building the infrastructure. We believe you have enough people, and we will give you enough coin to last one year to build your homes and supply your needs until your fields, orchards, and land become self-sufficient. And that is what I am celebrating with my friends tonight—a future for all of us."

We were loud, we were laughing, and there were tears shed and unshed. That night, I realized Miya, Chul, and Piffik were all the same type of person, and best of all, they knew it too. Wealth and privilege had scattered unevenly among them, but they all had minds which saw beyond what everyone else did. They did not belittle others or cheat another to reach for the stars, they didn't need to. They knew how to teach others, and ask for help. They honored their own truth, and asked to understand others.

Because of them, my own understanding had been blown wide open. I wasn't defined by poverty, or lack of education, or my size, or anything else. That's what Ngahuru and Rell and Siba had been telling me all along; I could be whatever I wanted to be.

Miya saw me standing so still and gently laid his arm across my shoulder.

"Zren Janin, you have many choices ahead of you. Will you move to Vikland's far east with the Conrosans to their new home? Accompany Ngahuru to the West Islands and see Koanga again? Travel to Matasi to join Solkka Ulani? Or sail with Jinhai and I to Conrosa?"

I blinked at him in surprise. "You would take me to Conrosa?"

"I keep my word, if that is where you wish to go."

"No," I reassured him. "Jinhai will have you all to herself."

I tipped my head and considered. "I will help Ngahuru settle any of her Wrens who wish to stay in Vikland, and then travel with her and the others over the Silver Mountains through Matasi. I will see them off on their ship, and then I will join Solkka Ulani wherever the Diplo sends him. After Matasi, I hope he is posted to the West Islands, or Conrosa, or maybe we will sail into Vikland's new port."

I hesitated wondering how Miya would take my words. "Vikland is not my home, but neither is Kerek. I don't know where my journey will end, but I know there will be stories, and good food." I grinned at him. "I do know none of us has so many friends we can throw any of them away."

He grinned back, and we watched the others bent over the map and the Empress's papers, looking at the future ahead of us.

ACKNOWLEDGEMENTS
(BUT I PREFER TO CALL THEM GRATITUDES)

The concept of Exile: A New Beginning—*whom do you serve* and *what should be the appropriate cost/reward*—was the result of a conversation with Marlene Harder Horst almost ten years ago around her kitchen table in Boone, North Carolina. Social justice can be a tricky thing.

In essence, determining that everyone has a seat at the table is not the same as fighting for that right. Social Justice can be a dragon of righteousness, a sword of courage against wrongdoing, or a knight in armor defending the villagers who are protecting their way of life. When the heroes and the villains are only determined by who is telling the story, who is right and who is wrong? When does reality morph into mythology?

I am only the storyteller.

It is up to you to decide whose deeds of renown are told at dawn and never forgotten, and those whose names and actions bring a sorrowful shake of the head.

There are many people who helped me tell these stories:

Thank you to the team at Paper Raven Books. Karen, Megan, Ashley, Stef, Amanda – you are so patient as you try to steer my enthusiasm and keep me focused on each new book in the series, *The Tales of Zren Janin*. I have been excited for *Exile* for a very long time. Thank you!

To my beta readers – Wow! You demanded so much from the characters! I was stunned when I received pages of feedback explaining motivations, casting aspirations, and painting morally grey stripes on all kinds of actions committed by those who live in these pages. And yet, and yet… when I held conversations with you, with the characters, and with myself, I realized you were right. No one is a villain in their own story. I sent you pages, and the well-marked manuscripts you sent back were far and away a better book.

To my reviewers, Booktokkers, and cheerleaders who have spread the message across social media – Thank you! Your creativity knows no ends and truthfully, you sometimes give me too much credit for weaving a story with so many layers. I learn from you all every day.

To the amazing team at Target – Thank you! You have been so much a part of this journey; I don't even know where to start. Compassion starts from the top down, and whether it was demonstrating the value of listening, leading with integrity, or assuming positive intent, so many of you have given me inspiration, validation, and support. To name you all would make this book as big as a doorstop, but know that I appreciate all that you have done for me.

To John Santoski, Susan Guevara, Bob DeVoe, Lat Anantaphong, Brandi McNamara Bailey, Adam Boser, Mark Scott, Sara Reininger, JaNaye Dee Peterson, and Justin Molina. But most of all, Kimberly Wick – You have all taught me that wisdom and grace mean the difference between a life and a life well lived. Your influence continues even though we no longer work together.

To Teresa Neby Lind, and Shirley Martin – Thank you for your incredible ability to connect and reconnect. You listen to all my stories over the years, and then when I dash off in yet another direction you patiently understand until I come back to where I need to be (again). As Zren Janin said in the last chapter, "I did not know what I had done to deserve such friends, but I knew enough to be very grateful for them." I am so very grateful for you.

As always, David and Bridget (and Sylvia!), Ryan and Briana, Jenny and Zach, Katie and Nelson, Almond, Brandon, Liz, Kaeden, Callie, Peyton, Philip, Lauren, Ryla, Rinoa, Gunther, Lark, Hayden, Max, Nordica, Penelope, Cory, Catherine, and

Hallie – You are brave, and talented, and kind, and funny. Thanks for putting on those superhero capes and saving the world.

My heart, my prince, Steven – Every day you remind me of why we work to make the world a better place. To whom much has been given, much is expected. My heart is too full to say everything that needs to be said.

Turn the page for *Exile: A New Beginning*

bonus materials including:

Reading Guide

TWO bonus short stories:

How to Find a Softfoot

and

The Value of a Daughter

Also a preview of *The Wrens Fly Away*

Book 5 in *The Tales of Zren Janin*

READING GUIDE

Book club/ Book review?

Try using these questions to start the conversations!

1. Imagine you are seeing ghostfire for the first time. How do you think this will change the war? How did this change how Zren Janin thinks of Rani the softfoot and his role?

2. Both Ross and Arden have been injured by the very ones they are trying to help. How is our perception of the war changing?

3. Zren's encounter with the bandits and with the Kereki soldiers forces him to reassess his biases. How does he show he is beginning to understand his own prejudices are as great as those who have been biased against him? How does this culminate with the encounter on the Sary bridge?

4. Zren and Bima Ritwik have a complicated relationship throughout the series. Zren has one more encounter with him early in the book, and then we see other sides of Bima from Miyamoto Suki and Solkka Ulani—both adding additional insight to Bima's character. How do you feel about Bima? Hero? Anti-hero? Villain? Why?

5. The Kerek King flees when his son is murdered in the streets of Kerek City. Yet it doesn't seem to have much effect on the war in the outlands. Why do you think this is?

6. Piffik's last rescue of the Wrens ties together three storylines: Falan's defiance of Kereki custom and her betrayal by those in Balza, Jenny as a soldier and not a Wren, and the deep talent of Kid's cleverness and his courage. How have the experiences the Wrens suffered in Kerek City prepared them for their heroism during the war?

7. Rell is missing for the last two thirds of the story. Yet we continue to feel her presence through Piffik's grief and Zren's feeling of loss. What do you think Rell's absence is teaching Zren? How will this make an impact on his life?

8. Zren learns several stories and rescues of the Wrens as the book progresses. Through these retellings we learn how independently all of the Wrens are acting from Tiju Tia's directions. How does the inability to communicate

with each other increase the danger and independence of the Wrens?

9. Did your impression of the Wrens change as you learned more of their rescues?

10. Why do you think it was so hard for the Wrens to adjust to Rishka and Axefield?

11. Who is your favorite Wren? Why? Are they similar or dissimilar to you?

12. A critical component of the book series is something the author calls "otherness" defined as an unrelenting attitude towards others that says they do not deserve the same treatment or kindness for any reason—lack of wealth, skin color, tenets of belief, gender/sexuality, abilities, lack of opportunities/privilege, or even no reason at all. In *Exile: A New Beginning,* we see how Zren's own perceptions have created a bias against Kerekis. We see that all of the countries have players that are morally gray and those who have good intentions that don't follow through. What are some of these examples?

13. Zren spends a significant amount of time trying to figure out how Inezi was murdered. He assumes she was not clever enough to stage her disappearance. What other

instances in *Exile* do you see where underestimating a person led to wrong assumptions?

14. Zren finally meets the Ulani family and Jenny. Why do you think Devi Ulani and Tedros tell the Ulani family history to Zren? What do you think Zren would say to Solkka if they meet again?

15. The last chapters deal with the rewards from the Empress. While the Empress feels she is generous, the gifts do not prepare the Wrens for a future of their own. No one speaks for Zren or Rygee. Because you as the reader know the Wrens from earlier books, what do you think will happen to them in *The Wrens Fly Away*?

HOW TO FIND A SOFTFOOT

(This story begins nine years before the events of *War and Wrens*)

Bima Ritwik and Rani the softfoot walked through the streets of the Sinner's District. It was early morning—the quietest and safest time of the day to walk through any part of Kerek City. The men were dressed in their Viklander blacks with a short bong strapped across their backs and two West Islands steel daggers hidden in their cloak pockets. They didn't expect trouble; they counted on the Viklander reputation to protect them as well as their steel and bongs. But they were prepared.

Conversation was brief. Both knew what they were looking for: men and women, as young as children, who would be willing to trade overheard conversations, stolen documents, and observations to the Viklander softfoots for food, protection, or other consideration.

Cart sellers were folding up their blankets from their sleeping places or arranging their goods. A man had set up his chair and was cutting hair in the open air. As the Viklanders got closer, he held his scissors high in the air and snapped the blades together—the West Islands steel glittered in the sun. He called to Bima and offered to cut their braids for them. Bima laughed and mimicked him cutting their throats instead. The barber chuckled and turned back to the man in his chair.

"One of ours?" Rani asked.

"No. West Islands. Their King has his sister as ambassador, and she has her fingers so deep here in the district, I am surprised we get any information at all." Bima scowled.

"How does the barber get anything worth sharing if everyone knows he sells secrets to the West Islands?"

Bima turned and gave him a wicked smile. "Perhaps no one else knows but you and me."

The men walked silently for a while, and then Rani put his hand on Bima's arm to stop him. Ahead of them was a patrol, five soldiers bunched loosely together as they ambled down the street. *New to Kerek City,* Rani guessed. Each of them wore their pocket of coins and papers tied on the outside of their uniforms. Easy to reach for the soldiers, easy to cut away for the thieves.

Rani and Bima looked at each other and smiled. They knew before the morning was over there would be at least one pickpocket who would risk a soldier's beating for a chance to steal a tied-on pocket loaded with coin. The Viklanders carefully stayed behind the patrol and started watching the alleys and doorways.

Rani tipped his chin to an alley. There was a young boy, skinny, but cleaner than expected for a throwaway. Bima and Rani both looked for a protector and saw a man hiding a little deeper in the shadows. The softfoots stopped to watch the thievery unfold.

As the patrol crossed the alley, a soldier lagged to look down the opening for trouble. At that moment, the boy burst out running and collided with first one and then another soldier. When they tried to grab him, he sidestepped as neatly as a dancer.

"Sorry! Sorry!" he called out. "My mother called me!" He mimicked waving a fist in the air and dashed across the street and down another alley. A soldier laughed.

The boy was too young to have any finesse. All too soon, one of the soldiers realized his pocket had been cut from his strings. He shouted in anger and frustration, but the boy was gone, and the shopkeepers and cart sellers all kept themselves busy ignoring what had happened.

Rani looked at Bima. "If we could catch that one in a year or two, he might be worth something."

"Or we could grab him now and train him for what we need. He looked like a Spice Islander which means he speaks Wester, and possibly Mata. I, for one, would love to know what rich Matasi businessmen consider important enough to write down before they go to sleep at night. And it would be a shame for the West Islands to keep all their secrets to themselves just because we cannot get close enough."

"A Spice Islander." Rani snorted. "What would you bribe them with? They aren't motivated by coin. I've been to the Spice Island, Bima, everyone lives in their small houses, just a stone's throw away from everyone else in the family. When the fishing is good, they fish. When it is not, they sit around and talk with their neighbors. If one person cooks a chicken and some rice, the entire family shows up at the door with an empty bowl."

"And yet," Bima reminded him. "You pick a fight with one, you find yourself in a battle with the entire family. The Kerek King desperately needs allies. He was no fool when he chose to marry a daughter of the Spice Island. They will protect her when he can't—or won't."

Rani was skeptical. "And the boy's protector? His handler? I saw the man in the shadows. I wouldn't want to cross him in the dark."

"If the Empress makes it worth his while, he could run an entire school of children for us. Rani, to bend a Spice Islander to your will, you must look for their weakness. And their weakness is always going to be their family—by blood and bone, or by the salt of the sea." Bima looked about. "We won't find the boy today, but keep your eyes open, he's fast enough to be worth a gold ring or two."

Days later, at the beginning of the Wet, Bima left for Matasi. Rani continued the search through the season that followed. He wasn't as foolhardy as Bima—he traveled with an entire patrol whenever they wandered through Dockside and Lowertown.

He searched for apprentices, those who would want to hang their own shingle out soon and needed more coin than they had set aside for a place to work and live. He bought drink in the taverns and listened for those who like to hear themselves talk or wanted to make themselves important by sharing too much of what they saw and heard. He visited with Patrons in their shops and watched for those who worked there with sullen and angry faces.

He learned these people didn't care about overthrowing a corrupt King. They cared that there wasn't enough food on the table, they couldn't own their carts, their houses, their shops without paying someone for protection. They worried for their wives and daughters and mothers every time the women left the safety of the house. They didn't care about the King; they cared that the King's taxes meant there was always a need for coin lenders and Patrons who could provide payments and protection when the purse was thin. They cared there were too many people crammed into too small of a space in Lowertown and Dockside chasing after work that left them dirty, or broken, or dying. Sinner's District, the Flower District—all of the Districts—took more coin to live than one could make in an almost honest living.

The best and worst softfoots, First Soldier Joon always said, were those motivated by discontent, not patriotism. Zealots, he claimed, only made good martyrs.

Rani didn't have Bima's gift for enticing those who would make a good Viklander softfoot. He couldn't look at a person and know exactly the right words to twist their wants into meeting Vikland's needs. But Rani knew his own worth. His talent was an eye for those who didn't act as expected and a memory for faces. He may have been better at determining who was already stealing secrets in the streets and for whom, but even that was information Bima could use.

It was already the end of the Wet when Rani and a patrol were hurrying through Dockside to meet the Matasi ship from Salisport. "No use in having every one of the new transfers lose their coin to Docksiders with clever fingers before the soldiers reach the Vikland embasado," the Ambassador had sighed. With any luck, Bima Ritwik would be on this ship or the one after.

Rani stopped abruptly when he recognized the boy again. Standing in an alley with a small bundle of black fur in his arms, the boy only had eyes for a Matasi businessman and his bodyguard. Rani looked around carefully for the boy's protector. He didn't see him, but there was a girl with a basket on her arm in a shop door across the way. She looked a little too interested in the unfolding scene.

"Oh!"

Rani snapped back to the boy as the dog dashed in front of the businessman and the bodyguard and the boy ran after it.

"Don't hurt my puppy!" he cried as he collided with first the businessman, then the bodyguard. The girl in the doorway bent down and tried to grab the puppy. It slipped through her fingers, and dashed around the corner. The boy couldn't stop in time and bumped into the girl still bending over. Rani saw something get tipped into her seagrass bag resting on the ground. She scolded the boy for his clumsiness as she picked up her bag and entered into the shop.

The bodyguard grabbed the boy.

"My puppy!" the boy wailed. "I can't lose my puppy!"

The bodyguard held the boy as the businessman roughly patted him down. The Matasian shook his head but didn't say anything. The man released him. The boy raced down the alley after his puppy, and the sudden excitement of the street faded into the buzz of midday business.

Rani slipped into the shop. The girl was still there, looking about, holding a list as if she was merely gathering the day's needs. Her bag had a slight bulge. Rani smiled and slid quietly next to her.

"I think you and I might have something to discuss," he began.

She looked at him coldly. "I am not a fancy. I have a male protector. If you leave before my father sees you, I will say nothing and spare your life."

Rani smiled thinly and repeated his words in Wester. "I saw what just happened. The dog ran to you. You gave the dog a bite of food before it ran around the corner. If the businessman would have looked down the alley, I presume he would have seen another child who held the dog until the boy could retrieve it. This is not the casual work of children too hungry to care if they are caught. You and I have a lot to talk about. But let's not do it here." He took her by the elbow and gently guided her outside.

The boy was just coming around the corner, carrying the puppy again. His eyes widened as he saw Rani holding the girl's arm.

He quickly started petting his dog, murmuring in Wester, "Are you unhurt, my little puppy? Is everything all right? Are you afraid? Should someone follow you when you leave me?" The boy stubbornly blocked their way as he kept his head down and snuggled the black puppy resting contentedly in his arms.

Rani shook his head at him, but spoke to the girl, "Is this your brother? I assume he is acting as your protector on these streets. Small, but quick feet as well as quick thinking. We are interested in him too. The coin Vikland could provide for the both of you for your skills in…" he smiled, "…gathering information would get you and your family out of Dockside and into a much better place to live. The both of you should listen to what I have to say."

The boy suddenly looked up. He spoke Keresh with a soft accent. "Come tomorrow. This place, this time. We will bring our father to speak for us, and you can bring another if you wish. We will say nothing to my father that you touched my sister." He grinned. "We are generous in our kindness already, my friend. I am far more afraid of him than I am of you."

Rani hesitated and then nodded. It could be a trap, but then Bima should be on the ship now in the harbor. It would be good to have the both of them—and a patrol hiding nearby—tomorrow as they spoke to the Spice Island family. This might be just what Vikland needed.

Arden and his sister first appeared in Book 3 "War and Wrens."

THE VALUE OF A DAUGHTER

(This story takes place one season before the events in *War and Wrens*)

Linna heard her father's voice first. She pushed the blankets away from her ears and listened. Voices. Her father's, her mother's, but who was the third? She carefully slid out of bed and made her way to the stairway and looked down into the room below.

The man was still in a traveler's cloak, but the hood was down. Linna could see short curly brown hair. She thought it might be one of the Matasians her father paid to bring him goods from other ports beyond Kerek City. Her father worked with many ship captains and middlemen, but she never bothered to learn who they were. Kereki custom would not allow her to inherit her father's business, so what was the point? Her younger brother was already reminding her of his bright future as a wealthy shop owner in the Flower District.

The voices were somber. Her mother was silent. Linna looked back at her bed. Her younger sister was still asleep. Why would someone come in the middle of the night to talk to her father?

The man stood up. "I'm sorry, this is not news you want to hear. This is news no one wants to hear." He sighed and repeated, "I'm sorry." He walked softly to the door and let himself out.

Linna's parents still sat at the table. They said nothing; they hardly moved. Linna wondered what could have possibly happened to make them look so old so quickly. She pulled on her boot linings and hurried down the stairs.

"I heard voices. What happened?"

"Pirates struck a ship before it sailed into Kerek City. It was not sunk or captured, but the cargo was lost. I won't know more until the Harbor Master releases the news, but it will be a little tight for us for a while. Don't worry about it. This was only a friend to let us know what to expect."

Linna pinched her lips together. She knew her father paid protection coin to others to keep their shop open and free from conflict. She also knew he paid men to protect her and her younger sister every time they left the shop to make a delivery or do business across the city. She wondered what the words "a little tight" would mean.

"Linna!" her mother said suddenly. "You are in your nightgown! Run upstairs and get back into bed, or get dressed before you come down again!" She looked fearfully at the windows, heavily shuttered against the night. Linna sighed. Her mother seemed afraid of her own shadow sometimes. Linna smiled and pushed herself up from the table.

"If you tell me there is nothing to worry about, then I will not worry. I am for my bed. I will see you in the morning." She climbed the stairs and looked back over the railing.

Her parents had not moved from their places at the table.

***

Linna felt the Wet dampen her mood even more as she quietly worked in the shop. Her parents were cheerful and chatty when customers came in, but as soon as they left a gloom would settle over the group. Even her brother toned down his voice and loud personality until he seemed as quiet as Linna herself.

Oro stopped by once during the days while they waited for the Harbor Master's report. Her parents stepped out 'to see a man' they said, and the next person in was Oro. Linna grinned. He had to have been waiting for her father to leave. Linna glanced over at Kent, but she knew he wouldn't tell. He knew how Linna felt about Oro and only smiled back at her. Nonetheless, he smacked the cudgel in his palm and gave Oro a menacing look. All three of them laughed.

They chatted. They always only chatted, Linna sighed. Oro was tall, he towered over Kent and the other men her father hired to protect her, the store, and his other possessions. But while the others were nearly as broad as the doorway, Oro carried his fine Viklander face on a body so lanky, her mother fussed that the boy was too delicate and one Linna should stay far away from.

Her father was not as subtle in his disapproval.

"That boy will bring you nothing. He is only a second son. He will not own a shop and he will not marry into mine. What will he do to put a roof over your head? Does he expect you to work here to support him all the days of your life? He has no ship to bring him coin, no lands to bring him crops. He is not sturdy enough to keep Trouble from your door. I beg you, find another. One who can keep you safe."

Linna sighed. That was the problem with Kerek City. Everyone was measured by their power to cause hurt or harm. Women were trapped in tiny houses, tiny shops, and by men with tiny minds. She wanted more than a tiny life in the Flower District. She longed to see more. She wanted to see the frontier of Kerek. She wanted to travel on a ship to the islands. She would travel with Oro if he wished to find his family. She fretted that she would never get out of the city.

Oro's news wasn't good. The Harbor Master had made a decision on the Matasi ship. Based on what the ship had been carrying before the looting by pirates, the taxes were more than the remaining goods. The ship had been seized. The crew was released, but without a ship they could not sail, and without coin they could not live in Kerek City. Rumor said they had been taken in by the Matasi missionaries and were fleeing by land to safety over the border before they could be arrested and thrown into the King's prison for nonpayment and vagrancy.

Kent looked concerned, no, fearful. Both Oro and Linna questioned him on what he knew.

"Your father owes a lot of people, Linna. He brings in a lot of coin but most of it goes out again. I cannot imagine he has enough set aside to recover from this."

"He'll ask for new terms. He will offer collateral. He told me it will be tight. He did not say all is lost." Linna tried to sound confident.

Kent shrugged but went and stood by the door. As soon as he caught sight of his Patron, he signaled Linna. She quickly led Oro out the back of the shop through their house to a door that exited out onto a different street. He bent over her and just as she thought he would finally kiss her, he whispered he would come see her again.

She huffed in frustration as she walked back into the store and promptly stopped.

Her father was so pale he looked like the skinned fish sold at the dock markets. Her mother was crying silently, tears running down her cheeks.

"What happened?"

"Your father owes more coin than we have. If we do not pay the taxes on the lost cargo, your father would lose the business. If your father does not pay those who own the streets, we could be burned out or worse. If he does not pay those who protect us, your sister and you will be in danger. We have no other options."

Linna pounced. "You said 'no other options.' That means you have one."

Her father sighed. "A man has offered to pay our duty to the King and pay for protection for all of you. We would also be free of payments to keep our shop open and free from harm until our next ship comes in with our goods."

"But that's what we need, isn't it?" She paused, trying to think why they would be so upset. "What is he asking for collateral? The shop?"

"He will marry you when you turn eighteen."

Linna recoiled. "Never! I love Oro."

"Oro is not worthy of you," her father answered sharply. "I don't want to fight about this now. It doesn't matter. The King must have his coin. And I must find a way to pay it."

Linna was so shocked she was speechless, and then furious. "You are pretending there is a choice, but there is not. I am seventeen years old, and you are telling me I will be sold to a man to pay your debts."

"We are not selling you," her father snapped. "Don't be so dramatic."

"And if I refuse? Or run away?"

"We have time, Linna. It will be more than a season before you are eighteen." Her mother tried to soothe her. "Your father and I are counting on several shipments that will arrive before this day and that day. Your father's Patron will listen to reason, once your father has coin in hand. This offer has bought us time. We won't have to go to the coin lenders. We all need time, Linna. We only have to pretend we are in agreement until our next shipments. You must play your part. We must be clever until we have coin of our own again."

Linna reached for her apron and carefully retied it over her skirt. She was so tired of others telling her what to do. Just once, she thought, she would like to burn everyone with scathing words and when there was nothing left but cinders and smoke all about her, she would just step over the ashes and walk away.

Linna squared her shoulders. Her life wasn't over yet. Her parents didn't know, but she had been passing news and information to Ngahuru of the West Islands for two seasons. She had set aside the coin she received from the softfoot—she had planned to surprise Oro—but now she could use it to run away. She still had time before she turned eighteen.

She would give Ngahuru a letter telling her everything and how it had all gone wrong. Perhaps the softfoot could give her the coin for her parents. Perhaps she would have an idea of what could be done. Her mother was right. She needed to be clever. From this day, this moment, Linna would take charge of her own life. There had to be a way she and Oro could be together.

Linna and Oro first appeared in Book 3 "War and Wrens."

And now a preview of

The Wrens Fly Away

CHAPTER 1

DREAMS AND PLANS

Axefield had been a small town blessed with a perfect location on a low-level plain. It was a half-day's ride from the palace at Juisiti on a smooth road. South of Axefield the road branched into four directions: southwest to the border with Kerek and the Vikland garrison Nebulin, south to the estates and the Conrosan refugee camp at Rishka, southeast to the orchards and fields of the Selena Plains, and east to the Summer Plains, the breadbasket of Vikland.

Raul Huena had grown up here, the son of a hostler who had a small station boarding and hiring out horses to those coming to and from Juisiti. Like many of the children who grew up spending more time working with their families and on business than on their schooling, he had arrived at the academies far behind the others who came from backgrounds of tutors and coin. He worked hard to catch up, but he'd left in his second year to complete his military service.

That was his real education. He had traveled. He was experienced enough to handle the high-spirited horses used for ceremonies by the diplomatic corps and ambassadors in West Islands, the Spice Island, Kerek, and Matasi. It was in Matasi he met his wife, Melia, another Viklander in the last year of her military service. After, they had returned to Axefield.

Armed with the wisdom of their travels, they built the first Huena Inn. They started a family, planted gardens, increased the stables, and they were blessed with commerce and each other. Melia had an eye for beauty and a palate for the flavors of the known world. Raul had the gift of hospitality and a sympathy for those coming from the outlands to the larger cities. He shared his knowledge freely, and he worked with other people in town to pass along business to wheelwrights, carriage makers, teachers, and tailors who knew how one needed to dress and act at the palace, and provisioners who knew what one needed traveling from the city to the Selena and Summer Plains.

And now his only daughter, Rell, had given him a gift like no other. He had wanted to expand for years but knew his talents were not up to the task. Then, during the war between Vikland and Kerek, Rell introduced him to Piffik Qanaq, a young man with the mind of a scholar, the will of a general, and the hands of a skilled builder.

At first, Raul and Melia hadn't known what to make of Piffik and of Zren Janin, the other young man Rell had brought to meet them. Piffik was a man who thought deeply, read widely, and acted on his convictions.

Piffik had been running his family business since he was far younger than their son Dylis, and he was responsible for many at Manumina. Piffik spoke three languages and the language of business, Melia told her husband, and it was clear to anyone who had eyes in their head, Piffik thought their daughter was a cherished gift. He would not try to bend or break her. Rell had chosen well and could have chosen far, far worse.

Zren Janin, on the other hand, was cheerful and friendly and never stopped talking. He asked questions immediately if he didn't understand something and said whatever he thought. At first it was a little disconcerting, and then it was just refreshing to meet a man so completely without guile. He was funny and appreciative of every little kindness, and had the same gift of well-turned words as Piffik had. If these two were indicative of the other Conrosans of Manumina, well then it was good the Empress had offered them a home.

***

At first, Raul had faltered when Piffik and the Conrosans arrived to build the second inn. Melia had asked him if he was sure he knew what he was in for when they set up their tent city, built long wooden sheds for their cooking and dining halls, laundries, and tool shop. But within days, he realized his good fortune. By bringing his own people, Piffik didn't waste time trying to find people, hiring the wrong ones, and fixing expensive mistakes. Piffik had told Raul their terms: they would work for five and a half days, be paid at midday on the sixth so they could do their shopping, and have a Rest Day. After the seventh day, they would start all over again. It was the Conrosan way and the way they worked best, Piffik explained.

The people worked as fast as the lumber and supplies came in. Women and men dressed in shabby Kereki pants or faded and patched Conrosan clothes. And they worked. When Piffik paid them after midday, they shopped. Soon Axefield business owners knew if they stayed open in the evening of the sixth day, their tills would equal the previous four days. On the seventh day, the workers played, they rested, they walked along the streets of Axefield, they picnicked in the gardens after visiting the street vendors. And even though his daughter Rell was far away in Kerek working with the Diplo at Evensong, Raul Huena blessed her every day.

And so it was, when Falan, one of the Kereki children traveling with the Conrosans, came to him and asked to have a room for the Wrens to meet for a little while, he gave her one of the private dining rooms, and only asked to have the room empty a decon before the end of day meal.

***

Falan watched as Ross and Nelo were the last to enter the room. The other Wrens were scattered about: some sat at the square tables; Josef and Kid stood, backs against opposite walls; Arden sitting in the left corner with Mother flopped on the floor to the right of him—the dog just out of the way if Arden would need to leap to his feet for a fight.

The room was tense, not in anticipation of a fight, but in response to Tiju Tia's news. The Empress of Vikland had given them a soldier's pay—enough coin for a year—and an invitation to make a home in Vikland. There were no plans to educate them, help them find shelter, or prepare them for a position to make enough coin to feed and clothe themselves in the future. The generosity of living in Vikland was supposed to be enough. They had been told this by Tiju Tia and now they gathered to talk about it—without Tiju Tia.

"I found Ross in the kitchen with Mother Huena. I told him we had been given this room to meet and when we were finished, he could return to her," Nelo offered.

"Oooooh, did you bring fingersweets?" Josef called out. "I cannot believe Falan would call us all together like this and not serve us coffee and fingersweets."

Ross said nothing, and Nelo gave an exasperated sigh. "Ross, I *saw* her give them to you. Don't stand there pretending you don't know what Josef is talking about. I am not going to let you keep them all for yourself." Ross slowly drew out a cloth napkin and put it on the table. Callis unwrapped it, and the Wrens eagerly reached for a treat.

"Now we are all here," Josef said, "and now we have been fed. Tell us, Falan why *did* you insist we drop our tools and plans and spend time with you?"

Falan gave him a troubled look. "I wanted to talk with all of you about Tiju Tia's generosity and what you all plan to do."

Dica crossed her arms. "I am not going back into service." Then she gave a deep sigh. "But I speak too little Vik for another position."

"I'm not sure Vikland is a good place for us." Arden looked at the others. "Anyone who looks at our faces will be reminded of someone who did not come home from the war. Others will narrow their eyes and assume—correctly, I might add—we are living in Vikland because we betrayed Kerek, and so how trustworthy can we be?"

"So Vikland's out?" Callis questioned. "A soldier's pay is not going to go far if we must travel across the known world."

"Maybe so, maybe no." Kid pushed himself off the wall. "My plan is to find the family Ulani. I know our Jenny is there, and I have saved one of their boys twice. I have no interest in becoming an heir, but I wish to be tutored as Jenny is, to go to the academies in Juisiti when I am able, and join the Vikland Diplo service to become a softfoot. If I must serve three years of military service as all Viklanders do, so be it. If I must repay the Ulani family for the cost of my education *after* I am in the Diplo service and a softfoot, so be it. But I know how heavily the Viklanders took losses in the war, and my fine face will fit in well as a softfoot for the Viklanders in Kerek City."

Josef gaped at him, and then laughed. "That's bold. That's beyond..." he didn't finish his sentence. "I like it though. Perhaps we all have been thinking too small."

"What if they say no?" Tyra asked.

"Then they say no, and I am no worse off than I am at this moment standing in front of you." Kid shrugged. The room was silent while everyone matched their own expectations against Kid's plan.

Falan waited for a few moments and then looked about her. "Did anyone hear the argument between Piffik, Rygee, and Tiju Tia yesterday?"

The Wrens broke out in sly smiles.

"I've never seen Piffik angry before. I didn't know he *could* get angry," Tyra said in a small voice.

"I saw him furious at Zren once, but he took it out on a Kereki traveling with the Sary Justice. This was much better—Rygee roared back," Josef said cheekily. "Tell everyone what they missed, Falan."

Falan said she had been fetching tools for the builders when Rygee had come flying out of the bakery yelling for Piffik. Ngahuru had been trailing behind, unable to keep up with Rygee's long legs. They had stepped away into the tack room in the stables, but anyone who wanted to—and Falan had wanted to—could hear them.

"It seems Piffik and the Council of Wisdom negotiated for the Conrosans, and received almost an entire district of land in the back of beyond to settle and build a deep-water port, and Tiju Tia sold us all for coin and dumped us on Vikland's doorstep, but no one spoke for poor Rygee." Falan shook her head in mock dismay.

"He said it was his coin that bought our houses and settlements, his neck he risked for Nelo, and his farming knowledge that kept Manumina and the Wrens from starving. He said Ngahuru's wish for revenge and Piffik's wish for peace made them blind to what was needed, not just wanted. He expected them both to think over what they could do to repay him. He wasn't leaving Vikland empty-handed."

The room was silent. "I don't think you gathered us to tell us this story as casual talk, Falan. What is it you want us to know?" Nelo leaned against the doorframe.

"Today I learned Piffik has offered all of the property and homesteads he, Rygee, and Tiju Tia purchased from the forfeited tax rolls. Rygee now owns the places Linna, Callis, Josef, and Nelo lived in and the settlement south of the Northern Track between Balza and Huk. He can sell or lease them as he wishes."

Falan took a deep breath. "Callis and I have talked it over. We are going back to Kerek. The house in Cloa is the only one in a town. We are going to ask Rygee to lease or sell it to us if Callis can apprentice with the healer there. I will try to take the position in the general store which Linna held during the war."

Everyone sucked in their breath and a few snuck furtive glances at Arden.

He blew out a noisy sound. "You can say her name, people, you can talk about her. I'm not made of fairy dust and dew drops that I am going to fall to ashes at your feet. Please, stop pretending Linna didn't exist. I'm sure wherever she and Oro moved to in Juisiti, they talk about all of you."

"Yes, but..." Josef joked. "I rather liked the idea of using Linna's name as a curse whenever Falan vexed me." He shot Arden a wide grin. Arden shook his head, but a small smile played about his lips.

Falan rolled her eyes. "Does anyone else want to say what they are doing, or where they are going? Or must we feed Josef's desire for an audience all day?"

Nelo cleared his throat. "Ross, why don't you say what you were doing when I found you?"

Ross shot him a mulish look. "Why don't you go first?" he shot back.

"I will and thank you." Nelo paused. "I am going with Piffik. I like building things, and I like working for him. I am going to move with the Conrosans to build a harbor." He nodded at Arden. "I think you are right—the Viklanders won't love me, but I plan to tuck myself into all of those Conrosans and see if my past can be forgotten."

Tyra gave him a serious look. "I am planning to go also. I am too young to live on my own, and like Dica, I do not want to be a servant in someone's great house. With the Conrosans, Siba Namikk said I can learn what I want in their schools, and not be concerned with food and shelter." She dropped her eyes and then looked at Nelo again. "Is this all right with you?"

Nelo smiled, a look so unusual to his harsh features Falan stared. "Of course, it is. Piffik is not so little a man that he can only manage one of us at a time. I believe Therin is staying with the Conrosans as well. The family that cares for him wishes him to remain."

Tyra looked relieved.

Falan nodded her head at Ross. "You said you wanted Nelo to speak first. He spoke. Now what were you and Mother Huena planning?"

"I'm going to stay at Axefield and raise rabbits. They get first pick for the table. A son, I forgot his name, will build me more rabbit hutches and I can sell my extras and keep the coin. I'll have a small room in the old inn and I won't have to share with anyone. When her boys go to the academies or for their military service, I can pick up their extra work for coin." He looked at the room defiantly.

"Well done, Ross!" Callis smiled. "You may be the most successful one of us all."

His face softened, not smiling, but not glowering either.

Falan looked about the room. This was not a surprise to her, to hear all of the Wrens had started making plans as soon as Tiju Tia had told them of her meeting with the Empress. They had survived the war by making plans as soon as they had news. She was relieved the littlest ones, Tyra and Therin, would be with the Conrosans and not her responsibility. Dica was still too young to live on her own, which it seemed she knew, but didn't have an answer for.

"Dica? We know what you *don't* want to do, care to share what you do want?"

Dica stiffened. "I want to be a shop girl. I don't want anyone telling me what to do."

Falan gave her an incredulous look. "That's all anyone does, Dica! The Patron who owns the shop tells you when to work and when you can finally go home. The people who shop think you exist only to magic whatever they want at a price they want to pay." She waved her hand. "You'll find that out soon enough. You'll go to Juisiti then?"

Dica shook her head. "I only know a little Vik."

Callis gave her a troubled smile. "Falan and I think Cloa will be safe enough for us because the Matasi army now guards the Northern Track. Even so, the two of us plan to travel together. I would not go to Matasi or Kerek alone."

Dica said nothing.

Callis looked to Josef. "You have been silent about your plans. Or is there to be three in the bed in our house in Cloa, and Falan has not yet told me the news."

Josef smiled broadly. "As much fun as that would be, Callis, I will have to turn down your invitation. I have been thinking of Kid's words ever since they fell from his mouth. I thought I wanted to buy and sell horses, but I could not work out how I could make that happen. So. I am going to ask Rygee for his thoughts on how this could be done, and I hope he offers me a position with him when he returns to his father. I remember he said they had horsebreakers on their farm. It was how he knew what happened to Zren when he broke his collarbone and rattled his brain. So, if they have horsebreakers, they have horses."

"Ah, Zren," Falan snorted. "Does anyone know what the half-wit is doing?"

"He's not a half-wit, Falan, his mind just works differently than anyone else's does," Arden said quietly.

Callis gave him a long look. "I never thought I would hear *you* defend him."

Arden shrugged, but it was Nelo who spoke, "Arden's right. Zren asks too many questions to be lacking sense. His brain is odd, it's true, but he's a hard worker, there is not a cruel bone in his body, and he does what he's told. As long as he is fed often and given a story to puzzle over, he'll be happy wherever he goes. We needn't worry for him."

Dica looked at Nelo. "Is he going with Piffik or Ngahuru?"

"Don't know," Nelo admitted.

Tyra turned to Arden. "Where are you going?"

Arden smiled. "I am going to travel for a bit. I thought I would like to see Matasi. Perhaps after Mother and I have wearied of that, we will sail to the West Islands, or to the new port of Vikland. But I tell you, my friends, sometime between this world and the next, I hope to show my face at each of your doorsteps and we can share tales of our adventures."